**"I can't stand the thought of my
daughter being afraid of me,"** Caleb
whispered.

"She's not," Noelle whispered back. "After all, she
let you hold her in the pool, remember?"

He shook his head. "She wanted to swim so badly
I think she would have let anyone hold her."

Noelle sank down into the chair next to him,
unable to refute his logic. "She needs a little time,
that's all."

He lifted his gaze to hers. "Maybe I can find a safe
place for the two of you to stay for a while. Then
I'll head off on my own to try to figure out who's
trying to kill me."

For some odd reason, Noelle found she was
beginning to believe Caleb was in fact innocent of
the crime he'd been accused of.

But knowing that didn't reassure her the way she
thought it would.

Because whoever had tried to kill Caleb outside
her house was very likely still looking for him.
And she was deeply afraid that the killer wouldn't
hesitate to take the life of a woman and child, too,
if necessary.

LAURA SCOTT

Wrongly Accused
&
Down to the Wire

HARLEQUIN® LOVE INSPIRED®CLASSICS

LOVE INSPIRED BOOKS

Recycling programs for this product may not exist in your area.

ISBN-13: 978-1-335-23257-1

Wrongly Accused & Down to the Wire

Copyright © 2019 by Harlequin Books S.A.

The publisher acknowledges the copyright holder of the individual works as follows:

Wrongly Accused
Copyright © 2014 by Laura Iding

Down to the Wire
Copyright © 2014 by Laura Iding

www.Harlequin.com

Printed in U.S.A.

CONTENTS

Laura Scott is a nurse by day and an author by night. She has always loved romance and read faith-based books by Grace Livingston Hill in her teenage years. She's thrilled to have published over twelve books for Love Inspired Suspense. She has two adult children and lives in Milwaukee, Wisconsin, with her husband of thirty years. Please visit Laura at laurascottbooks.com, as she loves to hear from her readers.

Books by Laura Scott

Love Inspired Suspense

Military K-9 Unit

Battle Tested

Callahan Confidential

Shielding His Christmas Witness
The Only Witness
Christmas Amnesia
Shattered Lullaby
Primary Suspect

Classified K-9 Unit

Sheriff

Visit the Author Profile page at Harlequin.com for more titles.

WRONGLY ACCUSED

For I, the Lord, love justice; I hate robbery and wrongdoing. In my faithfulness I will reward my people and make an everlasting covenant with them.
—*Isaiah* 61:8

This book is dedicated to Pat and Ted Iding.
Thank you for all the wonderful years
you've loved me as one of your own.

ONE

Caleb O'Malley's stomach knotted painfully at the thought of seeing his daughter, Kaitlin, for the first time in over a year. Since the day he'd been sent to jail for a crime he didn't commit.

He parked his beat-up truck in front of the fourth house from the corner and killed the engine. Taking a deep breath, he shoved his car door open and forced himself to get out and walk up the sidewalk to the front door of Noelle Whitman's house, trying not to resent the woman who'd been his daughter's foster mother while he'd been behind bars.

To be honest, it was his own fault he hadn't seen Kaitlin in so long. At first, he'd thought he'd be let out as soon as they realized he was innocent. But then week after week passed by, and he'd grimly realized there was a very real possibility he'd be found guilty. At that point, he'd been unable to bear the thought of having his young daughter see him in jail.

He'd been shocked to hear from his lawyer that the case against him had been dropped due to the strange disappearance of the eyewitness. And deeply glad to know he was free at last.

He rapped sharply on the door and waited impatiently for the Whitman woman to answer.

He squinted against the harsh glare of the summer sun. After not being in the sunlight for so long, he enjoyed the warmth soaking into his skin, even though the temperature was hovering at a steamy ninety degrees.

His lawyer, Jack Owens, had promised to let Ms. Whitman know Caleb was on his way to pick up Kaitlin, so there was no reason for her not to be here. Hard to believe that he'd only been out of jail for a few hours. His release had been so sudden he hadn't had time to make plans. It was Friday and once he picked up Kaitlin, he'd go home and take the weekend to figure out how to start their life over again.

He lifted his hand to knock again at the exact moment the door swung open, so he pulled back his hand just in time. The woman standing before him was much younger than he'd anticipated, probably barely thirty, with reddish-gold hair and fair skin. She was dressed casually in a green short-sleeved sweater and calf-length blue jeans. In her arms was his five-year-old daughter, wearing a pretty pink dress and pink barrettes clipped to her glossy chin-length blond hair. She clutched a small stuffed giraffe to her chest.

The minute Kaitlin saw him she dropped the giraffe, wrapped her arms around Noelle's neck and burst into tears. "Nooo, I don't wanna go wif Daddy!"

His stomach tightened painfully as his worst nightmare played out in front of him. Ms. Whitman held Kaitlin close at the same time she took a step back, a wary expression on her face.

"You'd better come in," she said over Kaitlin's sobs. He stepped forward and bent down to pick up the giraffe.

A split second later, he heard the crack of a rifle and the soft thud of a bullet hitting the doorframe of the house, inches from where his head had been.

"Get back," he shouted, barging into her house with the finesse and strength of a bull, before slamming the door behind him.

Another bullet pierced the door, followed by yet another. He covered Noelle's body with his as he practically pushed her toward the relative safety of the kitchen.

"What's going on?" Noelle asked hoarsely, her green eyes wide with fear as he shoved her down behind the island. He hated the way Kaitlin's crying grew louder.

"We have to get out of here." There wasn't time to explain what he didn't even understand himself. He had no clue why someone was shooting at him, but right now all that mattered was getting out of here in one piece. He lunged for the keys he saw lying on the counter and mentally visualized where the garage was located. "Does that door lead out to the garage?"

"Yes."

"Let's go."

"No! Wait! We have to call 911!" She shrank away from him, pressing herself against the island and curling protectively around his daughter.

He hesitated, trying to think rationally. He didn't trust the police, but if he left on his own would the shooter follow him and leave Ms. Whitman and Kaitlin alone?

Or use his daughter as bait as a way to draw him out? The very possibility made his blood run cold.

"Look, we need to get out of here. There's a chance that guy out there will try to use Kaitlin as a way to get to me. I have to keep her safe!"

The sound of breaking glass made him glance back

toward the living room. A familiar round canister landed and rolled on the carpet with smoke rising up toward the ceiling.

"Tear gas! Listen, lady, if you want to live, come with me. I promise to keep you and Kaitlin safe. But we have to move. Now!" His eyes were already starting to burn as he grabbed the pink backpack that was on the counter next to the keys, gripped her arm and dragged her toward the door to the garage. "Hurry!"

Thankfully she followed him into the fresh air of the garage. She slid into the backseat and talked softly to Kaitlin as she buckled his daughter into her booster seat. He tossed the pink backpack inside and climbed into the driver's seat.

"Buckle up," he said tersely as he cranked the key in the ignition. The moment he heard her seat belt click he put the SUV in gear. Thankfully she drove a sturdy vehicle, which would help them escape the shooter. The thought of backing out the driveway in full view of the shooter filled him with dread. But he mentally visualized the neighborhood, marking a path that should help keep them safe.

"Hang on," he warned before he hit the garage door opener. As the door slowly opened he decided not to wait for it to get all the way up before he stomped hard on the accelerator and flew out of the driveway, clipping the bottom of the garage door with the top of her car.

The sound of gunfire filled the air as he swiftly spun the SUV around and headed straight across the street through a neighbor's yard.

Noelle let out a small scream as he barreled out of the garage, wrecking her garage door as he sailed down the driveway. At the sound of gunfire, she leaned over, trying to protect Kaitlin as Caleb O'Malley drove like a maniac across the street and through her neighbor's yard. She momentarily closed her eyes and frantically prayed.

Dear Lord, please keep me and Kaitlin safe!

The vehicle jerked sharply from side to side as they went up and over the edge of her neighbor's flower bed. Within moments, they were heading down that neighbor's driveway to the street behind hers.

Kaitlin's father didn't speak as he drove, taking several sharp turns as he took them farther away from her house. The way he kept glancing at the rearview mirror told her he was worried they were being followed.

Should she mention how she'd noticed a black pickup truck following behind her for the past few days? Was it possible that person had just been waiting for Kaitlin's father to show up?

She swiped at her eyes and glanced back, wishing desperately there was a cop somewhere close by. Where were the police when you needed them? Hopefully one of her neighbors had heard the gunshots and called the cops. If only she hadn't left her cell phone and her purse in her bedroom. But how was she to have known something like this would happen?

She pulled herself together with an effort. She could not let this man know how afraid she really was.

Kaitlin finally stopped crying, but her thumb was planted firmly in her mouth, a sure sign that the child was upset.

When Kaitlin's father headed toward the freeway, she forced herself to speak. "Why aren't we going to the closest police station?"

"Because I don't trust the police."

Her stomach knotted further and she had to work to keep her tone steady. "Where are you taking us?"

"Somewhere safe," he said, barely glancing back at her.

Somewhere safe? She swallowed a hysterical laugh. Everyone in Milwaukee knew he'd been arrested for killing his wife fourteen months ago. Caleb O'Malley had made headline news, not just in the city but across the country. *Former sharpshooter for the Milwaukee County Sheriff's Department SWAT team arrested for murdering his wife.*

Unfortunately, all charges against Caleb O'Malley had been dropped when the eyewitness, who claimed to have seen O'Malley shoot his wife and then take off from the scene of the crime, abruptly disappeared a week before the trial. Without the witness there wasn't enough of a case against him. At least that was what his lawyer, Jack Owens, had told her.

Noelle had been sick at the thought of handing Kaitlin back over to her father, but there hadn't been much she could do to prevent him from exercising his custodial right to take his daughter. Supposedly he wasn't a criminal anymore.

Still, she knew there was no statute of limitations for murder. There was a part of her that believed the police would eventually find the evidence they needed to lock up Caleb O'Malley for good. If he was guilty, of course, which she was fairly certain he was.

Had she gone with one killer to escape another?

"Why don't you let me and Kaitlin go?" she said, striving to sound reasonable. "Surely you don't want to expose your daughter to danger."

He concentrated on the road. "I told you, I can't ignore

the possibility they would use her to get to me. I thought about dropping you off somewhere, but obviously Kaitlin needs you so that's not an option. I promise I'm not going to hurt you."

He was right about one thing: Kaitlin did need her. No way was she leaving the child alone with a potential murderer. Yet she knew she was risking her life by staying. Granted, he'd tried to protect her back at the house when the bullets had started flying, but what did she really know about this man? Nothing except what she learned through the media.

And none of that had been good.

Trusting men wasn't exactly easy for her, either.

"Did you see anything out on the street?" he asked, breaking into her thoughts.

"You mean before the gunshots?" She thought back to those moments when she'd faced Caleb O'Malley across the threshold. Ironically, there hadn't been the usual black car she'd noticed over the past few days. "There was a red pickup parked on the street."

"That's my truck. Did you see anything else? Another vehicle? A person? Anything?"

"No." She'd been far more preoccupied with trying to find a way to ease the transition for Kaitlin. Noelle had planned to invite him in, hoping he'd spend some time getting to know his daughter again before leaving with her. Especially after the way Kaitlin had clung to her, sobbing.

As much as she feared the dark-haired stranger, she wasn't leaving Kaitlin alone with him any time soon. Kaitlin was the sole reason she'd come along in the first place. The poor child had already been through so much, losing her mother and then her father. Kaitlin had suf-

fered night terrors the first weeks she'd been with Noelle, but the child hadn't had a nightmare for almost five
months.

Noelle would be shocked if today's events didn't bring
them back. She'd be surprised if her own nightmares of
the past didn't return, too.

There was another long silence and she realized they
were already well outside the city limits. Grimly she
knew they could go for several hundred miles without
stopping on the gas tank she'd filled yesterday.

"I'd let you both go if I could," he said in a low voice.
"But I'm afraid it's too late. You and Kaitlin are in danger now, too."

"In danger from whom?" she asked helplessly.

"I wish I knew," he said, his tone weary. "Probably
from the same person who killed Heather."

She knew Heather had been his wife and Kaitlin's
mother. And if he thought she was going to believe that
line of baloney, he was as crazy as the media had portrayed him to be.

During an interview on TV, one of his SWAT teammates had mentioned Caleb's hair-trigger temper. She
could imagine how difficult it must have been for him
to discover his wife was cheating on him.

Not that his wife had deserved to die for her sins, leaving Kaitlin without a mother, or a father once Caleb had
been arrested. As Kaitlin's preschool teacher and an ap-
proved foster parent, she'd fought for and won temporary
custody of the little girl. At first she thought it would only
be a few weeks until other family had been notified but
no one had been found. Over the past year she'd grown
to love Kaitlin. And being forced to turn the child over
to Caleb had nearly broken her heart.

"I guess you don't believe in the theory of innocent until proven guilty," he said, breaking into her thoughts.

"I never said you were guilty," she said hastily. No sense in baiting the tiger. She needed to keep on his good side in order to convince him to let her and Kaitlin go. So far, she wasn't entirely sure she believed in his theory that she and Kaitlin were in danger.

"So you believe I'm innocent?" he asked after several long moments.

She licked her dry lips and tried to smile. "The judge let you go, which is good enough for me."

He let out a noise that sounded suspiciously like a snort, but didn't say anything more. She stared out the window as the miles zipped past. Glancing over at Kaitlin, she noted the girl's eyelids were starting to droop. Long car rides tended to make the little girl sleepy and no doubt she'd worn herself out with her crying jag.

Twenty minutes later, Noelle realized Kaitlin's father had left the freeway and turned onto a country highway.

She couldn't quell a hint of panic when she didn't recognize the area. They were in a rural part of Wisconsin. Where was he taking them? What did he intend to do?

She'd gone along with him to protect Kaitlin, not to mention to get away from the rolling tear gas and flying bullets. But now, she was second-guessing her decision.

She and Kaitlin would likely be safer on their own. She trusted the police would protect them. Why wouldn't they?

Somehow, she needed to find a way to escape.

Caleb dragged a hand over his face as the SUV ate up the miles, and tried to think rationally. He didn't know who'd fired those shots at him, but if he hadn't picked up Kaitlin's stuffed giraffe, he'd be dead.

Leaving Kaitlin an orphan.

Somehow, he felt stupid for not realizing that whoever had killed his wife would still be out there somewhere, waiting for him. But the attempt on his life didn't make much sense. Why not try to plant more evidence to get him back behind bars? What would they gain from killing him?

"Where's Giffy?" he heard Kaitlin ask. The little girl had napped for a while but was obviously awake now.

"Right here, sweetheart." In the rearview mirror, he saw Kaitlin hug the stuffed giraffe close.

"Ah, Mr. O'Malley?" Noelle's voice was soft, almost hesitant. He hated seeing the shadow of fear in her eyes, but he didn't know how to reassure her he was innocent of the crime he'd been accused of. He could talk all he wanted, but without proof that he was being framed, there wasn't much he could do.

"Caleb," he corrected curtly. "Call me Caleb."

"Uh, sure. Caleb. It's past five-thirty and Kaitlin usually eats dinner about this time," she said with a hint of nervousness.

He flushed, squelching a flash of guilt. He should have realized that his daughter would need to eat soon. After fourteen long months in jail he'd forgotten how to be a father. "Sounds like a plan. What would you like?"

"Kaitlin, what do you want for dinner?" Noelle asked.

The little girl pulled her thumb out of her mouth. "Chicken bites."

In the rearview mirror he caught the fleeting grimace that passed over Noelle's face, but she readily agreed with Kaitlin's decision. "That would be great."

"Looks like there's a fast-food restaurant five miles ahead," he said, gesturing to a road sign. "We'll get something there."

"Thank you."

He swallowed a frustrated sigh. Noelle acted as if he was some sort of ogre keeping her and Kaitlin prisoner. Yet what could he have done differently? If he had left Kaitlin behind and something had happened to his daughter, he'd never have forgiven himself. No question he'd give up his life for Kaitlin.

And he couldn't bring himself to trust the police, either. Not when he fully believed that someone from his SWAT team had set him up for his wife's murder.

Feeling grim, he imagined that the cops were right now swarming Noelle's house, gathering evidence. What would they think when they found the slugs from a high-powered rifle and a canister of tear gas in her house? Would that prove his innocence? Or would they turn the whole thing around to somehow make him the bad guy?

He couldn't help believing the latter. It wouldn't be long before the killer was hot on their tail. He needed to figure out a good place to hide until he could find someone to trust.

Not that he could think of too many people he trusted at the moment. He'd put his faith in his lawyer, Jack Owens, but Jack had been the only person who'd known Caleb's plan of going to Noelle's house. Not that he could understand why Jack would try to kill him after working more than a year to set him free.

His wife's killer had clearly set him up to rot in prison for the rest of his life. And now that Caleb had been given a get-out-of-jail-free card, it was possible that the same person had tried to kill him. Unless his wife had other lovers who he didn't know about, someone who'd taken shots at him in an effort to seek revenge?

He sighed and turned off the highway, heading onto a side road leading to the popular fast-food restaurant. He pulled in and headed down the drive-through lane.

"I hav'ta go potty," Kaitlin announced.

He inwardly winced, feeling guilty for not anticipating his daughter's needs. He made a quick U-turn in the parking lot so he could pull into a spot located near the front of the building.

He slid out from behind the wheel but before he could try to help Kaitlin out of her booster seat, Noelle took control, undoing the buckles to free his daughter. She carried Kaitlin out and set her down on the ground.

"I hav'ta go now!" Kaitlin said, rushing toward the door. Noelle sprinted to catch up, quickly capturing Kaitlin's hand.

"I'll take you to the bathroom, okay, sweetie?"

Caleb followed them inside, feeling like an outsider. He'd lost so much time with his daughter. The fact that she didn't want to be near him was like a knife to his heart.

Standing at the back of the lobby area, he stared blindly at the menu selections. Food wasn't nearly as important as keeping his daughter safe from harm. He felt exposed standing here in the middle of a fast-food joint, considering how just three hours ago, someone tried to kill him. Yet he'd kept a careful eye out to make sure they hadn't been followed.

But they weren't safe yet, not by a long shot.

Noelle and Kaitlin returned from the bathroom and he couldn't help smiling at the way his daughter was giggling.

"I had no idea public restrooms could be fun," he said with a smile.

Noelle shrugged. "She found the air hand-drying machine entertaining."

"So, Katydid, what would you like for dinner?" he asked, capturing his daughter's gaze. He hoped she remembered his pet name for her.

She tilted her head to the side and gave him an exasperated look. "I already tole you, chicken bites."

She hadn't reacted to the nickname, but at least she wasn't crying, either. He tried to take heart at the minor step forward. "Okay, one order of chicken bites. Noelle, what would you like?"

"I'll have a grilled chicken sandwich."

"What about to drink? I'll get Kaitlin some milk, but what would you like?"

"Water is fine."

He nodded and decided to order a thick cheeseburger for himself. Soon they had their food piled on a plastic tray. Noelle and Kaitlin picked out a small rectangle table and he made sure to sit where he could keep an eye on the door.

He found himself distracted by Kaitlin, who'd grown so much in the time he'd been stuck behind bars. Before he could dig into his food, Noelle surprised him by taking Kaitlin's hand in hers and bowing her head.

"Dear Lord, we thank You for providing this food for us to eat and we ask for Your protection and Your guidance in showing us the right path. Amen."

"Amen," his daughter echoed.

He paused, unsure of how he felt about the fact that Noelle was teaching his daughter to pray. He and Heather hadn't been particularly religious and he instinctively knew Heather would have been upset at Noelle's teaching Kaitlin about God. But he decided there were worst things than being a Christian so he didn't say anything. Although he couldn't help wondering what else Noelle had taught Kaitlin while he'd been gone.

He bit into his cheeseburger, enjoying the juicy taste he'd long been denied. He divided his attention between Kaitlin and the door. His daughter ate sparingly, spending more time playing with her chicken bites, pretending they were animals talking to each other. Regret burned in the back of his throat for the time he'd lost. He wanted nothing more than to gather his daughter into his arms and hold her close, but he'd rather cut off his arm than scare her again.

"Eat your dinner, Kaitlin," Noelle said in a soft but stern tone.

"Are we goin' home soon?" Kaitlin asked.

Noelle lifted her eyebrow and glanced at him. He cleared his throat and smiled. "We're going to spend the night in a motel. Won't that be fun?"

His daughter's big blue eyes, mirror images of her mother's, widened with excitement. "Wif a swimming pool?"

"I don't know, maybe." There were plenty of hotels with pools, but he'd wanted to find something small and off the main thoroughfares. Maybe he'd get lucky and find a small motel with an outdoor pool. After all, it was mid-June, warm enough for outdoor swimming. He was eager to gain whatever ground he could with his daughter. "But first you have to finish your dinner."

"Okay." She grinned saucily and popped another chicken bite into her mouth, smearing ketchup across her cheek. He was glad to see she was growing more at ease with him.

He reached for his napkin but Noelle was quicker, already wiping the red stain away. He curled his fingers into a helpless fist.

And couldn't help wondering if Noelle was really trying to help. Or if this was a subtle way of sabotaging his relationship with his daughter.

Noelle finished her sandwich about the same time as Caleb. She gathered all the trash into a neat pile on the tray while they waited for Kaitlin. When they'd first entered the restaurant, she'd considered asking one of the patrons for help, but there weren't many people inside. And what if they simply looked at her as if she were crazy? Technically, Caleb had legal custody of his daughter, while she didn't have any right to the child. For now, she'd decided to go along with pretending to be a family.

The stark longing in Caleb's eyes as he gazed at his daughter made her wonder if she'd misjudged him. Clearly he loved Kaitlin and during the course of the meal she found herself torn between wanting to get as far away from him as she could and wanting to help him repair his relationship with the daughter who barely remembered him.

She couldn't imagine who'd tried to shoot him, but at least now the black truck that had trailed her for days made sense. Whoever was driving it must have been waiting for Caleb to arrive. If Caleb was truly innocent of the crime he'd been accused of, why would someone still want him dead? Was it possible he had really been framed? Or was that wishful thinking on her part?

"We need to go," Caleb said.

"All right," she agreed. Kaitlin was obviously finished with her food, so she quickly wiped off the little girl's sticky fingers and then stood up. Caleb took the tray of garbage and headed over to the trash can. Then he waited for her by the door, holding it open for the two of them.

They walked toward her car and as Caleb opened the back passenger door, she caught a glimpse of a police car pulling into the parking lot of the restaurant. She froze, wondering if she could manage to capture the cop's attention. Would the cop believe her story? Or would he run a check on Caleb only to find that he did have legal custody of his daughter?

"You're welcome to leave, but you won't take my daughter," Caleb warned, clamping his hand on her elbow to prevent her from leaving. "So make up your mind, and quick."

She hesitated, full of uncertainty.

"Just get Kaitlin into the car, all right?" he pressed.

"Uh, sure." She lifted Kaitlin into the booster seat. Her fingers were shaking so badly that she had trouble buckling the girl in.

When Kaitlin was safely secured in the seat she shut the door and made her way around to the other side, trying to see where the cop car was located. The officer had pulled into the drive-through lane and had his window rolled down as he perused the menu.

If she started screaming like a lunatic, would he help her?

"Sit up front next to me," Caleb said when she reached for the back door handle.

She felt trapped but since there was no way she was going anywhere without Kaitlin, she climbed into the front passenger seat.

When she glanced over to the police car, it was farther away, having moved forward to the next window.

Within moments Caleb drove back out onto the road, leaving the police car and any hope of getting help behind.

TWO

Noelle was grateful that after another two hours of driving, Caleb pulled off onto an exit that advertised a motel with a swimming pool.

The motel was small, but not so small that there weren't other guests, at least based on the cars in the parking lot. She was berating herself for not taking a chance by going to the police.

Too late now. She'd agreed to stay with him for Kaitlin's sake. Her own deep-seeded fears meant nothing compared to keeping the little girl safe from harm.

Caleb kept her close by his side, as if worried she might try something rash. She found his presence overwhelming. She wasn't used to being so close to a man, hadn't dated anyone in years. The three of them walked into the lobby together, and she knew he wanted to give the clerk the impression that they were a family, especially when he'd requested one room with two beds.

"How's the water in the pool?" Caleb asked the older man behind the desk as he paid in cash for the room. The guy barely glanced at his driver's license.

The guy shrugged. "Probably a bit on the cold side by now," he said in a disinterested tone. There was a small television behind the desk and his gaze kept straying back toward the baseball game he had on.

"Thanks," Caleb said cheerfully.

"Can we go swimming? Please?" Kaitlin asked.

"Soon," he promised, taking the room key and then holding the door open for Noelle and Kaitlin as they made their way back outside. There were two levels of the motel but Noelle noted their room was on the first floor, closest to the outdoor pool.

The room was nothing special, but it appeared clean enough. Kaitlin disappeared into the bathroom. When the child was out of earshot Noelle turned to Caleb. "Now what?" she asked in a low tone.

His enigmatic gaze didn't reveal much. "There must be spare clothes in that backpack that Kaitlin can use to swim in."

"There's one change of clothes, the rest is in her suitcase we left behind. And I don't have any other clothes and neither do you. She's too young to swim by herself."

"There's a strip mall a few miles down the street. We'll stop by tomorrow to pick up a few things," he said. "And the pool isn't that deep. At the very least she can dangle her feet in the water."

As annoyed as she was with him, she couldn't help appreciating the way he was trying so hard to make his daughter happy. But at the same time, she also wished he'd simply let them go.

Was he right in thinking that the person who'd shot at him would use Kaitlin to get to Caleb? Or was that just a handy excuse? She wished she knew.

Kaitlin came out of the bathroom and jumped up beside her on the bed. "Can we swim now, Noa? Puleeze?"

Looking down into Kaitlin's big blue eyes, she couldn't bear to disappoint the little girl. "Sure, sweetie."

"Why does she call you Noa?" Caleb asked, a small frown puckering his brow.

Did he resent their closeness? It certainly wasn't her fault he'd been arrested.

She dug in the backpack for a pair of shorts and a top that Kaitlin could use in lieu of a swimsuit. "Because she couldn't pronounce my name. Noa was as close as she could get to Noelle."

"How is it that you became her foster mother?"

She had no intention of giving him her life story. Especially since that would include confessing her horrible past along with her more recent failures. Trusting him as much as she had so far had been difficult enough. Under normal circumstances she avoided men, especially macho, dangerous types like Caleb. She forced a casual tone. "I'm your daughter's preschool teacher and happen to be licensed as a foster parent. I asked for custody and the state agreed."

If he was embarrassed that he didn't recognize her from the preschool, he didn't show it. She wasn't necessarily surprised that he hadn't remembered her, because his wife had been the one who'd come in to drop off and pick up Kaitlin, at least 80 percent of the time. The few times Caleb had come, he hadn't seemed to notice her.

She still remembered the last time she'd seen Heather, the day before she'd died. Caleb's wife had come in late on that Friday, almost twenty minutes past closing. Heather had looked nervous and hadn't been alone. There had been another man with her, who'd waited impatiently near the doorway.

It wasn't until after Heather's affair had hit the news that she'd understood what she'd seen that evening.

Tearing her thoughts away from the past, she turned her attention to helping Kaitlin change her clothes into a shorts-and-top set.

"But this isn't my swimming suit," Kaitlin protested with a frown. "My swimming suit has sparkles."

"We left your swimming suit at home, remember?" she said patiently. "Do you want to check out the water or not?"

"I do! I do!" The little girl jumped up and down for emphasis.

"All right, let's go." She ducked into the bathroom, grabbed a towel off the rack and then came back out to take Kaitlin's hand in hers.

Caleb silently held the door open once again. *A criminal with manners,* she thought, fighting a sense of hysteria as they walked over to the pool area. He unlatched the fence, and she was surprised and a bit disappointed to find there weren't any other guests there.

Kaitlin ran over to the edge of the pool.

"Wait for me," Noelle called out, quickly taking off her sandals. "We have to check the water first."

She glanced over at Caleb, surprised to see he was taking off his running shoes, too. He then proceeded to roll his jeans halfway up his calves, which would have looked geeky on anyone else.

But there was nothing geeky about Caleb. He must have worked out while he was in jail because he was lean and muscular, without an ounce of fat to be seen. His dark hair was short and she wondered if that was by choice. Or if he'd been forced to get it cut.

Did they have barbers in jail?

He plopped down on the edge of the pool and put his feet in the water. "Come over and test the water, Katy-did."

Kaitlin hung back, staying next to Noelle. She urged the little girl over, taking a seat on the edge of the pool next to Caleb, leaving enough room between them for Kaitlin. The little girl sat down and then shrieked when she put her feet in the water. "It's cold!"

"Probably because the sun is going down," Caleb said. "I bet it will be warmer tomorrow. See that plastic cover rolled up over there? They put that on at night, and in the morning the sun shines through the bubbles to warm up the water."

Kaitlin kicked her feet, giggling as she splashed the adults. Noelle tensed, but Caleb didn't yell or tell Kaitlin to stop. In fact, he playfully kicked his feet, too, mimicking his daughter.

"Can I go in farther, Noa? Can I?" Kaitlin pleaded.

"You can if you hold on to me," Caleb answered, holding out his hands in a nonthreatening gesture.

Noelle held her breath as Kaitlin silently stared up at her father. The lure of the water must have been more than she could resist, though, because she nodded.

Caleb gently lifted her up, as if she weighed nothing more than Kaitlin's stuffed giraffe, and propped his elbows on his knees for stability. Slowly he lowered Kaitlin into the water, her tiny hands clutching his forearms.

"It's c-c-cold," she said, her teeth chattering.

"Do you want to get out?" Caleb asked.

"N-no, not yet." Kaitlin wiggled around in the water, as if she could swim with her father holding her, and then scrunched up her nose when a bit of water splashed in her face. He grinned and lifted her up and down, like a bobber on the end of a fishing pole.

She watched Caleb play with his daughter, her reserve melting away. His smile softened his harsh features to the point it was difficult to imagine him doing anything as terrible as killing his wife.

"Okay, I think that's enough, Katydid," Caleb said, lifting her out of the water and setting her back on the edge of the pool. "Your lips are turning blue."

"I'll get the towel," Noelle murmured, glad to have an excuse to put some distance between them. Why did she suddenly doubt the image the media had portrayed? An eyewitness had watched Caleb kill his wife and then flee the scene.

An eyewitness who'd disappeared. Why? What did that mean?

She hid her confusion by wrapping Kaitlin up in the towel. The little girl snuggled against her and yawned.

"I think it's bedtime, young lady," she said, glancing up at Caleb. He nodded, rose to his feet and padded across the concrete to where he'd left his shoes and socks.

As they made their way back to the room, she reminded herself that it was easy to believe Caleb's father-of-the-year act because she hadn't seen him angry. She'd suffered at the hands of an angry man in the past and the last thing she wanted to do was to find herself in a similar situation with Caleb. So far, she had not seen any evidence of his so-called hair-trigger temper.

And silently prayed that she never would.

Caleb stretched out on the bed fully dressed, and stared up at the ceiling of the small motel room. Noelle and Kaitlin were snuggled together in the other bed, the one closest to the bathroom.

There were a few things he wanted to do, but he didn't dare leave until he knew they were both sound asleep. He was fairly certain Kaitlin was down for the count, but he sensed Noelle was fighting to stay awake. Finally her breathing deepened and he waited another hour just to be sure she was asleep before he quietly stood and made his way to the door.

He held his breath as he opened the door as silently as possible and slipped outside. Had the noise caused Noelle to wake up? He sincerely hoped not.

First, he needed to swap the license plates on Noelle's SUV. He drove down the road, looking for a car that he could use for the swap. He was afraid that anyone within the motel parking lot might notice, so he was determined to find a vehicle somewhere else.

About three miles down the road he spotted a tavern that suited his needs perfectly. He pulled up to a SUV similar to Noelle's and smiled grimly when he discovered the Illinois license plates. Even better. He made sure the tag was paid up, and then used his Swiss Army knife to swap the plates.

At least this way, he could buy some time if whoever shot at him had an APB out on Noelle's car. It wouldn't work forever, but he'd take what he could get.

He returned to the motel, relieved to have that task finished. He parked and shut off the car, but stayed in his seat as he turned on his cell phone to place a call to his lawyer, Jack Owens. It was well past midnight, but he didn't care. He wanted answers.

The phone rang several times before Jack answered.

"O'Malley, where are you?" he asked in a sleep-laden voice.

"Somewhere safe. I'm sure you know by now that someone tried to kill me," he said. "What's going on?"

"I don't know, but the police want to talk to you, Caleb. They've been hounding me all evening."

"Too bad." The last thing he intended to do was to trust the police. Not after the way his SWAT teammates had been so eager to believe the worst about him. And there was a tiny voice in the back of his mind reminding him that Jack was the only person who'd known he was heading over to pick up his daughter. Granted anyone could have made a reasonable assumption, but still. "Did they find the slugs embedded in the house? And the canister of tear gas?"

"They haven't told me much," Jack confessed. "Other than they want to talk to you."

"Kind of hard to shoot at myself, don't you think?" he asked, trying not to sound as sarcastic as he felt. "I'd estimate the shooter was standing about a hundred and fifty yards away."

"I believe you. You're the sharpshooter. But you really do need to come back, at least long enough to give your statement," Jack pleaded. "After all, you have nothing to hide. You're the victim this time, remember?"

He wished it were that easy, but knew full well it wasn't. "What are they saying about Noelle Whitman and Kaitlin?" he asked, changing the subject.

"Not much, at least as far as I know. Although the police want to interview Ms. Whitman, too."

Of course they did. And despite the way he'd watched her pray over their meal, he wasn't ready to trust her completely, either. He sighed, feeling as if the weight of the world were on his shoulders. "I have to go. Let me know if you find out anything about the crime scene," he said. "I'll be in touch in a few days."

"Caleb—" Jack started, but Caleb pushed the button to end the call, and then turned off his phone not just to avoid further conversation with Jack but to preserve the battery life and to prevent anyone tracing him through the GPS.

For several long moments he stared sightlessly through the windshield of Noelle's SUV. He wanted to trust his lawyer—after all, Jack had been the only one to stick by him throughout the entire nightmare of being charged for murder. Of course, Caleb had paid the man a tidy sum of money to represent him, so that might not mean much. But he couldn't come up with any reason his own lawyer would want him dead.

No, somehow the attempt on his life outside Noelle's house had to be connected with Heather's murder. It was the only thing that made sense. Someone who was afraid he'd discover the truth? Someone who was feeling desperate, now that the so-called eyewitness had disappeared? And why had the guy disappeared? A sudden attack of cold feet about committing perjury? Or something more sinister?

He took a deep breath and slid out of the car, closing the door behind him as silently as possible. Using the magnetic key, he quietly opened the door and slipped inside. He stood for several long seconds, allowing his eyesight to adjust to the darkness and listening to make sure Noelle and Kaitlin were still asleep.

Reassured by the steady breathing, he ventured farther into the room, estimating the location of the bed.

And then nearly fell flat on his face when Kaitlin screamed.

* * *

Noelle bolted upright in bed and gathered the little girl close. "Shh, it's okay, sweetie. I'm here, it's okay," she crooned.

"What's wrong?" Caleb asked hoarsely.

"Nightmare. Shh, Kaitlin, please don't cry. It's okay, sweetie, you're fine. Everything's fine."

She felt the mattress dip as Caleb came over to sit beside them. "Is there anything I can do?" he asked softly.

"For night terrors? I'm afraid not," she responded, still smoothing her hand down Kaitlin's back. After what seemed like ages, the little girl's screams subsided into hiccuping sobs, her tiny face still pressed tightly against her neck. "I'm sure she'll calm down soon."

There was a long pause as she rocked Kaitlin back and forth, still murmuring words of reassurance.

"She's done this before, hasn't she?" he asked.

"Yes, but not lately." *Not for over six months,* but she didn't tell him that. She'd suspected the gunfire, tear gas and subsequent wild ride out the back of her garage would bring them back. "Unfortunately, with everything that happened today, I'm not surprised they returned."

Please, Lord, bring peace to this sweet little girl. She's an innocent victim in all of this.

Noelle lost track of time as she held Kaitlin, waiting for her to fall asleep once again. When Kaitlin's breathing slowed and her tiny body went slack, she stopped rocking and gently lowered the child to the bed. Caleb moved away, and now that her eyes had adjusted to the darkness, she watched him scrub his hands over his face.

She knew just how helpless he felt; she'd experienced the same thing during those first few months that Kaitlin had come to live with her.

"Excuse me," she whispered, making her way into the bathroom. She used the facilities and splashed cold water on her face to brace herself before heading back out to face him.

Caleb had opened the curtains a half inch, allowing the light from the outside parking lot to shine into the room. He was seated on a chair near the window, holding his head in his hands.

He lifted his head when she approached. "This is my fault, isn't it?" he asked.

Why she wanted to make him feel better, she had no idea. "It's not your fault someone shot at you."

"I can't stand the thought of Kaitlin being afraid of me," he whispered.

"She's not," she whispered back. "After all, she let you hold her in the pool, remember?"

He shook his head. "She wanted to swim so badly I think she would have let anyone hold her."

Noelle sank down onto the chair next to him, unable to refute his logic. "She needs a little time, that's all."

He lifted his gaze to hers. "Maybe I can find a safe place for the two of you to stay for a while. Then I'll head off on my own to try and figure out who's trying to kill me."

As much as she wanted him to let them go, she couldn't seem to stop herself from arguing. "Don't you think that's a job for the police? They have more resources than you do."

"Not if they're in on it," he muttered. "Don't you understand? I can't trust the police, not after the way everything went down. The entire community thinks I'm guilty. And I can't take the chance the shooter will use my daughter to get to me."

"Who is the shooter? And why would anyone do something so terrible? I don't understand what's going on, Caleb."

He stared at her in the darkness, and she wished she could see his eyes more clearly. Strange that her earlier distrust of Caleb seemed to have faded in the wake of Kaitlin's nightmare.

"I don't understand what's going on, either," he said. "Other than someone wants to kill me. Likely the same person who killed my wife. And why wouldn't that person try to use Kaitlin? She's my one and only weakness. Anyone who knows me, which includes all the guys on my former SWAT team, would know that I'd do anything to keep my daughter safe."

She wasn't sure what to say to that. "You really think someone on your team killed your wife?"

"Yes, I do. I've thought of nothing but Heather's murder for the fourteen months and it's the only theory that makes sense. I know you don't believe me, but I promise you I didn't kill her. I'd considered filing for divorce, when I discovered she was cheating on me, but I didn't kill her. And I especially wouldn't do that while Kaitlin was sleeping in her bedroom. I wasn't there that night because I'd moved into a motel room. And no matter what that neighbor claimed he saw, I did not go back to the house to kill Heather."

She'd known that Kaitlin being there the night of her mother's murder had been the source of the child's night terrors. The poor child had likely woken to the gunshots and had been found covered with blood in her mother's room.

After seeing Caleb interact with his daughter, she found it hard to believe everything had happened the way the eyewitness had claimed. That Caleb had killed his wife and then had run away from the house, carrying a gun and leaving his daughter behind.

A gun that still hadn't been found.

Not to mention an eyewitness who'd disappeared.

Had Caleb really been sleeping in a motel room while someone else killed his wife?

"You'd better try to get some sleep," he finally said.

"All right." She rose to her feet and crossed over to the bed she shared with Kaitlin.

But sleep was a long time coming, because for some odd reason, she found she was beginning to believe Caleb was in fact innocent of the crime he'd been accused of.

But knowing that didn't reassure her the way she thought it would.

Because whoever had tried to kill Caleb outside her house was very likely still looking for him. And she was deeply afraid that the killer wouldn't hesitate to take the life of a woman and child, too, if necessary.

THREE

Caleb woke up after five hours of sleep, feeling surprisingly refreshed. Maybe because it was his first night of sleep as a free man. He'd never slept well in jail, too much noise from the other inmates and guards constantly making rounds. Even a low-budget motel room was better than what he'd left behind.

The sun was up, but it was still early, barely seven-thirty in the morning. Noelle and Kaitlin were sleeping in, so he quietly made his way to the bathroom, gently closing the door behind him. He felt better after a hot shower, but wished he had a razor and toothpaste.

He planned to make good on his promise to do some shopping right after breakfast. Then maybe they could take Kaitlin swimming again, before they had to hit the road. As much as he wanted to stay here another day, he didn't dare stick around in one spot for too long. He'd just have to find another motel with a pool for Kaitlin.

Remembering his daughter's nightmare made him frown. It had been the first hint of what his daughter had gone through emotionally and psychologically after his arrest. He was sincerely glad to know that Noelle had been there for Kaitlin the past fourteen months. The way she'd soothed his daughter last night during her nightmare had touched his heart.

Noelle was a much better mother than Heather had been.

The instant the thought sank in, he thrust it away. He closed his eyes and dragged his hands over his rough cheeks. The demise of his marriage hadn't been all Heather's fault and he needed to stop thinking negative thoughts about his former wife. No matter how she'd betrayed him, and violated their marriage vows, she hadn't deserved to be murdered.

He shoved the past away and finished cleaning up. When he emerged from the bathroom, Noelle was sitting at the side of the bed, finger-combing her hair. "Good morning," she whispered.

"Morning." The hint of fear that had shadowed her eyes since he arrived on her doorstep seemed to have vanished. He was afraid to hope that maybe, just maybe, she was starting to believe him. "I thought we'd get something to eat and then find a store. I'm sure you'd like some toothpaste as much as I would."

A shy smile bloomed on her face. "Yes, that would be wonderful."

Kaitlin opened her eyes and rolled onto her back, a tiny frown furrowing her brow as she looked around in confusion. "Noa?"

"I'm here, sweetheart," Noelle said as she pulled the little girl close and gave her a hug.

He wanted to give his daughter a hug, too, but stayed where he was, hoping she'd remember the way he'd held her in the pool rather than the way they'd escaped the gunman at Noelle's house. "Hey, Katydid, are you hungry?"

Kaitlin gazed at him solemnly before nodding her head. "Yes."

"Me, too," Noelle said. "Let's wash up in the bathroom first, okay, Kaitlin? Then we'll get some breakfast."

Kaitlin let go of Noelle and scrambled off the bed. She went into the bathroom and Noelle grabbed the pink backpack before following his daughter.

While he waited, he took out his wallet to double-check the amount of cash he had left. Thankfully Jack had stopped at the bank on the way home so that Caleb could draw out a chunk of his savings, partially to pay his legal fees along with having some cash to live on. Good thing, since staying alive was obviously a priority at the moment.

Heather had made a good living as a model before they'd gotten married, and after Kaitlin's birth she'd worked out like a maniac to get back in shape to resume her career. He'd tried to tell her she didn't need to keep modeling, but she'd insisted. The amount of money she made was more than what he made as a member of the SWAT team, but he'd rather Heather would have been content to do something else. It wasn't as if she was going to be able to model for the rest of her life. But she'd refused to consider a second career. He hadn't wanted to leave Kaitlin in the preschool center full-time, but Heather had insisted.

As a result of their combined incomes, they'd had a substantial amount of money saved up. Enough that he'd been able to continue paying the mortgage while he was behind bars. With Jack's help he'd listed the house on the market, but apparently no one was anxious to buy a home where a murder had taken place.

Not that he could blame them.

The amount of cash he had would probably only last them a week, maybe more if he was frugal. He considered calling Jack for assistance in getting more money, but decided he'd wait until the following Monday. Considering it was a Saturday, there wasn't enough time to get back into Milwaukee before the banks closed. Besides, he didn't really want to head back into town so soon after leaving. Not when he suspected the cops would be looking for him and for Noelle's SUV.

He was sure to be a *person of interest* despite Jack's assurances that he was a victim. When he'd been arrested after Heather's death, he'd assumed that he'd be found innocent because he was. But then the eyewitness had stepped forward and he had no choice but to grapple with the possibility of spending the rest of his life behind bars.

No way was he making the same mistake twice.

The bathroom door opened, letting a cloud of steam into the room. Noelle's hair was damp from her shower, and Kaitlin was wearing her previous clothes. He quickly stuffed the money back into his wallet and turned toward them. "Ready for breakfast?"

"Absolutely," Noelle said cheerfully. For a moment her gaze locked on his and he wished he knew what she was thinking. Had she changed her mind about him at all? Or was that wishful thinking? And why did he care?

"Let's go," he said, crossing over to open the motel room door. Kaitlin eagerly dashed outside, as if the nightmare from last night was already forgotten. Noelle seemed content to walk beside him.

After they reached the car, Noelle helped Kaitlin into her booster seat before taking her place beside him up front without his having to ask. He headed down the road to a well-known chain restaurant that served breakfast, trying not to read too much into Noelle's small gesture of trust.

No matter how much he wanted to.

Noelle finished her breakfast, a yummy veggie omelet, before she realized that she hadn't once looked for an opportunity to escape.

Was she crazy to put her trust in Caleb? She sipped her coffee, trying to sort out her feelings.

Caleb's despair last night hadn't been faked. He'd truly felt awful about Kaitlin's nightmare. But did the fact that he loved his daughter make him innocent of the crime he'd been arrested for? Of course not.

So why did she suddenly believe him?

She closed her eyes for a moment and prayed. *Dear Lord, I don't know what to believe. Please help guide me. Please show me the way.*

A sense of peace settled over her and she realized that if Caleb had intended to hurt them, he would have done that already. Instead he'd done nothing but provide food and shelter. Not to mention, finding a pool to make his daughter happy.

Even now, he was coloring the paper cartoon place mat with Kaitlin, as if he didn't have a care in the world.

"No, Daddy, purple," Kaitlin insisted, shoving the green crayon aside. "Not green, purple."

"You're right, Katydid, purple is way prettier than green," Caleb agreed.

Noelle hid a smile behind her coffee mug. If she wasn't seeing the way he tried so hard to bond with his daughter with her own eyes, she wasn't sure she would have believed it. Especially when she hadn't watched Caleb interact with his daughter very much before he'd been accused of murder.

"Kaitlin, why don't you finish your scrambled eggs and bacon before they get cold," she suggested.

"We're almost done," Kaitlin muttered, filling in the last of the cartoon character's bright purple dress. "See?" She held the paper up high. "Isn't it pretty?"

"Very pretty," she agreed. Caleb set down his crayon and reached for his own cup of coffee.

"Here, this is for you, Daddy." In a surprise gesture, Kaitlin handed the picture to Caleb and then picked up a piece of bacon.

"Thanks, Katydid," Caleb murmured in a husky tone. For a moment she thought there was a glint of tears in his eyes, but then it was gone. He gave Kaitlin a broad smile and carefully set the place mat in the center of the table, where it wouldn't get stained with food or drink. "This is the best present, ever."

She simply couldn't believe a man who cared so much about his daughter that he nearly cried after getting a picture from her was cold and callous enough to kill his ex-wife. In the past twenty-four hours, there'd been no sign of his so-called hair-trigger temper, either.

At this point, she had no reason not to give him the benefit of the doubt.

"Do you want anything more?" Caleb asked.

"No way, I'm stuffed," Noelle murmured, sitting back in her chair and feeling a bit guilty at how much she'd eaten. "That was delicious. Thanks, Caleb."

"You're welcome." He quickly finished his own meal, and then gestured for the waitress to bring the bill. He glanced at the amount and pulled out his wallet, leafing through the bills.

For the first time since this mad escape had started she found herself wondering how long they could stay on the run like this. She didn't have her purse, so she couldn't help pay for anything. What would happen when they ran out of cash? What if they messed up and the shooter who'd tried to kill Caleb found them?

She shivered, suddenly cold. Should she tell Caleb about the black truck that had been following her in the days prior to his release? Should she tell him about the man who'd accompanied his wife to pick up Kaitlin the Friday evening before she'd died? She'd told the police, but since she didn't have a name, there wasn't much they could do. The officer she spoke with assumed the guy was the same man Heather was having an affair with.

Wasn't it possible that man had killed Heather, rather than Caleb?

"Are you all right?" Caleb asked with a slight frown.

"Sure," she said, forcing a smile. The way he seemed to be tuned in to her emotions shouldn't make her believe in him even more. But it did. She reminded herself that Caleb wasn't her type. She didn't date men, especially handsome men. There was no way she should even think about Caleb on a personal level. Trusting a man enough to have a relationship was far too difficult for her.

"All finished, Katydid?" Caleb asked his daughter.

The little girl nodded and pushed her plate away. She'd eaten most of her food this morning, which gave Noelle some encouragement. Maybe if they kept things calm today, the little girl wouldn't suffer another night terror at bedtime.

They left the restaurant and stopped at the strip mall that was only a couple of miles away. Despite her concerns about money, Caleb seemed determined to get them each a change of clothes, including sweatshirts for the cooler nights, swimsuits and toiletries. Kaitlin was thrilled to have another sparkly swimsuit, jumping up and down with excitement when Caleb agreed to buy it for her. Noelle winced at the total, but he readily paid in cash.

It wasn't until they were walking back out to the parking lot, with Kaitlin skipping between them, that she noticed the license plates on her car. She stopped abruptly and stared.

Caleb instantly noticed her reaction. "Noelle, I only swapped them to keep us safe."

Logically she knew that, but he'd broken the law just the same. Apprehension swelled in her chest. "What if we get caught?"

His gaze was full of empathy. "Please try to trust me in this. I won't do anything to hurt you or Kaitlin. We'll take Kaitlin swimming and then hit the road. We'll be far away from here soon enough."

She took a ragged breath and gave a jerky nod. When Caleb opened the back of her car she stored the bag inside, hoping he didn't notice the way her hands were shaking.

Never in her life had she committed a crime. She always followed the rules. As a preschool teacher she took her job as being a role model for her students seriously. Granted she wasn't perfect. After all, she'd failed her previous foster child. She'd thought for sure she was getting through to the youngster but Stephanie had run away and had been found dead of a drug overdose.

No matter how much she'd prayed for peace, Noelle still carried the guilt over Stephanie's death. She'd done her best to make amends by helping Kaitlin.

She lifted Kaitlin into her booster seat and wondered

if she'd made a grave mistake by trusting her instincts as far as Caleb was concerned.

Caleb glanced over at Noelle for the third time in five minutes, wishing she would say something. Anything. But she didn't. She merely sat there, looking devastated. The shadow of fear was back in her eyes and he knew that his actions had put it there.

He shouldn't care what she thought about him, but he did. For so long, no one had believed him. Not the D.A. Not his teammates. Certainly not the media. He wasn't sure that Jack had really believed him, despite what the lawyer had claimed.

Even his closest friend, Declan Shaw, hadn't believed him.

So why was he surprised that Noelle, a virtual stranger, was suddenly acting as if he deserved to go back to prison?

The silence between them stretched as they made their way back to the motel. Most of the cars that had been parked outside were gone, probably because it was near the designated checkout time.

But he wasn't leaving until Kaitlin had a chance to swim. He parked in front of their room and slid out from behind the wheel. "Why don't you change into your swimsuits and I'll meet you out at the pool?" he suggested.

"Yay! I getta swim in my sparkly suit!" Kaitlin shrieked. He smiled grimly. At least one of them was happy.

"Sure." Noelle's less than enthusiastic response made him feel bad, but there wasn't much he could do to change what he'd done. Especially since he wasn't about to apologize for swapping out the plates. As far as he was concerned it was a small price to pay for keeping his daughter safe.

He carried the bag inside and then left them to change. He walked down to the office, relieved to see a woman sitting behind the counter, rather than the crabby old guy. He waited for her to finish with another couple who were checking out before he stepped up to the counter.

"Hi, we're in room twelve and we're checking out today, but would you mind if we did a late checkout so my daughter can swim before we leave? It would really mean a lot to her."

The woman scowled and shook her head. "Rules are rules. I'm afraid I'll have to charge you an extra fee for a late checkout."

He narrowed his gaze, but didn't bother arguing with her. He wondered what she and the old man had to be so crabby about anyway? "Fine, I'll load up the car now, then. Here's the amount we owe." He handed over the cash, tapping his foot impatiently as she took her time counting out the bills.

"Leave your key in the room," she instructed.

"I will." He turned and left, trying not to be annoyed. The girls were finished changing by the time he arrived. Noelle had a towel draped over her shoulders. "We'll just head out to the pool, okay?"

"Sure. We have to pack our stuff and vacate the room, so I'll be down in a few minutes."

Noelle didn't meet his gaze, but took Kaitlin's hand and headed outside. He quickly changed into a pair of swim trunks and a T-shirt before putting everything they'd purchased back in the plastic bag. He moved the car so that it wasn't right in front of the room, and parked it off to the far side of the parking lot, but within view of the pool. Then he took the bag to the pool area with him, figuring they could change their clothes in the restrooms located in the small building adjacent to the swimming area.

When he arrived he found Noelle and Kaitlin in the shallow end of the pool. Noelle was holding Kaitlin as she moved around in the water, while his daughter giggled and splashed.

He wished he was the one holding his daughter. He'd been secretly thrilled when she'd given him the coloring picture at the restaurant, but that brief moment of closeness seemed to have vanished.

And he would have done anything to bring it back.

He set their bag off to the side and joined them in the water, swimming laps while Noelle and Kaitlin played. After about an hour, he noticed his daughter was shivering and decided it was time for them to leave.

"But I don't wanna leave," Kaitlin wailed.

Noelle wrapped a towel around his daughter. "Kaitlin, you're shivering and your lips are blue. Let's go and change our clothes, okay?"

"B-but I'm n-not c-cold," Kaitlin protested, despite the way her teeth were chattering.

He had to smile at his daughter's stubborn streak. He had no idea how much she enjoyed the water, and he knew that he needed to find another hotel with a pool. Maybe if he acted as if this was nothing more than a fun vacation, she wouldn't have any more nightmares.

He took his own clothes inside the men's room and quickly changed. When he returned he wrapped his wet things in one of the smaller plastic bags.

Noelle and Kaitlin emerged from the women's room

a few minutes later. "Here, I'll take your wet things," he said.

"Thanks," Noelle murmured as she handed over their wet clothes. Some of the tension seemed to have eased between them as she lifted her face to the sun. "Feels good to be warm."

"I know." He felt bad about dragging them away from the cozy motel, but he couldn't help the nagging feeling that they needed to keep moving. Even though he'd changed the license plates, it wasn't as if they still couldn't be found. For all he knew, the guy whose plates he swapped with had already informed the authorities. The cops could already be, right now, looking for the stolen tags he'd put on Noelle's car.

"No, I don't wanna go for a ride!" Kaitlin ran in the opposite direction, toward the plastic deck chairs lining the far side of the pool. Today, Noelle had dressed her in purple, his daughter's favorite color, with matching purple barrettes in her hair. Her cleft chin was thrust forward in a stubborn way that made him smile. Maybe he was a tad biased but he thought Kaitlin was the cutest kid on the planet.

Noelle let out an exasperated sigh at his adorable daughter's antics.

"Do you want me to get her?" he offered.

"No, I'll do it." Noelle walked slowly over to where Kaitlin stood, halfway hidden behind a deck chair. He lifted the plastic bag over his shoulder and followed.

A loud explosion caused him to instinctively duck and rush over to where Noelle and Kaitlin were standing. "Are you okay?" he asked hoarsely.

Kaitlin was crying but Noelle nodded. "Look!" she said with a gasp, pointing over his shoulder.

He turned and stared in shock at the ball of fire that engulfed Noelle's SUV.

Horror seeped through his bones. If not for Kaitlin's refusal to go along with them, they all would have been killed!

FOUR

Noelle couldn't tear her gaze away from the terrible black smoke and orange flames obscuring her car. How could this happen? Who had blown up her car? How had they been found?

"Come on, we have to get out of here!" Caleb picked up Kaitlin. "Grab the bag," he said as he headed over toward the fence. She picked up their meager belongings and hurried after him, trying to think logically.

"We can't just leave!" she whispered.

"Yes, we can. Whoever lit up your car could still be around." Caleb's terse tone made it clear he wasn't about to be swayed by any argument. "You go over the fence first, and I'll hand Kaitlin over."

She hadn't crawled over a fence since she was a teenager on the run from her foster home, but fear was a strong incentive. Caleb gave her a boost and she scrambled up and over. When she was safe on the other side, he lifted Kaitlin up and held her over the other side until Noelle had her. When she set the child on her feet, he tossed her the bag. Within moments he'd vaulted the fence and was standing beside her.

"See that outcropping of trees over there?" he asked in a low tone.

The trees were about fifty yards away. "Yes."

"I'll take Kaitlin. You take the bag. Keep your head down and run as fast as you can."

Miraculously Kaitlin didn't put up a fuss when Caleb scooped her into his arms. Noelle grasped the bag, took a deep breath and ran.

She stayed hunched over as much as possible, bracing herself for the sound of gunfire. She could feel Caleb's warm breath on her back as he ran behind her. When they reached the relative safety of the trees, she stopped and bent over to catch her breath.

"We have to keep going," Caleb urged, lightly grasping her arm. "Follow me."

She swallowed hard and nodded. She followed in his wake, running as best she could, darting between the trees with the plastic bag bumping against her legs along the way. She toyed with the idea of dumping it but figured she'd hang on as long as she could.

The woods ended abruptly in front of a cornfield. The stalks of corn weren't very high, but Caleb went into the narrow path between the rows regardless. She followed, darting a glance over her shoulder.

She didn't see anyone following them, but then again, she hadn't seen anyone before her car blew up, either. What choice did they have but to put as much distance between themselves and the motel as possible?

Strangely enough, she trusted Caleb to lead them to safety.

The wailing sounds of police sirens split the air and she saw Caleb tense before he increased the pace. She was already running as fast as she could, but she struggled to keep up. She wasn't a runner by nature. She hated jogging.

"This way," Caleb said as he veered off to the right. There was an old farmhouse up ahead. She instinctively slowed. Why on earth would he risk going to a farmhouse? There had to be people living there, otherwise who'd planted the corn?

"Wait," she said between gasping breaths. "What are you doing?"

"I've been watching the place for a few minutes now. It looks pretty dilapidated. So far, I haven't seen anything indicating someone is living there," Caleb explained. "Once we're at the farmhouse we can rest for a few minutes."

She was apprehensive about following him but as they approached, she relaxed as the state of disrepair became more obvious. The wood siding that had once been a light green or yellow, hard to tell as it hadn't been painted in at least a decade, and several windows were broken. The yard was seriously overgrown with tall grass and mega-weeds. The front porch was sagging so badly she had to assume the boards were rotting away underneath. There was no indication anyone was living there, and Caleb led them around to the back of the house, where there was plenty of shade providing relief from the sun. He gently set Kaitlin on her feet and the little girl rushed over to Noelle.

Noelle hugged her close and sank down into the long grass. *Thank You, Lord, for saving us!*

Caleb knew Kaitlin and Noelle needed some time to rest and recover, but he couldn't help feeling nervous as he glanced around to make sure they weren't followed.

He'd ditched his cell phone back in the cornfield, not a big loss as the thing was out of battery anyway, but still, he wouldn't be happy until they were far away from here.

The sirens had gone silent and he assumed that meant the police and the fire trucks had reached the motel. How long before the cops fanned out to look for them? Surely the desk clerk would be able to give adequate descriptions. Of him, for sure, although now that he thought about it, only the old man had seen Noelle and Kaitlin.

Still, they needed to get to safety. But how? The odds of getting away on foot weren't good. Especially since he would have to carry Kaitlin.

Squinting at their surroundings, he searched for familiar landmarks. When he recognized the buildings way off in the distance, he realized he'd headed in the same direction as the strip mall where they'd gone shopping earlier that morning. The mall provided at least one opportunity. As a cop he didn't like breaking the law, but what else could he do? If he didn't steal a car they'd never survive.

Oddly enough, he didn't like the thought of disappointing Noelle, either, but their safety was more important than worrying about his ridiculous feelings. He'd do whatever it took to keep them safe.

"I'm thirsty," Kaitlin said.

Regret welled in his chest. "I'm sorry, Katydid, but I'll get you some water as soon as possible, okay?"

"What's the plan?" Noelle asked with a weary smile.

He had to admit she'd held up through their mad dash through the woods like a trouper. "The mall where we shopped earlier today is a couple of miles down the road to the north," he said, indicating the general direction with a wave of his hand. "I think that's our best option."

Her gaze was troubled as she looked up at him. "We're

not going to get very far without a car, are we?" she asked, a note of defeat in her tone.

"We'll think of something," he assured her. No point in worrying about the next step until they had to. "Are you ready to keep going?"

"Sure." She stood and picked up the plastic bag. "Let's go."

He buried a flash of admiration for her strength and determination as he looked at Kaitlin. "Do you want to ride on my shoulders, Katydid?"

His daughter regarded him steadily for a moment and he hoped she might remember when he'd carried her like that when they attended the state fair a few short weeks before his wife's murder and his nightmare had begun. How he longed for those days. After what seemed like forever, she nodded and held up her arms. "Up!" she commanded.

His heart swelled with love as he put his hands around her tiny frame, lifted her up and set her gently on his shoulders. She clutched at his head, her tiny fingers finding his ears as a way to hang on when he started walking.

He ignored the discomfort, too happy to know his daughter was finally getting over her fear of him.

"Look, Daddy, birdies!" Kaitlin exclaimed.

"I see them, Katydid."

"Caleb, the road is over there," Noelle said, waving to the right.

"I know, but we'll save time if we cut through the cornfields." Being careful not to dislodge his daughter, he swept his gaze around the area, making sure they weren't attracting attention. "I'm guessing this farmland is being leased out to someone. It would explain the abandoned farmhouse."

"I guess you could be right. But, Caleb, why didn't the license plate swap work?" Noelle asked in a low tone. "Is it possible we were being followed the whole time?"

He let his breath out in a sigh. "I guess anything's possible, but I can't see how I would have missed a tail. And if someone had followed us, why wait so long to make a move? We'd been at the motel for over twenty-four hours. There was plenty of time to go after us then." The more he thought about it, the more he realized how unlikely that was. "No, I can't believe we were followed."

"Then how did they find us?" she persisted.

Admitting his lack of poor judgment wasn't easy. "I made a mistake," he admitted in a grim tone.

"What mistake?"

"Last night, I called my lawyer, Jack. I thought I kept the call short enough, but considering what happened, I have to assume that he managed to get a trace on me."

"But why? Why would your lawyer do something like this?" she asked.

"Giddyup, Daddy," Kaitlin said, kicking her heels. "You're my horsey!"

The interruption made him chuckle, despite the seriousness of their situation. "This horsey isn't going any faster, Katydid. You might fall off." He glanced over at Noelle. "I don't know why Jack would do something like this," he said in a low tone. "It doesn't make any sense, especially since he worked so hard to get me released from jail."

Noelle switched the bag over to her other hand and he knew the bag was getting heavy. "Could someone else have tapped into your lawyer's phone to trace you here?"

He turned the possibility over in his mind. "A cop would have the technology and the equipment to do that," he said slowly. "I'm already convinced the guy who took a shot at me outside your house is someone from the team. That was a long but unerringly accurate shot."

"Except he missed," she said.

"Only because of Giffy," he muttered wryly.

"Or maybe because God has other plans for you," she persisted. "I'm so thankful God has been watching over us."

He wasn't sure what to say to that, so he kept silent. Was God watching over them? Watching over Noelle and Kaitlin, maybe, but him? Doubtful.

His shoulders were feeling the strain of carrying Kaitlin over the uneven turf so he kept his sights focused on the shopping mall. He didn't want to point out that God wasn't going to be too happy with him after he hotwired a car.

Because truthfully, Noelle's disappointment would hurt more than anything God could dish out.

Noelle's arm muscles were screaming in protest from lugging their bag of belongings, but since Caleb was carrying Kaitlin she refused to complain.

She tried to keep focused on getting to safety. The buildings making up the shopping mall were slowly but surely getting closer. Once again, Caleb had saved her life. She'd never depended on a man before, not even when she was a teenager on the run from a physically abusive foster home. To this day she thanked God for sending her to a women's shelter run by Abigail Carrington. Abby had helped her turn her life around. She never would have gotten her GED and gone on to college if not for Abby's support.

After getting her preschool job and buying her very

first home, she decided to try and give back to the community, the way Abby had given so selflessly to her. So she'd gone through the red tape of becoming a foster parent and had opened her home to Stephanie, a troubled young girl who'd been in rehab for drug abuse at the tender age of thirteen.

She veered away from thoughts of Stephanie; the pain of losing the young girl was still too raw even after two years. She hated knowing how badly she'd failed the young girl.

"Are you okay up there, Katydid?" Caleb asked.

"I wanna get down," Kaitlin whined.

"All right." Caleb stopped and carefully lifted the little girl off his shoulders. He held Kaitlin in his arms but she squirmed.

"I wanna walk by myself," she said with a pout.

Caleb shot her a helpless look and Noelle smiled and nodded. "I'm sure she'll be okay for a while."

"Here, I'll carry our stuff, then," he said, reaching for the bag. Their fingers brushed and clung as she untangled her fingers from the plastic.

"Thanks," she said breathlessly, avoiding his gaze. What was wrong with her? She should be immune to men, especially a guy like Caleb. She'd only had one boyfriend during college and that relationship had ended after a few short months because she just couldn't bring herself to trust Daniel. He quickly moved on to someone else, which convinced her she'd made the right decision. What she didn't know about men would fill an entire library.

She reminded herself that Caleb had been married to Heather, a beautiful, striking model with a slender figure and long, silky blond hair. He'd never be interested in someone plain, like her. And she should be absolutely glad about that.

So why wasn't she?

Stress. It had to be stress making her think these crazy thoughts. Stress of being on the run from someone who'd tried to kill them. Twice. Any normal woman would be stressed under these circumstances, right? Right.

Yet she couldn't deny that being with Caleb like this was far better than those horrible weeks she'd been on the streets alone back when she was seventeen.

"Hey, don't worry, we're almost there," Caleb said in an encouraging tone.

She realized she must have been scowling, so she relaxed her features. "I know."

"So far there's no sign of the police searching for us," he added. "I have to admit I'm a little surprised."

"Me, too. I thought they'd bring out the bloodhounds," she joked.

"Be glad they didn't," he said soberly.

Kaitlin was skipping ahead but she tripped and fell, letting out a screech. "Owwwieee!"

Noelle rushed over and scooped the girl up. "Shh, it's okay, sweetheart. Let me see. There now, there's no blood. It's okay. You're okay."

Thankfully Kaitlin's cries diminished to mere sniffles when she saw that indeed there was no blood. Noelle picked Kaitlin up, intending to carry the child for a little while.

"I can take her," Caleb offered. "She's too heavy for you to carry for long."

She reluctantly handed Kaitlin over, knowing he was right. Their bag of clothing and toiletries wasn't very heavy, either, at first but after a mile it had felt like a ton of bricks.

They were only twenty feet away from the mall parking lot now, and as they approached she noticed there was a big chartered bus parked in the center of the lot. And then she saw the soft-drink vending machine. Just seeing the cold drinks inside made her keenly aware of how parched she was.

"First stop, water," she said to Caleb as their footsteps hit the pavement.

"I'm with you," he murmured. He set Kaitlin down again, but this time held on to his daughter's hand so she couldn't run off as they crossed the parking lot.

As Caleb fed dollar bills into the vending machine, Noelle couldn't help watching the bus. There appeared to be several elderly people nearby, making her wonder if they'd come here on some sort of senior shopping trip.

"Here," Caleb said, handing her an ice-cold water bottle.

"Thanks. Kaitlin, do you want a drink?" she asked as she unscrewed the cap.

"Yes." Kaitlin tried to grab the water, but she held firm, so it wouldn't spill as the child took several big gulps. When the little girl was finished, she took a long sip herself.

"Wow, that hit the spot," Caleb murmured as he recapped his water. "Why don't you two rest in the shade for a while? I'll be back soon."

Back? Where was he going? And then she knew he intended to steal a car. "Caleb, wait." She reached out to grasp his arm to prevent him from leaving. His skin was so hot she was half-afraid she'd be seared by the touch.

Yet she refused to let go. "Why don't you let me talk to the bus driver first?"

"The bus driver?" he repeated. He looked over and frowned. "Noelle, that's a private bus, chartered for a specific event. There's no way they're going to give us a ride," he protested.

She knew the odds weren't good, but she didn't care. "Have faith, Caleb. At the very least it can't hurt to ask. Wait here a moment, okay?"

She could tell he didn't want to let her go over there alone, but really after everything they'd been through it wasn't as if a bus driver and an elderly woman presented any sort of danger. Wishing she wasn't quite so hot and sweaty, she walked over to where the bus driver, a bald man who looked to be in his mid-sixties, was talking to a woman who was probably a decade older. From the gist of the conversation it appeared they were intending to leave soon.

Please, Lord, guide me through this.

"Hi there," she greeted them warmly. "My name is Noelle and we had a little car trouble a few miles back. Is there any way you would consider giving us a ride to wherever you're headed? We'd be so grateful."

"That's against the rules," the bus driver said quickly. "Sorry."

"Oh my dear, that's terrible," the elderly woman said with clear sympathy. "Do you want to borrow my phone to call a tow truck?"

"No, thanks, we really can't afford a tow truck and the car wasn't really worth much anyway," Noelle said sadly. She forced a smile and glanced again at the bus driver. If she could convince him to take them along, she thought for sure the elderly woman wouldn't mind.

"I understand it's against the rules, but Kaitlin is only five and she's exhausted and hungry. We aren't asking you to go out of your way. Please?"

"That's not an option," he said firmly.

She swallowed a frustrated sigh. She had no idea what she could say to make this stubborn old man change his mind.

"Look, Harry, give this poor girl a break, will you? She's a nice Christian woman," the elderly woman said.

Noelle's jaw dropped open. "How did you know?" she asked.

The elderly woman gave her arm a gentle pat. "You're wearing a cross around your neck, my dear," she said in a soothing tone. "Now, Harry, what can it hurt to give this nice family a ride back to Madison? Three additional people aren't going to make one bit of difference to you. We've already paid you for the trip, haven't we?"

The old man scowled and scratched his jaw. "Don't see what good a ride will do, they have to get a tow truck eventually," he groused.

"What do you care if they do or they don't?" the elderly woman asked with exasperation. "Now, listen here, Harry, giving these young folks a helping hand is the right thing to do. Now, are you going to give them a ride or not?"

The bus driver must have realized he'd soon be outnumbered because he let out a huff and threw up his hands. "Okay, okay. I'll give them a ride."

Relief threatened to buckle Noelle's knees. "Oh, thank you! Thank you so much!"

"My name is Lydia Rawlings," the elderly woman said. "But you can call me Lydia. Now bring that cute little girl and that handsome husband of yours over and introduce us properly."

Husband? Noelle blinked in surprise, but didn't correct Lydia's assumption as she gestured for Caleb and Kaitlin to come over. Caleb's gaze was questioning as he approached.

She wet her lips nervously. "Caleb, I'd like you to meet Lydia Rawlings, who has graciously agreed to give us a ride to Madison. Lydia, this is Caleb and Kaitlin."

"Pleased to meet you, ma'am," Caleb said, offering his hand. "We're very grateful for the lift."

"Well, the Lord always finds a way to provide, doesn't He?" Lydia said with a laugh. "It's a pleasure to meet you, too, such a beautiful family. Now go ahead and climb inside. I can see the rest of the group is already making their way over."

Caleb's gaze clashed with hers and she lifted her shoulder in a tiny shrug in response to his unspoken question. She hadn't told Lydia they were a family and certainly it wasn't her fault the woman had jumped to that conclusion.

But as she climbed inside the blessed coolness of the bus, she found herself wishing they were a real family, instead of a make-believe one.

FIVE

Caleb followed Noelle and Kaitlin to the back of the bus, taking the seat directly behind the one they slid into together. He had to admit being very surprised Noelle had managed to convince the bus driver to take them along. And he was glad he didn't have to steal a car.

At least not yet.

Many of the elderly patrons of the bus filed in behind them, greeting the newcomers as they took their seats. Noelle chatted cheerfully, giving a good impression that they had nothing to hide as she thanked them again for allowing them to ride along.

Now that they were relatively safe, he couldn't help trying to figure out how they'd been tracked to the motel. Jack Owens had to be the leak. There was no other explanation. Caleb had kept his phone off, turning it on to make the one call to Jack, before shutting the phone down again.

Grimly, he knew if they'd checked out of the motel on time, hitting the road as he'd initially intended, they would have been driving along the interstate when the vehicle exploded. He wished he could go back and review the wreckage to look for proof. The more he thought about it, he had to assume the explosive device had been on some sort of timer. Because if someone had been keeping them under surveillance, that person would have made sure the three of them were tucked inside the SUV before the blast.

He scrubbed his hands over his face. If he hadn't insisted on taking Kaitlin for a swim, they would all be dead. Mission accomplished for the bad guy.

But why? That was the part he couldn't quite figure out. Obviously this had to be linked to his wife's murder, but he was having trouble connecting the dots. Other than the fact that whoever had killed his wife must be worried that Caleb would figure it out. Avoiding life in prison was a strong motive for the bad guy to kill him.

Unfortunately he really didn't have a clue who that person was. Someone from the SWAT team, sure, but which one? They all had experience with explosives so it was not as if the bombing of the SUV was a good clue. Most of them were sharpshooters, too. Although he figured he could cross a couple of the guys off the sharpshooter list. Declan had been one of his best friends but the guy couldn't hit the center of a target at one hundred and fifty feet if his life depended on it. Declan had other skills for sure, including nerves of steel when it came to defusing bombs. But as a sharpshooter? No way.

The thought of Deck making a bomb and sticking it under their vehicle made him feel sick to his stomach. He and Deck had trained together. Deck had been the best man at his wedding.

Had his best friend betrayed him?

He stared out the tinted windows, watching the elderly shoppers making their way toward the bus. They would be on the road soon, which suited him just fine.

But his gut twisted when a squad car rolled into the parking lot of the shopping mall.

Slouching down in his seat, he silently willed the elderly shoppers to hurry. The bus was more than half full, but these people were moving slower than snails, stopping and chatting along the way.

He could tell Noelle had seen the squad car, too, when she shot him a panicked look over her shoulder. He silently shook his head, indicating there was nothing they could do but to wait and hope the bus driver would get on the road. Soon. Thankfully the tinted windows would help hide them.

But what if the cops came onto the bus to search for them? They were sitting ducks here in their seats. He couldn't bear to think about it.

Honestly he was surprised it took the cops this long to fan out and search for them. He'd kept a keen eye out the entire trip here from the farmhouse to make sure the cops weren't following their tail. The only rational explanation was that they'd needed to get the fire under control first, to verify they weren't actually inside the car.

Unfortunately, the cops were here now.

He couldn't tear his gaze from the squad car, tracking its progress as it headed toward the storefront.

Hurry, hurry! he silently urged the shoppers. The squad car slowed to a stop and two deputies stepped out, both holding photos in their hands.

Pictures of him, and possibly Noelle and Kaitlin, too. A wave of helpless anger washed over him. He should have realized there were cameras in the lobby of the motel. These days there were cameras everywhere. He was trained as a cop, an elite member of the SWAT team.

Being in jail for the past year was no excuse. If he didn't get his head in the game, he'd get them all killed.

One of the deputies turned and glanced over at the bus. He was saying something, but Caleb couldn't figure out what. He clenched his jaw so tight he was surprised he didn't crack a molar. There were only a couple of elderly shoppers left, but the very last woman was walking with excruciating slowness, leaning heavily on her cane for support.

Come on! Hurry!

He wondered if the bus driver hadn't somehow felt his intense vibe to leave as the older guy stepped off the bus to give the woman with her cane a helping hand. The second deputy gestured toward the drugstore where they'd stopped yesterday to pick up their toiletries. After a long heartbeat, the two men went inside the store.

Grimly, he realized the female clerk would likely identify them to the cops, as she'd made a big fuss over Kaitlin at the time. And they'd only been there a few hours ago.

The cane woman finally dropped into a seat toward the front of the bus. The driver stood in the aisle and counted his passengers, making sure not to leave anyone behind.

"Please, Lord, help keep us safe," Noelle whispered. And he found himself echoing her prayer.

The driver took his seat and closed the doors. "Everyone ready?" he called out.

"Yes!" the chorus of replies rang out from the shoppers.

The driver put the bus in gear and slowly stepped on the gas, sending the bus waddling like an overweight hippo toward the exit. Caleb couldn't help glancing back at the squad car, willing the deputies not to come out too soon.

It wasn't until the bus hit the highway, kicking up speed, that he allowed himself to relax. Granted they weren't out of the woods yet, but if the drugstore clerk did recognize them, there was a good chance the deputies might check the other stores, as well. They'd been at the drugstore earlier that morning but maybe the cops would try to see if anyone remembered seeing them more recently, like early this afternoon. Thankfully they'd gotten on the bus and hadn't gone into any of the stores.

After several miles had passed and they took the on-ramp to the interstate, Caleb took a deep breath and let it out slowly. They were safe for now.

Thank You, God!

Noelle unclenched her fingers as they rode along the interstate. Close call. Too close.

She'd sensed the tension radiating off Caleb from the seat behind her and knew he'd been worried, too. But the closer they got to Madison, the better she felt. No matter how much she'd feared Caleb initially, he'd kept her and Kaitlin safe so far.

She'd prayed the whole time the cop car had been parked at the shopping mall and had to believe God was watching over them.

"I'm hungry," Kaitlin whined, interrupting her thoughts.

"We'll eat soon," Noelle reassured the little girl. "As soon as the bus drops us off, okay?"

"I wanna eat now," Kaitlin persisted. The thrill of riding the bus was fading fast.

Noelle racked her brain for a distraction. "Why don't

we play the alphabet game?" she suggested. "There's a sign for Acorn Road. That's *A*. Can you find a sign with the letter *B*?" Kaitlin could only read simple sentences, but she knew her letters by heart.

The old tried but true car-ride game kept Kaitlin pre-occupied for a while, and Noelle had to smile when Caleb and some of the elderly shoppers sitting nearby joined in the game. Soon the back half of the bus was shouting out letters of the alphabet until they were stumped on the letter *Z*.

"There! Henry Vilas Zoo!" someone shouted.

"I didn't know there was a zoo in Madison," someone else complained.

"Let's play again!" Kaitlin yelled.

But the bus had already slowed down to pull into the parking lot of a senior-living high-rise.

"We're home," Lydia murmured. Noelle wished they really were home rather than heading to another imper-sonal hotel room.

Being in the back of the bus meant waiting for every-one else to get off first, before they could make their way outside. She glimpsed Caleb pressing a folded bill into the bus driver's hand as a way of saying thanks.

Her muscles were sore from all the running she'd done earlier, but she ignored the discomfort as she got off the bus and then faced Caleb. "I saw a fast-food restaurant a few blocks back," she murmured. "Kaitlin needs to eat."

"I saw it, too," he said. "Let's go."

For the first time in hours they relaxed and enjoyed a quick meal. Caleb asked one of the restaurant workers about motels nearby and thankfully, there was one just a half mile away.

Kaitlin's energy had rebounded after lunch and she

skipped between them as they walked toward the hotel. There was no pool advertised but there was a nice playground, which would hopefully keep Kaitlin happy.

"Swings!" Kaitlin shouted, running toward them.

Caleb took off after his daughter. "Wait up, Katydid."

Noelle followed more slowly, smiling as Caleb pushed his daughter on the swing. Noelle dropped onto a park bench to watch, knowing Caleb deserved some time to bond with his daughter.

She could leave now, she rationalized. Kaitlin didn't seem afraid of her father anymore. Of course, that could be partially because Noelle was there with them. Would the little girl freak out if she left? There was a part of her that wanted to believe Kaitlin would.

No, she couldn't leave Kaitlin just yet. What if the little girl suffered more night terrors? A very strong possibility after they'd barely escaped the explosion. The sound of the explosion was probably all too similar to the gunshot that had taken her mother's life.

"Noelle? Is something wrong?" Caleb asked.

Since when was he so tuned in to her emotions? She forced a smile. "No, I'm fine. Just tired." Massive understatement, but complaining didn't get the job done. In fact, she and Caleb needed to talk. Maybe later, after Kaitlin fell asleep. Because Caleb needed to hear about the black truck that she'd noticed following her. And about the man she'd seen with his wife shortly before she was murdered.

No matter how painful it was for him. Although why she cared about Caleb's feelings she had no idea.

She was so far outside her comfort zone right now that she had to pinch herself to make sure this wasn't some sort of nightmare. But no, here she was, on the run with a little girl and her father, a strange man who she barely knew yet trusted to keep her safe.

"Noa, come swing wif me!" Kaitlin shouted.

Unable to say no to the child, she rose to her feet and crossed over to sit beside Kaitlin. She gave herself a small push with her foot, enough to cause her to swing back and forth in a gentle motion. She vaguely remembered swinging on the swings as a child. Some happy memories before the abuse started.

"Come on, surely you can do better than that," Caleb teased. "Hang on," he advised. She tightened her grip seconds before she felt the heat of his strong hands in the small of her back, giving her a big push.

"Higher, Noa, higher!"

Knowing Caleb would only push her again if she didn't go higher, she pumped her legs to keep up the momentum. And when Kaitlin let out a shrill laugh she found herself joining in.

Maybe she was losing her mind. How else could she explain feeling so lighthearted and happy mere hours after running for her life?

Very simply, she couldn't. And right now, she decided to enjoy the moment.

Noelle didn't say anything about the mysterious black truck that had followed her before the shooting until after they finished dinner and then put an exhausted Kaitlin down to bed shortly after eight o'clock. It was still light outside thanks to the approaching summer solstice so she pulled the heavy curtains over the window and set the air conditioner on low.

The hum of the fan provided white noise that would hopefully prevent their voices from waking up Kaitlin.

"You should try to get some sleep," Caleb said in a low voice.

"So should you." She slid into a seat next to him at the small table in the corner of the room. Their knees brushed and she swiftly moved back out of the way. "There's something you need to know, Caleb," she said, partially to distract herself from his nearness.

His gaze narrowed and he went tense. "Oh yeah?"

She licked her dry lips. "In the week prior to you getting out of jail and coming over to pick up Kaitlin, I noticed a black truck following me."

"What?" He spoke so loud she jumped in her seat. She sent a worried glance over at Kaitlin, but thankfully the girl didn't stir. He lowered his tone. "Did you call the police?"

"Actually I did, but the officer I spoke to told me I needed to get the license plate number before they could do anything." She hunched her shoulders defensively. "But that doesn't matter. The black truck must belong to the shooter. He must have been somewhere close by that day you came to pick up Kaitlin."

"Why didn't you say something before now?" he asked with a frown.

"For one thing, I wasn't entirely sure I could trust you," she admitted. Hard to believe she'd only known Caleb for roughly twenty-four hours. And even more amazing to know she learned to trust him in that same short time frame. "And after the explosion there wasn't time to talk privately."

His expression cleared. "I guess I can't blame you for not trusting me right away," he murmured. "All you had was my word that I was innocent of the crime I'd been arrested for."

She wanted to reach out to put her hand on his arm to offer comfort and had to twist her fingers together to stop herself. "It's obvious to me that someone wants to silence you and the only thing that makes sense is that the same person likely killed your wife."

For a long moment his dark gaze bored into hers. "Does that mean you believe me?"

She couldn't deny what he seemed to desperately want to hear, the reassurance that someone was on his side. Besides, the more she watched him interact with his daughter the more she knew there was no way he would have murdered his wife with Kaitlin sleeping in a bedroom nearby. And for sure, he wouldn't take off, leaving his daughter behind.

"Yes. I believe you."

He stared at her another long moment before he glanced away. "Thank you," he said in a husky tone. "Now, if I could only figure out who was driving that black truck, we'd actually have something to go on."

"I never did get the plate number. But there is something else you should know. I was working at the preschool on that Friday before your wife was killed. Earlier that day, Heather was late picking up Kaitlin."

Caleb sighed. "I was working the evening shift that day. But that sounds like her. Heather was always running late."

She leaned forward in an attempt to get him to understand. "Twenty minutes late, Caleb. And when she showed up, she wasn't alone."

He seemed to brace himself, his gaze resigned. "She was with a man, wasn't she?"

She hated being the one to tell him this, but she nodded. "Yes. It wasn't until much later, after the murder and your arrest that I realized the significance. I went to the police and told them what I saw, but without a name there wasn't much they could do."

"They didn't ask you to work with a sketch artist?" he asked incredulously.

She shook her head.

He narrowed his gaze. "Describe him for me."

It wasn't easy to go back more than a year to dredge up the memory. "He was tall, over six feet, I'd say. He had dirty-blond hair that was cut short." He stared at her so intently she sensed she was failing the description test. "He had narrow, beady eyes and was hovering at the door scowling while Heather picked up Kaitlin."

"How was he dressed? In a uniform?"

"No. Dress slacks and a blue polo shirt."

"Any tattoos? Piercings?"

Helplessly she shook her head. "Nothing that I can remember. I'm sorry, Caleb. I wish I could give you something more."

"It's not your fault," he said with a sigh. "I can't help but think he must be one of the guys from the team. I can probably eliminate a few of them based on your description but there are too many possibilities left over to start throwing around accusations. I need proof."

She couldn't bear the way Caleb sounded so dejected. At the moment they still didn't know much more than they had when this mess started.

There had to be a way to figure out the identity of the mystery man she'd seen at the preschool that evening.

The man who had likely been having an affair with Caleb's wife. And since she didn't want to believe Caleb had killed Heather, she figured a jilted lover would have just as much of a motive.

But how on earth would they be able to prove it?

SIX

Caleb stared up at the ceiling, long after Noelle had crawled into bed with Kaitlin, unable to wipe the pleased grin off his face. Noelle believed him.

She believed him!

How ironic that the person who'd known him the least amount of time was the one who stood by him now. Even his best friend hadn't done that.

Thinking of Declan made his smile fade. He wished Declan had trusted him, because he could use some help in getting to the bottom of this mess. At least Declan had dark hair. Deck couldn't possibly be the guy Noelle had seen at the day care center. Even if Deck hadn't believed in Caleb's innocence, he wasn't the type of guy to have an affair with his best friend's wife. He and Deck had often worked the same shifts anyway, and the last time they'd been together their photographs had been splashed across the front page of the newspaper after they'd rescued a child from the Underwood Creek.

That's it! He abruptly sat up. Maybe he could get Noelle to identify the man with Heather if he searched on the internet for photos of various members of the SWAT team. If they couldn't find a photo of the guy, at least they could eliminate some of the others right off the bat.

But where to find a computer? With a sigh, he stretched back out on the bed. He might have enough money to buy a tablet for computer access, but they were already running short on cash. He didn't remember seeing a computer in the hotel lobby, but there might be a small business center with a computer that they could use.

He crept out of bed, intending to go down to find out, when Kaitlin screamed. He spun around, his heart lodged in his throat at the horrible sound. He made his way over to where Noelle was holding his daughter close, trying to soothe away the night terrors.

Watching helplessly, he took a seat at the side of the bed next to Noelle, trying to be supportive as his daughter sobbed with heart-wrenching agony. Noelle murmured comforting words to Kaitlin, and soon the intensity of his daughter's crying lessened to the point they faded away.

Still, Noelle continued to hold Kaitlin close. He ached to offer his daughter comfort, too.

After what seemed like an hour, Noelle gently tucked Kaitlin beneath the covers.

"Are you okay?" he whispered.

"I'm fine. What about you?" she whispered back.

He didn't think he could ever be fine, not until his daughter's night terrors went away for good. "I hate hearing her cry like that. Do you think the explosion caused this nightmare?"

"Probably," she agreed. There was a long moment as they stared at each other in the darkness. "Try to get some sleep, Caleb, there's nothing more we can do now, okay?"

"Okay. Good night," he whispered, rising to his feet

and heading over to the other bed. His previous happy mood vanished in the wake of his daughter's nightmare.

And despite his lack of faith, he found himself praying for God to bring Kaitlin the peace she deserved.

The next morning, Caleb climbed out of bed first and quickly made use of the bathroom. Shaving the stubble off his face felt great and despite the seriousness of their situation, he was anxious to get started on his investigation. The guy who murdered his wife must have targeted Caleb because he thought Caleb might figure out the truth. Which made him determined to do just that. First item on the agenda was to get downstairs to search for a computer.

When he emerged from the bathroom, he found Noelle and Kaitlin were awake now, too.

"Good morning," he greeted them.

"I'm hungry, Daddy." Kaitlin's smile didn't show any evidence of her earlier nightmare.

Just hearing her call him daddy warmed his heart. He smiled. "The hotel offers a free continental breakfast, so we can eat whenever you're ready."

"Sounds like a plan," Noelle said cheerfully. "After breakfast we can go to church. I saw one located just a few blocks down the street. Are you ready to get washed up, Kaitlin?"

Noelle grabbed clean clothes for the both of them out of the plastic bag before disappearing into the bathroom. He shouldn't have been surprised about Noelle's intent to go to church but somehow he was. He considered letting them go to the service alone, so that he could get started on the computer search. But then he remembered how he'd prayed during those long moments in the bus while watching the cops drive through the parking lot.

No, he couldn't let them go alone. Not that he'd really planned on keeping up with Noelle's Christian teachings once this nightmare was over. Surely he could hold off doing his computer search for an hour or so.

As he waited for Noelle and Kaitlin he cleaned up the hotel room, putting the dry clothes away and leaving out the ones that were still slightly damp that Noelle had set out to dry the night before. He turned on the news, anxious to hear what the media had to say, but there were only talk shows, which didn't interest him in the least.

Thirty minutes later, Noelle and Kaitlin were ready and they all headed down to the lobby for breakfast. He caught sight of a small room off to the side that housed a computer and a printer, and couldn't wait to get started.

Church first, he reminded himself. The computer would be here when they got back.

As they filled up on cold cereal, fruit and bagels he explained his plan to Noelle. "After church, I'd like you to take Kaitlin outside to play on the swing set while I search for photos of the SWAT team members. I'll save them on the hard drive and then let you review them, see if you recognize anyone." He'd thought about printing them out, but decided that it might be easier for Noelle to see the faces on the computer screen.

"All right," she agreed cautiously. "Are we checking out today? Or staying another night?"

Good question. As much as he felt the need to keep moving, the fact that this place had free breakfast and computer access made him want to stay. "Maybe we'll stay one more night," he said slowly. "By then we should have something to go on."

Noelle's expression was troubled and she looked as if she wanted to say something, but then glanced down at Kaitlin and simply nodded. "All right."

They finished the meal and then walked outside to head down to the church. The distance was farther than he'd originally thought, and the church bells chimed as they walked up.

He felt a little bit like a fraud as he followed Noelle and Kaitlin inside. Kaitlin didn't seem upset about going to the church service so he knew that his daughter was used to accompanying Noelle.

Glancing around, he noticed that the small church was surprisingly full. When Noelle picked up the hymnal, he followed her lead.

She sang the opening hymn, her voice clear and beautiful. He didn't know the words at all, but was content enough to listen to Noelle sing. To his surprise, Kaitlin joined in, too, but only during the chorus, which was probably the only part of the song she knew by heart.

Caleb could admit that he'd planned on being bored during the service, but he wasn't. In fact, he wondered if the pastor had known exactly what he needed to hear, especially when his sermon was centered all about learning to keep God's faith and following God's plan. He'd never considered looking to God for guidance. And when the pastor read from the book of Psalms, the words reverberated through his heart and his soul.

Teach me, Lord, the way of your decree, that I may follow it to the end. Give me understanding, so that I may keep your law and obey it with all my heart (Psalms 119:33-34).

From beside him, Noelle murmured the words under her breath, as if she knew them by heart. He was ashamed that he'd never bothered to read anything from the Bible. For one thing, he'd always thought it would be dull and boring. But the passage from the Psalms was lyrical and enlightening.

What else had he missed?

The closing hymn was another upbeat song that Noelle sang along to with gusto. He found himself wishing he knew the words and the melody so he could join along. He was content, though, to listen to Noelle's and Kaitlin's voices blend together.

When the service was over, he rose to his feet and followed Noelle and Kaitlin outside, feeling lighter and filled with hope despite everything that had happened.

Was this why people went to church? Not just to pray but to hand their burdens over to God?

Maybe. If so, he figured he should attend church more often.

"Thank you for going along with us," Noelle said as they walked leisurely back to their hotel. "I think it was nice that we could share the service together with Kaitlin."

"You've taken her to church often, haven't you?" he asked, even though he already knew the answer.

"Yes." She slanted him a sidelong look. "I hope you don't expect me to apologize for it."

He had to laugh. "No, I don't expect you to apologize. I'm actually very grateful that you were there for my daughter during the months I couldn't be. And I'm glad she's learned to love God and to pray."

"You are?" Surprise echoed from her tone.

"Yes, Noelle, I am."

"Does that mean you believe in God, too?"

He pondered her question for a moment. "I think deep

down I believed in the concept of God," he admitted. "But my parents didn't go to church much, so I never really gave religion much thought. Heather wasn't very religious, either, so we didn't make God or church a big part of our life."

"I guessed that Heather wasn't much of a believer," Noelle said.

He let out a soft sigh. "The demise of our marriage wasn't all her fault."

"I know. But you weren't the one who had an affair, right?"

"Right." How had they gotten on this subject? The last thing he wanted to do was to discuss his failures. He saw the park with the playground up ahead and pointed it out to Kaitlin. "Would you like to play outside for a while?" he asked.

"Yes! Can we, Noa? Can we?"

"Sure," Noelle agreed, smiling down at Kaitlin. Then she turned toward him. "Promise me that you'll let me know what you find out."

"I will. I need you to help ID this guy, remember?" They parted ways at the playground. Caleb quickened his pace to get back to the hotel's computer room. After he settled down in front of the computer, he clicked on the internet and began searching for various news stories.

Finding clear photographs of his former teammates wasn't easy, many didn't show their faces, but after an hour he had at least a half dozen, including a photo of Declan.

He stared at the picture of his best friend for a long minute. What would happen if he contacted Deck now? Would his buddy believe him? Or hang up on him?

Surprisingly, he was tempted to find out. Maybe if he

was alone, he'd take the risk. But no way was he going to put Noelle or Kaitlin in danger.

With a sigh, he moved on to another search attempt, but this time, a news caption on the home page caught his eye.

Body found floating in Lake Michigan believed to be that of Kenneth James, eyewitness to the murder of Heather O'Malley.

With a deep sense of foreboding, Caleb clicked on the headline and read the article. The body of his neighbor Kenneth James had been found almost ten days after his disappearance. And who had the most to gain by Kenneth's death?

Caleb O'Malley. After all, he was now a free man because there was no eyewitness against him.

He sat back in disbelief. Even though he'd been in jail when Ken had disappeared, the reporter believed it was possible Caleb had arranged the murder from prison.

Once again, he was a prime suspect in this latest murder investigation. And if he were arrested again, he felt certain he'd be convicted.

Noelle enjoyed being outside in the sun with Kaitlin, who'd found another little girl to play with on the swing set. Yet she couldn't help feeling like she needed to get back inside the hotel to help Caleb search for members of the SWAT team.

She glanced at her watch for the third time, and decided that an hour was plenty of time for Caleb to have found some photographs. After everything they'd been through, she found she desperately wanted to help clear his name. She needed to go in and review what he'd discovered.

"Come on, Kaitlin, it's time to go inside," she called.

"Not yet, Noa," Kaitlin protested. "We're having fun, aren't we, Izzy?"

The little blonde nodded eagerly. "Lotsa fun," Izzy said.

"Ten minutes," Noelle said firmly. "You can always come back to play later."

"But Izzy won't be here later," Kaitlin said, thrusting out her lower lip in a pout.

Noelle suppressed a sigh, and fought back a wave of impatience. There was no rush. Caleb had agreed to stay here another day. Certainly there was plenty of time to search the internet.

"Izzy," a blonde woman called out. "Time to go home. We have to get ready to go to your cousin's birthday party."

"Okay." The little girl obediently slid off the swing. "Bye, Kaitlin."

"Bye, Izzy." Kaitlin's sad eyes followed her new friend as Izzy ran over to her mother.

"Come on, Kaitlin, let's go inside for a while," she said, holding out her hand. Kaitlin reluctantly came over, her head hanging down dejectedly. Her heart squeezed in sympathy, knowing that if they were home right now, they'd be making playdates with other girls from pre-school.

She took Kaitlin into the lobby and walked over to the small computer station. Caleb glanced up at her, his expression grim. "What's wrong?" she asked.

He glanced at Kaitlin and shook his head. "I have some photos for you to look at," he said, rising to his feet so she could sit down. She noticed he had a short list of names written on a single piece of paper. "They're in order from left to right."

"All right." She clicked on the first image and couldn't help a small gasp when she realized the photograph was of Caleb and another man next to a small child who was wrapped in a blanket. "Who is this guy standing next to you?" she asked.

"Declan Shaw."

He didn't say anything more and she shook her head. "That's not him."

Caleb nodded and she saw a flash of relief in his eyes before she clicked on the next photograph. The image wasn't as clear and she stared at it for a long time before slowly shaking her head. "Nope, that's not him, either."

As she went through the next five photographs, Caleb made notes on the list. She sat back with a sigh. "None of these is the guy I saw. Maybe you're wrong about him being on the SWAT team?"

"I don't think so," he said shortly. "There are several guys whose photos I haven't been able to find yet."

"What's wrong, Caleb?" she asked, glancing over to make sure Kaitlin was still preoccupied with drawing her picture. There weren't any crayons, but Kaitlin didn't seem to mind as she used a pencil to draw a picture of a clown. "You look upset."

He hesitated, and then bent over to use the mouse to click on a newspaper article. The headline made her feel sick to her stomach.

"I don't believe it," she murmured as she scanned the article about the death of Kenneth James, the missing eyewitness from Heather O'Malley's murder investigation. "I don't understand why anyone would think this."

"I do," Caleb muttered harshly. "This is another attempt to get me convicted of murder."

The thought of someone going to such great lengths to do just that made her blood run cold. She shivered and tried to think rationally. "But, Caleb, you were obviously in jail when this happened. What possible proof could they have that you arranged this from behind bars?"

"I don't know. The only man I had regular contact with while in jail was my lawyer, Jack Owens. And he's the only one I called from the hotel where our car suddenly exploded. As much as I hate to admit it, Jack Owens is the key. Although, this new twist certainly doesn't help him any. He's being implicated in this murder investigation, too."

"That doesn't make any sense," Noelle said in a low tone. She swiveled in her seat to stare up at Caleb. "Remember what you said about someone from the SWAT team having the knowledge and ability to tap into Jack's phone? What if that same guy who murdered Heather did that and more? What if he's truly setting up both of you for this murder?"

Caleb abruptly straightened. "You could be right. I have to warn Jack."

"Wait." She caught his hand before he could leave. "How are you going to do that? If you call him they might track the call and find us. And we don't have a vehicle to drive over to find him."

"I'll take a bus," he said. "You and Kaitlin can wait here."

"No way," she protested, jumping to her feet. "What if something happens to you? We'd be stuck here without money or a way to get to safety. We're going, too."

"Too dangerous," he argued. "I'll leave you some cash.

If I'm not back before nightfall you can go to the closest police station for help."

The thought of sitting here and waiting hours for him to return was excruciating. Not knowing what was going on was worse than the fear of going along with him to the place this all started. "Caleb, please. Let us go with you to the city. We'll find someplace safe to wait while you talk to Jack. Don't make us sit here in a different city, alone."

He shook his head but didn't say anything more. She couldn't help feeling that splitting up was the worst thing they could do. But how could she convince Caleb?

Caleb knew that the best thing for Noelle and Kaitlin was to stay hidden in Madison. Yet leaving them here alone didn't sit well with him, either.

He didn't think they'd been followed here. How could they have been? They came on a bus chartered by a group of senior citizens. There was no reason to believe that Noelle and Kaitlin wouldn't be safe here. While taking them along with him would be far too risky.

They walked back to their room, a heavy silence hanging between them. He understood Noelle's frustration, but he needed to do the right thing to keep them safe. No matter how much he wanted to have their company.

"You can't stop us from buying bus tickets, too," Noelle said once they were inside the room. She stood near the doorway, with her arms crossed defensively over her chest. "We'll come along regardless."

"You don't have any money, Noelle," he reminded her.

"I'll use my credit card. I know the number by heart."

He batted down a flash of anger. "That wouldn't be smart and you know it. Whoever tried to kill me knows we're together. He'll find you in a heartbeat if you use your credit card. Don't you see? I have to warn Jack that he's at risk and I don't want you and Kaitlin in any danger. It's best for all of us if I go alone."

"Daddy?" Kaitlin came over and held her arms up. "Up!"

Flustered, he reached for his daughter, lifting her against his chest and holding her close. She'd never asked him to hold her before and he was thrilled that she was growing less afraid of him.

As if Kaitlin sensed what was going on, she placed both of her palms on either side of his face and peered at him with a serious expression. "We go with you."

"Ah, well. I don't think so…" His voice trailed off. He could take them with him and find a hotel in Milwaukee that wouldn't be too far from Jack's house. They could stay long enough to warn his lawyer and maybe get some extra money, too. He hadn't paid for the second night yet. Why not spend one night in Milwaukee? He'd have to be close by if he intended on digging into his wife's death anyway.

"All right, we'll all go," he said with a sigh. "But we have to hurry as it's almost past checkout time."

"Thank you," Noelle murmured. Most of their things were already packed, but she quickly gathered the rest and tucked everything inside the bag.

He tried to tell himself this wasn't a mistake as they made their way down to the lobby. On one hand, it would be easier to keep both of them safe if they were close by. But the bigger reason he'd agreed was that he needed to be closer to Milwaukee in order to figure out what was going on. And that meant finding a safe place to stay in the city.

Once they'd checked out, he looked at the map and

found the directions to the bus station. Their timing was almost perfect as the next bus to Milwaukee left in fifteen minutes.

The bus ride took about an hour and a half, longer than driving in a car but then again, the bus driver didn't go anywhere near the posted speed limit, which added time to the trip. When they reached the bus station and stood to get off, his gut twisted with nerves.

"Where to?" Noelle asked.

He took a deep breath and pulled himself together. "Jack lives in a condo downtown, but there's a cheap motel nearby where we'll stay for tonight."

"All right," Noelle agreed.

They walked the two blocks to the inn and went inside. "We need a room for tonight," he said.

"Sorry, no vacancies right now, but I can put you on a waiting list in case of a cancelation."

No vacancies? He couldn't hide his surprise. "Not even one room is available?"

"Not with the Milwaukee Lakefront Marathon going on." The clerk shrugged. "Sorry."

Caleb put a fake name on the waiting list and headed outside. He wanted to get Noelle and Kaitlin someplace safe before he headed over to Jack's place. Seeing as it was Sunday, he figured the attorney would be home, rather than at his office.

"Let's just get a taxi and head over there," Noelle said. "We'll stay in the taxi and drive around the block or something while you meet with Jack."

As if on cue a taxi pulled up. "All right, get in."

The three of them slid into the backseat, Kaitlin tucked between them. Caleb gave the taxi driver the address and thanks to the marathon, they had to go the long way to get to Jack's condo.

"Wait here," he said when the taxi pulled up in front of Jack's condo.

"I keep the meter running," the taxi driver warned.

"That's fine." Going around the block wasn't an option as most of the roads were closed anyway. He went inside and buzzed Jack's doorbell.

No answer. He pushed the buzzer again. A young woman wearing shorts and a T-shirt came out through the main door. He caught the door before it closed. "I'm here to see my friend Jack," he muttered as he strode past.

The woman shrugged and continued on her way. He took the elevator up to the third floor and walked down the hall to room 303. He rapped on the door, but there was no answer. He turned to leave, but then tried the door handle just in case, surprised to find it unlocked.

"Jack?" he called, taking a hesitant step inside. "Are you home?"

A horrible smell assaulted him as he walked farther into the room, filling him with a sense of dread. He stopped short, not surprised when he saw Jack's body lying on the floor in a pool of blood.

SEVEN

Noelle tried to wait patiently while Caleb was inside talking to Jack, but it wasn't easy. She looked out the taxi window at the crowds of people walking along the street getting ready for the marathon. Useless to even attempt to look for anyone out of place.

After what seemed like an hour but was only ten minutes, Caleb came out of the condo. He paused, holding the main door open as he swept the bottom of his T-shirt along the side of the door before stepping back and letting it swing shut behind him.

His expression was tense as he jumped back into the taxi. "Please take us to the bus station," he told the driver.

Why on earth would they be going back to the bus station? "Did you see Jack?" she asked in a low tone.

Caleb's lips thinned and he scrubbed his hands wearily over his face. "I'll fill you in later," he said.

His grim tone was not at all reassuring. But of course Caleb wouldn't want to say anything in front of his daughter. And she didn't blame him, considering Kaitlin's night terrors.

"Wait, stop here," Caleb said as they passed a small park.

"Forty-five dollars," the taxi driver said, after he'd pulled over to the side of the street.

She almost choked at the high fee but Caleb handed the guy some cash and then climbed out from the taxi, pulling out their bag of belongings and then holding the door for her and Kaitlin.

"Look, Noa, a slide!" Kaitlin shouted. She took off running, heading straight toward it.

She and Caleb followed more slowly. "What happened back there, Caleb?" she asked.

He stopped about ten feet from the slide and set the bag down while watching as Kaitlin went up and down the slide with a whoop. "I found Jack dead in his condo. I'm fairly certain he was murdered."

"What?" She gaped at him in horror. Whatever she expected, it wasn't this. "How do you know?"

"The bullet hole in his gut was a good clue."

She put a hand over her mouth, trying to hold back a wave of nausea. "We have to call the police," she whispered.

"I know. But the fact that I stumbled on the body isn't going to look good for me," he said. "I tried to wipe my prints off the doorframe and the door handle, but for all I know, my prints will be found inside somewhere. After all, he was my lawyer."

And now he was dead.

She shook her head emphatically. "No one will believe you had anything to do with that."

"Do you think it's a coincidence that the body of Kenneth James conveniently showed up in Lake Michigan shortly around the time frame that Jack Owens was murdered?" he asked. "Not hardly. And you can bet Jack's death will be used as another nail in my coffin."

She didn't want to believe it, but she could see only too well how this would play out in the media. And if she hadn't gotten to know Caleb O'Malley over these past few days, the man who would do anything to make his daughter happy, the man who'd gone out of his way to protect her, she likely would have believed he'd done all these horrible deeds.

But he was innocent, of that she was sure. And not just because she secretly admired him.

"We need to do something," she said helplessly.

"Yeah, well, I'm open for ideas."

"I'm your alibi, right? We've been together since we left my house."

"Yes, I've considered that," he admitted. "But if I'm being framed, do you think the murderer hasn't already come up with some sort of plan? I'm worried your name will be dragged through the mud right along with mine."

"My name? Why?"

Caleb silently watched his daughter play for several long minutes. "Think about the night my wife was murdered. There was an eyewitness, right? Someone who must have been bribed to lie to the police. What's to prevent the real murderer from planting more lies? Lies about you and I having some sort of secret affair? Anything to discredit you as a solid alibi."

She could barely wrap her mind around what he was saying. "No one who knows me would ever believe something like that."

"Anyone will believe anything with enough evidence," he said bluntly. "Trust me, I thought the same thing once. I thought for sure proving my innocence was a slam dunk. Instead I spent over a year behind bars."

"Push me, Daddy," Kaitlin called out from the swings. "I wanna go higher!"

When Caleb went over to do as his daughter asked, she stayed where she was, his words tumbling over and over through her mind. She didn't want to believe he was right. That people would actually think the worst about her.

But she couldn't deny the horror Caleb had lived through for the past fourteen months, either. And now his lawyer was dead. Murdered. Why wouldn't the real murderer try to frame Caleb for that, too?

Caleb was right. He would be the primary suspect. And so was she, now that her name was linked to his. What could they possibly do to prove their innocence?

Noelle tried to shrug off the sense of impending doom as they spent the afternoon at the park, eating hot dogs and popcorn from a nearby sidewalk vendor for dinner. They walked a few blocks to the city bus stop and Caleb studied the map for a long moment before deciding on a route.

When the number ten bus pulled up, she was surprised to see Caleb gesture for her and Kaitlin to precede him inside. She knew that one of her preschool teachers came in from the number ten bus and the preschool center wasn't far from where she lived. Were they heading back toward the scene of the original crime? Why else would Caleb have decided to take this bus? Unless it intersected with another route that would take them far away from the city?

She was about to take a seat near the front, but Caleb urged her to head to the back.

"Where are we headed?" she asked. Kaitlin wanted

the window so she let the child climb in first, before taking the aisle seat.

"I know a reasonable place to stay on the outskirts of the city," he said.

The outskirts of the city? Wasn't that area under the jurisdiction of the Milwaukee County Sheriff's Department, where his former SWAT team worked? She swiveled in her seat to face him. "Are you crazy?" she whispered. "Why would you take us back there?"

His gaze was enigmatic. "Trust me," he murmured.

She let out a sigh and tried to do that. Caleb must have some sort of plan, right? She closed her eyes and tried to pray. *Dear Lord, please guide us on Your path while keeping us safe in Your care. Amen.*

Kaitlin seemed to enjoy riding the bus although her eyelids were starting to get heavy by the time they arrived at their destination. They had to walk a few blocks, but soon they were approaching the Forty Winks Motel. Caleb requested another room with two double beds and used a story about getting mugged to avoid handing over his ID. The fact that they were there together acting the part of a family helped and the clerk accepted the cash.

"We need a plan," she said in a low voice while making sure Kaitlin was preoccupied with watching the Disney Channel.

"I know. I'm thinking of calling my buddy Declan."

She remembered the photo of Caleb and his teammate standing side by side holding a small child they'd pulled to safety from the creek. "Are you sure you can trust him?" she asked.

"No, I'm not sure of anything right now," he admitted. "But what choice do I have? We can't stay on the run forever and we're going through my cash reserves pretty quickly."

Her stomach knotted with anxiety especially knowing that this room was pricier than their previous ones. "Maybe I can pull some money out of my bank account. Wouldn't that be safer than trusting one of your former teammates?"

"And then what? We go on the run for how long?" he asked wearily. "The cops will catch up to us eventually, especially if they put out an APB. The three of us can't hide forever. No, we need help investigating these murders."

"And you can trust this guy, Declan?"

"Deck was once my closest friend not to mention the best man at my wedding." Caleb's tortured gaze made her want to wrap her arms around him. "If I can't convince Declan that I'm innocent I won't be able to convince anyone."

She didn't know what to say to that, because she sensed he was right. "What's the plan?"

"I'd like you to stay here with Kaitlin while I try to get in touch with Declan."

Instinctively she wanted to protest, but what was the alternative? Kaitlin was already looking sleepy from all the time she spent playing outside. There was no way she could leave Kaitlin alone. And the poor child deserved at least the chance for a good night's sleep. One that hopefully wouldn't be disturbed by night terrors.

"All right," she agreed with a small sigh. "But try to hurry back, okay? I won't be able to sleep until I know you're safe."

"I'll come back as soon as possible," he promised with an intense gaze. "I'm lucky to have you."

She ducked her head, trying to hide a blush. He didn't mean it the way it sounded and she was stupid to think even for a moment that he had. "That's not exactly true. I feel like I'm holding you back."

Caleb reached out to take her hand in his, his grip radiating heat. "Noelle, you're helping me more than you realize by keeping my daughter safe. And I'm sorry I dragged you into this mess with me. If I'd known…" His voice trailed off.

"You wouldn't have done anything differently," she pointed out. "Besides, I'm convinced that God has a plan for us. We've managed to get out of tight spots before, haven't we?"

A smile tugged at the corner of his mouth and she had to resist the urge to throw herself into his arms. "A few weeks ago I might have scoffed at that notion, but now I'm beginning to think you may be right."

His admission warmed her heart. "I'll pray for your safety and for Declan to believe in you."

"I'll gladly take all the help I can get." His fingers tightened briefly around hers before he released her and rose to his feet. "Don't answer the door to anyone but me, okay?"

"I won't."

He glanced back at Kaitlin once more as if debating whether to go and give her a hug and a kiss. But he didn't, maybe because Kaitlin was curled up in the bed, hugging her Giffy, her eyes at half-mast. She knew it wouldn't be long before Kaitlin was sound asleep and Caleb must have known it, too.

He pocketed one of the room keys and opened the door.

"Be safe," she whispered. He nodded and then slipped outside before she could say anything more.

After making sure the door was secure, she climbed into the bed beside Kaitlin and settled in to wait.

Please, Lord, keep Caleb safe in Your care.

Leaving Noelle and Kaitlin was more difficult than he'd anticipated, but he tried not to dwell on it as he silently jogged through the streets of Wauwatosa. He took a zigzag route, more to keep away from prying eyes than any fear of being followed.

He didn't have much of a plan, other than trying to catch up with Deck at his home. If his buddy was working, he'd be forced to wait until the end of his shift.

As he made his way to the familiar neighborhood of Declan's place, he mentally went through a few scenarios in his mind, trying to think of a way to convince Deck he was innocent. That is, if Deck even gave him a chance to say anything at all.

He shoved aside the depressing thought and slowed down to a walk as he approached Declan's modest house.

Darkness hadn't fallen yet so he couldn't be sure that Deck was actually home. But then he caught sight of a bluish glow from the television in the living room. Even from this distance he could tell Declan was watching a baseball game.

For a moment he battled a wave of regret, wishing for simpler times when watching a baseball game was commonplace instead of being completely outside the realm of possibilities. He felt conspicuous as he stood for a moment, trying to garner the courage to face his friend.

A car drove by, spurring him into action. He went up the driveway, bypassing the front of the house to knock at the side door. It took a minute for his buddy to respond and when Declan finally opened the door, the expression of pure shock on his face made his heart sink a bit.

"Hi, Deck, do you have a minute? I need a friend."

Declan's mouth opened and then closed again without a word. Caleb was afraid Deck was going to shut the door in his face, but then he pushed it open and stepped back, allowing him room to come in.

"Thanks," Caleb said. "I know you probably believe the worst, but I swear I'm innocent. I didn't kill Heather and I certainly didn't kill anyone else, either."

Declan stared at him for a long moment. "Give me one reason I should believe you."

Fair enough. "Because you know how much I love my daughter, Kaitlin, and you know I'd never kill my wife and then leave Kaitlin there alone with her dead mother."

Declan pursed his lips for a moment and then shrugged. "I never could figure out why you'd kill Heather," he finally admitted. "But when Ken James came forward stating he saw you, I figured you must have snapped or something."

"I didn't snap. I was framed."

Declan sighed and stared up at the ceiling for a long moment. "Why do I get the feeling I'm not going to like your theory?"

Relieved that Declan hadn't booted him outside, he chuckled. "Because you're a smart man, that's why."

"You'd better come in, then," Declan said, gesturing toward the living room. "The Brewers are losing anyway."

Caleb hovered in the doorway. "I'd rather we talked somewhere private so that no one can see me," he said. "For your own safety more than mine."

"My safety?" Declan scoffed. "I'm not the one accused of murder." Despite the comment Deck walked through the living room to pick up the TV remote. He shut it off and then turned back to face Caleb. "Do you want to sit here or in the kitchen?"

"Kitchen." Caleb wanted to be far away from the front living room window where anyone walking by could see inside. Declan's kitchen overlooked the backyard, which in turn butted up against his neighbor's backyard. Caleb took a seat at the table and tried to gather his thoughts.

Deck pulled two water bottles out of the fridge and handed one to Caleb. "Start at the beginning," he suggested.

Declan knew about the very beginning, his being arrested for Heather's murder, so Caleb started with getting out of jail and heading over to pick up his daughter from Noelle's house. Declan didn't say a word throughout the entire dissertation until he got to the part where he went inside Jack's condo to find him dead.

"Whoa, whoa, back up. Are you serious? Your lawyer was murdered?"

Caleb battled a wave of defeat. If Deck didn't believe him he was sunk. "Yes, he died from what looked to be a slug in the gut. And you can bet that my fingerprints will be conveniently found at the scene of the crime."

"Wow." Declan took a long gulp of his water. "I don't know anyone who hates you that much."

A flash of anger bubbled up before he could stop it. "Why in the world would I make all this up, Deck? And who said it's about hating me? What if this guy is just going to great lengths to hide his tracks? I have to believe he's running scared, otherwise why would he risk leaving a trail of dead bodies in his wake?"

"You have a point," Declan grudgingly admitted. "But, Caleb, you have to admit this is a whopper of a story. I mean, seriously, even Hollywood couldn't come up with a plot this convoluted."

His shoulders slumped and he dropped his head in his hands. "I know I'm asking a lot," he said in a low voice. Caleb forced himself to meet Deck's skeptical gaze. "But if you don't want to believe this guy is going to extreme measures to set me up, then give me something. Tell me what motive I have for risking my freedom by killing Jack. Especially now when I've finally been released from jail."

Declan slowly shook his head. "There is the possibility that you used Jack to arrange for Ken's murder. That Jack was going to rat you out so you killed him, too."

Hope deflated in his chest like a popped balloon. *This is it,* Caleb thought. *This is when Deck will throw me out of his house without offering any help.*

"Who am I kidding?" Deck abruptly said, throwing up his hands in defeat. "No way am I buying that story. For one thing, it doesn't even make sense. Why would Jack help you commit murder, for Pete's sake, and then suddenly get cold feet and threaten to turn you in? Why even risk his law license in the first place? No, you're right. This whole thing reeks of a setup."

The wave of relief was so overwhelming that it took several seconds for Deck's words to sink in.

"Really?" Caleb asked in a hoarse voice. "You really believe me?"

"Yeah, I believe you." Deck held up his fist so Caleb could bump knuckles with him. "I should have gone with my gut all along," Declan continued. "You're not the type to resort to violence."

Thank You, Lord!

First Noelle and now Declan. He didn't think it was a coincidence that he managed to get two people on his side. Maybe this was God's will.

"You have no idea what your support means to me," Caleb finally managed. To have Noelle's support was one thing, but to have his best friend back was even better. "I feel like I've been fighting alone for so long."

"Well, you're not alone any longer," Deck said with a grim smile. "So tell me, what can I do to help?"

Caleb swallowed hard. "I need assistance with investigating Heather's murder. And I need more cash. You know I'm good for it, Deck, or I wouldn't ask."

"I'm fine with lending you cash, but what's the point of investigating your wife's murder? If the scene was staged to frame you, there's no point. The clues are already tainted."

"Yeah, but consider this—Noelle saw Heather with a man the night she was murdered," he reminded Deck. "That's a place to start."

"Maybe," Declan said as he looked away.

The hairs on the back of his neck lifted in warning. "What?" he demanded. "What do you know about Heather?"

Declan winced, and shook his head. "Nothing you need to know."

"Deck, you have to tell me. If it could have anything at all to do with Heather's murder, then you have to tell me!"

Declan let out a heavy sigh. "I'm sorry, Caleb. But Heather was seeing more than one guy. From what I heard she was stringing several guys along."

Several? Caleb felt sick as he searched Declan's gaze, trying to figure out if his buddy was lying to him.

Because if Deck wasn't lying, and his wife really had been seeing multiple men, then they were no closer to finding out who'd framed him for Heather's murder.

EIGHT

Noelle was too wired to fall asleep. Images of Caleb's dead lawyer lying on the floor bleeding kept flashing through her mind and she feared this time she was the one who'd suffer a night terror instead of Kaitlin.

When there was a soft rap on the door, she literally shot to her feet, her heart thundering in her chest. Using the peephole she verified that it was Caleb standing there before she unlatched the dead bolt and opened the door.

She tensed when she realized Caleb wasn't alone, although it didn't take long for her to recognize that the man standing next to him was the same guy from the photograph in the newspaper. The one where they'd rescued a small child.

"Grab your key and come outside for a moment," Caleb whispered.

She did as he requested, staying near the closed door so that she'd be sure to hear Kaitlin if the little girl woke up crying. "What's going on?" she asked.

"Noelle, this is Declan Shaw," Caleb said, glancing up and down the front of the motel, and she knew by now he was trying to make sure there wasn't anyone listening to their conversation. "Deck, this is Noelle Whitman.

She's Kaitlin's preschool teacher and was my daughter's temporary guardian, too."

"Nice to meet you, Declan," Noelle said in a polite tone. "Does this mean you finally believe Caleb's innocence?"

Deck lifted an eyebrow. "Wow, she doesn't pull any punches, does she?"

Caleb grinned, looking younger and more relaxed than she could ever remember seeing him look before. "Noelle has been a huge help to me. I wouldn't even be here now if it wasn't for her."

Being reminded of everything they'd been through over the past few days sparked a rare surge of anger. "And why wouldn't you have stood by your best friend through all this anyway?" she demanded in a low, fierce tone, glaring at Declan. "Caleb shouldn't have had to go through this alone."

"Easy, Noelle, it's not all his fault," Caleb murmured, putting a hand on her arm.

"No, she's right, Caleb. I deserve her anger." Declan's gaze was contrite when he looked at her. "I'm sorry. I should have stuck by Caleb, and probably would have if there wasn't an eyewitness who vowed he saw Caleb shoot Heather. Not that it's a good excuse, but since I knew about his wife's affairs, I figured it wasn't a stretch that he might have snapped."

"By affairs, you mean more than one?" She couldn't believe what she was hearing. Could this situation get any worse?

"Yeah, unfortunately, that puts a crimp in our theory that the guy you saw with Heather that night was actually the one who may have killed her," Caleb said. "For all we know that guy she was with wasn't anyone from the SWAT team."

She leaned back against the door, battling a wave of helplessness. "But you were so convinced that someone from the SWAT team set you up. And what about having the resources to find my car even after you swapped the license plates? Who else could do something like that?"

"We'll figure it out. Don't worry," Caleb said reassuringly. "We're not alone anymore. Deck is going to help us. In fact, he's allowing us to borrow his laptop."

She wished she could be as hopeful as Caleb seemed to be now that they had Declan's support. But she couldn't quite shake a sense of unease. It felt like they were taking several steps backward for every inch they moved forward.

"You really think someone from the team set you up?" Declan asked.

"Yeah, I do." Caleb lifted his chin. "Obviously someone knew enough about police work to plant evidence and bribe an eyewitness. Someone who knew I might not be arrested unless there was an eyewitness."

Declan raked his hands through his hair. "Marc Brickner."

"You actually saw Heather and Marc together?" Caleb asked.

"Only once," Declan confirmed. "But now that you mention suspecting someone from the team, Marc was pretty vocal about believing you were guilty. He kept going on and on about what a horrible husband you were to Heather. And about your out-of-control temper."

"I need to find a picture of him for Noelle," Caleb muttered.

"Here, I'll find one." Declan used his smartphone to

search the internet and then handed the device over to Noelle. "Is this the same guy you saw with Heather?" he asked.

She stared at the photo on the screen, feeling a bit light-headed to have finally put a name with the face. She slowly nodded. "Yes, that's him."

"Well, that gives us a place to start," Caleb said.

"Yeah, especially since Brickner was seen with Heather the night she was murdered," Declan agreed.

Noelle couldn't seem to tear her gaze from the photo on Declan's phone. Somehow she thought she'd feel relieved once they knew exactly who was behind all of this.

But she didn't. Instead her sense of foreboding only deepened. Because, somehow, she knew that identifying this man was only the beginning. And she feared Caleb might end up like Jack Owens.

Dead.

Miraculously, Kaitlin slept through the night without waking up once. Noelle wished she could say the same. But when she heard Caleb get up and head into the bathroom, she rubbed her gritty eyes and swung up to a sitting position at the side of the bed she shared with Kaitlin.

Caleb had left Declan's computer on the desk, so she turned it on and quickly found the motel's free wireless network. She did a quick search on Marc Brickner and found several more photos of him. He looked different wearing all his SWAT gear, but there was no mistaking that he was the same man who'd been with Heather that Friday night she was twenty minutes late to pick up Kaitlin.

The guy never seemed to smile. In each and every photograph his mouth was compressed in a thin line.

Compared to the photograph of Caleb and Declan smiling and holding the young child they'd rescued, this Marc guy looked like he was capable of doing illegal activities.

But did that include killing his teammate's wife? His mistress?

Maybe. Yet even she knew they needed some sort of motive.

She typed Heather's name into the search engine, and immediately several photographs popped up on the screen. Caleb's wife had truly been a beautiful woman, at least on the outside.

"Noa?" Kaitlin called and she quickly shut the top of the computer down, so that the young girl wouldn't see the photographs of her mother.

"Good morning, Kaitlin," she said, getting up from the desk. "Did you sleep well?"

"Yes, but I hav'ta go to the bathroom."

As if on cue the door opened and Caleb came out, fully dressed with the only evidence of his shower being the drops of water glistening on his hair. "The bathroom's all yours, ladies," he said cheerfully.

Kaitlin scampered inside but Noelle didn't immediately follow. Instead she went back over to the computer, opened it up and disconnected from the internet.

"Find anything?" Caleb asked.

"Not really. I just wanted to be certain that Marc Brickner was really the man I saw with Heather."

"You already knew that, didn't you?"

She suppressed a sigh. "Yes, but I felt the need to be sure, in case I made a mistake." She paused and then added, "I can't explain it, but I'm scared, Caleb. I'm afraid that, somehow, he's going to find us before we find him."

Caleb lifted his hand and lightly cupped her cheek.

"I'll protect you and Kaitlin with my life if necessary, No-elle. I will do everything possible to keep you both safe."

She leaned into his hand for a moment, wishing he'd take her into his arms and hold her. She could use a bit of his strength.

"Noa, are you coming?" Kaitlin asked from the bath-room, breaking the moment.

"Yes, I'm coming." She reluctantly drew away from Caleb, hoping he wouldn't notice her pink cheeks. Why was she longing to be close to Caleb? She'd made up her mind to avoid relationships, because she didn't trust a man not to hurt her.

But, unfortunately, she trusted Caleb.

She picked up the bag of clothes and ducked into the bathroom to shower and change, reminding herself that Caleb wasn't the type of guy to be interested in some-one plain like her. After all, his wife had been a beauti-ful model.

With her chaotic feelings firmly in check, she and Kaitlin finished getting washed up. When they emerged from the bathroom about twenty minutes later, she was surprised to find that Caleb had breakfast spread out on the small table in the corner of the room.

"Where did you get all this?" she asked.

"Deck brought us breakfast," he said with a wry grin. "I think you made him feel guilty last night and he's try-ing to make amends."

"He should feel guilty," she muttered. She couldn't help her spurt of anger at the man who'd claimed to be Caleb's best friend. The aroma of scrambled eggs and bacon made her mouth water, distracting her.

"Yay, bacon!" Kaitlin exclaimed, climbing up onto one of the chairs.

"Hold on, we have to pray first, remember?" Noelle said.

Kaitlin sat back on her heels and put her hands together. Caleb mimicked his daughter's movements.

She took a deep breath and let it out slowly, gathering her thoughts. "Dear Lord, we thank You for providing this food for us to eat and for bringing us the help we need to clear Caleb's name. And we ask You to guide us on Your chosen path. Amen."

"Amen," Caleb and Kaitlin said simultaneously.

They enjoyed the meal, and while she wanted to grill Caleb about where Declan was now, she didn't want to say too much in front of Kaitlin. When they finished eating, she cleaned up the mess while Caleb packed their things. Kaitlin was glued once again to the Disney Channel.

"I take it we're moving on?" she asked, trying not to be too depressed about going to yet another impersonal motel room. Who would have thought that being on the run was so incredibly wearying?

"Deck thought we might be better off staying at his place for a while," Caleb said. "He has two spare bedrooms and we wouldn't have to use up our cash."

Ridiculous to feel annoyed because Caleb made arrangements with Declan without asking for her input. She should be glad that they had someone helping them. That Caleb had someone else who actually believed in him.

There was a soft knock at the door. Caleb peered through the peephole before allowing his buddy to come in.

"We have a problem," Declan said, his expression grim.

"What?" Caleb asked.

"There's been a warrant issued for your arrest related to the murder of Jack Owens."

Caleb shouldn't have been shocked at the news, but there was no denying that he felt as if someone socked him in the solar plexus. "Brickner must be the driving force behind that," he muttered.

"Now what?" Noelle asked helplessly.

He didn't have a good answer. He turned back toward his daughter. "Kaitlin? Do you remember Uncle Declan?"

Kaitlin ducked her head shyly and he realized that in the year he'd been gone, Kaitlin's life had been turned totally upside down. Was it any wonder she didn't remember everything from their former life together? Especially since she'd likely blocked a lot of the horror from her mind?

"Hi, Kaitlin," Declan said with a broad smile. "You've grown up a lot since the last time I saw you."

Kaitlin ran over to Noelle as if seeking support. Noelle pulled her close in a reassuring hug.

"Uncle Declan is a friend of your daddy's," Noelle said softly. "There's no reason to be afraid."

Caleb turned toward Deck. "So what do you think we should do? I don't blame you if you've decided against hiding a fugitive in your home."

"Don't worry about me. There's no reason for anyone to suspect that after all this time, I've decided to help you out," Declan said thoughtfully. "But we need to make sure that no one sees you going inside my place."

Caleb wished he'd gone to Declan's last night, but even when his buddy had suggested it, he hadn't wanted to wake up Kaitlin. The last thing he'd wanted was to cause another night terror for his daughter. He should have factored in the possibility of having a warrant out for his arrest.

"I guess I could ask the hotel if we can stay another night," he said, trying to hide his reluctance.

"I was thinking more along the lines of sneaking you in the back of my car," Deck said with a frown. "I think the sooner we get you hidden inside my place, the better."

"But it's broad daylight," Noelle protested.

"I know, but I made sure I wasn't followed here," Declan said. "And my place has an attached garage so if you hide on the floor, no one will be able to see you. Especially if you stay hidden on the floor until we're safely inside the garage."

"Let's go, then," Caleb said, anxious to get moving. He couldn't help feeling as if the minute anyone saw his face they'd start shouting for the police to arrest him.

"I'm parked right in front of the motel," Declan assured him. "And I'm ready if you are."

Noelle looked worried, but she gathered up the bag when he lifted Kaitlin in his arms. Moving swiftly, they slipped outside and headed for Declan's SUV.

He gestured for Noelle to get in the front seat. She put the bag on the seat and then crouched down on the floor of the car, keeping her head low and using the plastic bag for additional cover. He was impressed because he couldn't see her unless he was right next to the passenger door.

"We're going to play a hide-and-seek game, Katydid," he said as he set his daughter down in the back. "Can you crouch down on the floor of the car like this?" He demonstrated what he wanted his daughter to do.

"You're too big to fit, Daddy." She giggled as she

crouched down behind the driver's seat. "I'm a better hider."

"That you are," Caleb agreed.

As soon as they were safely inside, Declan put the car in gear and backed out of the parking lot. Caleb didn't like the fact that he couldn't see where they were going, but he knew he had to trust Declan.

His life, as well as Noelle's and Kaitlin's, depended on it.

For a moment he wondered if he should turn himself in to the police. Declan would be able to keep Noelle and Kaitlin safe, and maybe playing by the rules would work for him instead of against him.

But as soon as the thought formed, he rejected it. Too much had happened to turn himself in now. Especially since he didn't know how much evidence they'd fabricated against him.

The car swayed as Deck took several twists and turns, no doubt taking the extra-long way home.

"I don't wanna play this game anymore, Daddy," Kaitlin whined. "I want to sit up on the seat."

"Not yet, let's just stay down here a little longer, okay?" He reached over to take his daughter's hand, willing her to stay put. He didn't want to have to hold her down there against her will.

"We're almost there," Declan called from the front seat.

A few minutes later, Caleb heard the garage door going up. "There, see?" he said to Kaitlin. "Very soon we'll be able to get out."

"Is there a swing set?" Kaitlin asked.

He fought a wave of guilt. "I don't think so," he said.

Kaitlin thrust out her lower lip. "A swimming pool?"

"No, I'm afraid not." He wanted to give his daughter something to look forward to, but Declan was a bachelor and likely didn't have any toys lying around.

"I don't wanna stay here." Kaitlin pouted. "I wanna go back to the motel."

Declan pulled into the garage and they stayed where they were until the garage door shut behind them.

No one spoke until they were inside the house. The minute the door closed behind them, Declan turned toward Kaitlin. "Would you like to play with a dollhouse, Kaitlin?"

Caleb gaped at his friend. "Why on earth do you have a dollhouse?"

"I have twin nieces that I babysit for once in a while," Delcan said with a shrug. "I found out that having a dollhouse made for much nicer visits, at least for me."

"Yes! I wanna see the dollhouse!" Kaitlin literally danced from one foot to the other. "Where is it, Unca Deck! Where's the dollhouse?"

"In the spare bedroom. Come on, I'll show you." Declan took Kaitlin by the hand and took her upstairs.

"I bet she'd go with a stranger if they held out a dollhouse," Caleb said darkly as he followed Kaitlin's departure.

"I don't think so," Noelle said. "I think deep down she remembers Declan, the same way she remembered you. Besides, we're lucky Declan has nieces or this little adventure would be much worse."

That much was true. He'd panicked when Kaitlin asked for a swing set and a swimming pool. He could only hope the dollhouse would keep her occupied at least for a while.

"We'll need to stay away from the living room window," he said, trying to think through their plan. "And once the sun goes down, we'll have to remember not to put on any lights. We absolutely have to make sure that it looks as if Declan is living here alone."

"I understand." Noelle glanced around the small kitchen. "At least we can cook our meals rather than wasting our money on fast food."

"Yeah, but right now, I'd like to see the news." There was a small radio under the counter. "Or at least listen to it."

He fiddled with the dial, finding the sports station easy enough, but that wasn't what he needed. He turned the dial again until he finally found a talk show. Noelle sat down and he took the chair across from her.

Declan came back into the room and joined them at the table. "We have to talk while Kaitlin is occupied upstairs."

Caleb stood and turned down the volume on the radio. "What happened?"

"When I heard the APB put out for you, I asked a few questions. They found Jack's body and your fingerprints were at the scene of the crime."

Caleb curled his fingers into helpless fists. "So what? He was my lawyer. How big of a stretch is it to believe I was at his house at some point in time?"

"On the murder weapon?" Declan asked.

The murder weapon? He thought back, trying to imagine the crime scene. There was a lot of blood and the awful smell. He didn't remember seeing a weapon, but then again, he hadn't searched the place looking for it, either. He shook his head. "So where was the gun found?"

Declan frowned, his gaze narrowing with suspicion. "How did you know Owens was killed with a gun?"

For a moment he stared at his friend in horror. What was going on? Did Deck really suspect him after all?

Had he brought Noelle and Kaitlin here for safety, only to be turned in to the authorities by the man he'd once believed was his best friend?

NINE

"Because he saw the bullet wound, that's how!" Noelle shouted, jumping to her feet and glaring at Declan. She wanted to smack him for being so suspicious. "What are you saying? That you really believe Caleb is capable of cold-blooded murder?"

"I didn't say that…" Declan started but she wasn't in the mood to listen.

"How dare you bring us here as if you're willing to help, only to accuse him of killing his lawyer. Are the police on their way here right now? Is that what this is about?" Noelle was so mad her entire body was trembling and she barely registered the fact that Caleb had risen to his feet and put a reassuring arm around her waist.

"Calm down!" Declan said, holding up his hands as if he might need to defend himself. "I never accused Caleb of anything. I just thought it was odd that he knew about the gun."

"Noelle is only stating what I already thought," Caleb said reasonably. "And she's right about one thing. This isn't going to work without trust."

"Okay, okay." Declan jammed his fingers through his hair and sat back in his seat with a frustrated sigh.

"I'm sorry. You're right. I shouldn't have sounded as if I believed that you had anything to do with murdering Owens. I know you wouldn't do that, Caleb. I just…lost my head for a moment."

Caleb's arm around her waist proved to be a distraction, helped ground her so that her anger faded as quickly as it had ignited. She wanted so badly to lean on Caleb but this wasn't the time to show any weakness.

Could they really afford to trust Declan?

"Apology accepted," Caleb said, giving her a slight squeeze. "Right, Noelle?"

"I don't know," she muttered half under her breath. She allowed herself to lean against Caleb at least a little. "Maybe."

Caleb brushed a soft kiss against her temple and for a moment she forgot Declan was even there. She hadn't let any man get close to her for so long. Why did being with Caleb feel so right? She knew logically she should move away, but she couldn't bring herself to do it.

"Thanks for sticking up for me," he whispered.

She couldn't help but smile. "You're welcome."

Declan cleared his throat loudly and when she glanced over at him, she thought there was a flash of envy in his gaze. "I hate to interrupt, but we need to get to work if we're going to make any headway in this investigation."

Reluctantly she moved away from Caleb, missing his warmth as she dropped back onto the chair she'd vacated. Every one of her senses was tuned in to Caleb as he sat beside her.

"I'm listening," Caleb said.

"As I was saying, the murder weapon was found in the Dumpster outside the condo with your fingerprints on the handle of the gun."

Noelle rolled her eyes. "I'm not a cop and even I think that's ridiculous. Why would an experienced former SWAT team member be so stupid as to leave the gun right outside the scene of the crime?"

"Yeah, I hear you, but obviously someone believes it or there wouldn't be a warrant out for Caleb's arrest," Declan said dryly.

"Any idea who found the body?" Caleb asked. He reached over to take her hand in his, once again distracting her from the conversation. She didn't know why he kept touching her, and she sternly told herself not to read too much into his small, subconscious gestures.

"A neighbor reported a bad smell coming from Jack's condo. The Milwaukee police went in and found him."

"So now the MPD is working with the sheriff's department?" Caleb mused.

Declan snorted. "Yeah, not likely. You can be sure the sheriff will take over the case from MPD."

"And Sheriff Cramer never liked me much," Caleb said with a sigh. "I shouldn't be surprised at the way he chose to believe the worst."

"Cramer doesn't like me, either," Declan pointed out. "Don't read too much into that. It's likely Captain Royce fed him an earful about you. Remember how he called us hotshots after we rescued that kid? As if we did that just for the media exposure? The guy's a jerk."

Noelle frowned. "So what do Sheriff Cramer and Captain Royce think about your buddy Marc Brickner?" Noelle asked, dragging her attention back to the conversation.

The two men exchanged a knowing glance and she knew that couldn't be good.

"Well?" she demanded.

"Brickner is Royce's protégé," Caleb admitted. "And since Royce was promoted by Sheriff Cramer, it's likely they both think Brickner is the best guy on the team."

"Great. Just great." Could the scenario get any worse? "Any chance that Sheriff Cramer knew about Brickner's affair with Heather?" she asked.

Caleb shrugged. "No way to tell, but even if he did know about it, I don't think Cramer would suspect Brickner of murder."

Of course he wouldn't. That would be too easy. She glanced between the two men. "So what's our next step? Where do we go from here?"

"Maybe we should try to follow Brickner during his off-duty time, see what he's up to?" Declan suggested. "He's not scheduled to work tonight."

"We'd only find something if Brickner is doing his own dirty work, which right now, isn't a good assumption," Caleb said. "Why would he do anything suspicious now? There's a warrant out for my arrest. You can bet he'll sit back and wait for the system to work."

The thought was far too depressing. "What if Heather was involved in something illegal?" she asked.

Both Caleb and Declan stared at her as if she'd lost her marbles.

"What makes you think that?" Declan asked.

"Look, everything started with Heather's murder, right?" Both men nodded in agreement. "What's the motive? Jealousy? It seems like this cover-up is a bit extreme for something so simple."

"Heather was a model," Caleb protested. "Hardly illegal."

"Or maybe her modeling was a cover for something

else," Declan mused. "Noelle could be on to something. We have to consider all angles."

Caleb removed his hand from hers and she knew that she'd upset him. She sent him an imploring look, understanding where he was coming from. It was one thing to know your wife was having an affair, or even more than one affair. But to think that the mother of your child was involved in something illegal was entirely different. Especially since Caleb was a cop, sworn to uphold the law.

She didn't blame him for not wanting to assume the worst about his deceased wife.

Caleb stared at Declan, trying to fight the natural instinct to defend Heather. If he were honest, he would admit that what Declan and Noelle were suggesting wasn't outside the realm of possibility. "She did bring in a lot of money," Caleb finally said. "But what kind of illegal activity could she have been involved with? Drugs?"

And then it hit him. What else would explain why she was seen with more than one man?

"Prostitution?" He forced the horrible word past his constricted throat.

"We don't have to jump to conclusions," Noelle interjected, looking distressed. "Drugs could be the answer."

He shook his head, appreciating the fact that Noelle cared enough to try and spare his feelings. "I think there would have been some evidence if this was about drugs. Her autopsy showed she was clean. The D.A.'s office used the fact that she wasn't drugged as evidence that she likely knew her murderer."

"So what? That doesn't mean she wasn't some sort of drug runner," Noelle repeated stubbornly.

"Heather was far too noticeable to be a mule," Declan said. "She attracted attention everywhere she went."

"There's no point in speculating." Caleb glanced at his friend. "We could spend hours going through different scenarios, but without proof we're stuck. Deck, is there anything else you can tell me from the police report of Heather's murder?"

"No, there wasn't much evidence at the crime scene," Declan mused. "The eyewitness testimony played a big role in your arrest."

No kidding. "No murder weapon was ever found?" he pressed.

"Nope." Deck shook his head. "They had nothing else to use to pin it on you."

"Interesting, considering the gun used to kill Jack was found nearby," Caleb murmured. "Why didn't they use a similar ruse back then for Heather's murder?"

"Good question," Deck admitted. "Maybe it was a crime of passion, that whoever killed her didn't really plan it. And when he did, it was too late to plant the gun."

He had to admit, Deck's theory made sense. Ironic that Brickner had spouted off about Caleb's temper when Brickner's was far worse. He could easily imagine Brickner losing control and killing Heather in a fit of rage.

Too bad he needed a way to prove it. "Could I borrow your computer for a while?" he asked Deck.

"Sure." If Deck was curious as to what he was searching for, he didn't let on. Declan pulled the laptop out of its case and handed it over to Caleb. "Do you need any help?"

"No, just give me some time, okay?" He didn't want Declan or Noelle, for that matter, to watch over his shoulder. "Would you mind checking on Kaitlin?" he asked.

Noelle hesitated, but then nodded. "Sure."

Caleb waited until both Deck and Noelle left the kitchen, before he began his search. There was something niggling at him from the back of his mind. A website that he'd stumbled across by accident, shortly before he'd moved out of the house. At the time he hadn't thought much about it.

He tried several different combinations of words before he found what he was looking for.

Eileen's Elite Escort Services.

Caleb closed his eyes for a moment, dreading what he was about to find. But hiding from the truth wasn't going to help him clear his name. So he took a deep breath and entered the website, which required the viewers to be eighteen in order to move through the various screens. The meager attempt to prevent minors from going in was laughable.

It didn't take him long to find Heather's photograph, although he was a bit surprised that it was still on the site, considering she'd died fourteen months ago. Maybe they kept it for marketing reasons? She was beautiful, dressed in a sexy, scanty outfit that made him feel sick to his stomach. And he found it interesting to note that the name under her photograph was Hannah, not Heather.

A fake name? Why not?

He closed the laptop with a wave of disgust. His wife had been a paid escort. And what exactly did her services entail? He wasn't so sure he wanted to know. Considering the types of photographs he saw, he imagined the worst.

The only good thing to come out of this latest clue that he could see was that it was another possible motive for her murder.

* * *

Caleb didn't tell Declan or Noelle what he'd found, at least not right away. Partially because he was humiliated.

But more so because the site was probably just another dead end. Other than giving a clue as to another potential motive for murder, what could they do with the information?

While Noelle made lunch, Kaitlin chattered on and on about the dollhouse and the various dress-up dolls she'd found. He was grateful Deck had something to keep Kaitlin entertained.

"When do you work next?" he asked Deck.

Declan carried his dirty dishes over to the sink, glancing at Caleb over his shoulder. "Tonight, second shift, which means I have to leave a couple of hours. The three of you will need to keep a low profile."

"Understood. We'll make sure that we don't use any lights while you're gone and will keep our movements to a minimum." After the past few days, he couldn't deny the fact they could all use some decent sleep.

Declan scrubbed his chin. "I was thinking about that. There's only one small window in the basement, and we could board that up if you wanted to keep working on the computer. We could even move the dollhouse and the television down there, too. You could do whatever you want without anybody knowing that you're here."

"That would be great," he agreed. "We could even bring the mattress down from one of the beds."

"Let's do it," Declan said, setting his glass down with a thud. "Before I leave."

Eager to have something constructive to do, Noelle and Kaitlin carried the dolls and other toys that Declan had upstairs in the spare bedroom down to the basement while he and Deck hauled the heavy stuff. Once they had the mattresses and television strategically set up next to an old card table he planned to use as a desk, he stepped back and surveyed their work with satisfaction.

The television was small, but it was better to use the old one than to take the big screen from the living room, just in case the absence was noticed. Declan brought a few more chairs out for them to use, and Noelle dusted them off while Caleb looked around for something to use to black out the small window.

Duct tape and cardboard should do the trick. Although he was a little worried the light might shine through the cardboard. He dug around until he found a can of black spray paint. Perfect. He used the edge of the can to break a corner of the window, so that having it covered up looked reasonable, and within minutes had the window effectively blacked out.

"Nice," Deck said. "Now you guys should be totally safe down here."

"I hope so." Caleb didn't want to take any chances, especially not with Noelle or Kaitlin.

But he wanted very much to get outside the confines of Declan's house, to do a little research of his own, once Noelle and Kaitlin were asleep.

Noelle kept herself busy cleaning dust off the card table and chairs the guys had dragged out for them to use. She told herself that staying in a dark basement with only a few lights on was better than being on the run, but so far she was having trouble believing it. She kept feeling as if there were spiders crawling up her arms.

Maybe because she'd killed at least a half dozen so far. Ridiculous to get worked up over a few spiders, but everyone had a weakness and creepy-crawlies just happened to be hers.

The time seemed to move by with excruciating slowness once Declan had left for work. She played a game of Go Fish with Kaitlin while Caleb surfed the internet on Declan's computer.

At six, she slipped back upstairs to rummage for something they could eat for dinner. She decided to make a frozen pizza, since that would be easy to carry downstairs. While the oven was preheating she found paper plates and napkins and took those back down to the basement.

Caleb had put aside the computer to play a card game with Kaitlin. She was pleased at how comfortable the little girl was around him now, compared to their first meeting outside her house.

Before the bullets started flying.

She shivered at the memory. Hard to believe that just a few days had passed since then when it seemed like a lifetime.

They ate the pepperoni pizza in the basement, and both Caleb and his daughter prayed with her before digging into the meal. Afterward, they played several more card games, which only served to make Noelle wonder what it would be like if the three of them really were a family.

Don't go there, she warned herself. They wouldn't be together for very long, just until they cleared Caleb's name.

She pushed the depressing thought aside to concentrate on the game. After they'd each won several rounds, Caleb announced it was bedtime.

Kaitlin protested, but Noelle understood what Caleb

was thinking. They needed to take advantage of the ability to get some rest while they had it. Even though they were safe for now, she couldn't shake the feeling that their peace was short-lived.

Caleb turned out the two small lamps they were using and instantly the basement was plunged into total darkness.

"I don't like it so dark," Kaitlin whined.

"Is this better?" Caleb turned on the smaller of the lamps and carried it off to the farthest corner of the basement, tucking it behind some boxes to help dim the light.

"Much better, Daddy."

Sleep didn't come easy, despite the comfy mattress she shared with Kaitlin. She prayed for guidance and safety, which helped her relax. She was just beginning to doze off when she heard the soft brush of fabric and the almost imperceptible thud of a footstep.

Her eyes shot open and she turned her head in time to see Caleb heading upstairs. She almost called out to him, but held back so that she wouldn't wake up Kaitlin.

Where was he going? She rolled off the edge of the mattress, moving as silently as possible. They'd been sleeping fully dressed so all she needed to do was to pull on her running shoes before following Caleb up the stairs.

She didn't know how Caleb managed to be so silent, because the wood stairs creaked as she climbed them. She wasn't surprised to find Caleb waiting for her in the kitchen.

"Go back downstairs," he whispered when she reached the doorway.

"Not until you tell me where you're going." She heard him sigh.

"I'm just going to look around for a bit, that's all. Nothing for you to worry about."

"Why would you take that risk?" she asked, trying not to show her frustration. "Especially when there's a warrant out for your arrest? All it would take is for one person to recognize you."

"I'm just going to see if Brickner's home, that's all. I'll be back in an hour or so."

"You were the one who said that following Brickner wasn't going to do any good. So why go out now?"

Caleb's expression wasn't easy to read in the dark. "Stay here with Kaitlin, okay? I promise I'll be back soon."

"Wait," she said, grasping his arm. "What kind of car does Brickner drive?"

"I'm not sure. I never paid attention since we didn't hang out together."

"If you're going to head over there, see if he's driving a black extended cab pickup truck."

Caleb paused for a moment and then scowled. "Just like the one that was following you in the days prior to my release."

"Yes." She didn't want him to go, but sensed there was nothing she could say or do to make him change his mind. "That might give us a hint of something to go on."

"Sounds like a plan." Before she could say anything more, Caleb slipped out the garage door, closing it softly behind him.

She stayed in the kitchen, looking out the window at the backyard, where she assumed he'd go rather than heading out front. But even though she watched intently, she never saw any sign of Caleb.

Which should have reassured her. But she couldn't

suppress a shiver and rubbed her hands over her arms for warmth.

Please, Lord, watch over Caleb. Keep him safe.

TEN

Caleb slipped through Deck's backyard, taking care to stay hidden in the shadows. He didn't rush, but chose his path carefully. As much as he'd tried to reassure Noelle that he would be fine, the last thing he wanted to do was to be identified by some nosy neighbor and sent back to jail.

If that happened, he felt certain he'd never get out. Ever.

He headed for the running/biking trail and increased his pace to an easy jog for roughly two miles before veering off onto the side street that would take him past Brickner's house.

Caleb had only been there once about two and a half years ago, shortly after Brickner's divorce was final. Marc had thrown a huge Super Bowl party to celebrate his new single status. All the guys from the SWAT team were invited, so Caleb had tagged along with Declan and another buddy, Isaac Morrison. Caleb remembered the night clearly because Brickner had been a bit of a jerk, bragging about how he'd taken the house from his ex-wife. Caleb remembered thinking at the time it was a good thing Brickner didn't have any kids. The game had been boring, and Brickner had started drinking heavily, so he, Deck and Isaac ended up leaving at halftime. Now that Caleb thought about that night, he couldn't help wondering if Brickner had been having an affair with Heather even back then? And if so, what on earth had his wife seen in the guy?

Steering away from those thoughts, because really what difference did any of that make now, Caleb concentrated instead on walking past Brickner's house, trying to appear casual and not overly interested in his surroundings. From the corner of his eye, he could see there were no obvious lights on, at least none that were visible from the street.

At the next intersection, he purposefully turned the corner in the opposite direction and headed down several streets before he backtracked to the row of houses that were located directly behind Brickner's place. From this side, he could make out a small light that was on over what appeared to be the kitchen area.

One small light didn't mean much. Brickner could easily be home or out somewhere, so Caleb checked over his shoulder to make sure no one was watching before he slipped between two houses with dark windows and no sign of anyone being home to sneak up to Brickner's place.

He prayed he wouldn't be arrested for being a Peeping Tom as he flattened himself against Brickner's house and peered in through the lighted window.

He didn't see anyone, so he made his way around to a couple of the other darkened windows, hiding behind trees or bushes if any cars came down the street. When he rounded the corner of the garage, he glanced in the window and verified the garage was empty.

He hunkered down to wait a bit, even though logically he knew that if Brickner was working, the guy wouldn't be home for a good hour yet, since the second-shift guys worked until eleven-thirty at night. And if Brickner wasn't working, he likely would be out even later.

After about thirty minutes, Caleb decided to head back to Declan's place when headlights pierced the darkness. He kept hidden as the vehicle came closer, slowed down and then turned into the driveway. The garage door opened and with the light on, he could easily identify the make and model of Brickner's vehicle.

Noelle's guess had been dead-on. Marc Brickner drove a black extended cab pickup truck. He memorized the license plate, even though he vaguely remembered Noelle stating she'd never gotten the tag number.

He waited for what seemed like a long time but was only thirty minutes, when Brickner came back out, dressed in a very sharp suit, a white shirt and a tie. Not at all the usual garb worn by the guys on the SWAT team. Where was Brickner headed? Who was he meeting with? The questions barely formed in his mind when Brickner backed down the driveway and left, heading east.

Leaving Caleb to wish he had a set of wheels to follow him.

Caleb returned to Declan's house a while later, not a bit surprised to find Noelle up and waiting for him.

"You were gone a long time," she accused, meeting him once again in the kitchen. She hadn't turned any lights on, but his eyes were so accustomed to the darkness he could see her fairly well.

"I'm sorry, but Brickner came home so I hung around longer than I intended." He reached into the cupboard for a glass and poured a large glass of water to soothe his parched throat. "You were right, though. Brickner drives a black extended cab pickup truck."

Noelle's sour mood evaporated. "That's great news. Surely that helps our case."

He didn't want to burst her bubble but he also didn't want to give her false hope, either. "He's not the only guy driving a black extended cab pickup truck. We'll need more than that coincidence to convince the authorities that I'm not the killer."

"I know, but he's the same guy I saw with Heather the night of her murder. All we need to know is a little more about what was going on between them. It has to be drugs. Nothing else makes sense."

He wasn't convinced, but filled her in on the way Marc was dressed when he'd left the house. "Brickner was either meeting a woman or a boss of some sort. No one dresses like that without a good reason."

"Too bad you couldn't follow him," she murmured.

"Maybe next time," he said. He caught sight of the flash of headlights outside, so he drew Noelle into an alcove so they couldn't be seen. The peach scent of her shampoo was distracting, although he tried to keep his gaze focused on the living room window.

The vehicle outside slowed and very nearly stopped directly in front of Declan's house before it picked up speed and drove away.

"I thought for sure the car meant Declan was home," Noelle whispered close to his ear.

"No, but it was another dark-colored pickup truck," he said grimly. He released her and took a step away to put some badly needed distance between them.

She sucked in a harsh breath. "Brickner?"

"Maybe." He wished he could have gotten a good look at the driver, but that was impossible with the glare of the headlights. His gut knotted with tension at the realization. "Or there's some other guy with a dark pickup truck involved in this case. The same guy who was following you. Someone that isn't Brickner."

He didn't even want to consider the possibility that they were on the wrong track. That Brickner wasn't the one who'd murdered Heather after all.

Because without a hint of a clue, the case of his wife's murder was dead in the water.

Noelle huddled next to Kaitlin on the mattress, her mind too busy to sleep. What if Caleb was right about the black extended cab pickup truck? What if they couldn't figure out who was behind these murders?

They couldn't hide out in Declan's basement forever. She knew they were already putting Declan in a bad situation by staying here in the first place. If anyone found out he was hiding a fugitive, he'd lose his job and face being arrested, too.

She imagined Marc Brickner dressed in a suit and tie, heading off to—where? A date? Or an illegal business meeting? She supposed there was a chance he was headed to a legal business meeting, but somehow she didn't think that was likely.

The garage door opened, signaling that Declan was home. She heard Caleb get up and head up the stairs to meet his friend. Unwilling to be left out, she followed.

"We had a hostage situation," Declan was saying as she reached the top of the stairs. "I stayed late to help cover because we were a man short."

"How did it end?" Caleb asked.

"Our perp surrendered without harming his wife and kids," Declan said. "But it was touch and go there for a bit."

"Who was the negotiator?" Caleb asked.

"Isaac Morrison," Declan said, glancing over at her as she entered the room. "You'll be interested to know that Brickner was originally supposed to work tonight, but he called in sick."

"Sick?" Caleb echoed. "Well, that's funny, since I saw him leaving his house about ninety minutes ago, dressed in a suit and tie. He certainly didn't look sick to me."

Noelle was relieved at the news. "We are on the right track. I knew he was the one who was following me."

"We still don't know that for sure," Caleb protested and she understood he was trying to keep an open mind. From spending just these few days with Caleb, she was already getting a sense of the type of cop he'd been before this happened. Good cops always kept their minds open to other possibilities, a trait she couldn't fault him for. Too bad the guys who'd arrested him hadn't given him the benefit of the doubt. "Besides, it doesn't make sense that Brickner would drive past Deck's house on a night he knew Deck was likely working."

Declan straightened away from where he'd been leaning against the counter. "Brickner came here?" he asked in shock.

"A black extended cab pickup truck slowed down in front of the house and then drove away," Caleb corrected. "And really it wasn't easy to see in the darkness, for all I know it could have been dark gray or a dark blue in color rather than black."

Declan was silent for a moment. "Brickner may not

have looked at the schedule, or he knew I was working and was making sure there was no one here."

"Like us," Noelle said softly.

"Yeah," Declan admitted slowly. "Maybe. Brickner knew Caleb and I were friends."

"Do you think he's been swinging by here on a regular basis?" Caleb asked.

"I don't know," Declan said in a frustrated tone. "I haven't been paying that much attention to the traffic on my street. This is a normal, safe neighborhood. The only thing I know for sure is no one has been following me."

"Did you happen to notice when Brickner is scheduled to be off again?" Noelle asked.

"Yeah, he's off the next two days in a row."

"Good," Caleb said with satisfaction. "That means we can follow him tomorrow night."

"If he goes someplace," Declan agreed.

Noelle sighed, knowing that she would be expected to stay here with Kaitlin while they followed Brickner. Not that she minded taking care of Kaitlin, but the thought of being left here in the basement without any way of knowing if they were okay filled her with dread.

She'd just have to put Caleb's and Declan's fates in God's hands.

The next morning, Noelle's eyes were gritty from lack of sleep. She dragged herself out of bed to take care of Kaitlin and within minutes Caleb was up, too. She took Kaitlin upstairs to use the bathroom facilities while Caleb straightened up their temporary living space. She brought cold cereal and milk down for breakfast and this time Caleb led the prayer.

"Dear Lord, thank You for providing this food we are about to eat and keep us safe in Your care. Amen."

"Amen," she and Kaitlin echoed simultaneously, which made Kaitlin giggle.

The thought of spending the entire day in the basement did not fill Noelle with enthusiasm. She understood the need to be safe, but it was barely an hour and she already missed having natural sunlight.

Caleb must have understood her feelings, because he gestured to the staircase with his spoon. "I think we are probably okay to head upstairs for a while after breakfast, as long as we stay out of the living room. With the bright sunlight outside, it won't be easy for anyone to see inside unless they come right up to the windows."

"That would be great," she said thankfully.

Noelle managed to keep busy throughout the next few hours, doing dishes and playing dolls with Kaitlin. When she heard Declan and Caleb talking in low tones, she left Kaitlin to her dollhouse and went down into the basement to see what was going on.

Caleb's expression was grim as he stared at the computer. She nearly gasped out loud when she recognized the photograph of Heather, Caleb's wife, on the screen. The woman was dressed in a racy outfit that barely covered the essentials.

"Where did you find it?" she asked. She couldn't imagine what he must be thinking about seeing his wife dressed like that.

Caleb and Declan exchanged a long glance. "Eileen's Elite Escort Services dot com," Caleb admitted.

"Escort services?" Noelle frowned, not exactly sure what that meant. "What exactly does an escort do?"

Caleb shook his head. "I'm not sure I want to know."

Declan's expression was equally sober. "In theory the escorts are available for wealthy men who want a good-looking woman to appear at functions with them. However, we suspect there is far more to the escort's duties than that."

She remembered what Caleb had said yesterday, about prostitution. She hadn't wanted to believe the worst, wanting to spare him the pain and humiliation. But obviously now that they found Heather's photo on this website, there was no denying the truth.

"But why would Heather's photograph still be on this site if she's been dead for over a year?" she asked.

"That's a good point," Caleb admitted. He refused to meet her gaze and she worried that he somehow felt responsible for what his former wife had done. "Either the owners aren't good at updating their website or they chose to keep the photo there for advertising purposes."

"At least we know that this is another possible motive for murder," Declan said.

"Is there a way to find out who owns this business?" Noelle asked as Caleb minimized the site as if to hide the photograph of his dead wife. She wanted to reassure him that this wasn't his fault, but considering the stiff set to his shoulders and the way he was avoiding her gaze, she didn't get the sense he would accept anything remotely resembling sympathy.

"I bet Brickner's involved somehow," Caleb muttered harshly. "The way he was dressed last night was far from subtle."

"He could be the middle man," Declan agreed. "Maybe he was reporting to his higher-ups about the business?"

Noelle wasn't a police officer but what Caleb and Declan were proposing made sense. "We need to find a way to prove he's involved." Then another idea occurred to her. "What if Heather wasn't murdered out of jealousy or rage, but because she wanted out? Maybe she threatened to go to the authorities if they didn't let her go, so Brickner killed her?"

Caleb spun around in his chair to face her for the first time since she'd come downstairs. "You could be right about that. As Kaitlin was getting older and starting school, she may have had second thoughts about being involved in this escort business."

The frank hope in Caleb's eyes tugged at her heart. She just couldn't imagine what it must be like to realize you've been betrayed to this extent by the woman you promised to love and cherish. Any illegal activity was bad enough, considering Caleb was a sheriff's deputy, but an escort service that potentially doubled as a high-class call girl? She could barely wrap her mind around the concept.

"I'm sure you're right," she agreed softly.

"Hopefully we'll find something tonight," Declan said as he moved across the room. "I'm heading to the grocery store, and will be back in about an hour."

When she and Caleb were alone, she placed a reassuring hand on his shoulder. "I'm sorry you have to go through this," she said.

His mouth thinned and he looked exceptionally weary as he shrugged. "I knew our marriage was falling apart, but I can't help thinking I should have done more. Tried harder. Figured out that something like this was going on sooner."

"Caleb, beating yourself up like this isn't going to change anything. Besides, Heather is responsible for her own behavior," she said.

He hung his head and took a long, shuddering breath. "I didn't love her the way I should have," he said in a voice so low she could barely hear him.

She put her arm around his shoulders and gave him a hug. "Maybe not, but she must not have loved you the way she should have, either."

"You're probably right about that," he admitted. "We were young and I was infatuated with how beautiful she was. I remember thinking I was such a lucky guy to have a woman like her. But after we got married and Heather discovered she was pregnant, everything changed. Heather became obsessed with her looks, with her weight. She only gained fifteen pounds with Kaitlin and she worked out like a maniac afterward." He paused and then continued, "And when Kaitlin was barely a year old she began her modeling career again. Which I'm sure was a big, fat lie."

"We don't know for sure that Heather wasn't modeling back then," she pointed out. "Maybe it was only later that she went into the escort business."

"Maybe." He shrugged. "The timing doesn't matter, so I need to just let it go."

"Your daughter needs you, Caleb. Have you noticed that she's not afraid of you anymore? Heather betrayed you and your wedding vows, but your goal right now is to clear your name so that you and Kaitlin can become a family again."

"Thank you," he murmured. She stepped back so that he could stand up, but she wasn't prepared when he gently cupped her face in his hands and stared down at her intently. "Noelle, I don't know what I would have done without you," he said mere seconds before he gently kissed her.

ELEVEN

Caleb's heart pounded in his chest as Noelle returned his kiss with a sweetness he craved. It seemed like a lifetime since he'd held a woman, especially someone as pure and good as Noelle. But their brief moment of togetherness was interrupted when Kaitlin began to wail.

"Noa! My tummy hurts!"

Noelle broke away from Caleb and he wished the lighting in the basement was better so he could search her expression. Was she upset with him for overstepping his bounds? He hadn't intended to kiss her, but then again, he couldn't deny that he wanted to kiss her again.

"I better go check on Kaitlin," she murmured, running a hand through her hair.

"We'll both go," he said, determined to take an active role in raising his daughter. If he could clear his name, or rather *when* he cleared his name, he had every intention of being a good father to his daughter.

Noelle cuddled Kaitlin close, pressing a kiss to his daughter's forehead. "She feels a bit warm."

"What should we do?" he asked. "Take her in to the doctor's office?"

"I don't think we need to panic yet. She isn't throwing up or anything. We'll just have to keep an eye on her. I'll make something light for lunch, like soup and toast."

"Cin'mon toast," Kaitlin corrected. "I like cin'mon toast."

"All right, we'll see if Uncle Declan has cinnamon for your toast," Noelle agreed.

Caleb stood there for a moment, feeling stupid. How was it that he hadn't known that his daughter liked cinnamon toast? And what else didn't he know? What else had he missed?

Too much. He realized now he should have stayed more involved in raising Kaitlin, especially after Heather returned to her so-called modeling career. He was ashamed to admit that he'd resented Heather for always getting a babysitter, when he never considered cutting back his own hours.

For a moment he wondered if spending fourteen months in jail and almost losing his daughter was God's way of sending him a wake-up call.

And if so, he was grateful for being given a second chance.

The rest of the day seemed to crawl by in slow motion, and Caleb wasn't sure if it was because Kaitlin was more fretful than usual or if he was just anxious to be doing something active to clear his name.

He spent time on Deck's computer, trying to search for more information on Eileen's Elite Escort Services, but every avenue he'd tried resulted in a dead end. He finally gave up, realizing that he and Declan would just have to put their energies into following Brickner and finding leads that way.

He played card games with Kaitlin, giving Noelle a

break from the uncharacteristically clingy child. He knew Kaitlin wasn't feeling well when she only ate half of her cinnamon toast and chicken noodle soup.

Declan brought home more than just groceries, he'd purchased three prepaid phones and used a fake email address to activate them.

"Thank you," Noelle said, taking her phone gratefully. "At least now I have a way of getting in touch with you guys if needed."

"These are mostly to be used in an emergency," Deck cautioned.

"I know."

Caleb cleared his throat. "I'd like to go back to Noelle's house, see if we can figure out where the shooter was located."

"I'm not sure if that's a good idea, especially now that your mug shot has been splashed all over the news," Deck said.

"I know, but hear me out for a minute. If you and I dress in our uniforms, then no one will question us. We'll look like a couple of cops gathering clues."

"Yeah, except that the police have already done that." Deck did not look enthusiastic about his plan.

"Who are the best sharpshooters on the team?" Caleb asked.

"You were one of the best," Declan admitted. "But now Marc Brickner has the top slot."

"I just want to take a look at the trajectory," Caleb said, trying to find a way to change Deck's mind. "I think there are only a few guys who could have made that shot."

"Come on, Caleb, anyone from the team could have attempted the shot. Obviously, they missed."

"The miss was sheer luck," Caleb said. Although now

that he'd learned a bit about prayer, he couldn't help wondering if maybe God had spared him for a reason. "I bent over to pick up Kaitlin's stuffed giraffe. If I hadn't, I'm pretty sure I'd be dead."

Deck seemed to consider that information before he reluctantly nodded. "All right, but I don't think going into your old house to get a uniform is very smart. I'm sure there are hidden cameras set up to monitor the place."

Caleb knew Declan was right. "I'll borrow one of yours. We're not that different in size."

"All right," Deck reluctantly agreed.

As Caleb dressed in one of Declan's spare uniforms, he realized that he'd lost weight in prison. Where once Deck's uniform might have been a bit snug, it now hung loosely on his frame.

"I need to hit the gym," he muttered in disgust as he tightened the belt.

He checked on Noelle and Kaitlin before leaving, and Noelle's eyebrows shot up in surprise when she saw him. "Wow, you look great in uniform," she said.

He knew better than to be pleased by how she'd noticed, especially since there was no guarantee that he'd be offered another job with the SWAT team even if he managed to clear his name.

Although he secretly hoped Sheriff Cramer would hire him back.

One step at a time, he reminded himself sternly. He followed Deck out to the garage, and hid down in the seat as Declan backed out of the driveway and headed out of the subdivision.

He stayed hidden for at least ten minutes while Deck drove around making sure that he wasn't followed. Deck was in his private vehicle and not a squad car, but hopefully the neighbors would assume it was an unmarked vehicle.

"You can sit up now," Declan said after he made another right-handed turn. "We'll be at Noelle's house in about five minutes."

Caleb couldn't deny he was nervous about doing this, but he really needed to see the scene to be sure that he understood the facts. So far, they were building a case against Brickner, although it was circumstantial at best. Proving that Brickner had made the shot that nearly killed him wouldn't be easy, but as a former sharpshooter himself, he knew that the crime scene could reveal a lot about the shooter.

He climbed out of the passenger side of Declan's vehicle, trying to look as if he belonged. His beat-up red truck was gone, obviously it had likely been towed and swept over by the crime scene techs.

Had they planted more evidence to make him look guilty? He didn't want to know.

As they approached Noelle's house, he noticed that someone had nailed up a board over the broken window of her living room. At least someone had tried to protect her house from vandalism.

"Here are the bullet holes," Declan said, waving a hand at Noelle's front door. Caleb examined the one along the doorframe first, and if he stood straight the bullet hole was just below eye level.

"Thinks he's hot stuff to attempt a head shot," Caleb grumbled. Every cop knew that head shots were not usually attempted because of the small area. Chest and abdomen shots were the preferred target range.

It would be just like Brickner, a man with an overly healthy ego, to attempt a head shot.

Caleb slid a straw into the hole to figure out the track of the bullet. Turning, he carefully swept his gaze across the street. Where had the shooter been?

Then he saw the large tree between two houses, with thick branches low enough to grab onto. "How much do you bet he was up in that tree?" he asked Declan.

"Let's go check it out."

Caleb followed Declan across the street, hoping that no one was looking at him too closely. It was the middle of the day in summer and there was one elderly man mowing the lawn on a riding mower and a few doors down there were a handful of kids playing tag.

"Give me a leg up," he said to Declan.

His buddy didn't argue. With a leg up it was easier to get up into the tree, although he imagined that Brickner had managed the feat on his own.

He found the shooter's spot without too much difficulty. There was a large branch with another branch shooting off to the right, making the perfect prop for a long-range rifle. There was a small opening between the leaves through which he could see Noelle's front door.

Caleb took his time, finding the small section of the branch where the bark was worn away, likely from the weight of the rifle. He took a picture with the cell phone.

How long had the shooter sat up here waiting for his target? Several hours? Seemed unlikely in broad daylight. Even though there was an abundance of green leaves, anyone living in one of these two houses would have noticed a guy hiding in the tree.

"I bet he had an accomplice," Caleb muttered. Someone who'd tailed him from the time Caleb had left the jail? Possibly.

He swung down from the tree and dropped to the grass

beside Declan. As they left the scene and walked back to Declan's vehicle, he grew more certain that the shots were fired by Brickner.

But who was Brickner's accomplice?

Caleb was relieved when they returned to Declan's house without catching anyone's attention. He swept his arm across his sweat-dampened brow, thinking that being a criminal wasn't easy. All this skulking around, trying to hide from view? And for what? A little extra cash?

"How's Kaitlin?" he asked when he saw Noelle cleaning up the lunch dishes in the kitchen.

"She says her tummy hurts, but so far she seems okay. I found a thermometer in Declan's medicine cabinet and she has a very low-grade fever. Nothing to worry about yet."

He didn't like the thought of Kaitlin being sick. "We could send Declan out for medicine to help bring down her fever," he offered.

"That would probably be a good idea, just in case her fever spikes later tonight." The pucker between her brows was an indication of her worry. "And for sure if we have the medicine we won't need it," she added with a wry smile.

He wanted to pull her close and hug her, but he held back, unsure what she thought about their kiss earlier. He told himself not to push his luck. "Why don't you make a list of things you think we might need?"

"Good idea."

He changed his clothes while Noelle wrote out her list. He hung up Deck's uniform with a pang of envy. He told himself that a career didn't make the man, but he was too afraid that in his case it did.

What would he do for work if he couldn't get hired back on the SWAT team? He might be able to find a security job somewhere, maybe at one of the local hospitals. The idea didn't hold a lot of appeal, but he needed to remember that his daughter was his first priority.

Everything else was second.

After Declan returned from the local pharmacy with the items on Noelle's list, he took a tray of cheeseburgers outside to place on the grill. When Caleb protested, Deck insisted that he grilled for himself often and that no one would think it was suspicious that he was grilling so many.

Kaitlin didn't eat much, but Caleb hoped her appetite would return tomorrow. He and Noelle figured Kaitlin had caught some sort of twenty-four-hour virus.

When dinner was over, he and Declan cleaned up so that Noelle could play another card game with Kaitlin. Even though it was still light outside, he and Declan planned to leave soon, unwilling to take the chance that Brickner might slip away before they arrived.

"Call if you need something," Caleb said to Noelle as she and Kaitlin played a game of Go Fish on the mattress they used as a bed in the basement.

"Declan was pretty clear that I can only use the phone in case of an emergency."

"Yeah, well, I'd appreciate a text message so that I know Kaitlin is okay."

She smiled as if pleased that he cared enough to ask about his daughter. "All right, I'll text you."

"Good." He wished he had the right to kiss Noelle goodbye, but he had to be satisfied with getting a big hug and a kiss from his daughter.

"I love you, Daddy."

"I love you, too, Katydid." When he glanced at Noelle he thought he saw the gleam of tears in her eyes. "Stay safe," he murmured before heading upstairs to find Declan.

They parked the next block over and used Declan's binoculars to keep an eye on Brickner's house. As the sun disappeared behind the horizon, Brickner left the house in his shiny black pickup truck.

"We've got him," Caleb said to Declan. "He's heading east on Palmer."

His buddy drove around the block, keeping a decent amount of distance behind Brickner's truck. Declan followed him all the way out to what looked to be a gentleman's club, but Brickner surprised him by not going inside. Instead he parked in a corner of the lot that was farthest away from the light.

A small blue car drove up, and headed directly over to where Brickner's truck was. Using the binoculars, Caleb watched Brickner get out of the truck and meet the woman who was dressed much like the photograph he'd seen of Heather. Not the same clothes of course, but just as revealing.

"Write down this tag number," he said to Declan and rattled off the license plate for the blue car.

"A hot date?" Declan asked.

"I don't think so," Caleb murmured. "She's yelling at him about something. I can't read her lips, but he's yelling back at her. Wait, now he's hauling her into his truck!"

"Let me see," Declan demanded. "Is he actually kidnapping her?"

"Not exactly. She's sitting with her arms folded over her chest and gazing out the passenger window as if resigned to her fate." He handed the binoculars over to Declan. "We need to follow them."

Declan took a quick look before handing them back to Caleb. Deck started the car. "I think we're in for a long night."

Caleb kept the binoculars trained on the reluctant passenger in Brickner's truck for as long as he could, silently agreeing with his buddy's assessment of the situation.

He hoped and prayed they'd uncover something to crack the case wide open. Because he didn't want to let down Noelle.

Or his daughter.

Noelle didn't remember falling asleep, the bone-deep exhaustion from the night before must have caught up to her. But when Kaitlin began to cry, she jerked awake. "What is it, Kaitlin? What's wrong?"

"My tummy hurts," Kaitlin whimpered. Noelle had a bad feeling and barely made it out of the way before Kaitlin threw up all over.

"Oh, sweetie," she murmured, grabbing the edge of the blanket and using it to wipe up the mess. "Come on, we need to get upstairs to the bathroom."

She had her phone in her pocket, but she couldn't call Caleb, yet. She carried Kaitlin upstairs and this time managed to make it to the bathroom so that the little girl could be sick in the toilet.

"I don't feel good, Noa," Kaitlin whined.

"I'm sorry, honey. Here, let me wash you up." When she reached for the washcloth and towel hanging on the rack, she belatedly remembered to close the bathroom door so that the light wouldn't be as noticeable to anyone outside.

Although there wasn't much she could do about the small bathroom window, other than making sure the blinds were closed.

After a few minutes, Kaitlin seemed to be better, although Noelle knew that was likely temporary. She left Kaitlin in the bathroom for a few minutes while she went out and found new sheets and blankets for the mattress downstairs.

She didn't want to waste too much time, so she balled up all the soiled stuff and carried everything over to the washer and dryer. Once she had one load of wash in, she remade the bed, sprayed a liberal dose of air freshener and went back upstairs to get Kaitlin.

"I'm hungry," Kaitlin announced.

"We'll try some crackers and white soda first," Noelle told her. Kaitlin followed her into the kitchen, where Noelle found a can of white soda and a package of saltine crackers. Then she emptied out a wastebasket to use as a bucket.

"I wanna sit at the table," Kaitlin insisted, crawling up onto a chair.

Noelle hesitated, glancing fearfully outside. The backyard was completely dark, and the kitchen was tucked away toward the back of the house. If they kept only the bathroom light on, they might be okay there for a few minutes.

Kaitlin sipped the white soda and nibbled on a cracker. Noelle prayed the child's stomach would tolerate the light fare. She texted Caleb about how Kaitlin got sick, and frowned when she didn't get a response.

She hoped the lack of response meant that Caleb and Declan were busy following Marc Brickner. The sooner they found some evidence against the guy, the better.

A flash of headlights pierced the darkness and she leaped up to flip off the switch for the bathroom light, plunging the room in darkness.

"Noa? I'm scared," Kaitlin whispered.

"I'm here, sweetie, don't worry." It wasn't easy for her eyes to adjust to the lack of light, but she felt along the wall until she found Kaitlin. "We're going to go back downstairs, okay?"

"Okay," Kaitlin agreed.

Noelle handed Kaitlin the crackers and then lifted the child into her arms while balancing the can of white soda. She carefully descended the basement steps, leaning heavily on the rail while her heart pounded erratically against her ribs.

She breathed a tiny sigh of relief when she reached the bottom. The light was on over the washer, so she was able to move quickly now, setting Kaitlin on the mattress and then dousing the lights.

Inexplicably paranoid, she turned off the washing machine and strained to listen. For several long moments she didn't hear anything except Kaitlin munching a cracker.

Just when she'd convinced herself she was making a big deal about nothing, she heard the distinct thud of a footstep above them.

Someone was inside the house!

TWELVE

Caleb's attention was focused on the road Deck was following toward some sort of old, nondescript garage-type building. He could see Brickner's black extended cab truck parked along the side, partially hidden beneath an overhang of trees.

"I think this must be their headquarters or something," Declan was saying as he parked along the side of the road, refusing to go too close. "Let's go check it out."

Caleb's phone vibrated with an incoming text message, and he frowned as he read the message. Declan opened the car door, intending to get out, but Caleb clamped his hand on Deck's arm to hold him in place.

"Wait," Caleb said. He read the message twice to make sure he was seeing it correctly. "Noelle's in trouble. She thinks someone is in your house."

"What?" Declan stared at him in disbelief. "How is that possible?"

Caleb was busy texting a reply. Stay hidden in the basement.

We are now, but Kaitlin threw up so we were up in the bathroom with the lights on. Someone could have seen us.

Caleb's stomach clenched with fear at the news. Having the flu was bad enough for Kaitlin to suffer, but this was worse. If Brickner had assigned someone to watch over Declan's place, they'd know Noelle and Kaitlin were there. He quickly relayed the information to his buddy. "We have to go back, Deck. Now."

Declan didn't hesitate, but closed his car door and swung the vehicle around in a sharp U-turn in order to head back the way they'd come. Declan pushed the speed limit as much as he dared, but Caleb knew they were a good fifteen to twenty minutes away. He texted Noelle. We're coming.

Hurry.

They were hurrying, but clearly she was afraid. He could almost taste her fear. Feeling helpless, he closed his eyes and prayed.

Dear Lord, please keep Noelle and Kaitlin safe in Your care. Please!

Noelle desperately searched the basement for something to use as a weapon. There was a fishing pole, too flimsy. Several previously opened cans of paint, useless. Finally she saw a couple of cans of wasp spray and figured one of those was better than nothing.

After tucking the canister under her arm, she wrapped Kaitlin in a blanket and carried her to the darkest corner of the basement. They huddled on the cold cement floor, partially hidden behind some boxes. Unfortunately, there weren't too many places to hide within the basement, and no time to clean up the evidence that they'd been living down there. The mattress on the floor, the laptop computer set up on the card table and the chairs set up around it would give away the truth.

She gripped the can of wasp spray in her right hand, and held Kaitlin close with the other. Up above, the footsteps on the floor seemed incredibly loud as the intruder moved from room to room, as if he was making no attempt to be quiet. Because he knew they were trapped with nowhere to go? The only way out was up the stairs. She tightened her grip on the wasp spray, trying to gather her courage.

"I'm scared," Kaitlin whispered.

"Shh," Noelle said, pressing the little girl's face closer to her neck to help muffle the noise. "We have to be quiet until your daddy gets here."

Kaitlin nodded, seemingly reassured to know that Caleb was coming home. Noelle swallowed hard, hoping Caleb and Declan would arrive soon. She wanted to believe the men would get there before the intruder found them. And she hoped and prayed that Kaitlin wouldn't throw up again.

The seconds ticked by with excruciating slowness. The footsteps stopped and she breathed a sigh of relief.

But then she heard the door open at the top of the basement stairs and the *thunk, thunk, thunk* as someone came down the steps.

She shrank against the boxes as much as possible, hardly daring to breathe. The intruder must have flipped on the overhead switch because the area suddenly flooded with light and she could easily make out the huge, hulking body of a man holding a gun as he stood sweeping his gaze around the basement. At the moment his back was to them, but for how long?

"You can't hide from me," he said in a harsh, raspy

voice, making her cringe with fear. "Come out now and no one will get hurt."

Noelle's mouth was so dry she couldn't have made a sound if she wanted to. Not that she believed him anyway. He had a gun, certainly he intended to hurt them or at the very least, take them away. But why? She had no clue.

And other than the wasp spray there wasn't much she could use to defend herself and Kaitlin. Even if she tried to make a run for it, she'd have to carry Kaitlin, which would slow her down even if she could outrun the guy, which she didn't think was remotely possible.

It struck her in that moment that she may have to give up her life in order to save Caleb's daughter. And she silently prayed to God for strength and for protection.

The man moved away toward the opposite end of the basement. But her relief was short-lived as he quickly made his way around the room until he was headed in their direction. The light from a high-beam flashlight blinded her and she ducked her head and shivered when his evil laugh echoed through the room.

"Gotcha."

Noelle blinked and squinted, trying to see as the gunman approached. He purposefully kept the light aimed at her eyes as a way to keep her helpless. The canister of wasp spray was hidden at her side, and she knew he'd need to get close before it would be of any use. If she aimed toward the sound of his voice, she might be able to slow him down.

"Come out of there," he demanded.

She didn't move, willing him to take a few more steps. When he was so close she could smell his sweat, she brought up the canister, pointed it directly at the area where she assumed his face was located and pressed hard on the lever. He let out a yowl and brought his arm up to protect his eyes.

She jumped to her feet and made a break for the stairs, carrying Kaitlin while managing to hang on to the wasp spray. It wasn't easy to see and she hit the edge of the wall hard with her shoulder. Ignoring the pain, she forced herself to keep going. She could hear the thug swearing as he stumbled after her. She hoped he was blinded by the wasp spray since she needed every advantage she could get.

But when she reached the top of the stairs, he was already gaining on her. She darted through the kitchen, intending to head out to the backyard when he grabbed her shirt from behind and yanked her backward. In a last ditch effort, she brought up the wasp spray and shot a stream over her shoulder hoping to hit him again, but he clipped her against the side of her head and she went down, hard. At the last possible moment she turned her body so that her shoulder took the brunt of the fall as she attempted to cushion Kaitlin as much as possible. Her temple throbbed where she'd hit it on the doorframe.

She tried to scramble to her feet, still hanging on to Kaitlin, but he roughly grabbed her and yanked her upright. Kaitlin let out a scream of terror but he ignored it, pinning Noelle painfully against his massive body. When he pressed the tip of his gun against Kaitlin's head, Noelle froze, breathing heavily. Instantly, he ripped the can of wasp spray out of her hand and threw it down onto the floor with a resounding clunk.

"We're going outside and you're going to move nice and slow, understand?" he murmured harshly in her ear. "If you give me any more trouble, I'll just shoot you both here and then wait here for your boyfriend to show up. Either way, you all die. It's your choice."

She nodded as the will to fight drained out of her. There was no way on earth she would risk any harm to Kaitlin. Even though deep down she knew he'd still eventually kill them, going with him now would give them time.

Time to get away. Or time for Caleb and Declan to rescue them.

"Move," he said, giving her a nudge. She took one step and then another, grateful that the thug allowed her to keep holding Kaitlin as he half pushed, half guided her out of the kitchen and outside. The phone, squashed between her and Kaitlin, vibrated in the pocket of her sweatshirt, indicating she had a text message. She ignored it, and hoped the thug hadn't noticed. So far, he hadn't frisked her and she prayed he wouldn't think to do that now.

The intruder stayed close to her side, a hard arm clamped around her shoulders, no doubt making sure there weren't any nosy neighbors who might see the gun, as they walked across the damp grass toward another black truck parked on the street.

Noelle tried to look around to flag someone's attention, but no one was around. And within seconds, he had the back door of the extended cab open, and shoved her forward.

"Get in. And if you try to run again, I'll shoot you in the back and take the kid. A small prisoner would be easier to control anyway."

She had no intention of risking that, so she climbed into the truck, holding Kaitlin, who was now crying softly, in her lap. He held the gun ready as he quickly rounded the car and slid into the driver's seat. The minute he started the car, the automatic locks clicked into place.

"Tell her to shut up," he said harshly.

She didn't bother to acknowledge him, since there was no way to make Kaitlin stop crying. Noelle was on the verge of crying, too.

The thug drove slowly away from the curb as if they had all the time in the world. She kept her eyes trained on the rearview mirror for any sign of Caleb and Declan returning, but there was nothing but darkness behind them.

She closed her eyes and rested her cheek on the top of Kaitlin's head, trying to reassure the little girl.

Please, Lord, keep this innocent child safe in Your care. Amen.

Declan headed up the driveway and before he came to a complete stop, Caleb pushed open his car door and jumped out of the vehicle. He ran into the house through the unlocked garage door, coming to an abrupt halt when he saw the canister of wasp spray lying in the middle of the kitchen floor.

Dread seeped into his bones. "Noelle? Kaitlin?" he shouted. There was no answer. The door leading to the basement was open and the lights were on, but even as he clamored down the stairs he knew they were too late.

Noelle and Kaitlin were gone. Whoever had been inside the house had taken them.

"No," he whispered, falling to his knees on the edge of the mattress. This couldn't be happening. He and Deck had followed Brickner. So who'd taken Noelle and Kaitlin?

The accomplice, of course. Hadn't he already known that Brickner couldn't have done this without help? Not just help in getting a hold of Noelle and Kaitlin, but in setting him up for his wife's murder, the murder of Jack

Owens and the murder of Kenneth James, the alleged eyewitness.

How many other people had to die? *Please, God, not Noelle and Kaitlin.*

Caleb buried his face in his hands, wishing that he could trade places with them. He'd do anything to keep them safe.

Anything.

"Caleb? Come on, buddy, you need to pull yourself together." Declan's hand was heavy on his shoulder. "Check your phone. Has she responded to your text message?"

A flicker of hope burned through the heavy veil of despair. He slowly rose to his feet and pulled the phone out of his pocket to peer at the screen. "Not yet."

"Look over here—see the spray pattern on this vent?" Declan practically dragged Caleb over to the back corner of the basement. "Smells like wasp spray, most likely from the canister upstairs. It looks like Noelle tried to fight back and escape."

He stared at the spray pattern, admiring Noelle's spunk. He forced himself to think like the cop he once was. The cop he still was, deep in his heart and soul. "I see what you mean," he admitted. "And look at the way those boxes are knocked askew. She and Kaitlin must have been hiding here. Let's go back up to the kitchen."

Upstairs, Caleb carefully examined the area, trying to visualize what had taken place. "There's a thin smear of blood here," he said, gesturing to the rust-colored stain on the oak molding around the doorframe. He fought to keep his tone steady. "Must belong to Noelle or Kaitlin since they aren't here and obviously were trying to get away."

"I see it," Declan said in a grim tone.

The thought of his daughter being hurt made his stomach cramp painfully. "We have to find them, Deck."

"We will."

He knew his buddy was trying to reassure him, to keep him from going over the edge, but as Caleb stood there, it was obvious they had no clues. Nothing to go on. No way of knowing who Brickner's accomplice might be.

"Maybe we should go back to that building where we last saw Brickner," Declan said, breaking the long silence.

Caleb brightened at that thought. "Yeah, why not? At least then we can grab him and force him to tell us where Noelle and Kaitlin are."

"Not exactly," Declan drawled. "Take a deep breath, Caleb. This isn't the time to overreact."

It was on the tip of his tongue to yell at Deck, since the guy clearly had no clue what it felt like to have your daughter and the woman you cared for in danger, but he was sidetracked by his vibrating phone. His flash of anger subsided as he grabbed the phone and quickly read the text message.

Heading north on hwy 33.

His heart leaped in his chest. "It's Noelle! We have to get in the car. She's giving us directions."

They hurried outside and jumped back in Deck's vehicle. "Highway 33 is only seven miles from here," Caleb said. "Maybe they're not that far ahead of us."

"Tell her that we're on the way," Declan said as he concentrated on driving.

He was already in the process of doing that. We're on the road, keep the info coming.

After sending the text he stared at the phone, praying

for a response, even though he knew that Noelle wasn't about to take any chance of getting caught.

The fact that she was able to text him at all was a good sign. The guy who'd taken them must not have searched her, so he must not realize she had a phone. Hopefully that meant that Noelle's injury wasn't too bad. Unless the blood had come from Kaitlin? *No, don't go there.* Imaging his daughter hurt would only paralyze him.

He needed to think positive. Wasn't that what prayer was all about? To believe that God was watching over them?

"Junction Highway 33 up ahead," Declan said, breaking into his thoughts.

As much as he wanted to keep texting Noelle, he managed to refrain, unwilling to increase the possibility of getting caught. All they needed was to know her ultimate destination.

A familiar landmark caught his eye. "Deck, isn't this close to where we last saw Brickner?"

"Yeah, actually we came in from the other direction, but this is the same area." Declan didn't take his eyes off the road. "Caleb, he could be taking them to Brickner."

"Good." Caleb didn't bother to hide his satisfaction. "If that's true we should be able to blow this case wide open."

"Maybe we should call for backup," Declan said.

He glared at his buddy. "You're kidding, right? Have you forgotten there's a warrant out for my arrest? What makes you think anyone will believe me?"

"I believe you and I'm sure we could get Isaac to back us up," Deck said stubbornly. "We can't do this alone, Caleb."

Panic gripped him by the throat. Would Declan betray him now, calling for backup when they were so close?

His phone vibrated again. "'In a truck, at a four-car garage,'" he read Noelle's text out loud.

"That's the same place we saw Brickner," Declan said, pushing hard on the accelerator. "At least now we know where we're going and we should be able to get there in less than ten minutes."

Caleb texted that information back to Noelle but he didn't feel any better knowing Noelle and Kaitlin's destination. Because if Brickner was out there waiting for them, he wasn't alone. He likely had a lot of help.

He and Deck would be seriously outnumbered. Not to mention out-armed. Deck had his service weapon, but Caleb didn't have anything other than a Swiss Army knife.

Maybe Declan was right. Maybe they really did need some backup. And Isaac was a decent guy, someone he once considered a friend.

As much as he hadn't planned on trusting anyone within the sheriff's department, he couldn't deny that he'd do anything, even sacrifice his own life if necessary, to save Noelle and Kaitlin.

And if that meant he was arrested and tossed in jail for the rest of his life, then so be it.

He was about to tell Declan to go ahead and call for backup, when Deck eased on the brakes.

"I think the building is up ahead. We should probably go in on foot from here."

"I'll go," Caleb said. "There's no sense in both of us going. I'll stall until you get backup in place."

Declan looked as if he might argue, but Caleb wasn't

going to sit around. He opened the car door and slid out, shutting it quietly behind him.

Declan was smart. He'd do what needed to be done.

And so would Caleb.

THIRTEEN

Noelle held Kaitlin close as the thug who'd kidnapped them drummed his fingers on the steering wheel, obviously waiting for someone to come out of the garage building to meet him. She'd managed to text Caleb a few details about where they were, but that didn't mean he'd be able to find them.

Kaitlin had stopped crying about fifteen minutes ago, after she'd soothed her fears as best she could. Noelle could only hope that the little girl was feeling a little better. She sensed the thug who'd taken them would not be happy if Kaitlin started throwing up again. Her greatest fear was that he'd do something to hurt Kaitlin, just to make her shut up.

A man came out of the building and walked toward the black truck. She thought he might be Brickner, but it was difficult to tell. The thug in the truck held his gun on her and gestured to the door. "Get out."

She swallowed hard and fumbled for the door handle while keeping a tight grip on Kaitlin. The door was heavy and she had to push it with her foot to get it open.

"Well, if it isn't Miss Whitman and O'Malley's daughter." The man's voice was low and once again she tried to get a good look at him. But he remained in the shadows. She suspected, although she couldn't see it, that he had a gun, too. "So glad you could join us."

As if they had a choice? She did her best to control the flash of anger.

There was no way to even consider making a run for it, considering the two men were armed, so she slid awkwardly to the ground, still holding Kaitlin. The truck was high off the ground and she stumbled a bit when she landed on the pavement. The child was getting heavy, but she ignored the cramping of her arm muscles.

"Take several steps forward," the man standing in the shadows commanded.

Noelle did as she was told, resisting the urge to glance around for any sign of Caleb or Declan. Even if the two men were somewhere close by, which she highly doubted, they certainly wouldn't be easily seen. She needed to figure out how to stall long enough for help to arrive.

"What do you want?" she asked as she cautiously approached the stranger. "I don't understand what's going on. Why did you bring us here?"

"I'm surprised you didn't figure it out for yourself," he said in a scathing tone. He must have been closer than she realized because suddenly he was gripping her arm hard enough to leave bruises. He forcibly dragged her toward a side door on the building. "No? Guess you're not too smart, are you? Obviously we need the kid to lure O'Malley out of hiding. You're nothing more than a glorified babysitter."

Knowing the truth should have made her feel better, but it didn't. She had no idea how she and Kaitlin could manage to escape, or if Declan and Caleb would be able to find them.

The only good thing was that the stranger, who she was now convinced was Brickner, probably wouldn't kill them yet. He'd wait until Caleb arrived. But she wished she hadn't sent Caleb the text messages. She felt certain he would give up his life for his daughter.

The only problem was that they would likely all die here. No way would Brickner let Noelle and Kaitlin go, even if Caleb did show up.

She wanted to text Caleb to let him know it was a trap, but she didn't dare do anything that would catch Brickner's attention. He roughly dragged her into the large building, which conveniently didn't appear to have any windows. There were a few lightbulbs hanging off the ceiling though, so it wasn't completely dark. In the light, she could make out the familiar face of Marc Brickner. He wasn't trying to hide his face now, so obviously he intended to kill them all.

She glanced around the building, realizing that it was smaller on the inside compared to the outside. Then she realized that there was a wall dividing the large space in half. Their half was mostly empty except for another black truck parked off to the side. She stared at the wall, wondering what was located on the other side. More men with weapons? Probably. She couldn't afford to assume there weren't others around.

"Sit over there," Brickner said, giving her a slight shove toward the farthest corner of the building.

He released her arm and she resisted the urge to rub her bruised flesh. She sat down in the corner, the concrete floor definitely uncomfortable, not that she planned to complain. When Brickner moved away she lowered her mouth to Kaitlin's ear. "How are you feeling?" she asked in a whisper. "Does your tummy still hurt?"

"A little," Kaitlin whispered back. "Can I eat a cracker?"

Noelle was surprised to realize that Kaitlin had managed to hang on to her package of crackers, although they were likely crushed into millions of small pieces after everything they'd been through. But if the crackers helped settle the child's stomach, she was all for it. "Sure," she responded.

Brickner and the thug who'd found them at Declan's house were standing together near the truck, talking in low voices. She couldn't hear what they were saying, but that didn't matter. While their attention was otherwise occupied, she risked sending another text message to Caleb.

Stay away, it's a trap.

She felt a little better after sending the message. Surely Declan wouldn't let Caleb do anything foolish. Kaitlin nibbled on a cracker while Noelle glanced around the interior of the building, searching for anything that she could potentially use as a weapon.

But there was nothing.

"I'm thirsty," Kaitlin whispered.

"I'll ask for something," she reassured the girl. Raising her voice she called out to the two men. "Excuse me, but Kaitlin's been sick, and I'd like to give her some white soda so she doesn't throw up again."

The two men swung around to face her and she shivered at the frank malice reflected in the eyes of the thug she'd sprayed with wasp killer. Even in the dim lighting she could see that his eyes were red and swollen from the harsh chemicals. If she hadn't been blinded by his flashlight, she might have actually managed to get away.

"This isn't a hotel," Brickner said with a dark scowl.

"I know, but if she gets sick, the whole place will reek like vomit," she pointed out. "Why would you want that?"

There was a long pause before Brickner turned to the guy next to him. "Ray, get the kid a soda."

Ray didn't look at all happy to be the gopher but he threw her one last look before he disappeared, she assumed, to the room on the other side of the wall.

After a few minutes Ray returned carrying a can of white soda. Brickner held his gun on her as Ray handed it to her. Up close the damage to his eyes looked even worse. "You'll pay for what you did to me," he said in his low, evil voice.

She swallowed hard, imagining the worst as she took the soda can from him, avoiding his gaze. She opened the can and held it for Kaitlin.

As thirsty as Noelle was, she decided to hold off drinking any of the soda herself. For one thing, she didn't see a bathroom anywhere. And for another, she didn't want to catch Kaitlin's bug. Besides, it was far more important for Kaitlin to remain hydrated than it was for her.

She had no illusions about how this might end up.

Kaitlin only took a few sips before pushing the can away. The little girl looked sleepy and Noelle hoped the child could manage to get some rest.

"Close your eyes. I'm right here," she said softly. "We're safe here for now."

"I love you, Noa."

Her throat closed and it took her a minute to respond. "I love you, too."

She hugged Kaitlin on her lap, running a soothing hand down the child's back, softly reassuring her that they'd be fine. Kaitlin seemed to believe her and soon the child's eyelids fluttered closed. Noelle sighed and leaned back against the coarse two-by-fours which made up the walls of the building.

Closing her eyes, she prayed.

Please, Lord, keep Kaitlin safe in Your care and Caleb, too. Amen.

Caleb forced himself to move slowly, even though adrenaline coursed through his bloodstream, making him want to run as quickly as possible. He knew Deck was calling for backup but there was no way in the world he could sit around waiting for their backup to arrive. Right now, his only thought was to find a way to convince Brickner to release Noelle and Kaitlin in order to take him instead.

The garagelike building came into view and he kept hidden among the trees and shrubs as much as possible. He racked his brain for some sort of viable plan, but so far he didn't have much. Without a weapon he couldn't even the odds in his favor. If he was captured and taken inside the building, where he was sure they were holding Noelle and Kaitlin, he might be able to use the knife. If Brickner didn't search him and find it.

Too many "ifs" for comfort.

When he was about twenty yards away, his cell phone vibrated with an incoming message. He glanced at the screen, expecting an update from Deck, but the message was from Noelle.

Stay away, it's a trap.

He stared at the message with a mixture of relief and exasperation. It was great that she was trying to warn him, but did she really think he would stay away, leaving her and his daughter to face Brickner alone?

Yeah, right. Not hardly.

I'm coming, he texted back.

With grim determination he crept closer to the building, trying to think of a way to force Brickner's hand. He wasn't armed, but Brickner didn't know that. Maybe, just maybe, he could bluff his way in.

But if that didn't work, he'd have to come up with a plan B.

Caleb waited at the corner of the building, not far from where the black truck was parked, for what seemed like forever. A glance at his watch confirmed only ten minutes had passed. Just when he was about to throw a few rocks toward the building to draw someone out, the side door opened and a tall, broad-shouldered figure came out and headed toward the black truck.

He was beginning to think that Brickner required all his goons to drive black trucks, to keep anyone from figuring out which truck Brickner might be in. Did this guy realize that he was being used as a patsy to keep Brickner's identity secret? Probably not.

Caleb waited until the guy had gotten inside the car and drove away before he made his move. There could obviously be other men inside, but there was at least one less person that he'd have to deal with. He sent Deck a quick text letting him know that the guy who'd taken Noelle and Kaitlin was leaving in the truck. With any luck, Deck and his backup team could arrest the guy and from there, they could potentially get him to squeal on Brickner.

Caleb left the corner of the building and made his

way to the small group of trees that were located at a right angle to the building. When he was situated, he dug a rock from his pocket and heaved it with all his might at the garage door located on the side of the building, choosing the door closest to where the guy had just left the building. The rock hit the garage door with a resounding *crack*.

He thought he heard some activity coming from inside the building, including a few loud bangs. Then the side door opened and he saw Brickner standing there, holding a gun to Kaitlin's head.

"Come on, O'Malley, you can do better than this," Brickner taunted. "What's the matter? Are you afraid to take a shot at me for fear of accidently hitting your daughter? You never were as good of a sharpshooter as me."

Caleb had to work hard to hold his anger in check, especially because he could see that Brickner had the gun pressed tightly against Kaitlin's temple and she was sobbing soft, ragged sounds that ripped his heart to shreds. Brickner was right. Even if he had a weapon, he wouldn't use it. He'd never take a chance on hitting his daughter.

"Let her go, Brickner." He hoped his voice didn't show the depth of his fear. "Let her go and I'll take her place."

"You'll surrender now, or I'll kill her," Brickner said in a harsh tone. "Shall I count to five?"

"Are you really going to take a chance that I'll miss?" Caleb asked with a calmness he didn't feel.

Brickner hesitated, and from where he stood, Caleb could see the other man was still searching for him. "You won't sacrifice the kid. One, two, three, four…"

"Okay, okay!" Caleb stepped out from his hiding spot and put his hands up in the air. "You have me, Brickner. Now let her go."

"I'm not letting her go. Get inside the building, now."

Caleb forced himself to walk toward Brickner, keeping his hands on his head in a show of good faith that he wasn't armed. He hoped that Brickner would frisk him for a gun, without finding the knife that he'd stashed in the bottom of his shoe.

"Dad-dy," Kaitlin sobbed, her tiny face streaked with tears.

"I love you, Katydid," he said reassuringly. "Everything is going to be fine."

"Very sweet," Brickner said snidely. When Caleb was inside the building, Brickner shoved Kaitlin at him. "Here, take the kid and go sit in the corner with your woman."

Caleb gladly took Kaitlin in his arms, hugging his daughter close while praying that Deck and his backup team would get here quickly. Brickner locked the door behind him, but Caleb didn't even think of trying to rush the guy right now. First he needed to know what he was up against.

He carried Kaitlin over to where Noelle was waiting. She met him partway, giving him a desperate hug. He wrapped one arm around her, the other one still holding his daughter. For a moment he couldn't speak.

When she loosened her grip, he still didn't release her. "I'm sorry I got you into this mess," he whispered.

"It's not your fault."

Noelle was being far too kind. It was his fault, and he knew it. Maybe if he'd called Declan sooner. Maybe if he'd kept Noelle and Kaitlin in a motel instead of taking them to Declan's basement. Maybe if he hadn't gone to pick up his daughter from Noelle's house in the first place, none of this would have happened.

But it was too late to go back and change the past now. No matter how he wished he could.

"I want you to know, that if we don't make it through this for some reason, I promise we'll meet again in heaven," he told her in a quiet voice that wouldn't carry over to Brickman.

"Oh, Caleb." Noelle's eyes filled with tears. "I'm glad you believe in God, but we're not finished yet. God is still with us, watching over us."

"I know." He reached up to cup her cheek with his hand, staring intently down into her eyes. "I've been praying for you. For Kaitlin. For us."

"Me, too."

He brushed a brief kiss across her mouth, wishing there was something he could do to help Noelle and Kaitlin escape. When he lifted his head, he was certain that his regrets were reflected in his gaze. He tried to smile as he transferred Kaitlin back into Noelle's arms.

"Stay behind me," he instructed in a low voice.

She made a soft sound that he took to be a protest.

"I need to get him to talk, to stall." He didn't dare mention Declan's name, but he could see by the expression on her face that she understood what he meant.

Noelle didn't say anything more before she melted back against the wall, sliding back down to sit in the corner with Kaitlin cuddled on her lap.

Caleb turned to face Brickner—the man he knew likely killed his wife, his lawyer and his former neighbor.

What Caleb didn't know was why.

FOURTEEN

Noelle held Kaitlin close, murmuring soothing words to the child as a way to hide the depth of her overwhelming despair. She understood that Caleb was stalling, waiting for Declan to arrive in order to help get them out of here. But it seemed as if too much time had already passed by and she couldn't help thinking that Declan would be too late. Especially now that Caleb was captured and being held here, too. Brickner had exactly what he'd wanted and she feared that their time had run out.

Even Caleb's brief kiss hadn't made her feel any better because the gesture had felt too much like goodbye. She was thrilled that Caleb believed in God, and as much as she hoped they would all meet in heaven some day, that didn't mean she was ready to die just yet.

Kaitlin deserved a chance at life. Surely God would spare the child's life?

Please, Lord, save us from harm. Keep us safe in Your care. Amen.

"Why are you doing this, Marc?" Caleb asked in an overly loud voice that startled her. "I mean, I get the fact that you tried to frame me for my wife's murder, but I don't understand why you came after me once I was released from jail."

Noelle held her breath as Brickner stared at Caleb, his gun steady in his grasp.

"I found your perch in the tree across the street from Noelle Whitman's house," Caleb continued as if they were having a two-way conversation, ignoring Brickner's steely gaze. "I have to say, that was really an amazing shot."

"Don't patronize me," Brickner said harshly. "If it had been an amazing shot you'd be dead and we wouldn't be here right now."

"Pure luck on my part," Caleb said, waving away the comment and keeping his tone filled with admiration. "How could you know that I would bend down to pick up Kaitlin's giraffe at that moment? You were always a better shot than me. By far, the best sharpshooter on the team."

Noelle couldn't tear her gaze away from Brickner, searching for any sign that Caleb was getting through to him. Although she wasn't really all that hopeful, since anyone who killed the way Brickner had couldn't possibly have a heart or a soul.

"But I still don't understand why," Caleb continued as if they were old friends discussing the weather and not murder. "Why take a shot at me outside Noelle's house? Who were you going to pin that one on? I just can't quite follow your logic on that."

Brickner glanced at his watch, as if he was waiting for someone else to arrive. After a long moment he met Caleb's gaze. "I was forced to change my approach after Ken weaseled out on the original plan."

"Yeah, I figured that much. But what happened?"

Caleb asked. "Why did Ken end up in Lake Michigan? Did he try to take the bribe money and run?"

"I caught him sneaking out of his house in the middle of the night, with a one-way plane ticket in his pocket. I didn't mean to kill him, but it was his fault for getting cold feet," Brickner admitted. "If he would have testified against you, I know the jury would have sent you away for life. That stupid idiot ruined everything."

Noelle couldn't suppress a shiver at how logical Brickner made everything sound. As if he had no choice but to commit murder. To kill Ken and dump his body into the lake.

"Your plan was perfect," Caleb agreed. "Well, almost perfect."

Brickner's expression turned ugly and for a moment Noelle feared that Caleb had pushed him too far. She subtly reached up and gripped the hem of Caleb's T-shirt and gave a gentle tug, trying to warn him.

But Caleb acted as if he didn't notice. "I have to assume that you were afraid I'd start digging for the truth about Heather's death. Is that why you took a shot at me? Because you were afraid I'd figure everything out?"

Noelle tugged on Caleb's shirt harder this time. What was he thinking to keep poking at Brickner?

"Don't overestimate your importance," Brickner sneered. "I was never afraid of you."

Caleb shrugged. "Maybe you should have been. Especially since I found your secret company, Marc. Let me think, what was the name of it again? Oh yeah, Eileen's Elite Escort Services. And of course I saw Heather's photo on there."

Brickner gave a tiny jerk, making Noelle think that he hadn't expected Caleb to find out about the website. Or the escort service. But other than the small involuntary movement, Brickner didn't say anything more.

"What happened that night, Marc?" Caleb pressed. "Why did you kill Heather? Was it because she wanted to get out of the business? Or did she break up with you?"

Noelle was practically holding her breath, waiting for his answer. She wished they had a tape recorder for the moment Brickner admitted he'd killed Caleb's wife.

"Don't be ridiculous," Brickner said in a strangled tone. Gone was his previous arrogance, instead there was a note of agony shimmering in his voice. "She didn't break up with me. I loved Heather, and she loved me, too! After she divorced you, we were going to leave and be together, forever. I would never hurt her. Never!"

Noelle felt her jaw drop and quickly closed her mouth to hide her shock. Brickner's voice practically vibrated with the truth. The hint of pain reflected in his tone seemed too real to be faked.

She could tell by how still Caleb went that he was surprised, too. And she knew exactly what he was thinking. If Brickner didn't kill Caleb's wife, then who did?

Caleb couldn't believe what he was hearing. How was it possible that Brickner wasn't the one who'd killed Heather? What on earth had happened that night?

He tried to gather his chaotic thoughts. "I'm sorry, Marc. That must have been rough on you when Heather was found shot to death." It felt odd to be talking about his wife loving another man, but deep down Caleb knew that his love for Heather had died long ago, well before she'd been murdered.

This wasn't the time to wallow in his regrets of the past. Heather was gone and he would do whatever was necessary to save Noelle and Kaitlin. He needed Brickner to confide in him. To keep talking, long enough for Deck to get here with his backup.

It was already taking far too long.

Brickner turned away, and Caleb considered rushing the guy to get Marc's weapon, but almost as soon as the thought formed, Brickner straightened and swung around to face him. "She never loved you," Brickner sneered. "Heather loved me. Only me!"

Caleb wasn't about to argue, because really what did Heather's feelings matter? She was gone and there was nothing to be gained by arguing. He'd known their marriage was over, but he'd tried to stick it out, for Kaitlin's sake.

"I believe you," Caleb said quietly. "But if you really loved Heather, why haven't you tried to seek revenge on the real murderer?"

"What makes you think I haven't?" Brickner asked. He glanced at his watch again and almost as if on cue, his cell phone rang. Brickner answered his phone, still holding the gun aimed at Caleb.

"Where have you been?" Brickner asked the caller in a terse tone. "I expected you to be here fifteen minutes ago."

There was the muffled sound of someone on the other end of the line, but no matter how hard he tried, Caleb couldn't decipher exactly what the other person was saying.

He couldn't help wondering about the identity of the person on the other end of the phone. The same person who'd killed Heather? Was this what Brickner meant when he mentioned getting revenge? Was Brickner right now setting up Heather's murderer just like he'd set up

Caleb fourteen months ago? Unfortunately it seemed highly likely.

"You're not the one running this show. I am," Brickner was saying in a caustic tone. "Now you know what it feels like to be the one taking orders."

Taking orders? Caleb turned the phrase over in his mind, trying to make sense of the one-sided conversation.

Was the person on the other end of the phone someone who was normally in charge? The guy who owned Eileen's Elite Escort Services? And if so, who? A silent partner? A new player he and Declan wouldn't know or recognize?

Or could it be Sheriff Cramer? No, surely the sheriff wouldn't get involved in something like this. Sheriff Cramer didn't like him much, but the guy only had a few more years until his retirement. Why would he risk his pension at this point in his career? No, Caleb didn't buy it.

If not the sheriff, then who?

The image of Captain Will Royce flashed in his mind, and he felt a little sick at the possibility that the administrative leader of the SWAT team was a far more likely candidate to be involved in Brickner's scheme. Royce sometimes filled in on the SWAT team, so he certainly knew the guys. And Royce fancied himself to be a ladies' man, too. Was it possible he was the co-owner of the escort service?

Or worse, had Royce killed Heather in a fit of anger?

"I don't like a last minute change of plans," Brickner was saying. "We go with the original plan or I'll just kill them all here and let you deal with the mess."

Caleb didn't like the sound of that. Obviously their time was running out. Whoever the guy was on the other

end of the line, he certainly wasn't doing Caleb and Noelle any favors.

"Glad you agree," Brickner said smugly. "You have
ten minutes to get here, understand?"

Caleb tried to consider the proposed ten minutes to
be a positive sign. At least Brickner wasn't going to start
shooting yet.

As long as the caller showed up, that is.

There was no way to know for sure, but if the caller
was Royce then Brickner's comments made sense in a
sick sort of way. For some reason, Brickner had something to hold over the caller to make him do whatever
Brickner wanted.

A cold chill snaked down his spine. If Royce really
was involved, he hoped and prayed that Declan wouldn't
tip off the captain when arranging for backup.

Because if Royce got a whiff of Declan's rescue plan,
then they were certainly doomed to die tonight.

Noelle glanced up as Caleb took a step backward,
turning his head and talking in a voice so soft she could
barely hear. "Text D," he whispered. "Tell him to stay
away from Royce."

Noelle nodded and eased her hand back into the pocket
of her sweatshirt, where she still had her phone hidden.
She had no idea how much battery life she had left, and
prayed that there would be enough for the text to go
through.

Texting without watching what she was doing wasn't
easy. She typed the message and then tried to glimpse at
what she'd written to make sure it was right. Using Kaitlin's body to help shield the light, she peered at the screen.

The message was a bit mangled so she quickly fixed

it and then pushed the send button. There was only one bar of battery left, but she didn't turn off the phone. She intended to give Declan the chance to track them here through the phone, if at all possible.

Where was Declan? Why wasn't he here already?

"Noa, my tummy hurts," Kaitlin whimpered.

Up until now, the child had been relatively quiet, her hysterical sobs had faded once Brickner had given her back to Caleb. Noelle was very worried that the little girl would start screaming at any moment from her night terrors, especially at the way Brickner kept putting the gun to her temple as a way to force them to do what he wanted. Noelle had almost forgotten about the flu bug.

"What's wrong?" Caleb asked.

"She feels sick to her stomach," Noelle murmured. "Here, Kaitlin, try another sip of the white soda."

Kaitlin obediently sat up and took the can between her palms and sipped from the opening. "Can I have another cracker?"

"Sure." Noelle picked up the horribly crumpled package of crackers and tried to find a piece amid the crumbs. She pulled out a half cracker and gave it to Kaitlin. "Try this, see if it helps your tummy."

"Listen, Marc, my daughter has the flu," Caleb said. "Why don't you let her go? You have me. You don't need her."

"Nobody goes anywhere until I tell you to," Brickner said firmly. "Don't worry, the flu bug isn't going to be bothering your daughter for long."

Noelle swallowed hard, knowing exactly what Brickner was insinuating.

"Kill me if you want, but let my daughter go. She's five years old, hardly a threat to you or anyone else."

"She's not a threat, but she is a part of my master plan," Brickner corrected. He glanced again at his watch and Noelle could almost see his frustration. "If he's not here in five minutes..." Brickner's voice trailed off.

"Then what?" Caleb challenged. "Then you're going to kill us all here? And what story will you leak to the press? Who will you blame for our murders?"

The faint sound of an engine broke the silence and Brickner smiled grimly. "He's lucky he made it in time."

"In time for what?" Caleb asked, and Noelle could hear the desperation in his tone.

"You'll find out soon enough," Brickner said.

There was a knock on the door, must have been some sort of prearranged code, two short knocks, then a pause, and then two more knocks again. Brickner took several steps backward in order to unlock and open the door.

Caleb tensed as the stranger walked into the room, also armed with a gun. Noelle struggled to her feet, still carrying Kaitlin, wanting to be ready for anything.

"I figured you'd show up sooner or later, Royce," Caleb said to the newcomer. "I knew Brickner wasn't smart enough to do all this on his own."

Noelle gasped when Brickner pulled the trigger on the gun. A shot rang out at the exact same moment Caleb hit the floor.

"Silence!" Brickner roared. "Or I'll shoot again and this time I won't miss!"

Noelle was shaking so badly she feared she'd drop Kaitlin, but Caleb came up to a low crouch and after a few minutes she realized he wasn't bleeding.

Caleb hadn't been hit.

But now, the odds of their ability to escape seemed even more impossible.

* * *

Caleb took several deep breaths, realizing he'd pushed Brickner just a bit too hard.

But where was Declan? Why hadn't Deck stopped Royce from coming inside?

"Is everything set?" Brickner asked Royce, as if the shooting incident hadn't happened. He was beginning to wonder if Brickner had some sort of psychological disorder the way he ran hot and cold in a matter of minutes.

"Yes. Everything is ready," Royce said, looking as if he were scared to death of Brickner. How had the captain gotten involved in all of this?

"Good." Brickner gestured at Caleb with his gun. "All three of you, get in the truck."

The black extended cab truck was parked over to the south side of the building. Caleb didn't move, knowing that once they got inside the truck, their chances of getting away dropped considerably.

"Why?" he asked. "Where are you taking us?"

The expression on Brickner's face reflected evil. "We're going back to where this all started. Now get inside, or I'll shoot you in the kneecap."

Caleb glanced back at Noelle and Kaitlin, his expression full of regret. "Let's go," he said softly.

Noelle looked as if she might collapse, but she moved toward the truck with surprising strength. He would have taken over carrying Kaitlin, but he wanted to have his hands free, just in case. He still had the knife in his shoe. Maybe when Royce was driving he could use it to help them escape.

"Move!" Brickner thundered, his patience obviously wearing thin.

Noelle instinctively picked up the pace, and he followed close behind, protecting her as best he could. He almost wished that Royce would end up being assigned as their driver, because he was fairly certain that Brickner had completely lost his marbles somewhere along the way.

Caleb took Kaitlin long enough for Noelle to scramble into the backseat. He gently set his daughter beside Noelle and then took the seat beside her, so that Kaitlin was safely tucked in between the two adults.

Caleb closed the truck door and then quickly reached into his shoe for the knife. It was only a small pocketknife but it was better than nothing.

To his dismay, both Royce and Brickner climbed into the front seats. Royce was the designated driver and Brickner sat at an angle where he could easily keep his weapon pointed at Noelle.

Royce twisted the key, bringing the engine to life with a loud roar. He pushed a button on the dash and the garage door opened. Royce drove out of the building, and hit the button again to close the overhead garage door behind them.

Caleb tried not to search for signs of Declan, because he didn't want to tip off either Royce or Brickner that help was on the way. Or so he hoped.

"Give up, O'Malley," Brickner said. "There's no one here to help you."

Caleb froze. Had he somehow given something away to Brickner?

"We took care of your friend Declan Shaw," Brickner said with a smile that didn't reach his eyes. "The three of you are on your own."

Caleb licked his dry lips, hoping, praying that Brickner was bluffing. Brickner knew that Noelle and Kaitlin were hiding at Declan's house. Brickner must have assumed that Declan had been with Caleb at some point.

Surely Deck was too smart to get caught in Brickner's trap. Caleb wanted, desperately, to believe Brickner was just playing mind games with him.

"Sit back, relax. We have a good fifteen-minute ride before we reach our destination," Brickner said.

"And where exactly is that?" Caleb forced himself to ask. "Where did this all start?"

Brickner laughed, but it was not a pleasant sound. "Your house, O'Malley. This all started at your house. And that's exactly where it's going to end."

FIFTEEN

Noelle struggled to keep calm, but she was shaking so badly she feared the men in the front seat could actually feel the seat move. She was losing hope that Declan would be able to save them. And with two armed men now, instead of just one, she didn't know how she and Caleb could save themselves.

She wished now that they'd made their move while they were in the garage with just Brickner there. Surely the odds had been better then?

But it was too late to go back now. Noelle had been praying nonstop since this nightmare began and she'd continue until she took her last breath. The way things were looking now, she was praying that death would come quickly and without undue suffering.

Especially for Kaitlin. She closed her eyes against the burn of tears. Facing her own death was one thing, but she couldn't bear to think of the little girl dying tonight.

"Why did you kill Jack Owens?" Caleb asked as the big black truck ate up the miles.

"He was a loose end," Brickner admitted. "Once we found you, we didn't need him anymore."

Noelle wished Caleb would stop asking questions, because the more she heard the greater the fear that clawed at her belly. These men were not going to let them live. What was the point of knowing exactly what had transpired earlier? What difference did any of that make now?

"Who botched the car explosion?" Caleb asked.

Royce's hands tightened on the steering wheel in a way that convinced Noelle that he was the one who'd set the bomb. She was tempted to cover her ears so she couldn't hear any more, but realized that asking questions like this must be Caleb's way of dealing with stress. To keep them talking.

Maybe even to distract them.

She took a deep breath and did her best to swallow the hard lump of fear choking her. She needed to stay strong. For Kaitlin's sake.

"Another mistake," Brickner said tersely. "But there will be no more, isn't that right, Royce? You're going to get the job done this time, aren't you?"

"Yes, sir," Royce muttered.

An incredulous expression filtered across Caleb's face and she knew that seeing his former boss like this, bowing down to Brickner's authority, must be strange. The interaction between the two men wasn't at all reassuring. Clearly, Royce was going to do whatever Brickner told him to do as the guy calling the shots. Why, she had no idea.

"You see, Caleb, once we're finished here tonight, everyone will believe that all three of you died in a murder/suicide," Brickner said in a matter-of-fact tone.

"Yeah, right. No one who knows me will believe that," Caleb said. "Everyone knows my daughter is my life."

"Oh, trust me, they will believe exactly what we want them to. We've planted enough evidence to make it look as if you and the preschool teacher were having a hot affair even prior to Heather's murder. And of course, she threatened to take your daughter away from you, so you had no choice but to kill them both before you tragically took your own life."

Noelle couldn't bear to hear any more. The way Brickner talked she knew that he'd indeed have planted enough evidence to make the authorities and the media buy their story. And why not, when he'd had the captain of the SWAT team to add credence to his lie? She didn't know why Royce was involved, and at this moment, she didn't care.

She glanced out the passenger-side window, but it was too dark to see much and what little she could make out didn't look at all familiar. Even if she had the chance to run away with Kaitlin, she wasn't sure where to go to find safety.

The truck slowed as Royce turned into a ritzy subdivision. The houses weren't packed close together the way they were in Declan's neighborhood. She was shocked at seeing the high-end lifestyle Caleb once enjoyed. She found it hard to imagine what his life must have been like during the years he was married to Heather.

Although looking at him now, with a grim expression etched on his face, she knew he'd give up everything he owned in a heartbeat if it meant keeping them safe. The knowledge made her feel a little better. Caleb was a different man now than what he'd been before.

"Almost home," Brickner said with fake cheerfulness.

Caleb reached over to take her hand, giving it a reassuring squeeze. The resolute expression on his face caused her stomach to knot, painfully. This was it. Now that they'd reached their final destination, she was certain that Caleb would make one last attempt to save them.

Or die trying.

She shook her head, trying to tell him without words not to do anything foolish. But he only nodded, reaffirming her fears while subtly pointing to the small space on the floor behind the driver.

She could tell exactly what he wanted her to do. Get Kaitlin down and out of the line of fire so that he could make his move on Brickner. She gave a small nod to indicate she understood.

Royce turned the truck into a long, curved driveway in front of a large redbrick house with white trim and black shutters. Caleb's house was located at the end of a cul-de-sac, tucked between several trees, a good hundred feet away from the road. It was surprisingly isolated and her hopes of being rescued plummeted even further.

This was it. Noelle put her arm around Kaitlin while keeping her gaze focused on Brickner. She had to assume that Caleb would do something drastic during the time they were about to get out of the vehicle, especially the minute Brickner's gun was no longer pointed directly at her, Noelle knew she had to do what was needed to protect Kaitlin. The child must survive no matter what happened.

This is it, Lord. We are putting our lives and our fate in Your hands. May Your will be done. Amen.

Caleb gripped his small penknife in his right hand, waiting for the exact moment to make his move. Brickner was seated directly in front him, but he didn't dare attempt to stab the guy while Marc's gun was pointed at Noelle.

Timing was critical. The second Brickner moved to get out of the vehicle he'd have to move his gun enough that Noelle wouldn't be in the line of fire. That was the moment he needed to strike. He silently prayed for forgiveness for what he was about to do.

Dear God, forgive me for my sins and give me strength to save Noelle and Kaitlin.

"Okay, we're going to get out of the car, nice and easy," Brickner instructed. "The woman and the kid go first."

Caleb could see the stark fear reflected in Noelle's eyes and wished he could reassure her. He tried to let her know that the plan was still to get down, and truthfully if Noelle and Kaitlin could safely get out of the truck they'd have a better chance at surviving if they could somehow crawl underneath the massive frame.

Noelle's gaze clung to his for a long moment as she moved slowly and deliberately, opening her passenger door and then sliding out until her feet were planted on the ground. She reached for Kaitlin and his daughter went willingly into Noelle's arms. Noelle bent down to set Kaitlin on her feet and the way she had her head bent toward the child, as if peering down at the ground, Caleb could tell that Noelle had already figured out that she needed to get Kaitlin hidden beneath the truck.

"Whoops, did you fall, Kaitlin?" Noelle asked, bending over Kaitlin as if she were helping the child when in fact she was practically shoving his daughter to her knees.

The minute Noelle was ducked down and Kaitlin was safely out of sight, Caleb reached up and stabbed Brickner in the neck with his small penknife, hoping to disable the guy rather than trying to kill him.

"Argh!" Brickner cried out in pain, and Caleb jerked at the sharp retort of Brickner's gun.

"Get down!" Caleb shouted, reassured when Noelle dropped down out of sight.

Another muffled gunshot echoed through the night, and Caleb ducked, trying to figure out who was shooting. It was too dark to see much. Did Brickner have backup planted here for an ambush? Had Caleb stepped from one bad situation into a second, more deadly one?

But then he saw Marc Brickner crumpled on the concrete driveway, blood soaking through his white shirt beneath his fancy suit.

Caleb stared at his former teammate in shock. Who'd taken the shot at Brickner?

"Royce," Brickner whispered.

Caleb frowned and leaned closer. "What did you say?"

Royce was still in the driver's seat of the truck. Was Brickner trying to tell him that Royce shot him?

"Make him pay. Royce...killed her. Killed...Heather." Brickner stared at Caleb as if willing him to believe. "Make him pay."

"Why?" Caleb asked.

"He...wanted her...for himself..." Brickner managed. He coughed and then his eyelids fluttered closed.

"Marc?" Caleb reached out to check Brickner's pulse, but he already knew. His former teammate was dead.

Caleb didn't know if he should believe Brickner, although remembering how the guy professed to love Heather, he was inclined to go along with his theory. Besides, it made sense that Brickner had something to hold over Royce's head, to get the captain to do his bidding.

What better motive than to threaten to go to the police with the truth about Heather's murder?

Another gunshot echoed through the night and Caleb ducked down when he heard the shattering of glass. He instinctively glanced up, but the window in the car door above his head was still intact.

"Don't shoot! I give up! I give up!" Royce shouted in a panicked tone as he climbed out from behind the wheel. "Do you hear me? I give up!"

"Toss down your weapon!" a familiar voice shouted from a cluster of trees. "Now!"

Declan?

Caleb lifted his head in time to see Royce toss his weapon halfway down the driveway and then lift both his hands in the air in the universal gesture of surrender.

Almost instantly, three of Caleb's former SWAT team members emerged from behind the trees on either side of the driveway. One guy swooped on Royce's gun, safely taking possession of the weapon. A guy who looked like Isaac Morrison grabbed Royce and turned him around so that he faced the hood of the truck, pulling Royce's hands behind his back in order to cuff him. He tensed, wondering if he was the next one to be arrested but Deck crossed over and slapped him on the back.

"Nice work," Declan said. "Stabbing Brickner like that was exactly what Isaac needed to get the guy in position to make his shot."

"I can't believe you're here," Caleb said, feeling as if he were in a daze. "How did you know we were coming to my place? Why didn't you meet us out at the garage?"

"It's a long story," Declan admitted. "We managed to convince Royce to cooperate. In turn, Royce fed Brickner information that I was captured, too. I think Royce sensed his time with Brickner was coming to an end. He told us he believed Brickner was going to kill him."

"Really? You convinced Royce to turn against Brickner?" Caleb shook his head. "I'm shocked."

"We'll have plenty of time to fill you in on the details, later." Declan glanced down at Brickner. "Is he dead?"

"I think so." Caleb couldn't drum up any sympathy for the man who'd killed so many. And in that moment, he didn't care about what had happened. Deck was right. They were finally safe and that's all that mattered.

"Noelle?" Caleb called. "It's safe for you and Kaitlin to come out now."

"Hey, Caleb?" Isaac called as he finished the job of cuffing their former boss. "You better get over here. I think she's bleeding."

"What?" Caleb frantically pushed past Declan and rounded the truck, where his heart nearly stopped in his chest when he saw Noelle's body sprawled facedown on the driveway. He dropped to his knees and reached for her, desperately trying to feel for her pulse. "Noelle? Are you all right? Can you hear me?"

Kaitlin was lying mostly beneath the truck, and when she saw him she began to cry. "Daddy, help Noa. Please help Noa!"

"I will, sweetheart. Come on out now, you're safe." He reached out a hand to his daughter, silently urging her to come out from beneath the truck. "The bad guys are gone now. We're all safe."

"Noa," Kaitlin sobbed. She crawled forward and grabbed Noelle's hand, giving it a hard shake. "Wake up, Noa. Wake up!"

In the background Caleb could hear Declan calling for an ambulance. He closed his eyes and concentrated, thankful to feel the faint flutter of Noelle's pulse. Relieved to know she was still alive, he gently turned Noelle over to try and find the source of the bleeding.

"Isaac, get me some light!" he said urgently.

Isaac pulled out his flashlight and aimed down on Noelle, who looked far too pale as she lay unconscious on the driveway.

"Don't die, Noelle," Caleb muttered half under his breath. "Please don't die."

"She's hit just beneath her shoulder," Isaac said, shining the light on the area. "Looks like the entry wound is on the front and the exit wound is in the back. You'll have to hold pressure on both sides to stop the bleeding."

Caleb was already stripping off his shirt. "Come on, Noelle, hang in there. You're going to be all right. Don't give up on us, do you hear me? Don't give up!"

He placed his balled-up shirt beneath her right shoulder, using the weight of her body to help put pressure on the bleeding. "Give me your shirt," he said to Isaac.

Isaac stripped off his shirt and passed it over to Caleb. "She'll be okay, Caleb. It's just a shoulder wound."

Caleb nodded, not bothering to argue that she could die of a shoulder injury if her lung was hit. He could barely tear his gaze from Noelle, even as he leaned on her shoulder wound to help stop the bleeding. She was an innocent bystander in all of this. A mess he'd dragged her into without giving her a choice.

He couldn't bear to lose her.

Not when he hadn't gotten a chance to tell her how much he loved her.

The wail of sirens filled the air, telling him that help was on the way.

"Please, Lord, keep Noelle safe in Your care. Please heal her wounds and spare her life," he whispered.

"Amen," Kaitlin responded in a tearful voice.

He was humbled by his daughter's ability to pray. Thanks to Noelle's teaching, his daughter knew more about faith and God than he did.

He was so thankful, not only for this second chance at having a future with his daughter, but for discovering faith and God. He owed Noelle so much more than he could ever repay.

When the ambulance pulled up and the paramedics jumped out, hurrying over with their medical gear, he reluctantly eased back so they could begin working on Noelle. In the glow of the ambulance headlights, they quickly placed two IV's in her arms to give her the badly needed lifesaving fluids. One of them even pulled out what looked like a unit of blood.

Caleb picked up his daughter and held her close, kissing her on the cheek, trying to reassure her that everything would be all right. Kaitlin clung to him the way she once clung to Noelle.

His heart filled with love. He and his daughter were truly reunited at last, and he was deeply grateful. But he was also greedy enough to want more.

He wanted Noelle to be with them, too.

Maybe God had already answered his quota of prayers for the night, but that didn't stop him from praying some more.

SIXTEEN

Engulfed in a shroud of pain, Noelle gradually became aware of her surroundings. The sharp scent of antiseptic along with the beeping sounds of a monitor confirmed she was in the hospital and her heart squeezed with fear. Her entire body hurt from the beatings. She tried to open her eyes to make sure her foster father wasn't anywhere around. What if he came to finish what he'd started? What if he made good on his threat to silence her forever?

"No," she forced the word through her parched throat, blinking her eyes to get rid of the blurred vision.

"Just relax, Noelle." The deep male voice came from somewhere near her left shoulder.

She jerked away, turning as far as she could over onto her right side, cowering against the side rail while she desperately searched for the call light. Where were the nurses? Didn't they understand Frank was the one who put her here in the first place? Why had they left her alone with this monster?

"Noelle, what's wrong? Are you in pain? Should I call the nurse?"

She felt a heavy hand on her shoulder and she flinched,

trying to get even farther away from the threat. *No! Help me! Please, Lord, help me!*

"You must be in pain, I'm getting the nurse. Try not to move around so much, you might pull out your stitches."

She'd already found her call light and had pushed the button frantically, hiding her hands amid the folds of the blanket covering her. When the heavy hand moved from her shoulder, she forced herself to turn her head to face the threat. Her vision swam, then sharpened, and she frowned when she realized that the man standing beside her wasn't Frank Petrol, her foster father.

It took another minute for her to recognize the stranger as Caleb O'Malley. She blinked again and tried to gather her scattered thoughts. "What happened?" she whispered in confusion. "Are we safe?"

Caleb's dark eyes were full of concern. "Yes, we're safe. But unfortunately you took a bullet in your left shoulder. Can you feel the padded dressing there? You just came out of surgery a few hours ago. The doctor said you'll be fine, even though you'll need to have a lot of physical therapy to get your full range of motion back."

Now that he mentioned it, the pain in her shoulder became almost unbearable, radiating down her arm and ricocheting through her back. Obviously rolling over in bed hadn't been the smartest move. She slowly eased onto her back and tried to take some slow, deep breaths to calm her racing heart.

She'd never had a flashback like this before, probably because she hadn't been a patient in a hospital since the initial incident ten years ago. But the memory had been horrifyingly real. In that moment she thought for sure she was the sixteen year old who'd been beaten with a cane, her foster father's favorite tool for doling out punishment. The coppery taste of fear still tasted bitter on her tongue and she shied away from the painful memories.

"The nurse should be here shortly," Caleb murmured. He stood a good foot from the side of her bed with his hands tucked into the front pockets of his jeans and it dawned on her that he thought she'd been afraid of him. And she had, but only when she'd thought he was Frank.

"I'm sorry," she whispered again through a throat that felt like it was on fire. "Water?"

"Good morning," a perky blond-haired nurse greeted them as she entered the room. "My name is Jennifer and I'll be your nurse for today. How are you feeling?"

"Hurts," Noelle admitted.

"I've brought you some pain medication, but first I need you to rate your pain on a scale from zero to ten, with ten being the worst pain you've ever felt in your entire life and zero being pain free." As she spoke Jennifer pulled up a laptop computer on wheels and logged in.

"Ten," Noelle said, wondering just how many patients actually gave a zero after having surgery. Was this some sort of torture test to make the patients wait for their pain medication?

"Can she have a sip of water, too?" Caleb asked.

"Sure, let me give her pain meds first." Jennifer used some sort of gadget to bar-code her wristband and then the medication, hitting more keys on the computer before she actually got to the point of inserting the syringe of pain medication into her IV port.

Noelle avoided Caleb's gaze as Jennifer helped her sit forward enough to take a sip of water. She was deeply appalled at how she'd responded when she first woke up. She couldn't imagine what Caleb had thought of her reaction. Even now, she could feel his curious gaze penetrating deep, as if he were willing her to tell him what happened.

Something she'd rather avoid if possible.

She'd thought she'd gotten over her past. But apparently she'd only buried it. Now she knew exactly what Kaitlin's night terrors were like for the little girl.

The coolness of the ice water slipping down her sore throat felt wonderful. She eased back against the pillows and glanced around. "Where's Kaitlin?"

"Sleeping right here behind me." Caleb took a step sideways so she could see the little girl curled in the seat of the recliner, Caleb's sweatshirt covering her like a blanket. "She's been out for several hours now. Not surprising, after all the excitement from last night."

"She's okay?" she asked, desperate for reassurance. "She wasn't hurt?"

"She's fine, mostly worried about you," Caleb admitted, his brown eyes intense. "She prayed for you, too. You've taught her well, Noelle."

Tears pricked Noelle's eyes at the thought of the precious little girl praying for her safety. The pain Noelle felt in her shoulder was well worth the outcome.

"I'm glad she's safe," Noelle murmured. "I was so scared for her."

"Do you need anything else?" Jennifer asked, in her annoyingly perky tone.

"No, I'm fine." Thankfully the pain medication had already taken the edge off, making the pain tolerable. Gingerly, she shifted in her bed, trying to get comfortable.

A strained silence hung suspended between them the moment the nurse left. She wished Caleb would leave and take Kaitlin home so the child could sleep in her own bed. There was nothing more he could do here.

"Brickner's dead?" she asked, breaking the silence.

"Yeah and Royce is under arrest. Declan and Isaac saved the day. And just before Brickner died, he claimed Royce was the one who killed Heather."

She swallowed hard and nodded. She vaguely remembered the sound of gunfire just before the burning pain that had sent her to her knees. Before she lost consciousness she heard Royce giving himself up.

"Will the police finally believe you?" she asked.

"I think so, especially now that I have Deck and Isaac to back me up."

"Good." She was sincerely happy for him. All Caleb wanted was to clear his name and find out who really killed his wife.

"Noelle, are you sure you're okay?" he asked in a low voice. "You looked scared to death when you woke up."

She closed her eyes for a moment, wishing she could avoid this conversation. But it was too late to hide her reaction, and maybe Caleb deserved to know the truth.

The sooner he knew, the sooner he'd leave her alone. Their time together was over. He was finally free to live his own life and she would go back to being a preschool teacher. Their nightmare was over.

So why did she want to cry?

"Noelle? Please, talk to me. I'm worried about you."

She couldn't ignore his plea, no matter how much she wanted to. Baring her soul would be difficult but if that was what he needed before he left once and for all, then she'd tell him.

"I...was in the hospital once before, about ten years ago," she admitted. "When I woke up, I thought I was sixteen again."

"What happened back then?" he pressed, gently. "Why were you so afraid?"

Caleb reached over to take her hand, but Noelle couldn't bear to look him in the eye. "When I heard your voice, I thought you were my foster father, Frank. He used to...hurt me."

"What? He sexually assaulted you?" Caleb asked hoarsely, his hand tightening on hers.

"No, he only beat me with a cane."

"That's bad enough, Noelle. I hope they arrested him and tossed him in jail."

She bit her bottom lip and shook her head. "I didn't hang around long enough to find out. I ran away, and lived on the street for a few weeks."

"Oh, Noelle," he murmured, brushing a strand of hair away from her cheek. Thankfully she didn't flinch again at his touch and she hoped the flashback was safely in the past where it belonged.

She shrugged her good shoulder. "Don't feel sorry for me. I was lucky to end up in a homeless shelter, where I found a wonderful woman by the name of Abby Carrington. Abby took me under her wing, taught me about faith and God, helped me get a job as a waitress and finish my GED. I even managed to get a small scholarship into college. So you see? I was one of the lucky ones."

"I admire you so much, Noelle," Caleb murmured. "After everything you've been through, you still found a way to believe in me, believe in my innocence. And then you did whatever was necessary to protect my daughter. I owe you so much. I don't know how I'll ever be able to repay you."

"Just take good care of Kaitlin," she said, trying to fight off the sedative effects of the narcotic. Her mind was getting foggier by the minute. "That's all I ask. Goodbye, Caleb."

She thought she heard Caleb say her name before she succumbed to sleep.

Goodbye? Caleb stared down at Noelle's peaceful features, resisting the urge to shake her awake. What did she mean goodbye? Was this it? Was this her way of saying she didn't want to see him anymore?

He sank down onto one of the uncomfortable plastic chairs in the corner of Noelle's hospital room and scrubbed his hands over his face. He tried to push back the wave of panic. Surely Noelle hadn't really meant to tell him goodbye. That must have been the narcotics talking.

He couldn't bear the thought of not having Noelle in his life. Yet he couldn't deny that she may not feel the same way. She hadn't pushed him away when he'd kissed her, but maybe now she was having second thoughts.

He rubbed his palms into his eye sockets trying to erase the image of Noelle flinching from his touch, cowering in her bed. The thought of someone beating her with a cane filled him with a helpless fury. What kind of foster parent would do that? Why hadn't anyone stood up for her? She'd been a child, and children were meant to be protected. Not abused.

He was lucky that Kaitlin had ended up with Noelle as a foster mother. The idea of his daughter being subjected to the same abuse that Noelle had suffered made him sick to his stomach. His thoughts drifted back to the first time they'd met, when Noelle had hugged Kaitlin and Kaitlin had shied away from him. Noelle's past had likely made her more determined to protect Kaitlin, even from him.

And he didn't blame Noelle one bit for being leery of him. In fact, knowing what he did now, he was amazed Noelle had managed to trust him at all.

"Caleb?"

He lifted his head to find Deck hovering in the doorway. "Yeah?"

"It's time for you to give your statement."

He grimaced and nodded. "Who's leading the investigation? Sheriff Cramer?"

"Internal Affairs has taken over the investigation," Declan confided. "Sheriff Cramer is on the hot seat at the moment. IAB is all over him. He has some explaining to do since Royce reported directly to him and, of course, Brickner was dirty, as well. I doubt Cramer will make it through unscathed, even if he didn't know about Brickner's and Royce's involvement with Eileen's Elite Escort Services. Cramer will never get reelected after this."

Caleb hadn't been overly fond of Sheriff Cramer, but that didn't mean he wanted to see the guy lose his job. Back when he'd been locked up in jail, he'd have been happy to get revenge, but now, he was simply glad to be alive and reunited with his daughter.

And even more grateful to have found Noelle and God.

"Lieutenant Erickson is waiting for you in a small conference room down the hall," Declan advised.

"Can you stay here with Kaitlin for a while?" Caleb asked, rising to his feet. "I don't want to wake her up just yet."

"No problem." Deck crossed over and took the chair Caleb had just vacated.

Caleb glanced over his shoulder at Noelle one last time before he slipped from the room.

He found the conference room without any trouble

and when he saw Lieutenant Erickson sitting there in his full dress uniform, Caleb paused and took a deep breath, hoping and praying he wasn't about to be arrested again.

Surely Deck would have warned him if there was any possibility of that. Wouldn't he?

"Come in, O'Malley," Lieutenant Erickson said, rising to his feet.

Caleb forced himself to step forward, taking Erickson's outstretched hand. "Lieutenant."

"Have a seat." Erickson waved him toward the empty chair located perpendicular to his. Erickson glanced down at his fat file folder for a moment before meeting Caleb's gaze. "I'm here to listen to your side of the story and I need for you to start at the beginning."

Caleb stared at the senior officer for a moment. "You mean the night of my wife's murder? Or just since I've been released from jail?"

"We have your statement from the night your wife was murdered," Erickson said, tapping the folder with his pen. Caleb understood he wasn't about to get an apology for what had transpired. "And from what your former teammates said, it appears you really were innocent of that crime. But I want to know exactly what transpired since the moment you left the jail with your lawyer, Jack Owens."

Caleb took it as a good sign that the lieutenant at least appeared willing to listen. He began his story, telling how Jack had taken him to run a few errands, including stopping at the bank and picking up a new cell phone, before dropping him off at home. Caleb described how he'd narrowly missed getting shot when he'd gone to pick up his daughter and how he'd convinced Noelle to go with him to escape the gunman.

"Why didn't you call the police?" the lieutenant demanded.

"With all due respect, sir, I didn't trust anyone, but I especially didn't trust the police."

Erickson grunted as if he couldn't think of a good argument to refute his statement. "Okay, so then what?"

Caleb described how they'd found a motel with a pool and that he'd exchanged license plates and then had talked to Owens late at night. He explained that they'd stayed longer the next day, to allow Kaitlin time to swim, which is how they managed to avoid being killed when the vehicle exploded.

Lieutenant Erickson was taking notes fast and furious while Caleb talked. "You escaped on foot?" he asked incredulously.

"Yes, sir." Caleb described their journey back to Madison on the chartered bus. He described how he'd searched on the internet to find the SWAT member Noelle had seen the night of Heather's murder, and how she'd recognized Marc Brickner.

"We'll get to Brickner and Royce in a moment," Erickson said. "What happened after Madison?"

"We took a bus to Milwaukee and headed over to meet with Jack Owens. But he was dead inside his condo."

"And yet you still didn't call the police?" Erickson asked with a deep scowl.

"No, sir. By then we already knew that the body of Kenneth James had been found in Lake Michigan and that I was a suspect for his murder. I knew that Jack's death would be pinned on me, as well. And I was right. After I contacted my buddy Declan Shaw, I discovered there was a warrant out for my arrest." It wasn't easy to keep the accusation from his tone. The more he talked about everything that happened, the more his resentment grew. Why hadn't anyone realized that he was being set up? Why hadn't anyone given him the benefit of the doubt?

"All right, then what happened?" Erickson asked.

He shook his head. "I don't know the details. You'll have to ask Noelle Whitman once she's recovered from being shot, but Brickner had someone kidnap Noelle and my daughter, Kaitlin. We were following Brickner and it was pure luck that we saw Noelle and Kaitlin being taken inside the garage where we'd found Brickner. We never did find out what was on the other side of the building. From that point on we were focused on getting Noelle and Kaitlin out of there alive."

"So you saw Brickner holding them hostage?" Erickson asked.

"Yes. He held his gun at my daughter's head, forcing me to give myself up." The memory was enough to make him break out into a cold sweat. "He spoke to Royce on the phone and then the two of them took us at gunpoint over to my house. Brickner told me the plan was to make my death along with Noelle's and Kaitlin's deaths look like a murder/suicide."

Erickson's mouth tightened with anger. "Did he confess to killing your wife, too?"

"No, sir. He admitted that he killed Kenneth James, because the guy was trying to skip town with the money he was paid to be an eyewitness against me. Brickner also admitted that he arranged for Jack's murder, so that he could pin everything on me." Caleb let out a heavy sigh. "But as he lay dying on my driveway, he told me to make Royce pay for killing Heather."

At this point, Erickson tossed his pen down and sat

back in his chair. "That doesn't mesh with Royce's side of the story."

A chill snaked down Caleb's spine. He leaned forward, knowing he needed to make Erickson believe him. "Listen, Lieutenant, Brickner was a sociopath and deserved to die. But I believe he really loved Heather. He told me they were planning to get married after our divorce was finalized. I can't think of one good reason he'd kill Heather."

Erickson crossed his beefy arms over his rotund abdomen. "You said it yourself. He was a sociopath. He probably killed her and then tried to put the blame on Royce."

Caleb couldn't believe what he was hearing. They were going to let Royce walk! They were feeling bad for the guy, no doubt believing whatever sob-story Royce fed them.

"But why would Brickner admit to the other murders but not to killing Heather?" he pressed. "I think he would have taken the credit if he had in fact done the crime."

"Could be that he was just trying to get back at you, make you feel bad about his affair with your wife," Erickson pointed out.

"Listen to me. The man was dying. He told me to make sure Royce paid for murdering Heather. Why would Marc make up a story when he was about to die?"

"Did anyone else hear him say that?" Erickson asked.

Caleb thought back, trying to remember. "Deck was there less than a minute later. He may have heard it."

Erickson glanced down at his notes. "Nope, he didn't. Okay, that's all for now, O'Malley. I'll get in touch if I have any other questions."

Caleb stared at the lieutenant for several heartbeats, wrestling with his temper. He bit his tongue and forced himself to leave the room without losing control.

He slowly walked back to Noelle's room, grappling with the fact that Royce was actually going to get away with murder.

And there was absolutely nothing he could do about it.

SEVENTEEN

Noelle woke up several times throughout the day, and each time there was no sign of Caleb or his daughter. Jennifer, her nurse, claimed they left about an hour before lunch. Noelle told herself that it was better this way, but that didn't ease the ache in her heart.

By late afternoon the nurses and therapists made her get up out of bed to walk the halls. The pain radiating from her shoulder was still bad, but somehow the physical pain didn't mean much in the wake of her emotional turmoil.

She shouldn't be surprised that Caleb had left with his daughter, after all she was the one who told him goodbye. So what if Caleb had kissed her? It wasn't like a mere kiss meant anything these days. They'd been running for their lives while trying to figure out who'd killed Caleb's wife and set him up for her murder. They were forced to spend time together, and that closeness had heightened their emotions. She knew very well that under normal circumstances a man like Caleb wouldn't look at her twice. After all, he hadn't recognized her as one of the preschool teachers who cared for his daughter.

Frank had been a firefighter, physically fit, the macho

type of guy who secretly used his fists on his wife and a cane on his foster child. She felt a little ashamed at how she'd thought Caleb might be like Frank. Caleb had never said much when he came to pick up Kaitlin, and he'd always looked gruff and impatient as if he had far better things to do.

Not that he'd ever been short with Kaitlin. In fact, his daughter had always raced over to throw herself into her father's arms.

But that was before he'd gone to jail for a crime he didn't commit.

She learned more about who Caleb really was during their brief time together. She knew she could trust Caleb not to hurt her physically. She'd never once seen him lose his temper or lash out at anyone. Frank used to hit the wall or the table when he was mad, and from there it wasn't long until he'd started hitting people.

No, in that respect Caleb would never hurt her or his daughter. But could she trust a man like Caleb with her heart? Through the time they'd spent together, she'd grown to care for him. Maybe, even had fallen in love with him. But what did she know about real love? She'd never had a serious relationship, always shying away from men. The very thought of opening herself up to rejection made her break out into a cold sweat.

She couldn't help thinking about Caleb though as she worked on the simple exercises the therapist left for her to do on her own. She suffered through a brief interrogation by Lieutenant Erickson, who wanted to know all the details about what had happened since Caleb had showed up on her doorstep that fateful Friday afternoon. She assumed that he'd spoken to Caleb, too, which explained his absence.

But she'd thought for sure Caleb would return to visit with Kaitlin after dinner, but the hours crept by slowly with no sign of them.

By eight o'clock in the evening, when there was an overhead announcement about the end of visiting hours, she knew they weren't coming. Disappointment slashed deep. It had obviously been the right choice to keep her feelings to herself. Caleb was already moving on with his life and honestly, she couldn't blame him. He'd already spent fourteen long months behind bars.

He deserved every moment of freedom. And she'd known all along that once this was over he wouldn't need her anymore.

She squeezed her eyes tight to keep from crying but a few tears leaked out and slid down her cheeks. So she did the only thing she could, she prayed.

Help me to move on with my life, too, Lord. Please guide me along Your path. Amen.

Caleb spent the afternoon with Kaitlin, Declan and Isaac at his house, once the crime scene from the driveway had been cleared. He played with his daughter, but then put in a Disney movie for her so that he could strategize with his former teammates.

"There has to be some proof we can find to nail Royce for Heather's murder," Caleb said in a low tone.

"Not easy since it seems like the only one who knew the truth is dead," Deck muttered with a scowl.

"I think Cramer is going to offer you your old job back," Isaac said. "He's already down two men and I think he wants to try and salvage his image."

"His image is beyond repair," Deck scoffed. "But giving Caleb his job back is the least Cramer could do. Caleb could easily sue the department for defamation of character and false imprisonment."

Caleb sighed. "Come on, you two, focus. While it would be great to get my job back, if we can't figure out a way to link Royce to Heather's murder he'll be a free man in less than ten years. All they have against him right now is being a party to the crime. And considering he's claiming Brickner threatened his life if he didn't cooperate, they'll likely go easy on him."

"You have to admit, Brickner could have been lying," Isaac pointed out.

"He wasn't." Caleb was positive Marc was telling the truth. "Why would he bother? And besides, there had to be something big that Brickner was hanging over Royce's head in order to make him cooperate. Why not Heather's murder? Maybe Brickner walked in on him shortly after Royce killed her and the two of them trumped up this scheme to set me up in order to keep Heather's involvement in the escort service a secret."

"You're right, but we'd have to prove Royce was having an affair with your wife," Deck said thoughtfully. Then he grimaced. "Sorry, Caleb."

Caleb flashed a wry grin. "I've already seen her photograph on that sleazy website. There's nothing more that would shock me."

"Daddy, *Shrek 1* is over. It's time for *Shrek 2!*" Kaitlin shouted from the other room. She ran into the kitchen and climbed up onto Caleb's lap. "When can we see Noa?" she asked.

He forced a smile. "She's still groggy from her surgery, remember? We'll go tomorrow, when she's feeling better, okay?"

"Okay. I'm hungry. Can I have a snack?"

At times like this he wished Noelle was here to guide him. Was Kaitlin supposed to have snacks in the late afternoon? Wouldn't that ruin her dinner? But then again, she slept in this morning after being up half the night, and she was recovering from the flu, so maybe a snack was a good idea?

Why didn't kids come with an instruction manual?

"Ah, sure, Katydid. What would you like?" he asked.

"Fish crackers and juice," she announced.

That sounded like something Noelle would give her so he set Kaitlin down and pulled out the crackers and filled a glass with juice. He let her take her snack into the living room, even though he knew Noelle would not approve. But he didn't want to talk about murder within earshot of his daughter.

"Try not to spill, okay?" he said.

"Okay."

When he walked back into the kitchen, Deck and Isaac were deep in a low conversation. A conversation that halted abruptly the moment he entered the room.

"What's up?" he asked when the two of them stared at him.

Deck and Isaac exchanged a long look before Deck cleared his throat. "Caleb, don't get mad, okay? But we think you should have a paternity test done on Kaitlin."

Anger flashed hard and swift. "Get out," he bit off between clenched teeth.

"Caleb, we're only trying to help," Declan began but he cut him off quickly.

"No. Get out," he repeated. "I'm not kidding. I'm not going to listen to your garbage for another minute."

His two teammates exchanged a tense look before they slowly rose to their feet and made their way to the door.

"Caleb, she'll always be your daughter. No one can take her away from you. But if there's a chance that her DNA matches Royce's…"

Caleb slammed the door, cutting Declan off midsentence. He paced the short length of the kitchen, wishing he could hit the gym to let off some steam.

"Daddy, I spilled," Kaitlin cried out from the living room.

He grabbed a dish towel and hurried into the other room, knowing that he only had himself to blame for the cherry stain on his carpet.

The mess was the least of his worries. He did his best to ignore Declan and Isaac's suggestion, but he found himself searching Kaitlin's features for any resemblance to him.

Kaitlin had her mother's glossy blond hair and her big blue eyes. Surely Kaitlin had his nose, and his chin. No, wait, she had a cleft chin and he didn't. Although neither did Heather.

But Royce did.

No, he wasn't going to do it. Cleft chins likely skipped a generation, that's all. He'd never met Heather's parents, but he'd bet her father had a cleft chin.

He wanted to smack Declan and Isaac for planting the seeds of doubt in his mind. He tried to concentrate on the movie, but after about twenty minutes he went to find the old family photo albums. He scoured the faces of Heather's parents and his own.

And the sick feeling in his gut told him the guys could be right. That there was a possibility he was not Kaitlin's biological father.

He closed his eyes and prayed for strength to do what was right. *Guide me, Lord. Should I really do this? I just don't know. Please help me do the right thing, Lord. Amen.*

* * *

Noelle was woken up at the ridiculous time of five-thirty in the morning to have her labs drawn and her vitals taken. Thankfully she fell asleep for another hour and a half, before she woke up to the grumbling of her stomach.

"You have bowel sounds," Jennifer said in an approving tone, as if this was some great trick. "Good job! That means you can order full liquids for breakfast."

"Yippee," Noelle said weakly. How pathetic was she, that the thought of drinking her breakfast actually sounded good?

"I'll call for your tray. It should be here in less than an hour. And the doctor wants to switch you to oral pain medication today. So I brought two Percocets for you."

Accustomed to the routine, she gave her pain score as a seven, and waited for them to be scanned before she swallowed the meds. She knew they'd make her walk around and do her exercises so skipping the pain pills wasn't an option.

The trauma surgeon came in about an hour later with his team of residents. She stoically braced herself as they took down the dressing and peered intently at her incision.

"No signs of infection," Dr. Lauder said with satisfaction. "We'll keep you here on IV antibiotics for another thirty-six hours and by then you'll be ready to go home."

"Great," she said with a strained smile. "Can't wait."

"Do you have someone at home that can help you?" Dr. Lauder asked as one of his underlings redressed her wound.

Her smile faded. "No, but I'll manage." She refused to even consider calling Caleb.

"Hmm, we'll have the social worker come in to set up some home health visits, then," Dr. Lauder informed her. "Any other questions?"

"No questions," she confirmed, wondering if she could somehow ask the nurse to tell the social worker she wasn't interested. The social worker assigned to her case as a child in the foster system hadn't been the least bit helpful and in fact, had refused to believe the stories of Frank's abuse.

She wasn't interested in talking to another one. She'd rather struggle along on her own.

The physical therapists kept her busy for a few hours and by the time they were finished, her shoulder felt like it weighed ten tons. She'd just returned to bed when there was a knock at her door. For a moment she was tempted to feign sleep, but then realized she wasn't a kid anymore. She could tell the social worker to leave if she wanted to.

"Come in," she called, steeling herself to be polite but firm.

"Noa!" Kaitlin cried, running into the room. "I've missed you!"

"Oh, Kaitlin, I'm so glad to see you, too!" She couldn't hide the surge of joy that engulfed her. Maybe Caleb had only come back for his daughter's sake, but right now, she didn't care. Kaitlin tried to climb onto the bed, but Caleb stopped her.

"Noelle still has a big owwie on her shoulder," he said. "You can't hurt her, okay?"

"Okay, I'm sorry, Noa."

"It's all right, Kaitlin. Here, let me give you a little hug, okay?"

She managed to hug Kaitlin with her right arm and to gently kiss the top of the little girl's head. She noticed that today Caleb had dressed his daughter in neon-pink, one of her favorite colors.

"How are you feeling, Noelle?" he asked, his gaze full of concern.

"Much better," she said. "I'm sore now, but that's because I just finished therapy."

"You look better," he said as he pulled up a chair next to her bed.

"Daddy, I'm going to color Noa a picture, okay?"

Noelle noticed that Caleb had come prepared with a coloring book and box of crayons to help keep Kaitlin busy. He was obviously doing a great job of being a single dad.

She was happy for him, and tried not to feel sad for herself.

"Noelle, I need your advice on something," Caleb said quietly. His voice was so soft, she sensed he didn't want his daughter to overhear.

"What's wrong?"

"Nothing's wrong," he assured her. "I don't know if you heard that Marc Brickner claimed that Royce killed Heather before he died."

She nodded. "Yes, I gave my statement to Lieutenant Erickson and he asked if I'd overheard Marc saying anything that night."

"Did you?" His gaze was full of hope.

"I'm sorry Caleb but I didn't hear him. I was on the other side of the vehicle. I remember trying to protect Kaitlin and then getting hit by the bullet, nothing more."

"I know." Caleb stared at his hands for a minute. "I already knew that Heather had an affair with Brickner, but according to Marc, Royce had also been with her and he flew into a jealous rage and killed her."

"I'm sorry, Caleb," she said, reaching out to take his hand. "I'm sorry you had to go through all this."

A faint smile tugged at the corner of his mouth. "We've both had difficult situations to get through, haven't we? As tough as it's been, I'm still very thankful for everything I have."

Her heart swelled with love and she had to bite her tongue to stop herself from blurting out her feelings.

"Noelle, Deck and Isaac suggested I get a paternity test done on Kaitlin. To see if there's any chance that Royce might be her blood father."

Her jaw dropped open, and she quickly glanced over to make sure Kaitlin wasn't paying attention to the conversation. "Are you going to do it?" she asked.

"I don't know what to do," he confessed, his gaze full of agony. "I love my daughter. She's the center of my life, regardless who fathered her."

"I know you love her, and she loves you, too." Her heart was breaking for him and she thought that if Declan walked through the door right now she might be tempted to throw something at him, like her box of tissues or her cup of ice chips. Why had he put the idea in Caleb's head? "There's no reason to torture yourself over this, Caleb. She's yours and that's all that matters."

He nodded, but then shrugged. "I never noticed it before, but Kaitlin really doesn't look like me. And she has a cleft chin, just like Royce. I searched through all the family photo albums last night, not a cleft chin to be seen on anyone else."

She didn't want to admit that she'd noticed the lack of resemblance, too. "Do you really think that this test will help prove Royce's guilt?"

"I think it's the best shot we have," he replied. "As

much as I detested Marc Brickner, I believe he really loved Heather. And he wanted me to know the truth because he wanted to make Royce pay for what he did."

"Sounds like you've talked yourself into it," she murmured.

"Yeah, maybe. It will take a while for the DNA to get back, regardless."

"Are you sure all this hasn't changed your feelings for Kaitlin?" she asked.

"I'm positive." This time, his smile reached his eyes. "I love her. And I want you to know, Noelle, that I care about you, too."

She blinked, wondering if she'd imagined that last part. "I care about you, too, Caleb," she said carefully. "We've been through a lot together over the past week."

He cradled her hand between his. "Noelle, I don't want to scare you, or to rush you, but I want you to know, that my feelings for you aren't going to fade away over time. I missed you terribly and we were apart for less than twenty-four hours. Staying away so that you could get the rest you needed was almost impossible. I can't tell you how many times I walked to the door, intending to head over here to see you. And it didn't help that Kaitlin asked about you, constantly."

She stared at him in shock. Was she dreaming? *If so, please don't let her wake up.*

"Noelle, I know you're sick and in pain, but I just want to know that you'll give us a chance. After you feel better, of course. But don't shut me out. Don't hide from me. I love you, Noelle."

"Oh, Caleb," she whispered, her eyes brimming with tears. "I want more than anything to be with you, but I'm also afraid. I've never been in a serious relationship before. And you know I have a lot of baggage."

"I do, too," he reminded her. "And I'll be patient, as long as you give me a chance. I'll wait as long as you need."

She was honored and humbled by his declaration. "Caleb, how did I get so lucky to meet you? I never knew what it meant to be in love until I met you."

"Lucky?" he asked in mock horror. "I'm pretty sure it's the other way around. I'm the one who's lucky enough to have found you."

"God gets the credit for bringing us together," she said firmly.

"You're right. And it's up to us to honor His gift." Caleb rose and leaned over to give her a gentle kiss. She reached up to hug him with her good arm, longing for the day she could hug him properly.

"Daddy! Are you kissing Noa?" Kaitlin's voice made Caleb jump back and Noelle stifled a giggle as she glanced over to see Kaitlin gawking at them, holding a purple crayon in her tiny fist.

"Yes, I'm definitely kissing Noa," he said. To prove his point, he kissed Noelle again before he turned to face his daughter. "Are you okay with that, Katydid?"

"Oh yes, because I love Noa, too."

Noelle smiled through her tears, knowing she was truly blessed to be surrounded with love.

EPILOGUE

Six months later...

Caleb stood at the front of the church, waiting for his two favorite women to make their appearance. The church was crowded with the parishioners they'd come to know and his SWAT team buddies, including Declan standing beside him as his best man. He'd been reinstated on the force with a new boss at the helm and things were going about as well as could be expected, considering the reputation of the team had taken a serious media hit.

Caleb resisted the urge to tug at the tight collar of his tux, because he'd wear anything, including this monkey suit, if it made Noelle happy.

He was the luckiest man in the world to have this second chance at a family. Royce had crumpled after discovering he was Kaitlin's biological father, but since his former captain was serving a life sentence for his crimes, Caleb could afford to feel a little sorry for the guy.

The music swelled and everyone stood, rose to their feet and turned expectantly toward the back of the church. Kaitlin walked down the aisle first, adorably serious as she took slow steps, deliberately dropping pink rose petals on the white runner.

When her tiny basket was empty she smiled at him and came over to stand next to him. He put his arm around her slim shoulders and said, "Good job, Katydid."

"I love you, Daddy," she whispered back.

Noelle's friend and maid of honor, Sarah Germaine, came down the aisle next with Declan. When Deck came over to stand beside Caleb, he patted the pocket holding their rings and winked.

Caleb practically held his breath waiting for Noelle. When she walked toward him, their gazes clung and instantly the crowd of people in the church faded away, leaving just the two of them.

Noelle was so beautiful, smiling confidently as she approached. When they first met, in those terrified hours after the shooting, she reminded him of a frightened gazelle determined to protect his daughter. But once the danger was over and they had a chance to relax and get to know each other, Noelle's strength and confidence had grown. The way she smiled and laughed convinced him she was truly happy.

He hoped the love he felt was evident in his eyes, the way her love glowed from hers. And he couldn't stop himself from taking a step forward to meet her.

"You're so beautiful, Noelle," he whispered. "I love you so much."

"I love you, too, Caleb," she whispered back with a quick smile.

His heart swelled in his chest as he tucked her hand in his arm and they turned together to face the pastor.

With Noelle on one side and his daughter on the other, he was more than ready to begin the next phase of his life.

Noelle and Kaitlin were his family. And he would never take his life and his freedom for granted ever again.

* * * * *

DOWN TO THE WIRE

This is the message we have heard from Him
and declare to you: God is light;
in Him there is no darkness at all.
—*1 John* 1:5

This book is dedicated to my wonderful husband, Scott, who has done everything possible to support my writing. I love you!

ONE

Tess Collins stood at the front of the classroom, looking out at her new group of fourth graders. More than half-way through their second week of school, things were beginning to settle down. These were her students for the next nine months. For better or worse, she thought wryly.

"Good morning, everyone," she greeted her children with a smile. "Please take your seats."

The twenty-two fourth graders radiated energy but obligingly wiggled into their assigned seats. She checked to make sure none of them were absent, before she turned back to her desk. One glance at her seating chart confirmed that a few of the little rascals had switched spots.

"Ellen and Tanya, please return to your proper seats. Hunter and Brett, I also need you to go back to your assigned seats."

The four kids gaped in surprise but giggled and shuffled around until they were seated at their correct desks. She decided not to make a big deal out of their prank, at least for now. If they continued to misbehave, she'd have to make them stay after school to have a little chat.

"Today we're going to start with a math quiz that should be a review from what you learned last year."

She ignored the low moans of protest. "Miles, will you please help me hand out the papers?"

Miles, a short redheaded boy with lots of freckles, jumped up and took half of the stack of quizzes from her hands. She handed out the papers on one side, looking over the rest of the class as he passed a quiz to each student on the other side.

"Olivia, please put your book away. Only pencils and erasers are allowed." Tess waited until the young girl put her paperback away before glancing up at the clock. "Everyone ready? You may begin."

Instantly, all the students turned their attention to her impromptu math quiz. Satisfied they were all working diligently, Tess took a seat behind her desk to check out her lesson plan for the rest of the day.

Click.

Tess froze, the tiny hairs on the back of her neck lifting in alarm when she realized her knee had bumped into something hard. Battling a wave of trepidation, she bent sideways to see her knee was pressed up against a small box with lots of wires sticking out from it. The box was somehow attached to the inner side of her desk and there was a tiny red digital display with numbers counting down.

A bomb?

For a moment she simply stared in horror, barely believing what she was seeing. Afraid to move, fearing that releasing the trigger might cause an immediate blast, she glanced out at her students, who were all concentrating intensely on the pop quiz. Watching all those innocent faces, she grimly realized there wasn't a moment to waste.

"All right, class, we have a change in plans. Turns out we're going to have a fire drill. I need everyone to line up with their buddy and walk down the hall toward the principal's office just like we did the first day of school. I want you to go all the way outside. *Now!*"

The kids looked around in confusion but were more than happy to abandon their math quizzes. She quietly urged her students to hurry, unable to bear the thought of anything happening to them.

"Miss Collins, aren't you going to come, too?"

Trust Miles to be concerned about her. He was the sweetest child and she was often struck by the resemblance to her brother, Bobby. Although Bobby was a sullen seventeen-year-old now, a far cry from the loving younger brother he used to be.

"Not right now. But, Miles, I want you to tell the principal to come and see me, okay? Now go outside, but walk, don't run."

Tess held her breath waiting for the students to follow her instructions, walking out of the classroom and then down the hall. She closed her eyes in relief when the last pupil was out of harm's way.

Thank You, Lord.

"Tess?" Evelyn Fischer, the elementary school principal, came into the classroom, a concerned frown furrowed on her brow. "What's going on?"

She swallowed hard and tried to remain calm. "Listen, you need to get every student and teacher out of the building, immediately. Tell them it's a fire drill. And then I need you to call 911, because I'm afraid I've triggered a bomb...and if this timer is correct, we only have thirty minutes until it blows."

Declan Shaw set aside his M4 .223 and pulled his ear protectors off with a disgusted sigh. "I'm still only hitting the bull's-eye at sixty-five percent."

"Hey, you're getting better," his buddy Isaac Morrison pointed out. "The rest of your shots are in the next closest rim. That's not half-bad."

"Yeah, I think you're improving, Deck," Caleb O'Malley added. "Stop being so rough on yourself."

"We're down a sharpshooter," Declan pointed out. "Which means I need to step up my game."

"Your game is fine," Caleb assured him.

Their phones rang simultaneously, and Declan reached for his, knowing this couldn't be good news. "What's up?"

"Bomb threat at Greenland Elementary School," their new boss, Griff Vaughn, said. "Get ready to roll."

Declan didn't hesitate but ended the call and shouldered the M4 before leading the way through the training facility to the front of the building housing the sheriff's department. Isaac and Caleb were close on his heels.

"Probably a false alarm," Isaac muttered as they quickly donned their protective vests and the rest of their SWAT gear. "Some student pulling a prank to get out of school."

"Doubtful," Declan said grimly as he headed out to the armored truck. "Have you forgotten how we've had two other very real bombs within the past month, including one at the minimart that injured my sister? I don't think it's a bogus call at all."

"Most likely the same perp who seems to be targeting areas where students hang out—the custard stand, the minimart and now the elementary school. We need to catch this guy, and quick," Caleb added as he automatically slid into the driver's seat.

Declan knew that he'd be the lead point person during this tactical situation. He might not rock at being the top sharpshooter on the team, but he was the best when it came to disarming bombs.

Provided they could get there in time.

Declan tucked in his earpiece and flipped the switch on his radio. "Give me the intel," he ordered.

"We have a box with a trigger and a timer fixed underneath the fourth grade teacher's desk. She heard a click when she sat down and was smart enough to send the kids outside right away."

His gut clenched as he realized there was a possible victim close to the device. His sister, Karen, was lucky to only have suffered bruises and a broken arm, when she could easily have died from the force of the blast, just like his teammate. Once again, he couldn't help wishing he'd been the one called to the scene at the minimart. He wanted to believe his being there might have made a difference.

"Have you swept the school to make sure everyone is out and there are no other explosive devices?"

"Affirmative. The teacher managed to get almost everyone evacuated before we arrived. We're going through the rest of the building now, but so far it looks as if there's only the one device. We won't be able to use the robot on this one."

"Keep searching the rest of the building, until it's clear. We'll be there in five," Declan assured him.

"So it's the real deal, huh?" Isaac asked.

"Sounds like it. And there's an innocent victim involved, too. So step on it, Caleb."

"Like he isn't already going pedal to the metal with lights and sirens?" Isaac muttered. "Cool your jets, man."

Declan bit back a sarcastic reply, knowing his buddy was right. He needed to get his mind in the zone if he was going to be successful at disarming the explosive device in that classroom.

He went through his pack, double-checking to make sure he had all the equipment he'd need. Two weeks ago, he'd successfully dismantled the bomb that was found behind the counter at the custard stand. He wanted to believe he'd be able to take care of this latest bomb, too. So far they'd been fortunate that they hadn't suffered more casualties. Although losing three people after the minimart blast, one cop and two civilians, was three too many.

Declan took a deep breath and let it out slowly. When they arrived, the area around the school was vacant. The first cops on the scene had done a good job of getting all the students and faculty as far away from the building as possible. Caleb pulled up to the front door and Declan was the first with boots on the ground, his pack slung over his shoulder.

"I'm going in," he told them. "Isaac, you and Caleb stay here but keep the lines of communication open. I may need some assistance."

"Roger that," Caleb said. "We'll be ready."

Declan gave a brief nod before following the cop back into the school. The hallways were lined with coat hooks that were hung at what seemed like dwarf level. Even though he'd gone to school here, the place didn't look at all familiar now that he was seeing the building through adult eyes. Then again, he hadn't set foot inside a school since barely managing to graduate from Greenland High ten years ago.

He'd signed up to join the marines and left town a couple of weeks later, without looking back. After completing his six-year commitment, including two tours in

Afghanistan, he'd returned home to join the Milwaukee County SWAT team to help support his older sister, Karen, and her young twin daughters.

"Third door on the right," the cop said, hanging back in a way that made it clear the guy didn't want to go much farther.

"Thanks." Declan nodded at him, then headed toward the classroom.

He strode through the doorway, sweeping his gaze over the empty desks, papers and pencils scattered all over the floor. He zeroed in on the slender woman seated at the teacher's desk. Her long wavy blond hair was pulled back from her face, and when she turned toward him, his gut wrenched with recognition.

"Tess?" He blinked, wondering if he'd made a mistake. But as he came closer, he knew he hadn't. Tess Collins had been a year behind him in high school, but they'd never really been friends. She was the class valedictorian, while he'd been the town troublemaker. They'd rarely spoken until the night he'd saved her from an assault mere weeks before he joined the service. He wasn't sure why she wasn't a doctor the way she'd planned, but there wasn't time to wander down memory lane.

"Don't move, okay? I'm going to take a look at this device and see what I can do to get you out of here."

"Declan," she whispered faintly. And despite the seriousness of the situation, he was secretly pleased that she'd remembered him, too. "I thought you joined the marines."

"I did, but now I'm back." He didn't want to scare her by pointing out how precarious her situation was, so he chose his words carefully as he gave an update through his radio. "Isaac, this looks to be a homemade device, although it appears the perp stuck a lot of extra wires into it, probably hoping to cause confusion."

"Roger, Deck. Is there a timer?"

"Affirmative. We have less than twenty minutes and counting." He knelt beside her and opened his pack. "I don't want you to worry, Tess. Just stay as still as possible."

"I'm trying," she said. "I've been telling my students for years to sit still, but I had no idea just how truly difficult a task that really was until right now."

After taking out his flashlight and peering at the device, he gave Isaac and Caleb more information. "This isn't the exact same makeup as the device from the custard stand, but I still think it's the same perp. I'm betting it has basic dynamite inside, along with tacks, just like the last one."

"Tacks?" Tess echoed in horror.

"Roger that, Deck," Caleb said. "Can you disarm it?"

"Affirmative." Declan wasn't about to say anything else that would scare Tess more than she already was. But the fact of the matter was that the placement of the bomb was ingenious. With it tucked up against the inside wall of the desk, and Tess's knee pressed against the trigger, his ability to work around the device was severely limited. Their perp was getting smarter and bolder at the same time. Not a good combination.

"I need someone to take the teacher's place," he said. "Any volunteers?"

"I'll do it," Caleb offered.

"No way," Isaac said. "You have a wife and daughter depending on you. I don't have anyone dependent on me so I'll do it."

"No," Tess spoke up. "I'm not switching places with

anyone. That's a waste of time. Just figure out how to shut it down, okay?"

Declan glanced up at her. "Tess, I want you to be safe."

"I'm not trading places, end of discussion." Her brown eyes were haunted. "I trust God and I trust you, Declan. We'll get through this."

Her faith, even after all this time, was as strong as ever and only proved once again how far out of his league she was. "Negative, Isaac. She's refusing to leave. Sixteen minutes and counting."

"I trust you, Declan," Tess said again.

Humbled by her faith, he wanted more than anything not to let her down. "I'm going to move your chair as far over as possible so I can get closer to this thing, okay?" Deck stuck his flashlight in his mouth and turned over on his back, scooting under the desk. He held the wire cutters and then painstakingly followed the various wires.

Sweat beaded on his brow, rolling down the side of his face. Normally he was glacier cold when it came to disarming bombs. He didn't mind putting his life on the line to save others. In fact, he figured this weird talent he seemed to have was his calling.

But knowing that Tess would suffer—and probably die if he failed—elevated the tension to a whole new level.

He twisted several of the wires and found the bogus ones, holding his breath as he clipped them and tugged them from the clay inside the box. When he was down to four wires remaining, he wiped his brow with his forearm.

"Five minutes and counting," Isaac said in his ear.

He didn't want to think about what Tess was going through right now. She hadn't said a word as he worked, not even to ask how close he was to disarming the bomb.

"I've got four wires left. The rest were decoys," he informed Isaac. "They're all the same color, so I have no way of knowing which one is the ground, which one is attached to the timer and which one is the live wire leading to the fuse."

"You can do it, Deck," his teammate said. "Go with your gut."

Normally that was good advice. But not now. Not when Tess was the one who'd die alongside him if he failed.

He closed his eyes and cleared his mind, trying to imagine what the device looked like on the inside. With Tess's knee pressed up against the trigger, he hadn't been able to get the casing off to see for himself.

"Three minutes and counting," Isaac said.

"Dear Lord, please guide Declan," Tess whispered. "If it be Your will, give him the wisdom and strength to disarm this bomb. We ask for Your mercy and grace, Amen."

Tess's prayer caught him off guard, but then again, praying certainly couldn't hurt. He opened his eyes, and lifted the wire cutters.

"Two minutes, ten seconds and counting," Isaac told him.

Declan stared at the wires. He grabbed the one that was farthest away from the timer. If he were the one creating the bomb, he would thread it through to come out the opposite end as a confusion tactic. He clipped it with the wire cutters. The timer stopped and he breathed a sigh of relief.

"I've got it," he muttered. He clipped the next wire and relaxed when the bomb didn't blow. "Tess, I want you to slowly move your knee away from the box."

"Are you sure?" she asked, fear evident in her tone.

"I'm sure."

She moved her knee and the trigger popped back out. And then nothing. Relief flooded him. He'd done it. But the danger wasn't over quite yet.

"I'm going to ease out from under here, okay?" Declan slid out on his back, until his head was clear. He rose to his feet and then slowly pulled her chair back until her knees were free. He helped her to her feet and she clutched his arms, as if her legs weren't strong enough to hold her up.

"I need you to get out of here. I still have to get rid of this thing."

"Come with me," she begged.

"Shh, it's okay." He pulled her close for a quick, reassuring hug, before he spoke into his radio. "The teacher is clear, I'm sending her out."

"Roger, Deck. Good work."

"Go now, and I'll be out shortly, okay?" He hated pushing her away, but he needed her to be safe.

She stumbled a bit but then managed to get out of the classroom under her own power.

After summoning Isaac inside to lend a hand, he shoved Tess's chair out of the way and peered beneath the desk. The device had been neutralized for the moment.

But until they'd safely taken it off the desk and placed it inside the cast-iron container, there was still a chance it could detonate.

Blowing him and everything around him to smithereens.

Tess shivered and rubbed her hands over her arms, chilled to the bone despite the warm September sunshine. She hadn't wanted to leave, not until she knew Declan and the rest of the SWAT team were safe. Thankfully, no one asked her to; in fact, they requested that she stay, explaining that she still needed to give a statement.

The parking area was deserted, although there were plenty of cops along the perimeter. She saw a flash of green out of the corner of her eye, and when she swung around to look, she glimpsed a man wearing a green baseball cap, brown shirt and blue jeans hurrying away. She stared for a moment, thinking he looked familiar, but then shrugged it off. No doubt, he'd been told to steer clear of the crime scene by one of the officers.

"What's taking so long?" she asked after a long thirty-five minutes had passed.

The guy in charge, who'd introduced himself as Griff Vaughn, barely spared her a glance. "They're trying to cut through your metal desk in order to remove the device. They need to get it inside the steel box for safe transport and disposal."

Logically, she understood what they needed to do, but she was still inwardly reeling from seeing Declan Shaw again. He looked different from the eighteen-year-old she remembered. Granted, he still had his dark brown hair and penetrating ice-blue eyes, but he was bigger, more muscular than before. And his face had matured, as well. Back when he was younger, he'd worn his dark hair long enough to brush his shoulders, but now it was cut military short, giving him a tough, no-nonsense look.

They'd been as completely opposite as two people could be, yet she felt oddly connected to him, just the same.

How ironic to meet him again in yet another circumstance where she needed to be rescued.

"They're coming out, boss."

"I see them. Caleb, get the woman out of here."

"Come on, ma'am," Caleb said, taking her arm.

She didn't want to leave the vicinity, but since she wasn't exactly given a choice, she allowed the tall, lean, dark-haired man to hustle her away. She glanced up at him, remembering the brief conversation between the guys, when Declan wanted someone to take her place. Caleb was the one who had just gotten remarried, and he had a young daughter. She found herself wondering what it was like for his wife to know he went into dangerous situations every day. She shivered and imagined it couldn't be easy.

"We're clear," Caleb said into his mic.

They were too far away for her to see much, but she shielded her eyes with her hand anyway, catching a glimpse of Declan and Isaac carefully carrying a large box between them as they stepped slowly across the school parking lot. They tucked the box inside the back of the armored truck and then shut the back doors.

The two men spoke for a few minutes before the sandy-haired one opened the driver's door and slid behind the wheel. Declan jogged over to where she and Caleb were waiting.

"Good job, Deck," Caleb said as he approached.

Declan brushed off the praise with a quick shrug and focused his intense gaze on her. "Tess, we need to talk."

This must be the part where she was to give her statement. She nodded and Declan took her arm, guiding her over to another sheriff's department vehicle parked in the shade of a tall maple tree that was just barely beginning to change colors in the warm autumn sun. She glanced over her shoulder, watching thankfully as the armored truck drove away with the bomb.

She slid into the backseat, feeling inexplicably nervous when Declan joined her. He turned sideways in the seat so he could face her.

"I need you to start at the beginning," Declan said as he pulled out his notebook.

Tess explained how the events transpired in the classroom before she inadvertently triggered the bomb.

"How often do you sit at your desk during the day?" he asked.

"Hardly ever," she admitted. "I tend to stand in front of the room and walk around as I'm teaching, but I do sit down for tests. And at noon, since I normally eat a bag lunch at my desk while grading papers."

He nodded, jotting down a few notes. "Do you have anyone who might be holding a grudge against you? A boyfriend? Maybe an ex-husband?"

She blushed and glanced down at her hands entwined in her lap. "No, I'm not seeing anyone and I've never been married."

"Tess, this is important," Declan persisted, his gaze serious. "I need you to tell me anything in your personal life that might be remotely connected to this."

She didn't understand what he was getting at. "What? Why?"

Declan paused for a moment. "I believe your desk was chosen on purpose. And if you're the target, we need to figure out what connection you have to the perp."

TWO

Tess instinctively wanted to protest, but the somber expression on Declan's face forced her to bite her tongue. She thought back over the past few months. Pathetic as it sounded, she led a boring, noneventful life. She volunteered at the church, playing piano for the choir, and couldn't imagine anyone who'd want to hurt her.

She didn't have any enemies that she was aware of. In fact, she couldn't even think of one single thing that she'd done to make anyone angry.

The thought that someone might have purposefully planted a bomb under her desk made her feel sick. She glanced at Declan, grateful to know she wasn't alone. Just like ten years ago, she felt safe with him sitting beside her.

"There isn't anyone I can think of," she said finally. "The last guy I dated was the vice principal of Greenland Middle School, but he moved last year to take a principal position down in Missouri. I'm sure Jeff would never do something like this."

"What's his full name?" Declan asked, a frown puckered in his brow.

She sighed. "Jeff Berg. And I'm telling you, he's not involved."

"How long were you two seeing each other?"

She grimaced, wondering if this interrogation was really necessary. "A little less than four months. We weren't engaged or anything. When he told me about the job offer, I was happy for him."

"You didn't want to follow him to Missouri?"

She crossed her arms over her chest, feeling defensive. Maybe she once had a silly schoolgirl crush on the younger version of Declan, especially after he'd saved her from that disastrous prom date with Steve Gains, but at the moment, she didn't much like the man he'd become. Declan was all business, determined to get to the bottom of whatever connection he thought she had to the person who'd planted the bomb under her desk. There wasn't a speck of personalization in his tone.

In that moment, he reminded her too much of her father. The thought was enough to get her ridiculous schoolgirl emotions back under control.

"No, I didn't. Are we finished now? I need to get back to my colleagues."

"We sent everyone home…there won't be any school for the rest of the week," Declan said bluntly. "But I'd be happy to take you home."

"I don't need a ride, I have my car here." She pushed open her door and slid out of the seat, determined to get away from Declan's overwhelming presence and clear her mind.

She didn't get very far, because within seconds he'd caught up with her, lightly grasping her arm. "Tess, wait."

She stopped and glared at him over her shoulder. "For what?"

"Just give me a few minutes, okay? Which car is yours?" he asked.

"The grayish blue Honda Civic parked beneath the large maple tree," she retorted. "Why? Don't tell me you think there's a bomb planted there, too?"

"I'm going to make sure there isn't," Declan answered grimly.

What? Tess gaped at him in shock. She hadn't been serious when she made that remark, but it was clear that Declan really believed she was in danger. As upset as she was with him, when he let go of her arm, she missed his warmth.

Tess folded her arms over her chest, feeling vulnerable and alone as Declan crossed over to talk to Caleb. The two of them jogged across the parking lot to where she'd left her car and dropped to the ground to search underneath it.

She didn't want to think that she was the target of some crazy bomber, but it was difficult not to be afraid when Declan so clearly believed she was.

Maybe Declan was just being overly cautious. She simply couldn't imagine what she'd done to cause someone to hate her enough to plant a bomb under her desk, risking not only her life but those of her students.

There had to be some mistake.

"I can't see much," Deck muttered, flashing his light across the undercarriage of Tess's car.

"The car is too close to the ground," Caleb agreed. "I can't even get my head under there, can you?"

He shook his head. "Nope. I can't see anything obvious, but we'll need to get it up on a ramp to be sure."

"Yeah, good plan," Caleb agreed.

Declan took one last look before he reluctantly rose to his feet. No way was he going to let Tess drive the vehicle until he was certain it was safe. He caught Caleb's gaze across the hood of her car. "Maybe we should send a team to check out her house, too."

His friend lifted an eyebrow. "You really think she's the target?"

Declan nodded, unable to explain the niggling sensation that told him he was on the right track. "I do. But I can't prove it, at least not yet."

Caleb let out a low whistle. "Good luck trying to get Griff to buy your theory."

"I know." Declan understood their boss dealt with facts, not feelings. "Although it doesn't really matter if he believes me, since he'll expect us to cover all possibilities as we investigate anyway. All I have to do is come up with a plan to keep Tess safe."

"Well, good luck with that, too," Caleb said, flashing him a wry grin.

Yeah, he already knew Tess wasn't going to like his idea of forcing her to go underground, but he wasn't going to accept no for an answer. Not when her life was potentially in danger.

As he walked closer to Tess, he couldn't seem to tear his gaze away from her. Even wearing her business casual teacher's attire—gray slacks paired with a bright pink sweater—she was more beautiful now than she'd been ten years ago, decked out in her fancy prom dress. Why on earth had that Jeff dude let her go so easily? Something didn't seem right with that scenario, and he silently promised himself to double-check the guy's whereabouts for the time frame in question.

"Did you find anything?" she asked, breaking into his thoughts.

He hated seeing the fear lurking in the depths of her amber eyes. "No, but we couldn't get underneath your car to really check things out."

"So now what?" she asked wearily. "I really need to get home."

He rubbed the back of his neck, wishing there was an easier way to get her to go along with his plan. "I'm going to take you to my place for a while," he said slowly. "Just until we can verify that your car and your home haven't been tampered with."

Her eyes widened. "I don't think so," she said firmly. "My younger brother gets out of school at three o'clock, and I intend to be home when he gets there."

"Your brother?" Now he was the one who was taken by surprise. "I didn't know you had a brother."

"Bobby is ten years younger than I am, so you wouldn't remember him," she explained. "He's a senior at Greenland High School."

Deck frowned. "And he lives with you and not your parents?"

She hesitated and then nodded. "My parents died in a car crash right after my college graduation. Bobby was only eleven, so I used my science degree to become a teacher and moved into my parents' home so he wouldn't have to switch schools."

He was impressed that she took on the responsibility of raising her brother, and that also explained why she didn't follow her dream to become a doctor. There'd be time to find out more about that later, because right now he needed to stay focused.

"Okay, then you can both come to stay at my place."

Declan understood Tess wasn't about to expose her brother to danger, and he didn't blame her. "At least until we know you're safe."

Tess sighed. "Look, I know you're being extra careful, and I do appreciate your concern, but I'm not at all convinced that I'm really in danger. Why is it so hard to believe this bomb was just as random as the other ones?"

"What makes you think the others were random?" Declan countered. "If my memory serves me correctly, you worked at the custard stand during high school. And I'm sure you stopped by the minimart at some point, too."

The way she dropped her gaze told him he was definitely on the right track.

"In fact, the more I think about it," he continued, "the more I'm convinced that you really are the target. And I plan to protect you while we figure out what connection you have to the mastermind behind the bombings."

Tess didn't like ultimatums, especially those given by a bossy, take-charge guy like Declan. He was crazy if he thought she was going to let him run her life.

She'd been taking care of herself and her younger brother just fine for the past six years. Jeff had tried to run her life, too, demanding she do things differently, which really meant *his way*. He'd specifically expected her to be stricter with Bobby which she refused to do. As a result, she'd broken things off with him a few weeks before he'd gotten his promotion. Jeff's moving away was a blessing in disguise as far as she was concerned.

She refused to believe she was a failure at being a parental role model. She knew firsthand what it was like growing up in a super strict household. Her father had controlled almost every aspect of her life and she'd refused to do the same thing with her brother. Granted, Bobby was going through a rebellious phase, but she didn't think his behavior was that much different than most teenagers'. Deep down, she knew her brother still loved her. Even if he didn't often show it.

"Tess?" The way Declan called her name made her realize she'd been lost in her thoughts.

"What? Oh, I'm not going home with you, Declan. I'll give you an hour to clear my car, and then I plan on picking up my brother and we'll go to a hotel if that makes you feel better."

She sensed he wanted to argue with her, but he gave a curt nod. "Fine, I'll agree with one minor change. You need to let me drive you to pick up your brother and take you both to a hotel, because I can't guarantee we'll be able to clear your car that fast."

"Deal. Where are you parked?" she asked, glancing around the area.

Her gaze fell on the man wearing the green baseball cap who was lingering near the maple tree where she'd parked her car. She narrowed her gaze, squinting against the sun. He had to be the same guy she saw earlier. And as before, she thought he seemed familiar. "Who is that guy?" she asked, talking more to herself than to Declan.

"Who?" Declan asked sharply.

"That man in the baseball cap standing near my car. I saw him earlier, too."

As if the guy in question could feel their gaze on him, he turned and disappeared behind the tree.

"Caleb!" Declan shouted, sprinting off after the guy. "Come on! We need to follow him."

"Who?" Caleb demanded as he ran after Declan.

Tess couldn't tear her gaze off the two men as they

raced toward the area where the stranger had disappeared. She was so intent on watching them that she didn't notice Griff Vaughn, Declan's boss, come up beside her.

"What's going on?" he demanded with a deep scowl.

"I saw a guy over there, the same one who was here earlier," she explained. "But I don't get why Declan is so concerned about him. I'm sure he's just some curious bystander who wants to know what's going on."

"Maybe, but sometimes criminals return to the scene of the crime because they like to watch the chaos they've caused."

"I never thought of that," Tess admitted with an involuntary shiver. She was about to tell Griff about how the guy seemed familiar, when she noticed Declan and Caleb were on their way back.

Their boss jogged over to meet them and the three of them spoke for several minutes before they all turned to face her.

Declan gestured for her to come over by him while Griff and Caleb headed over toward a large unmarked black van.

"I guess you didn't find him?" she asked as she approached Declan.

"No, but we want you to view the videotape of the scene to see if you can spot him for us," Declan explained.

"Video?" she echoed. "What kind of video?"

"Video surveillance of the crime scene, including anyone observing from the sidelines," Declan explained. "We routinely take several hours of film, just in case. We use the film from the media, too."

"Yes, your boss mentioned how criminals often return

to the scene to watch." She could barely comprehend this shocking new development, but she followed Declan to the back of the van. When he opened the doors, she was surprised to see the massive amount of technology that was located back there.

"Wow," she murmured. "I had no idea you had all this stuff going on."

Declan helped her inside. "Nate is a whiz with electronics," he said. "Do you have the video ready?" he asked.

"Sure thing, Deck." Nate Jarvis, a tall, lanky blond pulled up a stool and gestured for Tess to take a seat. "We're going to start at the beginning, and I want you to let me know if you see the guy you spotted just a few minutes ago."

Tess nodded, blinking to help her eyes adjust to the darker interior of the van. She leaned close, staring at the video screen full of dozens of people standing around the perimeter of the school parking lot, and tried to catch a glimpse of either the green ball cap or the guy's brown shirt. Of course he wore colors that blended in with the crowd and the trees.

For several long minutes no one said anything, and as much as she tried to stay focused on the videotape playing in front of her, she was far too conscious of Declan crouched beside her.

Ignore him, she told herself, keeping her eyes glued to the video screen. They were mere acquaintances, nothing more, a fact that suited her just fine.

She was so preoccupied she almost missed the brief flash of green. "There!" she said excitedly. "That might be him."

Nate fiddled with the controls, going backward to capture the image and then moving forward in slow motion. He froze the image. "Is this the guy?" he asked.

She gnawed on her lower lip, staring at the blurry figure. "Maybe, but the way he's looking down at the ground, I can't be positive."

"I can't seem to get a good image of this guy's face," his tech-savvy teammate muttered, going through several frames. "It's almost as if he knows we're videotaping the crowd."

"I think it's him, but maybe we should keep looking," Tess said, biting her lip.

"You're doing great," Declan murmured encouragingly. "Take your time."

She was glad he'd dropped the demanding tone. She continued watching the videotape but was disappointed when she didn't see the strange guy.

But then, just as the camera switched direction, she saw him. "There he is," she said urgently. "That's exactly when I saw him, too, as he was walking away from the area."

"Got him," Nate declared, freezing the image. "Too bad it's not his face, though. And it's hard to tell what color his hair is beneath that baseball cap."

"I know," Declan agreed.

"I'll see if I can keep working the images to make them sharper," his colleague said.

She glanced over her shoulder at Declan. "I remember thinking at the time that one of the cops must have told him to get lost," she admitted. "Do you think it's possible someone spoke to him?"

Declan shrugged. "We can ask," he murmured. "Although I don't know if anyone would remember him."

"How about if I print off a copy of the image?" Nate offered. "It's better than nothing at the moment."

"Sounds good."

Tess stared again at the indistinguishable figure, wishing she could pinpoint what seemed so familiar about the guy. Without seeing his face, it was impossible to guess his age. Was he one of Bobby's friends? Or a neighbor? Maybe Allan Gray, the rather odd neighbor who was always overly anxious to help her?

"Let's give this printout to Griff," Declan said. "He can ask all the cops here on the scene whether anyone else recognizes him."

Tess took Declan's offered hand to step down from the van, letting go as soon as she was on solid ground. Despite the jolt of awareness that had just sparked between them, she refused to give in to the schoolgirl crush she'd once had on him. Because, just as they had been back in high school, they were still two completely different people.

She couldn't afford a relationship, even if she wanted one, which she didn't. Maybe all men weren't as controlling as Jeff and her father, but Declan certainly seemed to be. Besides, she needed to stay focused on keeping her brother out of trouble. And that was truly a full-time job.

Declan walked up to his boss and handed over the photo. The two men spoke briefly, and Griff passed Declan a set of keys, before Declan turned back toward her. "Okay, we're clear to leave."

She smiled in relief. "Good."

"It's that SUV over there," Declan said, gesturing at the police vehicle that was parked closest to her car.

"You don't have assigned cars?" she asked as they headed across the parking lot.

"Yes, we do, and that's the one I normally drive, although today Sam Irving drove it here. Caleb agreed to give Sam a lift back."

"Are you sure all this is really necessary?" Tess asked.

Before Declan could respond, a ball of fire exploded in front of them, sending her stumbling backward. She hit the ground hard, moments before everything went black.

THREE

The force of the blast sent Declan flying backward against the pavement. The breath was knocked from his lungs and for a moment he couldn't draw in any air. Smoke filled the area around them, and pain reverberated through his body. After a few seconds his military survival instincts, along with a healthy dose of adrenaline, kicked in and he rolled over and belly crawled toward Tess, who was sprawled on the ground just a few feet away.

"Tess! Are you all right?"

She let out a low moan and lifted a hand to her head. "Hurts," she whispered.

"Stay down," he ordered, covering her body with his as much as possible. He had no way of knowing if the explosion was only a precursor to more violence or not, but he wasn't taking any chances.

Not when Tess's life was at stake.

"What happened?" she asked, her voice muffled against his chest.

"Another bomb," he said grimly, watching the SWAT members that were still on the scene disperse and cover the area, rifles held ready. He craned his neck in order to see behind him. A small fire still burned near the maple tree where Tess had seen the guy in the green ball cap.

Had that dude been the perp who'd set the bomb? Most likely, although Declan couldn't afford to ignore the possibility of the guy being nothing more than a curious onlooker, either. He'd try to keep an open mind even though the stranger was currently the best lead they had.

"I can't breathe," Tess gasped, pushing against his chest.

"Sorry." He shifted a bit so that he wasn't quite crushing her, but he wasn't willing to move away completely until he knew the area was clear.

"Deck, are you and Tess all right?" Caleb asked, coming over to kneel beside them.

"I think we're okay. Are you sure the area is secure?" He was only slightly reassured that he hadn't heard the sound of gunfire.

"So far there's no sign of anyone or any other devices," Caleb told him. "We need to get you both out of here, though. How badly are you hurt? We have an ambulance on the way."

Declan pushed himself upright but hovered protectively over Tess. "I'm fine," he assured Caleb. "Tess, where do you hurt?"

"Everywhere," she admitted with a grimace. She struggled to sit upright, and Declan eased his arm around her shoulders to offer support. The way she leaned heavily against him made him realize she might be hurt worse than he suspected.

"Take it easy," he murmured. "Did you hit your head?"

Tess put her hand to the back of her head. "Yes, I might have blacked out for a moment or two. I can feel a lump, but there doesn't seem to be any bleeding."

Declan battled back a wave of fury. That had been way too close. Tess could have been seriously injured by the blast. And this latest turn of events only convinced him more that she was the specific target.

"Come on, let's get her to safety," Caleb urged.

Declan was totally on board with that plan. He helped get Tess up and on her feet and with Caleb's assistance, walked her over to the back of the van where Nate had opened the doors for them.

"Sit down, Tess," he instructed. "Do you have a first aid kit handy?" he asked Nate. "She could use an ice pack."

"I'm fine," she said. "I'm sure you have a few bumps and bruises, too."

He did, but that was a by-product of his job. Tess was a fourth grade schoolteacher, and he was fairly certain she wasn't accustomed to being thrown off her feet by a bomb.

Nate handed him the ice pack and he quickly twisted the bag to activate the coolant inside and gently pressed it against the back of Tess's head. Despite her earlier protest, she put her hand back there to help hold the ice pack in place.

"Just relax, I'll hold it for you," he told her.

"Did you notice that both your SUV and Tess's car were damaged by the explosion?" Caleb asked in a low tone. "The maple tree was knocked over, too."

"Yeah, I did. And I don't believe in coincidences. I need to get Tess someplace safe."

"I'm not going anywhere without my brother," she said, joining the conversation.

"I know, we'll take him with us," Declan promised.

The wailing sound of a siren indicated the local authorities and the ambulance were getting closer. He appreciated the additional backup, but at the same time, he wanted nothing more than for Tess to get the medical care she needed and then to get her out of there.

Before the bomber made yet another attempt on Tess's life.

Ignoring the pounding inside her head wasn't easy, but Tess knew that was the only way she could avoid going to the hospital. She stared down at her trembling fingers, and did her best to remain calm even though she was still reeling from being so close to the explosion.

Dear Lord, thank You for keeping me and Declan safe from harm. And please watch over Bobby, too. Amen.

"Tess? Is something wrong?"

Declan's concern was touching, but she knew that she couldn't keep leaning on him for support like this. They were just temporary allies. As soon as he had her safely tucked away, she knew that he'd go back to his SWAT team, leaving her and Bobby alone.

"I'm fine, but I'm anxious to see my brother."

"First we need the EMTs to check you out…you said yourself that you blacked out for a minute."

"I said I *may* have blacked out for a minute, or it could be that my brain simply shut down for a moment, from the shock of the explosion." She didn't appreciate his using her own words against her. "It's not like I find myself in harm's way like this very often."

"I know, but you could have a concussion. Give me a little more time here, okay?"

As if she had a choice. The only reason she wasn't pushing the issue right now was that Bobby was in school, surrounded by teachers and dozens of kids. He'd be fine there until she could get there to pick him up. At least she was fairly certain he'd be fine.

She winced at the shrillness of the siren as the ambulance pulled up. Within moments two EMTs had taken up residence on either side of her.

"Anyone else injured?" one of them asked.

"No, just Tess. She has a lump on the back of her head," Declan said, removing the ice pack so they could examine her.

"We were both knocked off our feet," Tess felt compelled to point out. "You should check him for injuries, too."

"I'm not hurt," Declan said firmly.

Stubborn man, she thought, as the EMTs poked and prodded at her. They took a set of vital signs and asked her dozens of questions to make sure her brain hadn't been knocked off-kilter. She scowled, knowing there was a very good chance that Declan had a bump on the back of his head, too.

"We should take her to Trinity Medical Center to have a CT scan of her brain, just to make sure there's no internal bleeding," the EMT on her right said.

"Okay," Declan agreed.

"No, I don't want to go to the hospital." She glared at Declan, trying to get him to drop the idea. "I'm sure I'll be fine."

"There's no need to be nervous," Declan told her. "CT scans don't hurt and we'll still have time afterward to pick up your brother."

There was that commanding tone again, and just hearing it made the hairs on the back of her neck stand up. Why did so many men like to give orders? Why did everything have to be done their way? "Have you ever been to the E.R. at Trinity?" she asked in exasperation. "Getting cleared could take hours and be a complete waste of time. I'm not going, end of discussion."

Declan wasn't happy with her decision, and neither were the two EMTs.

"You'll have to sign a release form," the guy on her left informed her. He placed a metal clipboard in her lap and handed her a pen. "Sign here," he instructed. "This means you can't come after us if you suffer a massive head bleed later."

She sensed he was trying to scare her with that comment, so she ignored it, signed her name and handed the clipboard back to him.

"Do you have another ice pack in there? This one is already getting warm," Declan said. "I'd like to try to keep the swelling down."

"Sure." The EMT took a prefilled ice pack out of his kit and gave it to him. Once again, Declan applied it to the lump on the back of her head.

She was tempted to tell him to use the ice pack on himself, but held her tongue. No sense in antagonizing Declan now, not until they'd picked up Bobby from school.

And by then, she'd be glad to see the last of Declan Shaw for a while.

"Hey, Deck, you need to come over here and see this."

Declan glanced over at Caleb and nodded. "Sure. Nate, will you keep an eye on Tess for a few minutes?"

"I don't need a babysitter," Tess muttered.

"No problem," the other man said.

Declan wished there was a way to force Tess to go to the hospital, but since she signed herself out of the EMTs' care, he didn't think there was much more he could do. Her stubbornness might have been cute if it wasn't so annoying.

He headed over to where Caleb waited. Together they canvassed the scene of the explosion. The fire had been doused by the members of his team, but the burned-out area looked awful, especially with the maple tree being uprooted by the force of the blast.

"I think the center of the explosion was in this area here," Caleb said, pointing to the blackened area. "The perp must have covered it with leaves and branches or we would have seen it."

Declan nodded thoughtfully, agreeing with Caleb's assessment. "We went right past this area to chase the guy with the green baseball cap."

"I know. It's possible he set the bomb and then took off running," Caleb mused. "But he took a chance...what if we had caught him and brought him back this way? He risked blowing himself up at that point."

"I know, but we still need to find that guy, which would be much easier to do if we had a face shot."

"Nate is going to work on enhancing the image, so maybe we'll at least be able to get a hair color as an identifier."

Declan scowled. Knowing the guy's hair color wouldn't help them much. "All right. Anything else here that might give us a clue?"

Caleb shook his head. "Not yet. We'll keep looking, but right now it's appearing to be more of a crime of opportunity than a planned attack."

"Putting the bomb under Tess's desk seems to have been a definite plan, but I'm not so sure that the custard stand or the minimart bombings were thought out the same way. Who is this creep and why does he like setting off bombs?"

"I don't know, but we'll find him." Caleb's tone radiated confidence.

Declan wished he could say the same. Oh, he knew they'd find the guy eventually, but how many other casualties would there be before that happened?

"I'm going to drive Tess over to the high school to pick up her brother," he told Caleb. "I'll be in touch later."

"Sounds good."

Declan crossed over to his boss and arranged for a different vehicle to use for a couple of hours. Griff handed over a set of keys and he took them gratefully before heading back over to Tess, happy to see she was standing up under her own power.

"Are you finally ready to go?" she asked.

"Yeah, the boss gave us his wheels to use. Right over here," he said, heading toward one of the other SUVs on the scene.

"How on earth do you tell them apart?" she asked when he opened the door for her.

"No big secret, we go by the license plate numbers." He closed the passenger door and then went around and slid into the driver's seat. "We'll pick up your brother and get you both settled into a hotel, okay?"

"Okay." Tess seemed resigned to spending the next hour or so in his company, and if he was interested in some sort of relationship, his ego might have been bruised by her lack of enthusiasm.

But he had no intention of getting personally involved, especially not with a woman like Tess Collins. She was the type who would want a family, and that wasn't for him. His father had been an angry drunk, lashing out with his fists if Declan didn't move fast enough. He knew exactly what genes were in his DNA, and he wasn't about to tempt fate.

Besides, ten years ago, after he'd rescued her from that jerk of a prom date, all he could think of was kissing her, but instead she'd told him she'd pray for him. Really? Not that he didn't appreciate her intent, but still, what did he know about church and prayer?

Not one thing.

And he really had no interest in finding out. Caleb might have joined the church thanks to his wife Noelle's influence, but Declan wasn't about to follow along.

Tess didn't say much as he drove into the parking lot of Greenland High, but he noticed she scanned the cars as if looking for someone. "What kind of car does Bobby drive?" he asked as he parked in the visitor lot.

"A used blue GMC truck. It's about ten years old."

Declan filed that information away for future reference. They walked up to the front entrance and stepped inside the school. Tess headed for the office and he followed, thinking about all the time he'd spent in the principal's office back when he was a student. Not some of his fonder memories, that's for sure.

"Hi, Mrs. Beckstrom, I need to see Bobby Collins," Tess said.

"There's a bit of a family emergency," he added, when Mrs. Beckstrom frowned, obviously put out at taking a student out of class in the middle of the day.

The secretary took one look at his uniform and nodded her agreement. "Of course. I'll see if I can find him."

But when the secretary returned a few minutes later, she wasn't smiling. "I'm sorry but Bobby isn't in the cafeteria. He must have left the campus for lunch. I'm afraid you'll have to wait until he returns."

"All right, what time does his next class start?" Tess asked.

"Twelve-fifteen. He has the early lunch period."

"Would you please call my cell number if he returns before we get back?" Declan asked. He took out one of his cards and handed it to her.

"All right," the secretary agreed.

"Thank you," Tess said before turning away.

They walked out of the office and headed back outside. Declan glanced at her. "Do you have any idea where Bobby spends his lunch hour?"

Tess shook her head. "Not really. I forgot that seniors were given the option of leaving the school grounds during lunch. So, as far as I know, he could be anywhere."

"What about Greenland Park?" Declan asked.

Her spine went stiff, and he mentally smacked himself. Of course Tess wouldn't want to go to Greenland Park considering that was where her idiot prom date had tried to assault her.

He was about to tell her never mind when she abruptly agreed. "All right, let's check out the park."

"Are you sure?"

"Yes. We have almost twenty minutes before Bobby is due back in class. We may as well see if we can find him on our own."

Tess walked back to the truck, and the dejected stoop of her shoulders bothered him. The events of the morning were obviously catching up to her, especially if her head was pounding the way his was. But he knew she wasn't going to be able to relax until she was reunited with her brother.

"It would be easier if I had my cell phone," Tess muttered. "But it sounded as if your boss wasn't letting anyone back inside the school yet."

"Sorry, but we'll get your personal items as soon as possible," he assured her.

Greenland Park wasn't very far from the high school, which was why the students liked to hang out there. He wound his way along the parkway, and when he saw a blue GMC truck parked along the side of the road, he gestured at it. "Is that Bobby's?"

Tess slowly shook her head. "No, his is a much older model. I don't remember the entire license plate number, but it starts with three letters *UTS*."

He nodded, knowing that it was a long shot that they'd even find Bobby here. It took almost ten minutes to circle the park and then from there, he decided to take a quick drive past the local fast food joints that were close to the high school.

"I don't see his truck anywhere," Tess said, rubbing a spot along her temple. "Where could he be?"

He glanced at his watch. "It's almost a quarter after twelve now. Maybe we missed him. Your brother is probably already back at the high school."

"I sure hope you're right." Hearing the worry clearly evident in her tone, he frowned as he drove back toward the high school. Was there something more going on here? Was Bobby the type that might skip school, or who'd been hanging out with the wrong crowd? When the time was right, he planned to get more intel on her brother. By the time he'd parked the car, it was close to twelve twenty-five. His cell phone rang as he was about to open his door.

"Hello, is this Deputy Shaw?"

"Yes," he said, recognizing the school secretary's tone. "Do you have Bobby Collins there with you?"

"No, that's why I'm calling. Bobby never returned to his fifth-hour English class."

"I see. Will you please call me as soon as he does show up?" Declan asked, feeling Tess's concerned gaze boring into him. "Thanks."

"He's not there?" she asked, her voice rising in panic.

"No, Bobby didn't report to his English class. Tess, is it possible he skipped school?"

She stared at him. "I can't say for absolute certainty that he didn't skip on his own accord, but I don't think it's likely. Bobby knows he's on probation this semester, and he promised me he wouldn't ditch school. Believe it or not, he really wants to graduate."

He couldn't deny the sincerity of her tone. "Then where could he be?"

"I don't know," Tess whispered. "But, Declan, what if this crazy guy who's after me somehow got to Bobby first? What if he plans to use my brother as a way to get to me?"

Declan wanted to reassure Tess that it wasn't possible, but he couldn't lie to her.

Obviously anyone who wanted to hurt Tess would know she had a younger brother, one she'd raised for the past few years.

Finding Bobby just might lead them to the mastermind behind the bombings. He could only hope and pray they wouldn't be too late.

FOUR

Tess couldn't bear to think of Bobby being in danger because of her. He was seventeen, old enough to take care of himself, but not if he trusted the wrong people.

And how could he protect himself from a bomb?

"I need to get home," she said, straightening in her seat. "Right now."

"Tess, it's not safe for you to go home," Declan pointed out. "There have been two attempts on your life already."

"But that's the first place Bobby will go," she argued. Was he really going to just sit there and tell her what to do? She opened her passenger-side door. "Listen, I'm going home with or without your help. So what will it be? Should I get out and call a taxi? Or will you take me home?"

Declan blew out a heavy breath. "I'll call the guys from the SWAT team to meet us out there. We need to make sure there aren't any more surprises."

The thought of a bomb being planted inside her home made her stomach churn. All the more reason to get home before Bobby did, she told herself. She closed her door with a swift thud. "Go ahead and call them, but hurry. We need to get there before anyone else."

She listened as Declan called his fellow SWAT officers to arrange for them to search her property. She was surprised Declan still knew her address from the night he'd rescued her all those years ago and had taken her home in his beat-up truck, not unlike the one she'd purchased for Bobby. Declan finished his call and then put the truck in Reverse so he could back out of the parking spot.

"I really wish I had my cell phone," Tess murmured. "It could be that Bobby is trying to call me right now."

"Do you want to call him from my phone?" Declan offered.

She nodded and took his smart phone, quickly dialing Bobby's number. Of course her brother didn't answer, probably because he didn't recognize the strange number. Still, she left him a message, instructing him to call her back on Declan's phone.

Discouraged, she stared at the screen, trying to ignore the pounding headache she had, as Declan drove her home. He pulled up in front of her house and parked along the quiet, tree-lined street. When she moved to get out of the car, he caught her arm. "We have to wait for the SWAT team to clear your house first."

After everything that had happened that morning, she knew he was smart to be cautious, and tried to find comfort in the fact that she didn't see Bobby's truck in the driveway.

However, she did notice her neighbor Allan Gray coming out of his house to stand on his front porch, openly staring at Declan's police vehicle.

"Who's that guy?" Declan asked with a frown.

Before she could answer, Allan came striding toward them. "Are you okay, Tess?" he asked, peering at her through the passenger window.

This time, Declan didn't stop her when she pushed open her passenger side door. In fact, he climbed out of the vehicle, too, and came around to greet her neighbor.

"I'm fine, Allan," she said, forcing a smile. "How are you doing today?"

He bobbed his head and glanced nervously over at Declan, who still wore his work uniform. "I'm fine, Tess, but why is there a police officer with you?"

"Hi, my name is Declan Shaw." Greeting Allan causally, he stepped forward to shake the man's hand. "I'm a friend of Tess's."

Tess wondered why Declan was using the friend routine instead of grilling Allan about where he was earlier that day. Allan Gray was a nice guy roughly about her age. As far as she knew he'd never been married, although he did have a full-time job working as a night-shift security guard for the local hospital. Today he was dressed in his usual baggy jeans and striped button-down shirt with a white T-shirt underneath. Allan was generally a nice guy, constantly offering to help Tess out, but she always felt as if she was walking a fine line around him. She wanted to be a nice friendly neighbor, but she also didn't want to give Allan the impression she was interested in anything more than a platonic friendship. She couldn't help thinking that he might not be emotionally stable, although he hadn't done anything to truly make her uncomfortable.

"Allan, have you seen my brother, Bobby, today?" she asked in an effort to distract him from the fact that Declan had driven her home.

"Yes, I saw him this morning, Tess," Allan said, always anxious to please. He bobbed his head again, a weird mannerism that tended to drive her a little crazy. "He left for school about fifteen minutes before you did."

She tried to smile, even though the fact that Allan was clearly watching her way closer than she'd realized gave her the creeps. "But you haven't seen him since then, right?"

"No, I haven't seen him. Is there a problem, Tess?" Allan's attention was centered on her, as if Declan weren't standing right there beside her. "Do you need me to help you look for him?"

"There's no problem at all," Declan spoke up. "But thanks for your help, Allan. I'm glad you're keeping an eye on things here. Have you seen anything out of the ordinary this morning?"

Allan frowned. "What do you mean?"

"You haven't seen any strangers lurking around Tess's house, have you?" Declan asked. "Or noticed any vehicles that don't belong here?"

"Your vehicle doesn't belong here," Allan said in a blunt tone. "But other than that, no, I haven't noticed anything unusual."

"Okay, thanks. Here's my card. You can call me day or night if you detect something strange."

"I will." Allan took Declan's business card, looking a bit flustered. Tess knew Declan was trying to make a statement, basically warning Allan that he'd be nearby if anything happened. She only hoped Allan was savvy enough to understand Declan's subtle message.

Their brief conversation was interrupted by the arrival of several SWAT vehicles. The way Allan's jaw dropped in shock when he saw them made her grimace.

"What's going on?" Allan asked anxiously.

"It's nothing, really. They just want to go through my

house to make sure it's safe. Don't worry, I'm sure they won't find anything amiss."

Declan walked over to meet with the other members of his team, leaving her with Allan. She tried not to compare the two, but Declan was so much taller and broader across the shoulders than Allan, it was difficult not to notice.

Not that she was interested in Declan on a personal level. He reminded her too much of her father, who had been the city mayor for almost twenty years. With her father, everything was about control and image. Serving the public was admirable, but the way her father used to yell, often made her wonder if he'd used her as a way to let off steam from the pressures of his job.

Her mother had never stood up to him, either.

She shook off the painful memories, focusing instead on Declan and his team, who'd entered her house.

"What are they looking for?" Allan asked.

She glanced at him in surprise. "Surely you've heard about the bomb that was discovered at the elementary school? I imagine it was all over the news."

An odd expression filtered across his face, but then he nodded. "Oh, yes, it was. Terrible, just terrible." Allan reached out to pat her arm awkwardly. "I'm glad you're okay, Tess, that was a close call."

A shiver of icy trepidation ran down her spine as she stared at her geeky neighbor. Close call? Did Allan know that her desk was the one where the bomb was planted? Declan had led her to believe that the details of the investigation would not be revealed to the press.

Had Allan been the guy she'd seen hanging around the parking lot? The man had seemed familiar but now that she was looking at Allan, she didn't think so.

It could be that Allan was just making that statement

because she'd been in the school, not because he knew that the bomb had been planted beneath her desk. Yet she couldn't quite shake off the feeling of unease. Even though she knew it was highly unlikely that Allan had been involved, she was all too aware that she didn't feel safe standing out here without Declan.

"First floor is clear," Isaac said, meeting Declan in the kitchen.

"Agreed. Let's split up between the basement and the second floor," he directed.

"All right. Caleb and I will go down, leaving you and Nate to take the second level."

Declan acknowledged the plan with a curt nod and headed upstairs. He automatically went to the left, leaving Nate to check the rooms on the right. There were three bedrooms and one office upstairs, and since Tess kept everything neat and orderly, it didn't take them long to canvass the second level.

"Basement is clear!" Isaac shouted.

"Same goes for the second floor," Nate added.

"Which just leaves the grounds," Declan said. "Let's sweep the yard, just to be sure."

No one argued, and he suspected the bomb planted near the maple tree was fresh in their minds.

When Declan went out the front door, he noticed that Tess had made her way closer to the cluster of sheriff's department vehicles parked in her driveway. Was it his imagination or was she trying to get away from Allan Gray?

He kept his gaze focused on doing his job, but as soon as the team had finished checking the yard, he hurried over to Tess. "Everything is fine," he assured her.

"Good to know," she said softly. "Can I go inside now?"

Declan nodded, unwilling to say too much in front of her weird neighbor.

"See you later, Allan," Tess said, before turning away. Declan gave the guy a quick nod and then followed her inside.

"You can't stay here, Tess," he said the minute he'd shut the door behind him. "Just because we didn't find a bomb doesn't mean that you'll be safe here."

"You already said that, Declan," she responded testily. "I just want to see if there's any indication Bobby has been here since this morning, okay?"

Declan sensed he was skating on thin ice and tried to stay back, giving her plenty of room. Tess had been through a lot today, not to mention being worried about her missing brother. He knew better than to take her tense mood personally.

She disappeared upstairs and he stood in the living room, noticing how the side window gave a clear view of Allan's house.

Did the guy watch Tess on a regular basis? Did he have a pair of binoculars that he used to spy on her? Declan couldn't explain why he didn't like him. After all, Gray hadn't done anything overt, although he *had* admitted to watching Bobby and Tess leave earlier this morning.

Declan made a mental note to do a thorough background check on Allan Gray as soon as possible. Maybe he was overreacting, but it was clear to him that the guy was a bit obsessed with Tess.

But if the nosy neighbor was interested in Tess, why would he try to hurt her?

Declan didn't have an answer to that question, but

that didn't mean the guy didn't have something to hide, either. He glanced at his watch, realizing Tess had been upstairs for a long time. Despite promising himself he'd give her some space, he found himself taking the stairs two at a time, to get to the second floor.

"Tess? Is everything okay?" he called.

For several long seconds there was no response, and he had taken several steps toward her bedroom when she emerged carrying a small suitcase.

"Why wouldn't everything be okay?" she asked, stopping short when she saw him standing there.

Declan felt stupid for worrying. What was wrong with him? Hadn't he already checked the house and deemed it safe at least in the short term?

"I'll take your suitcase for you," he offered.

She handed it over and then brushed past him to precede him down the stairs. "I want to leave a note on the door for Bobby, because I'm sure he'll come looking for me."

"All right." He followed her back down to the main level, setting the suitcase beside the door while she disappeared into the kitchen to write her brother a note.

He couldn't help smiling when she chose a neon-green sheet of paper for her message, taping it to the front door where it could be easily seen from the driveway.

Isaac crossed over to meet them. "We'll be clearing both your vehicle and hers next, Deck. I'll let you know as soon as we're finished."

"Thanks." He clapped Isaac on the back and watched as the rest of his team made their way back to their vehicles. Then he turned to Tess. "All set?" he asked, taking the suitcase over to his car. He glanced over his shoulder, half expecting to see Allan Gray peering at them through his window.

"I guess," Tess murmured, in a less than enthusiastic tone. "I really hope Bobby contacts me soon."

He nodded, hoping for her sake that her brother would get in touch with her. The fact that they hadn't found anything at her house reassured him that the kid had probably skipped school on his own, rather than being a target for the bomber.

"Can I borrow your phone again?" Tess asked. "I'd like to send Bobby a text message."

"Sure." He handed over his phone, keeping his attention on the road. "We could stop and pick you up a new phone."

"Really?" The spark of hope in her eyes made him feel like a jerk for not thinking of this option sooner. "That would be a huge relief."

"No problem."

It didn't take long to stop at her wireless carrier store and upgrade her current phone to a new one. When they exchanged phone numbers, he was relieved to have a way of getting in touch with her.

"So, where are we going?" she asked once they were settled back in his vehicle.

"There's a small hotel called the Forty Winks, not far from where I live. Their rates are very reasonable, and the place is clean." He remembered the location from a while ago when Caleb had been on the run, trying to clear his name. Caleb, Noelle and his daughter, Kaitlin, had stayed there for a night, and he figured if it was good enough for Noelle, it should be okay for Tess.

"As long as it's not too far from my house, then I'm fine," she said.

Fifteen minutes later, he pulled up in front of the hotel and shut off the engine. Tess slid out of her seat, heading inside the lobby, but he stopped her with a hand on her arm.

"Tess, I think it's best if I pay for the room."

She scowled and shook her head. "I'd rather pay my own way."

"It's not about paying your way, it's about keeping you safe," he said, unable to contain his exasperation. "Please don't argue about this. Don't you understand that I don't want anyone to know where you are?"

Her gaze clashed with his for several long seconds. "Fine," she grumbled. "But I think you're being overly cautious."

"Thank you." He pulled her suitcase out of the back and then followed her into the lobby. The woman behind the counter agreed to take cash for the room, probably because of his cop uniform, but insisted on having a credit card on file in case there was any damage.

Tess's room was on the second floor. When she used her key to open the door, he was glad the place didn't smell old and musty. "Thanks, Declan," she said, when he swung her suitcase onto the bed.

"Stay safe, Tess. I'll get in touch with you as soon as possible."

"I'll be fine," she reiterated.

He hesitated, not liking the thought of leaving her here alone. If it wasn't for the fact that his boss was waiting for him to report back, he'd take her out to lunch.

His phone rang, and he suppressed a sigh when he saw that Griff was calling. "I'm on my way," he said in lieu of a greeting.

"You better be," his boss said in a gruff tone. "The FBI is here and they want to talk to you."

He couldn't hide his surprise. "We've been keeping them updated on the investigation, and they've admitted they don't think the bombs are related to terrorism. Have they changed their mind?"

"Not that I know of, but apparently they want to talk to you. So get back here, now."

"I'll be there in ten," Declan promised. He disconnected from the call and glanced at Tess. "I have to go, but you need to know that the FBI has been involved in this since we discovered the first bomb, and they may want to interview you."

She nodded grimly. "All right, let me know."

Declan had the insane urge to give her a reassuring hug, so he stepped back toward the door. "Remember, don't open for anyone but me."

"Or Bobby," she added.

"Call me if you need anything." He told himself to stop procrastinating and to leave already. After all, his boss and the FBI were waiting.

But leaving Tess wasn't easy, and he silently promised to return as soon as he'd fulfilled his SWAT duties.

Tess stared at the door, long after Declan had left her alone in the hotel room. Ridiculous to miss him when he'd been gone all of two minutes.

She gave herself a mental shake and quickly unpacked her small suitcase. She found a small bottle of over-the-counter painkillers and took a few, hoping that her headache would start to feel better. Then she sat on the edge of the bed, feeling as if she should be doing something to find Bobby.

But what could she do without a car? She could call for a taxi, that's what. Actually she'd rather rent a car, but that wouldn't work until she had her driver's license back. She made a mental note to make sure Declan returned her personal items from the school, before she used her brand-new smartphone to search for taxi services.

Twenty minutes later, she left her hotel room and went down to wait for the taxi to arrive. She was glad to have found her spare stash of cash back at the house, or she'd be totally dependent on Declan for everything.

"Where to?" the cabbie asked in a thick New York accent. She wondered why he'd moved to Wisconsin from New York.

"Jackson Park, it's on the corner of Elmhurst and Morrow."

The cabbie looked confused for a moment but then shrugged. "Okay, lady, it's your dime."

She clipped on her seat belt, staring through the window as they approached Jackson Park. There were batting cages there, and she knew Bobby used to go there when he was still playing for the Greenland High baseball team.

It was a long shot, but she couldn't think of where else her brother might be hanging out.

The cabbie pulled up to the entrance of the park, and she asked him to wait for her while she checked out the area. He didn't seem happy but reluctantly nodded.

She ran up to the batting cages, sweeping her gaze around the parking lot to see if she could spot Bobby's truck. There wasn't any sign of the truck or of Bobby himself, when she went from one batting cage to the next.

Discouraged, she returned to the taxi. She wasn't surprised he'd kept the meter running and she gave him the address of another park, one on the other side of the city.

But Bobby wasn't there, either. She had the cabbie swing by the school one last time, before heading back to the hotel. Eighty-five dollars later, she still hadn't found her brother.

As she used the key card to unlock her door, her new phone rang. When she glanced at the screen, her heart leaped with excitement when she recognized Bobby's number.

"Hello? Bobby?" she answered quickly.

"Tess?"

She gripped the phone tightly, as the rest of the message was garbled from a bad connection. And then the line went dead.

"No!" She quickly punched the redial button, hoping to catch her brother, but the call went straight to voice mail. She tried over and over again, but each time the call went to voice mail.

The brief connection to her brother had been severed.

And she still had no idea if Bobby was safe, or being held against his will.

She sat on the edge of the bed, staring at her phone, her eyes filling with helpless tears.

Please, Lord, please keep Bobby safe in Your care!

FIVE

Declan strove for patience as FBI agents Stuart Walker and Lynette Piermont asked him a series of questions. The same questions they'd barraged him with the last time he disarmed the bomb that had been planted beneath the counter of the custard stand. His boss, Griff Vaughn, sat beside him, a stern expression on his face.

He knew he didn't have anything to feel guilty about, but he couldn't help feeling as if he were the one on trial, instead of the perp who'd set all the bombs.

"Tell us again how you disarmed the device," Agent Walker said.

Declan suppressed a sigh. "First I found and removed all the dummy wires. Then I clipped the wire that was associated with the timer. From there, I cut the wire leading to the explosive."

"How did you know which wires to clip?" Agent Walker asked.

He shrugged and spread his hands. "I don't know what to tell you other than I seem to have a knack for defusing bombs."

"Deputy Shaw, don't you think it's odd that you always seem to know how to disarm these devices?" Agent

Walker asked, leaning forward. "After all, your fellow SWAT team member James Carron lost his life when he tried to disarm the bomb at the minimart."

Declan reined in his temper with considerable effort. "That was the same explosion that put my sister in the hospital, too, remember? I don't like what you're insinuating. So what if I happen to be good at disarming bombs? It's an uncanny gift and I don't see anyone else complaining."

Griff crossed his arms over his chest and scowled at the FBI agents. "Are you accusing one of my deputies of committing a crime?" he asked.

"No, of course not," Agent Lynette Piermont said in a consoling tone. "But you have to admit, it's a little strange that Deputy Shaw always manages to disarm these devices."

"Except for the one that went off today that nearly killed him," Griff Vaughn pointed out. "Or maybe you think that was just a ruse to derail the investigation?"

Declan appreciated his boss's support, although he was annoyed to be put in a position to need it. He tried to keep his tone even and nondefensive. "We have a suspect that was identified at the crime scene and that very likely set the bomb that caused damage to my vehicle as well as to Ms. Collin's car. We have videotape of this perp being there as well, and our crime scene tech is working to identify this man. So if you're not going to help us solve this series of crimes, then maybe you should leave us alone so we can get back to work." He didn't care that his tone bordered on rudeness.

"I agree with my deputy," Griff said. "Do you have anything besides allegations to contribute to our investigation? Because, if not, this interview is over."

"Do you have any reason to suspect that these bombings are related to terrorist activities?" Agent Piermont asked.

"No, we don't," Declan said. "I believe this is the work of someone who wants to be the center of attention. Someone who is choosing his targets because they mean something personally to him. I believe this perp is from the area."

The two agents exchanged a knowing look. Because they believed him? Or because he was from the area himself? It took every ounce of willpower to keep from lashing out in anger. How dare they insinuate he might be a suspect?

"Anything else?" Griff asked. "Because I need to debrief with my team."

"That's all for now," Agent Walker said, rising slowly to his feet. "But we'll need to be kept in the loop on your investigation. I'd like a progress report by the end of the day."

Griff grunted in what could have been an agreement or something else entirely.

Declan glanced at his boss after the two federal agents left the room. "Do you honestly believe I had something to do with this?"

"Of course not," Griff said wearily. "They're just mad that you've managed to disarm so many of these devices. And they're itching to get their hands into our investigation, which they really can't if there isn't any link to Homeland Security or say a bigger target than just these few local events. Forget about the feds for now, and let's concentrate on working this case."

Declan felt a little better, although the pall of being a suspect wouldn't go away. Was this how his buddy

Caleb had felt when everyone suspected him of being a murderer? Declan couldn't even begin to imagine being tossed in jail. He took a deep breath and gathered his scattered thoughts. "I have a couple of potential suspects that I'd like to follow up on, Allan Gray and Jeff Berg. Both have connections to Tess—one is a former boyfriend and the other is a neighbor who clearly has a crush on her."

"All right, anything else?"

Declan shook his head. "Not so far. We cleared her house, and according to Caleb and Isaac, her vehicle is clean, too. Her car suffered some cosmetic damage, but it still runs."

"What about your vehicle?" Griff asked.

"Not good. The engine didn't start, so Isaac and Caleb had it towed to the garage."

Griff sighed heavily and scrubbed his hands over his face. "The sheriff isn't going to like the negative impact on the budget."

Declan understood where his boss was coming from, but what could he say? They had no way of knowing that another bomb had been planted so close to the parking lot. It was just bad luck that his truck had taken the brunt of the blast.

"I'm sorry, I'll use whatever car you assign."

"Come with me to my office. I'll see what's available." Griff rose to his feet and made his way through the building to the other side of the office area. After shuffling through a stack of paperwork, Griff found the list. "Take 7918. It should be ready to roll."

"Thanks." For a moment he almost felt sorry for his boss; dealing with the massive amount of paperwork that government agencies demanded couldn't be easy. And

Griff was a huge step up from their former boss who'd tried to frame Caleb for murder.

"Get me the background information on your two suspects as soon as possible," Griff added. "I'll need to include them in my report to the feds."

"Yes, sir." Declan escaped his boss's office and went to his own cubicle to log on to the computer. He decided to run a background check on Allan Gray first, and was almost disappointed that he didn't find anything more than a couple of traffic violations.

Same thing happened when he ran the background check on Jeff Berg. He scowled and drummed his fingers on the desktop. Just because they didn't have criminal backgrounds didn't mean they weren't guilty.

He performed an internet search on Allan Gray and soon discovered that Gray actually graduated from Greenland High School the same year he had. Declan sat back in his chair for a moment, surprised by the information. What were the odds?

He stared at the photo on the screen, trying to remember back to his high school years. Declan had run with a group of troublemakers, while Allan looked to be the studious, chess club type.

No matter how hard he tried, Declan couldn't remember a single interaction with Gray, good or bad. He'd have to check out the class yearbook to see what sorts of activities Allan had done back then. Maybe that would spark some memories.

After glancing at his watch, he realized it was getting close to dinnertime and he wanted to run back over to the hotel to take Tess out for something to eat. But first he had to finish his report for his boss.

Normally he took his time, but tonight he was in a

hurry. Declan typed out a brief summary of the day's events and then included a brief background sketch of the two suspects. He hit the send and print buttons with a sense of satisfaction. Despite the electronic world, the bureaucrats insisted on having their reports on paper.

As he pushed away from his desk, another thought crossed his mind. Had Allan liked Tess back in high school, too? Had he asked her out? Or had she snubbed him in some way, causing him to resent her? Was that his motive for planting bombs?

Feeling grim, Declan dropped off his report on Griff's desk and left the building, realizing he might have to move Allan Gray up to the top of his suspect list.

And he intended to ask Tess about her relationship with him as soon as possible, to see if there was any way to back up his latest theory.

Tess was relieved when Isaac called to let her know that her car had been cleared. She'd already spent a small fortune on taxicabs going to all the places she could think that Bobby might be. Back at the hotel, she called a taxi one last time, having agreed to meet Isaac at the elementary school parking lot.

Isaac was waiting near her car when she arrived, looking a little out of place with her purse tucked under his arm. He smiled when he saw her. "Hi, Tess. I have your things and we've released your car."

"Thanks," she murmured, feeling self-conscious as she took her purse from the sandy-haired deputy's hand. "Will you drive me over to pick it up? I've been going crazy without having my own vehicle."

Isaac frowned. "I know Deck wants you to stay safe, so don't do anything foolish, okay?"

"Don't worry, I intend to stay out of danger," Tess assured him. Of course, she also intended to find her brother, too, but decided not to mention that part.

Her car had lots of dents and scratches, but right now that was the least of her worries. She slid behind the wheel and started the car, heading out to the street. Where could Bobby be? She hadn't found him at any of his usual hangouts, which only made her think that it was highly likely that someone had taken him against his will.

What if they'd drugged him? Or hurt him in some way?

She took several deep breaths, knowing it didn't help to think the worst. She needed to remain calm and rational if she was going to find him.

The ride back to the hotel wasn't nearly long enough to clear her mind, and she leaned back in her car rather than heading back inside to stare at the four walls of her hotel room.

Where else could Bobby be?

Abruptly she sat up. What if he was hanging out at one of his buddies' houses? But if that was the case, why would he ignore her calls? Because he thought she'd be upset with him for skipping school? Right now all that really mattered was knowing he was all right. They would deal with the rest later.

Mentally she went through the short list of his close friends. Finn McCain and Mitchell Turner were the only two whose last names she remembered.

For a moment she dropped her forehead to the edge of the steering wheel. What sort of mother figure was she that she couldn't remember the last names of her brother's friends?

Maybe she hadn't done the best job in raising her brother, but she refused to fail him now.

Pulling herself together, she put her car in gear and headed over to Finn McCain's house. Finn lived very close to the high school, and as she drew closer, she eagerly scanned the area for Bobby's truck.

But it was nowhere in sight.

With grim determination she parked in the driveway and walked up to the front door. There were raised voices inside, male and female, causing her to pause with her hand raised to knock, remembering what it had been like when her father had yelled at her for getting a *B* instead of an *A*.

She swallowed hard and pushed the painful memories away. She rapped sharply on the door. When there was no response she leaned on the doorbell, and that worked because the loud voices abruptly stopped.

After several lengthy moments, the door opened and a big burly man with a huge belly scowled at her from behind the screen. "We're not buying whatever you're selling," he said harshly.

"Mr. McCain, I'm looking for my brother, Bobby Collins. He's a friend of your son. Are Finn and Bobby here?"

"No." Without another word, the large man shut the door in her face.

She raised her hand to knock on the door again but then let out a sigh, knowing it was useless. Even if Bobby was here, she doubted Mr. McCain would open the door long enough to admit it.

Since she didn't see any sign of Bobby's truck, she turned around and headed back to her car.

Her head throbbed from a mixture of pain, anxiety

and hunger, but she wasn't going to stop for something to eat when she didn't even know for sure if her brother was safe.

She slid behind the wheel and swallowed hard. Mitchell Turner lived in the poor side of town, in the same neighborhood where Declan had grown up. She wasn't thrilled about going over there, but at least it was still light out. And based on her reception here at Finn's house, she didn't expect her next visit would take too long.

The houses lining the streets gradually became more dilapidated and grungy the closer she came to Mitchell Turner's address. After crossing an intersection, she spotted a large group of kids lounging in the doorway of a neighborhood liquor store, and she felt her heart drop, hoping that Bobby wasn't among them. She slowed down, peering at them intently in an effort to make sure that Bobby wasn't part of that crowd.

A few of the boys stared boldly back at her and she quickly averted her gaze, tightening her hands on the wheel. A quick glance confirmed that her automatic locks were engaged, just in case.

Broad daylight, she reminded herself. Nothing to be worried about.

She caught sight of Mitchell's house, complete with boarded-up windows and several rusty car parts scattered all over the front yard, which consisted mostly of weeds. Her attention was diverted when she heard a loud crash a moment before her windshield shattered into thousands of tiny pieces.

Wrestling with the steering wheel, she tried to stay on the street she couldn't see, but despite her best efforts, the car slammed into something hard, bringing her to a teeth-rattling stop. The engine hissed and groaned and she knew she wasn't going to be able to drive even if she could see through the spider-cracked glass, which she couldn't.

Fear skittered down her spine as she numbly realized what had just happened. Someone had thrown something at her car on purpose. She slowly unclenched her fingers, remembering the group of boys she'd noticed. Had one of them caused the crash? The force of the impact had caused her purse to tumble to the floor, so she removed her seat belt and leaned over, to search for her cell phone.

With shaking fingers, she quickly scrolled through the contact list to find Declan. She called his number, hoping and praying he'd answer.

SIX

Declan had just pulled into a fast food drive-through lane when his phone rang. He smiled when he realized Tess was calling. "Hi, Tess," he greeted her.

"There's been an—accident," she said in a wobbly voice. "I need you to come pick me up right away."

He frowned and yanked the steering wheel to the right so he could get out of the line of cars waiting for food. "Are you all right? Where are you?"

"I'm in your old neighborhood near Sixth and Forrest. Please hurry, Declan. I'm scared."

He battled back a flash of fear. "I'll be there as soon as possible," he promised. He flipped on the red lights and sirens in the vehicle so that everyone would move out of his way. He could tell by the quiver in Tess's voice that she was frightened, either because she was injured by the crash or because of the fact that she was a woman alone in the worst part of town.

Or both.

He made it to his old stomping grounds in record time, which was amazing since it was the height of rush hour. He saw Tess's car smashed up against a light post and his heart rattled in his chest as he pulled up alongside it. Through the driver's-side window, he could see Tess huddled in her seat, holding a can of hair spray.

The old neighborhood hadn't improved any over the years. He couldn't imagine what on earth Tess was doing here, but he climbed out of his car and rushed over to her. "Tess? Are you all right?"

Frank relief was mirrored in her eyes as she slowly nodded. "The door won't open," she said.

The front bumper was crushed up into the driver's-side door, so he jogged around to the other side. A good yank opened the passenger door. "Can you crawl over here?" he asked.

"Yes." She tossed the can of hair spray onto the floor of the passenger side and gingerly climbed over the console between the seats. He helped her out of the car and she clutched at his shoulders, sagging against him. "Thank you," she whispered.

He wrapped his arms around her, holding her close. He was grateful she wasn't hurt, but he didn't understand why she was here in the first place. Hadn't he asked her to stay at the hotel in order to be safe? Why on earth couldn't she have just listened to him?

"I think someone threw something at the windshield," Tess murmured, loosening her grip on his shirt. "When it shattered into millions of tiny cracks, I couldn't see."

"Did you see anyone suspicious before that?" he asked, raking his gaze around the area.

"There was a group of kids back there by the liquor store," she said in a low tone. "But they're gone now."

"We'll have to call a tow truck," he said, trying to keep his tone even. "Why don't you wait for me in my car?"

Tess shook her head, and then bent down to gather up the stuff that must have fallen out of her purse, including the can of hair spray. "I just need a few minutes to go over to Mitchell Tanner's house. He lives just a couple of houses down on the other side of the street."

Declan gritted his teeth in frustration. "Tess, you shouldn't even be out here at all!" he said, the words coming out sharper than he intended. "I thought I asked you to stay and wait for me at the hotel."

She acted as if she hadn't heard him, but before he realized what she intended, she'd looped her purse strap over her shoulder and strode down the street rather than getting into his car.

"Tess, wait!" He quickly caught up to her. "What are you doing?"

She spun around to face him, her eyes full of wounded reproach. "My brother is missing and I intend to go to his friend Mitchell's house to see if he's there."

"Tess…"

"Don't even go there," she warned. "If your sister was missing you'd be out looking for her, too."

She had a point, even though his being in danger was part of his job. He swallowed his anger and tried to keep his tone even. "Okay, fine, we'll both go."

"Suit yourself," she said with a shrug, before turning away.

Declan kept a keen eye out for any other troublemakers as they approached a run-down house. He didn't see any sign of Bobby's truck, but he knew that wouldn't stop Tess from making sure her brother wasn't here.

She didn't look at all nervous as she rapped loudly on the door. He lingered a little behind her and to the right, in case the situation went south.

There was no answer, so she knocked again, harder. After a long minute, the door opened and a woman stood there, smoldering cigarette in one hand and a glass full of amber liquid in the other. "Yeah? Wadda ya want?"

"My name is Tess Collins and I'm looking for my brother, Bobby. Have he and Mitchell been here?"

"I dunno." Mitchell's mother swayed in the doorway, and from the glazed look in her eyes, Declan knew she was intoxicated. "I don't think so."

"Please, Ms. Turner, this is important. I haven't seen Bobby all day and I'm very worried about him."

The woman tossed back the rest of her drink and then swiped her hand across her mouth. "If I see 'im, I'll have him call ya." She moved back and shut the door.

Tess's shoulders slumped as if the weight of the world rested upon them. Declan's earlier ire vanished and he put his arm around her shoulders. "Come on, Tess, I doubt Bobby and Mitchell are hanging around here."

She didn't protest as he guided her back down to the street and over toward his car. At the curb, they had to stop and wait for a car to pass by. He glanced at the driver, and then did a double take as he realized the man behind the wheel looked like Allan Gray.

"What is he doing here?" he asked, staring after the nondescript beige car. He quickly memorized the tag number, in case he'd made a mistake.

But he didn't think so. The driver had absolutely looked like Tess's neighbor. And if he didn't know better, he'd think the guy was following her.

Had he been the one to throw the rock at her windshield, too? Although, if that were the case, Gray had plenty of time to pretend to be the hero, coming to her rescue.

"This way," Declan said, turning Tess in the direction of his car. It didn't seem like the right time to mention how he thought he'd seen Gray. First he needed to run the license plate number in order to be sure.

"I have to find my brother," she whispered as he opened the car door for her.

"I know." There was no point in arguing, because he realized that Tess cared more about finding her brother than she did about her own safety.

And while he couldn't blame her, he still didn't approve of her decision to drive to the seediest part of town to look for Bobby, especially when she could just as easily have asked him to go with her. Or to have asked him to do the task himself.

Unless there was some reason she didn't want him around when she finally caught up to her brother. The thought pulled him up short. Was that it? Was there more to Bobby's disappearance than she was letting on?

And if so, what?

Tess kept her gaze averted from Declan so he wouldn't see how close she was to losing it. First she'd been in a car crash caused by vandalism and then he'd yelled at her, just as her father used to do. And now she was no closer to finding her brother than she had been earlier that morning.

She'd been so certain that she'd find Bobby at one of his friends' houses, but instead she discovered that Bobby's friends were in horrible home situations, worse than she ever could have imagined. Even worse than what she'd endured with her father.

How was it that Bobby identified so well with these two boys? Did he really think living with her was as bad as what these boys had to deal with? Maybe she wasn't perfect, but she wasn't that bad, either. She simply couldn't comprehend what was going on with her brother.

Despair overwhelmed her. She had no idea where to look for Bobby next. And having Declan go from holding her close to basically yelling at her was too much to handle.

She sniffed, trying to fight back her tears. There had to be something she could do. But what?

Pray. She dropped her chin to her chest and squeezed her eyes shut, blocking everything else out.

Dear Lord, if it be Thy will, please guide me in searching for Bobby. Please watch over him and keep him safe. Please grant me the patience and strength I'll need to get through these next few days, Amen.

A sense of peace crept over her and she took a deep breath and let it out slowly, knowing that God would carry her burdens if she simply asked Him.

Tess subtly swiped away the evidence of her tears and glanced over at Declan. Now that she'd had a chance to calm down a bit, she understood that he'd been upset with her for leaving mostly because he was worried about her. She probably needed to explain about her past, but she was too exhausted to broach the subject now.

She pulled herself together, knowing that this situation wasn't Declan's fault. Furthermore, she was truly grateful for the way he'd come the moment she called.

"I'm sorry," Declan said, reaching over to take her hand in his.

Surprised, she glanced up at him. "For what?"

"I shouldn't have gotten upset with you. It's just that this place…" He paused and then shook his head. "You know this neighborhood isn't a safe place to be, even during the day. Especially not for a woman like you."

"I've been here before. I dropped Bobby off here a while ago."

Declan actually winced. "Don't tell me stuff like that. I can't stand the thought of you being anywhere near here."

She realized he was embarrassed that he'd grown up in the neighborhood. "Was joining the marines worth it?" she asked softly.

"Yes," Declan responded without a moment's hesitation. "As hard as it was to become a marine and to fight in Afghanistan, I don't regret getting the chance to leave this all behind."

She nodded, understanding without being told that Declan's life experiences must have been all too similar to what they'd just witnessed with Mitchell's mother. And she found it amazing that Declan had turned his life around, to become a member of the SWAT team, no less.

Obviously being forced to give and obey orders helped mold him into the man he was today. So she had no business complaining. Besides, she didn't care if he yelled at her, as long as they found her brother.

She closed her eyes and prayed again for Bobby's safe return. Feeling a little more optimistic after her prayer, she sank back in her seat and stared again at her phone. If only Bobby would call or text her again.

"Let's stop for dinner," Declan suggested. "We need to refuel, and besides, if we're going to find your brother, we need some sort of plan."

"Really?" She glanced at him, afraid to hope. "You'll help me find him?"

A wounded expression flitted across his face before he nodded. "Of course I'll help you. Why wouldn't I? The only reason I left you alone in the first place was that I had to report in to work to talk to the feds."

"I know, but I thought you were mad at me." She couldn't explain how she was used to being controlled by anger and fear. *If you do exactly as I say, I'll let you stay overnight at your girlfriend's house. But if you disappoint me, you'll be grounded for a month.*

She shook off the memories, reminding herself that her father had been gone for over six years. She missed her mother, even though her mom had been kept under her father's thumb as much as Tess had been, if not worse.

"I'm not mad at you, frustrated maybe," Declan said, pulling into a well-known diner. "All I wanted was for you to wait for me so I could keep you safe."

"Yes, well, sitting in that hotel was driving me crazy," she admitted. "I needed to do something to find Bobby. But I checked everywhere I could think of without any luck."

"Where did you go?" Declan asked as he climbed out of the vehicle.

"The batting cages, a couple of other parks. And then the houses of his two best friends. Mitchell's house was my last resort." Tess tried to keep the depths of her despair from her tone.

"Come on, let's get something to eat."

She followed Declan inside the restaurant, and soon they were seated across from each other in a booth off to the side. She didn't think she was hungry, but the scent of food made her stomach growl.

"Everything looks so good," she murmured, looking through the glossy menu.

A few minutes later, a server came to give them water

and to take their order. Tess treated herself to a thick juicy burger while Declan ordered the pot roast.

As soon as they were alone again, he leaned forward, pinning her with his crystal-blue gaze. "There have to be other places where your brother could be," he said in a low tone. "He must have other friends, besides the two we've already checked out."

"He doesn't talk to me about his friends," she admitted, toying with her straw. "He always seems so alone."

"What activities is he involved in at school?" Declan pressed.

"He was dropped from the baseball team when his GPA dropped to less than 2.0," she said. "Most of his baseball buddies stopped hanging around with him after that."

"Tough break. I can see why he might be falling in with these other guys."

"Really? Because I don't get it at all," Tess said, tossing down her straw with a disgusted sigh. "Those boys come from rough backgrounds, and I just don't understand why Bobby would think that living with me is so terrible."

"Tess, it's probably not about you at all," Declan said, reaching across the table and taking her hand. "He must feel abandoned by his other friends, so he's picked the few guys who accept him for what he is."

She understood what Declan was saying, but inside she still rejected the concept. "Bobby struggles with school and I tried to tutor him myself, but that didn't work. So I hired someone else to do it, but he refused to go. If he had stuck it out with the tutor, he might not have been dropped from the team."

Declan gently squeezed her hand. "You can't go back

and change the past," he pointed out. "Right now we need to find Bobby and keep you both safe. Are you sure there isn't anyplace else he would go? A girlfriend that you might not know about? Some other place he likes to hang out, maybe to be by himself?"

She shook her head and shrugged. "I'd be the last to know about a girlfriend." The thought only depressed her more, so she shoved it away. "I checked all the places I could think of. I'm out of ideas for the moment."

Declan held her hand, his comforting touch filling her with solace until the server arrived with their food. As hungry as she was before, she found that her appetite had suddenly vanished. The few bites of her burger sat like a lump in her stomach.

"You need to keep up your strength, Tess," Declan reminded her.

"I know." She nibbled on a French fry in an effort to get something solid in her stomach. But as soon as Declan was finished eating, she pushed her half-eaten food away. "I'm ready to go," she announced.

She was impressed that he didn't harp on her again about eating. He paid the bill and she followed him out of the diner back outside.

"There used to be an old arcade in the old neighborhood," Declan said as he slid behind the wheel. "Maybe we should check that out before we go back to the hotel."

"Sure," she agreed, feeling a slight flare of hope. "Bobby loves video games."

"What kid doesn't?" Declan asked drily.

He didn't say much as they drove back to the neighborhood, and even with Declan beside her, she couldn't deny feeling nervous at the blatant looks thrown their way as they walked through the arcade.

She blew out her breath when she realized Bobby wasn't there.

"Maybe he's at the hotel waiting for you," Declan suggested after they left.

"I wish he'd call me again," she said.

Declan's eyebrows shot up in surprise. "You mean he already called you once?"

"Yes." She quickly explained that all she could hear was Bobby saying her name, before the call had been cut off.

"If he called once, I'm sure he'll call again," Declan said confidently.

She wished she could be so sure.

As Declan pulled up in front of her hotel, she turned in her seat to face him. "Thanks again, for everything."

"I'll walk you up," he said.

Since arguing would be a waste of breath, she slung her purse over her shoulder and took the steps up to the second floor where her room was located.

She pulled out her room key intending to unlock the door, but before she could slide it into the slot, she realized the door was already ajar.

"Get back," Declan said, putting out his arm to prevent her from going inside.

"I'm sure I closed it behind me," she said.

Declan held his Glock ready as he kicked the door until it was wide-open. He stayed along the edge of the wall, checking the small bathroom area first, before going farther into the room.

Tess hovered in the doorway. Even from there she could see that someone had been inside her room. Her small suitcase was lying empty on the floor and the few items she'd packed, clothes and toiletries, had been scattered carelessly around.

For a moment she could only stare at the mess in horror. Who would have done such a thing? And why?

She had no idea, but it was clear she wasn't safe here.

And the way things had gone so far today, she was beginning to believe she wouldn't be safe anywhere.

SEVEN

Declan scowled as he went through Tess's small hotel room making sure the perp wasn't still around, hiding. He was glad Tess hadn't been here when this happened, but he didn't like the fact that someone had obviously followed her here, either.

Once he'd cleared the room, double-checking everything, he glanced back at Tess and gestured for her to come inside. "Let's gather your stuff together. We need to get out of here."

Thankfully she didn't argue and between the two of them the task didn't take long. But even when she had the suitcase packed, he went over to the doorway and stood, scanning the parking lot for any sign of danger.

Was the person who'd ransacked her room still hanging out somewhere nearby?

He couldn't afford to discount the possibility.

There were several cars in the parking lot, and he took his time inspecting them, making sure each one was empty. Or at least appeared to be empty. From his perch on the second floor, he could see into the front row of cars that happened to be parked nearby. But there were still a half dozen vehicles he couldn't eliminate as potential threats.

"Stay behind me," he said in a low tone. "We're going to take the east set of stairs down to the ground level. You'll have to carry the suitcase so that I can hold my gun just in case."

"I understand," she murmured. "The suitcase isn't heavy."

He let out his breath and made his move. The sun had disappeared behind the trees, giving them a hint of dusk as protection. Full darkness would have been better, but he wasn't about to wait around any longer.

Keeping close to the wall of the building, he led the way down the east stairway. As soon as they were on the ground level, he breathed a little easier.

"Stay down as much as possible," he instructed as he eased along the sidewalk in front of the building, using the parked cars as protection. He was glad he'd parked in the front row, and as soon as they'd reached the vehicle, he opened the passenger-side door for Tess and urged her inside.

He tossed the suitcase in the backseat and then jogged to the driver's side. Once he was behind the wheel, he jammed the key in the ignition, cranked the engine and backed out of the parking space, mentally braced for the sound of gunfire.

But there was nothing but silence as he headed for the street. Still, he didn't fully relax until he'd driven a winding path through the subdivision, making sure they weren't followed, before he headed for the highway.

"Where are we going?" Tess asked.

Good question. He glanced over at her, wishing she'd just come and stay with him, but knowing she wasn't about to change her mind. "Another hotel, only this time, we're not telling anyone where you're staying."

Tess grimaced but nodded. "All right. But I didn't tell anyone where I was staying, either."

"Any idea what the intruder was looking for back there?" he asked.

"I have no idea. From what I could tell, there wasn't anything missing. I had my purse with me, so they didn't get any cash or my credit cards."

"You didn't put the name of the hotel on your neon-green flyer you taped on the front door of your house, did you?"

"No, the sign simply asked Bobby to call me as soon as possible."

He was glad she hadn't been more specific. First he had to rescue her from his old neighborhood and now this. As if they hadn't had enough danger so far today? A wave of frustration hit hard.

"I don't get it, why would anyone take the risk of breaking in?" Declan tried to make sense of the series of events. "If they were trying to get you, they would have been better off staking out the place and waiting for you to be in there alone."

So much for his attempt to keep her safe.

"I don't get it, either," she admitted.

"What about earlier today? Did you notice anyone following you?"

She shook her head. "I had the taxi driver take me all over the city, and I didn't notice anything unusual."

Declan drummed his fingers on the steering wheel, thinking back to that beige car he'd noticed in the old neighborhood. "I'm pretty sure I saw your neighbor Allan Gray after we left Mitchell's house. Could be that he followed you earlier. Otherwise how would he have known you'd be there?"

"Allan?" Tess echoed with a frown. "I didn't see him."

The more he thought about it, the more he figured that her neighbor had to be the key. But he shouldn't have said anything until he'd gotten proof of his license plate, like he'd originally planned. "Do you know what kind of car he drives?"

"I'm not sure, some sort of sedan, I think," she said in a doubtful tone. "But I can't be positive. I guess I don't make it a habit of spying on my neighbors." He knew what each of his neighbors drove, but being aware of those sorts of details was part of his job. Normal civilians like Tess didn't live that way. He reminded himself to look up Allan Gray's vehicle later. "Gray went to Greenland High School, too, and apparently he was in my graduating class. Did you know him back then?"

"Yes, I knew him in high school, although not very well. I think he might have been in my physics class, though."

Declan was surprised to hear they shared a class together. "Did he ever ask you out?"

"No, why would he?" She let out an exasperated sigh. "It's not as if I was a popular kid back then. I studied all the time because my father wouldn't accept anything less than straight *A's*. I spent way more time in the library than I did anywhere else. In fact, that was part of the reason I was so surprised that Steve asked me to prom. Little did I know how he planned to end the evening."

Declan frowned, remembering that night he'd stumbled upon Steve Gains attempting to force Tess into having sex with him. He was very glad he'd gotten there in time to prevent anything from happening, although truthfully, Tess had managed to save herself without a whole lot of help from him. The memory of the way she'd kicked Gains and then taken off running brought a reluctant smile.

But he was more interested in what Allan Gray was doing back in high school. "I don't remember Gray at all," he confessed. "I meant to stop at home to find my yearbook to see if anything might jog my memory. Do you know what he was involved in back then?"

"I'm pretty sure he was involved in the drama club," Tess said slowly. "I vaguely remember he asked me to join, too, so that we could be stagehands together. At the time I thought it might be fun, but my father put an end to that idea pretty quick."

This was the second time she'd mentioned her father, and Declan was beginning to realize that Tess hadn't achieved the status of being class valedictorian because it was something she wanted to do, but because her father expected it. "Did your father want you to be a doctor?"

Her lips thinned and she shook her head. "No, that was my dream. He wanted me to be a lawyer so that I could go into politics like he did."

"That's right, I remember now. Your dad was the town mayor, wasn't he?"

"Yes." The pinched expression on her face gave him the impression that these were not happy childhood memories. And since she'd been through enough, he decided to steer the conversation back to the situation at hand.

"So you knew Allan back in high school, which makes sense. But how is it that he ended up living next door to you?"

Tess was silent for a moment. "I don't know the exact details. But I do recall there used to be an elderly couple who lived next door, and they put their house up for sale after they decided to move into an assisted-living facility. I'm sure the price was reasonable, and I guess Allan figured it would be a good investment. I know for a fact that he's only lived there for about two years."

"Hmm, interesting." He wondered how much of Allan's decision to buy the place was related to the fact that Tess lived next door. Was it possible Gray harbored a secret obsession for Tess that had spanned ten years?

If so, Declan could only imagine what Allan Gray was capable of doing if he discovered Tess didn't return his feelings.

Tess rubbed her temple, trying to massage her headache away. She didn't want to think about Allan Gray or the fact that her neighbor might have been near the scene of her earlier accident.

She stared down at her phone, willing Bobby to call.

"We'll stay at that hotel up ahead, if that's okay with you."

"Sure, why not?" She glanced up and noticed that the hotel wasn't all that far from where her church was located. "Wait, pull in here," she said quickly.

"What? Why?" Declan asked, but he did as she asked and made a sharp right turn into the church parking lot.

"I need to go inside for a moment," she said, opening her door.

"Hang on a minute," Declan protested, lightly grasping her arm. "Are there services tonight? Is there some religious holiday that I don't know about?"

"No, I just need a few minutes of peace and quiet, that's all." She didn't want to explain the urge to go inside the church that she'd gone to for solace after a particularly difficult argument with her father. "Please let me go inside. I promise I won't be long."

"If you're going, then I'm going with you." Declan's expression was pulled into a tight frown, as if he didn't appreciate her request for a little side visit, but while she felt bad, the need to go inside outweighed her guilt.

She tugged on the door, glad to find that the church wasn't locked. Pastor Tom normally locked the place down overnight, but since the hour was only seven-thirty in the evening, the doors were still open. She headed down toward the front of the church and slid into the fourth pew on the right, where she normally sat during services.

Closing her eyes, she prayed for strength and support, followed by the Lord's Prayer. When she finished, she was conscious of Declan standing in the back of the church and couldn't help wishing he'd join her in prayer.

But he wasn't a Christian, at least as far as she knew. Was that part of the reason that God had brought Declan back into her life? Not only to keep her safe, but so that she could show him the way to being a Christian?

The more the idea rolled around in her mind, the more she believed that had to be part of God's plan. After ten minutes or so, she opened her eyes and gazed up at the empty altar, feeling a little better. Being in church was so soothing she wished she could spend the night here.

Not that Pastor Tom would approve. And besides, she couldn't ignore the fact that danger seemed to follow her wherever she went. The last thing she wanted to do was to put Pastor Tom in harm's way. The hotel that was just a couple blocks away was probably a better choice.

She was about to leave when she had an idea. Why not leave Bobby a note here? Bobby knew how much she enjoyed attending this church and that she always came early enough to sit in this pew. And he'd come on occasion, too. Maybe he'd return as a way to connect with her? Without giving herself a chance to second-guess her decision, she quickly pulled a small piece of paper and a pen from her purse, holding it in her lap so that Declan couldn't see what she was doing. Somehow she sensed he wouldn't approve.

She kept the note short. *Staying at the American Lodge. Come and find me. Tess.*

There was a crack along the edge of the pew and she quickly stuffed the note inside.

She frowned, staring at the note. Hopefully Bobby would come here seeking peace, the way he had in the past. After all, he got along pretty well with Pastor Tom. But what if he didn't? Or couldn't come?

Leaving the note was better than doing nothing and provided at least a glimmer of hope. With a sense of renewed determination, she slid out of the pew and then walked back down to where Declan waited. She caught his gaze, wondering if he'd noticed that she left the note.

Since he didn't say anything as they made their way back out to his car, she figured her secret was safe.

Dear Lord, keep Bobby safe in Your care and please guide him to the note I've left for him. Amen.

Declan had felt out of place even just standing at the back of the church, but since Tess was smiling, he figured the slight detour had been well worth it.

"Thanks," she murmured.

He flashed a reassuring grin. "You're welcome. Did it help?"

"Praying always manages to put things in perspective," she replied as he drove the couple of blocks to the hotel. "And I needed those few moments of prayer more than I can say. Your patience really means a lot to me."

"No problem," Declan said, feeling a bit uncomfortable with her gratitude. Obviously she didn't realize how close he'd been to refusing her request. "After the day you've had, you deserve a little peace and quiet."

"Do you attend church at all?" she asked as he pulled into the hotel parking lot.

He tried not to grimace. "Not really."

"I'd think in your line of work you'd pray a lot," she murmured. "Especially since your job places you in dangerous situations."

He wasn't sure what to say to that. He remembered listening to her prayer as he was defusing the bomb. At the time he'd been grateful for the assistance, from whatever the source. "I tried a few prayer services while I was deployed overseas," he confided. "But then after my buddy was killed, I never went back."

She glanced at him in sympathy. "I'm sorry to hear about your friend's death. I'm sure that must have been difficult."

"Yeah." Talk about a massive understatement. He'd been standing right next to Tony when he was shot. It was a quirk of chance that Declan was here today, while his buddy wasn't.

"After my parents died, I leaned on my faith a lot," she continued. "God is always there for us when we need Him."

He didn't think she'd appreciate hearing how he had returned home after losing Tony to drown his sorrows in a bottle of booze. He might still be drunk if not for the fact that Karen had needed his help to get away from her abusive ex-husband.

He hadn't touched a drop of alcohol in the four years since then, but he was keenly aware that it might not take much to send him tumbling down into that black hole. He was, after all, his father's son. And wasn't there something about how alcohol abuse tended to run in families?

Depressing thought. He refused to be anything like his father, no matter what. Just knowing they shared the same genes was terrifying enough.

"Thanks for offering to pray for me that night I drove you home after your prom date," he said.

"I prayed for you a lot," she said. "I was tempted to write to you but wasn't sure how to find your address."

That surprised him. "Really?"

"Really. I guess I should have asked around to see if anyone else knew how to reach you."

He didn't want to tell her that he was one of the few marines who hardly got any mail. Karen had written to him a few times, but then those letters had dropped off, too.

Humbling to think that Tess cared enough to at least consider writing to him. Not that she probably would have written the entire time he was gone.

Even one letter would have been great to have.

Okay, enough already. What was the point of wishing things had been different? Tess was far too good for him and a Christian, too. She deserved more than he could ever give her.

And it was annoying that he even considered trying to change for her.

"Let's go inside," he said abruptly, cutting off that

thought before he could make a fool of himself. "It's getting late."

"All right." Tess slid out of her door and walked toward the lobby. He pulled her suitcase out from the backseat and then caught up with her at the door. He held it open with one hand and quickly followed her inside.

"May I help you?" the desk clerk asked.

"Yes, I need a room," Tess said.

"Actually we'd like two connecting rooms," he spoke up, cutting off Tess's request.

"What are you doing?" she whispered under her breath. "There's no reason for you to stay."

"I'm not leaving, Tess." This was why he'd waited to even bring up the subject. "Don't worry, you'll have your privacy."

"We have two connecting rooms on the first floor, but you'll be facing the parking lot. Is that acceptable?" the clerk asked pleasantly.

"Yes, that would be fine." Declan handed over his credit card and ignored the scowl Tess sent his way. "Thanks."

"You'll be in room 110 and 112. Your rooms will be all the way down at the end of the hall."

"Great, thanks." Declan took one key and handed Tess the other one. He grabbed her suitcase and wheeled it down the hallway toward their rooms.

Tess waited to get away from the lobby before she spoke her mind. "This is ridiculous. There's no reason for you to stay here when you have a perfectly good house to go home to."

"Would you consider going home with me? I have a spare bedroom."

"No, I wouldn't." She crossed her arms over her chest,

obviously disgruntled. "I like this location. It's close to church."

Sunday was three days away, but he wasn't going to point that out now. "You may as well save your breath, because if you're not leaving, then neither am I."

She sighed, but he was thankful when she gave up her argument. The clerk had indeed allocated them rooms that were way at the end of the building, overlooking the parking lot which was probably a good thing in case they needed to leave in a hurry.

He set the suitcase down and then used his key to open his door. "Unlock your side of the connecting door when you get in, okay?"

"Hrumph." Tess didn't look pleased as she lugged her suitcase inside, letting the door close loudly behind her.

He went inside his room and then unlocked and opened his side of the connecting door. Since he didn't have any luggage with him, he decided he'd have to go back to the lobby to get a few bare essentials from the front desk.

By the time he returned with a comb, toothbrush, toothpaste and razor, he noticed that Tess had her connecting door open about an inch. He set his things inside the bathroom and then hesitantly knocked on her door.

"Come in."

He pushed the door open a bit farther and saw that Tess was sitting in a desk chair reading a Bible. It didn't look like the ones that were normally left in hotel rooms, so he assumed it was hers. "Everything okay?"

"Of course, why wouldn't it be?"

Good point. Why the sudden need to check on her? It wasn't as if there was any hint of danger. "Call me if you need anything."

"I will."

"Good night, Tess."

"Good night, Declan."

He closed her door just enough so that it didn't latch, and then did the same on his side. As he stretched out on the bed, he stared up at the ceiling. Was it possible that Tess was right about faith and church? Did believing in God really bring peace?

For the first time, he wondered if maybe he would have coped differently after Tony's death if he'd had faith and God to lean on.

But almost as quickly as the thought entered his mind, he pushed it away. After all the trouble he'd caused as a teenager, he was certain he'd sinned too much for God to forgive him. Even his own mother hadn't loved him enough to take him with her when she left his father. Instead, she'd taken Karen, leaving him behind.

Furthermore, he didn't have any business thinking of ways to get on Tess's good side. Granted the more time he spent with her, the more he admired her strength and endurance, but he already sensed she didn't feel the same way about him. And while he knew deep down that it was better that way, he couldn't help wishing that things could be different.

That he was the type of man who really could have a home and a family.

EIGHT

Tess tried to concentrate on the book of Psalms, which were her favorite, but she was acutely aware of Declan's presence in the room next door. She was oddly touched by the fact that he'd chosen to stay with her, so that he could offer his protection.

She couldn't remember the last time any man had cared about her safety and well-being. Of course, she hadn't been in danger like this before, either, at least not since that disastrous prom date ten years ago.

Declan had stepped up to protect her back then, too. She'd tried to repress her memory of that night, but now the images came rushing back. The way Steve's personality seemed to have changed over the course of the evening from being the nice guy she knew in her physics class to the nasty creep who'd demanded sex from her. He'd been drinking all night from a water bottle that really contained vodka, a fact that she realized far too late.

Steve had gripped her wrist so hard that he'd left bruises that had lasted for a full week. She knew Steve would have forced himself on her, but Declan had shown up and demanded that Steve let her go. When Steve was distracted by Declan's arrival, she'd kicked him and had taken off running. She'd heard someone jogging behind her and had tried to go faster. Soon she realized Declan was the one following her, making sure that Steve didn't try to follow.

Declan had offered to drive her home, and during that time, she'd shared her dream of being a doctor while Declan had informed her he was going into the marines. He'd given her a light, gentle kiss, a moment she still savored. Even though Declan had been the town troublemaker, she'd never felt as safe as she had that night.

Until now.

She gave up trying to read and crawled into bed. But she couldn't sleep. Memories of her eventful day kept crowding her mind. The bomb under her desk, the explosion outside, the crash in Declan's old neighborhood.

Searching for Bobby.

Her phone rang and she bolted upright in bed, her heart hammering wildly. She reached for the device and wanted to weep with relief when she saw Bobby's number. "Bobby? Where are you?"

"Tess, I need help." Her brother's voice was barely a whisper, so soft she had to strain to hear. "I need money. Can you meet me at Greenland Park?"

She swallowed hard, trying to ignore the stab of disappointment. "Where have you been? I've been searching all over for you. Do you have any idea how worried I've been about you?"

There was a slight pause before her brother responded, "I'm sorry...I can explain everything when you get here. Please, Tess, it's important. I need your help."

She closed her eyes, fighting a wave of nausea and a nagging headache. Bobby knew that she didn't like going to Greenland Park, the site of her near rape, but obviously he was in trouble. She was afraid to hear the details, yet she knew she'd have to help him. No matter what. "Okay, where do you want me to meet you?"

"I'll be waiting in picnic area number three. Thanks, Tess."

She barely had a chance to say goodbye before Bobby hung up. Her brother sounded as if he was under a lot of pressure for some reason. She didn't mind giving him money, but she needed to understand what he was involved in and how she could help him get back on track. He'd skipped school, for heaven's sake. What happened to the earnest young man who'd promised her he'd graduate?

Tess took a deep breath and let it out slowly. She didn't have a car, which left two choices. Call for a cab or wake Declan.

Her first instinct was to go with the cab option, but there was a good chance Declan would hear her. It made her a little nervous to tell him about Bobby's request, because who knew what legal trouble her brother had gotten into? But at the same time, she didn't really want to go to Greenland Park alone at eleven-thirty at night.

Before she could move toward the connecting door, Declan rapped on the frame to get her attention then poked his head inside. "Tess? I heard your phone. Was that Bobby?"

"Yes, he wants me to meet him at Greenland Park. Will you drive me?"

Declan frowned. "Of course, but why does he need us to go to him? Why can't he come here? What exactly is going on?"

"Bobby said he'd explain everything when we get there. I need you to trust me on this." She was afraid to mention the fact that Bobby wanted money. Deep down, she suspected that Declan might share Jeff's philosophy of how to manage a teenager. Her ex had made it clear she was too lenient when it came to her brother, yet she knew that being strict wasn't the answer, either. Of course a happy medium would be nice, but at times like this, she knew that was nothing more than wishful thinking.

"I don't like it," Declan muttered.

She didn't have an answer for that, so she grabbed her purse before following Declan out of the room. He headed outside to where he'd left the car.

Her stomach twisted painfully the closer they came to Greenland Park. Being there at night brought back memories she'd rather forget. She was relieved to be reuniting with her brother, yet at the same time, she'd rather be anywhere else than Greenland Park.

"Where are we meeting him?" Declan asked as he drove into the park's north entrance.

She forced the words through her dry throat. "Picnic area three."

The darkness enveloped them as the towering trees lining the park road blocked out the light from the moon and the stars. From what she could tell, the area was deserted and there weren't any other cars or people that she could see. Soon their headlights flashed on the sign labeled Picnic Three. "Pull over," she urged.

Declan stopped his car and hesitated before he turned off the engine, including the headlights, plunging them in complete darkness. "Maybe we should leave the lights on, so Bobby can see us?" she whispered.

"Not right now. First I need to be sure you're safe. Since we haven't seen Bobby yet, he's either hiding or hasn't arrived. There's no sign of his truck, but for all we know he could have parked elsewhere and is heading over on foot."

She didn't argue, because something about all of this didn't seem quite right. Granted she already knew Bobby was probably in trouble, but still, using the park as a meeting place felt—off.

"We're going to walk across to where those three picnic tables are clustered beneath the oak tree," Declan said. He reached up and fiddled with the dome light, and she was surprised when he removed the tiny bulb. "I want you to stay right next to me, okay?"

She nodded and looped her purse over her shoulder as she opened her door. Her foot hit the curb and she slipped, falling against the side of the SUV with a soft thud. Declan was there in a heartbeat, to steady her.

"Are you okay?" he whispered.

"Yes, I'm fine."

Declan held on to her hand as they gingerly made their way across the grassy embankment toward the three picnic tables. The dewy grass made her running shoes damp as they walked, making sure not to trip over branches or rocks. She peered through the darkness, trying to catch a glimpse of her brother. Was Bobby hiding somewhere nearby? Was he watching them right now? Was he disappointed that she hadn't come alone?

She shivered and hoped Bobby wouldn't try to do anything foolish, especially since she knew Declan was armed and a highly trained member of the SWAT team. When they reached the middle picnic table, they stood for a while, anxiously waiting for her brother to show.

But he didn't. Where was he? Had he expected her to take more time to arrive? Was he on his way here right now? Or had something prevented him from coming at all?

The latter thought was far too depressing. She sat down on the bench seat of the picnic table, but Declan stopped her.

"Wait," he said in a hushed tone.

She froze while Declan pulled out a small flashlight. He swept the tiny yet powerful beam over the area. There was no sign of anyone hiding nearby, although there were certainly enough trees and brush to hide behind.

She had no idea what he was looking for, but then she heard him suck in a harsh breath.

"What's wrong?" she whispered.

"Look," Declan said in a husky tone. Beneath the picnic table to their left was a small cardboard box. For a moment she didn't understand the significance, thinking that some previous picnicker had left it behind.

"I have to call this in," Declan said in a grim tone. "I think this could be another bomb."

Declan knew that the small cardboard box could be nothing, but ever since they'd arrived in the park his nerves had been on edge. No way was he taking a chance on the fact that this could be yet another explosive.

Using his radio, he called his boss and reported the potential threat. Griff agreed to send his SWAT team and the robot, as this was an isolated device, and the rest of his gear. Feeling better that he had backup on the way, Declan fished out his keys and glanced at Tess.

"Here, I need you to go back to the car and lock yourself in," he said, dropping the keys into the palm of her hand.

"I'd rather stay here with you," she protested.

No way, he didn't want her anywhere near the bomb. He was already worried that it could be ready to blow. "I'll walk you back," he said. "I want you to shut off your cell phone, because we have no way of knowing if this device is on a timer or if it could be detonated remotely. For all we know, someone is out there right now ready to set it off."

"Stay with me," she begged. "At least until your team arrives."

Her concern warmed his heart, even though he knew Tess would be worried about anyone who was in harm's way. "I'll stay clear, but I need to make sure no one else gets too close, either."

"There isn't anyone else here," she protested.

"Tess, you know as well as I do that there are likely a few homeless people roaming around this park. This is my job," he reminded her gently. "You can help me out by locking yourself inside the vehicle. In fact, I'd like you to drive back to the hotel, just in case."

He didn't want to scare her, but for all he knew there was either C-4 or dynamite in that box.

Or nothing at all.

"How will you get back?" she asked.

"Caleb or Isaac will drop me off. Please go. I need to know you're safe."

"All right," she reluctantly agreed. "But promise me you'll be careful."

"Always," he assured her. As she climbed behind the wheel, he realized how hard it must be for the guys' families, sitting at home, waiting for news. He wasn't sure how Noelle, Caleb's wife, managed the stress.

Would Tess be able to do the same?

He shook his head at his foolishness as members of

his team arrived. Isaac pulled up first and Declan headed over to grab the bomb gear.

"If this is another explosive, this would be a new record," Isaac muttered. "Three in one day? What in the world is going on? Why is this perp escalating?"

"Good question," Declan said as he donned the heavy protective gear. "I can only hope this is a false alarm."

"No such luck," Isaac mumbled. "The feds will go crazy over this."

Declan silently agreed. They sent the robot in first, but it soon became clear that it couldn't navigate beneath the picnic table. Resigned to doing the task himself, he put on a headlamp and led the way back to where the cardboard box was sitting beneath the picnic table.

Declan knelt a few feet away and used a long device to gingerly lift the cardboard flaps one at a time. When the box was open, he glanced at Isaac. "I'm going to look inside," he said in a muffled tone.

"Roger, Deck," Isaac responded.

Declan slowly eased forward, hoping that there wasn't some perp hiding out, waiting for him to get close enough before he triggered the device. He found himself repeating the prayer Tess had said when he'd worked on the mechanism under her desk.

Dear Lord, if it be Your will, give me the wisdom and strength to disarm this bomb. I ask for Your mercy and grace. Amen.

Declan craned his neck forward to see inside the box. His headlamp confirmed his suspicions. There were three sticks of dynamite wrapped together with electrical tape, along with an old-fashioned egg timer wired to the front.

There was only about fifteen minutes left on the timer before it was designated to blow.

He glanced over at Isaac. "Fourteen minutes and counting. I'll take the lead."

Isaac looked as if he might protest, but Declan didn't give him the opportunity. Feeling more confident now that he could see that the device didn't have a remote detonator, he crouched beside it and pulled out his wire cutters.

But as he examined the wires, his usual coolness deserted him. And for the first time in a long while, he realized just how much he wanted to live. Not that he ever had a death wish or anything, but still, he had more to live for now. Not just to bring this guy to justice for the lives that had been lost.

But because of Tess. Because as crazy as it sounded, he wanted a chance to get to know her better. To relate to her on a personal level once all this absurdity had been settled.

"Deck?" Isaac asked through the radio. "Something wrong?"

Declan shook his head, realizing he'd been standing there staring at the bomb for at least two minutes. "No, I'm fine. Twelve minutes and counting."

He cleared his mind and focused on the task at hand. The bomb was rigged in a standard, straightforward format, but he couldn't help thinking that the guy who'd made the previous bombs wouldn't have done something so simple. He gently tugged on the wire that logically would lead to the timer, and then moved on to the next one.

There were slight gaps between the sticks of dynamite, and he caught the barest glimpse of a black wire tucked into the back of the timer. He clipped that wire first and was relieved when the timer stopped.

"Bring me the steel box," Declan said to Isaac. "The timer has been shut down, but I'm not sure which wire leads to the trigger."

"Roger, Deck."

Within minutes Declan had lifted the explosive device and placed it gingerly inside the steel box. Then he and Isaac jointly carried it over to the armored truck. Declan didn't relax until they'd closed the explosive device inside.

"Good job, Deck," Isaac said, slapping him on the shoulder. "For a minute there, I thought you lost your nerve."

"Never that," Declan assured him. "Just needed to think it through, that's all."

He was embarrassed to admit that he'd taken the time to pray and to contemplate just how much he had to live for. Which reminded him he needed to call Tess. He took out his phone, turned it on, but was stopped by his boss.

"We need to talk," Griff said curtly. "Now."

Declan grimaced. Now that the threat had been neutralized, he knew his boss had several questions: first and foremost, how Declan had come to the park to find the device in the first place. As much as he wanted to talk to Tess, she'd have to wait.

Thankfully, she was likely safe inside the hotel right now. A few more minutes wouldn't matter much.

He followed his boss over to where the rest of the team waited and drew a deep breath as he prepared to give them the rundown on the latest turn of events.

Events that now put Tess's brother smack-dab center in the pool of possible suspects.

After leaving picnic area three, Tess drove slowly through Greenland Park looking for the exit. She caught sight of a blue GMC truck with the letters UTS on the license plate and slammed on the brakes in surprise.

Bobby's truck! He had come after all!

She pulled up behind the GMC but couldn't see anyone inside. Where was her brother? She slid out from behind the wheel and quietly closed the car door behind her.

"Bobby?" she called softly. "It's me, Tess."

She strained to listen but couldn't hear anything other than the rustling leaves and the occasional chirping of a cricket.

"Bobby?" She walked up to the truck, pressing her face against the window to peer inside. Had he fallen asleep?

The interior of the truck was a mess, littered with fast food wrappers and empty soda cans. No beer cans, as far as she could tell, which was reassuring.

But there was no sign of her brother.

She walked around to the front of the truck, looking to see if he was nearby, when she heard something rustle behind her.

"Bobby?" she said once again as she turned around.

She caught a glimpse of a dark figure looming over her seconds before something hard hit her on the head, sending pain reverberating through her skull. Before she could gather her thoughts, darkness claimed her.

NINE

Tess opened her eyes and blinked, trying to see through the darkness. What happened? Where was she?

Her head throbbed and she quickly found the source of her pain in a sizable lump along her temple. There were twinkling stars overhead and it took a minute for her to figure out that the damp feeling was because she was lying flat on her back on the grass alongside the park road.

She pushed herself upright, swaying a bit as the world tilted chaotically on its side. Bracing her hands on the ground, she looked around, sensing something was missing.

For a moment she couldn't think rationally but then realized Bobby's truck was gone. She frowned and stared through the darkness. The truck had been there, right? She hadn't imagined it, had she? Declan's SUV was parked alongside the road and she remembered parking behind Bobby's truck.

She didn't want to believe that her brother had assaulted her and then had taken off. Despite the tension between them, he'd never hurt her physically. It didn't make sense that he would start now. Staggering to her feet, she belatedly noticed her purse was on the ground a few feet away, lying open. When she crossed over to pick it up, her heart sank as she realized her wallet was gone, along with all the cash she possessed.

Tears burned her eyes as a wave of hopelessness washed over her. Why would Bobby do this? She'd brought the money he'd requested and would have given him what he needed. Why would he have hit her on the head and robbed her?

She fished around in her purse for the car keys, but couldn't find them. Had Bobby taken those, too? She tried to think back to her actions and remembered that she'd held the keys in her hand as she searched for her brother.

Crawling on her hands and knees, she brushed her hands over the damp grass, trying to feel for the keys, which had to be somewhere nearby. But after a few minutes of searching fruitlessly in the dark, she gave up. She struggled back up to her feet and went over to the police vehicle. Thankfully she hadn't locked the doors, so she slid inside and switched on the headlights. But even after she turned on the lights, she couldn't see much in the grass.

Discouraged, she shut the headlights off and climbed back out of the car to walk back the direction she'd come. Her head throbbed more with every step until she felt so sick to her stomach she stopped and sank down onto the grass, curling up in a ball and breathing deeply to fight back the urge to throw up.

She had no idea how long she sat there. It could have been a few minutes or close to an hour, but soon a car approached, the bright headlights cutting through the darkness.

The light made her blinding pain worse, so she ducked

her head, shielding her eyes from the glare. It occurred to her that she should run away and hide, but she couldn't find the will to move.

"Tess? What happened?"

Declan's reassuring voice broke through the fog in her head. She glanced up at him as he hovered over her. "I'm...sorry. Lost...the...keys—"

She couldn't finish her thought, but it didn't matter because Declan lifted her in his arms and carried her. She put her head on his shoulder and closed her eyes, giving in to the overwhelming fatigue now that she knew she was safe.

Declan held Tess close, his heart pounding with fear and worry as he headed over to the car. He didn't understand why she hadn't gone back to the hotel, or why she'd been lying along the side of the road, yards away from the sheriff's deputy vehicle he'd loaned her.

"What happened?" Isaac asked.

"Not sure but I need you to call 911." Declan gently set Tess on the passenger seat, but she slumped forward as if unconscious. "Hurry," he urged Isaac.

He held Tess upright listening as Isaac requested an ambulance for a suspected assault. Declan performed a cursory exam and found a lump along the side of her head.

Two head injuries in less than twenty-four hours couldn't be good.

"Is she okay?" Isaac asked, coming over to where Declan was kneeling beside the car. "Is there something I can do?"

Declan tore his gaze from Tess's pale face. "She mentioned something about lost keys," he said. "She must have misplaced the keys to my vehicle."

"I'll take a look around," Isaac said, pulling out his mega flashlight.

Declan nodded, his attention focused back on Tess. She was breathing okay and he could feel the rapid beat of her pulse, yet she didn't respond when he called her name.

He hated feeling helpless, unable to do anything for Tess other than to wait for the ambulance to arrive.

But then he remembered how he'd prayed when defusing the bomb, secretly amazed at the sense of peace. Why not try that again?

Dear Lord, thank You for watching over Tess and please heal her wounds. Amen.

Again he experienced a sense of peace, of rightness that he never felt before. And even though Tess wasn't responding to him, he spoke to her anyway.

"Hang in there, Tess. Help is on the way. I'm right here and I won't leave you. But this time you are for sure going to the hospital to be checked out, so don't even try to argue."

He continued his one-sided conversation until the wail of sirens reached his ears. Within a few minutes the ambulance pulled up just as Isaac jogged back over.

"I found your keys," he announced, holding them up triumphantly.

"Thanks," Declan murmured. He stayed right where he was until the two EMTs pulled their equipment from the back of the ambulance and crossed over to him. "What happened?"

"I'm not sure, but she had a lump along the side of her head," Declan explained.

"We'll take a look. If you don't mind, we'll need some room to maneuver in order to get her on the gurney."

"Sure." Declan stepped back, watching closely as the two men worked together to examine Tess once they had her safely strapped onto their gurney.

"Declan?"

He jumped forward when he heard Tess's voice. "I'm here, Tess."

Her hand grasped his tightly. "Bobby's truck...was here. All my money's gone."

The implication of what she was telling him sank into his brain. "He attacked you in order to steal the money?"

Her eyes glittered with tears. "I don't know for sure... that it was Bobby," she whispered. "Could have been... someone else."

He ground his teeth, willing himself not to lose his temper. "Try not to worry about it now, Tess," he said in an attempt to reassure her. "We'll keep searching for your brother. Right now I want you to concentrate on taking care of yourself, okay?"

"Okay," she agreed, although he could still see the worry in her pretty brown gaze.

"We're taking her to Trinity Medical Center," the EMT informed him.

"I'll meet you there." As much as he wanted to ride in the ambulance with Tess, he needed to drive so that he would have his car on the off chance they ended up discharging her.

He stood beside Isaac, watching as they loaded Tess into the back of the ambulance.

"Do you want me to come to the hospital?" Isaac offered.

He was touched by the offer but shook his head. "No, but thanks."

Isaac clapped him on the back. "I'll put out an APB for that GMC truck," he offered. "And don't forget Griff wants your report ASAP."

He grimaced. "Yeah, I know."

"Let me know if you need anything else," Isaac said before he headed over to his car. Declan nodded and then jogged the few yards back to where his vehicle was parked. He slid behind the wheel and made a U-turn in the road so he could follow the ambulance.

Griff's report could wait until he'd made sure that Tess was really okay. At least physically. Mentally, emotionally, he knew she'd suffer.

Because her brother was clearly involved in this mess, too. Declan figured Tess was holding on to false hope, that Bobby was really innocent despite all the evidence that was now stacked against the kid. But Declan didn't believe in coincidences. The fact that Bobby called her and asked her to meet him at the same place where a bomb was planted was too much to ignore. Not to mention the way she was subsequently attacked and robbed.

Declan could only hope that one of his colleagues found Bobby soon, before they stumbled across another bomb.

Because Tess's brother was already facing significant jail time.

He drove to the hospital parking lot and climbed out from behind the wheel. The antiseptic smell of the hospital assaulted him when Declan walked into the emergency department. His uniform was badly wrinkled, but his badge should still be enough to cut through the red tape.

"I need to see Tess Collins," he said to the woman behind the front desk.

"Ah, sure, let me see." She tapped on the computer keys and then nodded. "Oh, yes, Ms. Collins is in room twelve. Go through the doors and it's the last room on the right."

"Thanks." He strode through the double doors and found Tess's room without difficulty, although there was a doctor and a nurse in there, so he waited outside the door while they tended to her.

Tess looked pale and fragile dressed in a hospital gown. Her blond hair was tangled and her amber eyes were closed, her pinched expression betraying her pain.

He was relieved when he overheard the doctor order a CT scan of her head to assess for a brain injury. And he wasn't surprised to hear that they also discussed whether or not she would need to stay in the hospital for twenty-four hours of observation.

Tess would hate staying, but he didn't care. He needed to know she was medically stable, and Tess would likely be safer in the hospital than anywhere else right now.

Once the doctor and nurse left, he went inside and took her hand in his. "How are you feeling?"

"Declan?" She opened her eyes and turned to face him. "Have you found my brother?"

"Not yet, but don't worry. We'll find him." He didn't elaborate more, as he didn't want her to be upset about the fact that the entire police force would be out looking to arrest Bobby.

Her eyelids fluttered closed and her fingers relaxed their grip on his, but he didn't let her go until the radiology staff came to take her for her CT scan. Declan sank into an uncomfortable plastic chair, wishing he had a laptop so he could begin working on his report.

He tipped his head back against the wall and closed his eyes, feeling the effects of the adrenaline crash. He was exhausted and knew Tess must be even more so. She'd been through so much, and had never once complained.

His phone rang, jarring him back to reality, and he grimaced when he saw the caller was his boss. No point in ignoring the call, so he pushed the talk button. "Yeah, what's up, Griff?"

"The FBI wants to talk to you again. How quickly can you get here?"

He closed his eyes and sighed. "I'm at the hospital, and it's well past midnight. Can't this wait until morning?"

"You can't say no to the feds," his boss informed him. "And I need to give them a time frame."

Declan didn't want to leave, but Griff was right: the feds never took no for an answer. He glanced at his watch. "I can be there in ten to fifteen."

"Good." Griff abruptly hung up.

He tucked his phone back into his pocket and scrubbed his hands over the stubble on his jaw. He could use a shower, a shave and a change of clothes. Maybe leaving for a while wouldn't be the end of the world. He could let Tess's nurse know so she wouldn't worry. Besides, he didn't think Tess would be discharged anytime soon.

Decision made, he summoned the nurse into the room, filled her in on his plans and asked her to give him a call if Tess's condition changed. After she graciously complied, he flashed a tired smile and then made his way back outside. There was no reason to be nervous...Tess was in good hands. She probably needed rest and relaxation anyway.

Declan drove back to headquarters, mentally preparing himself for the interrogation to come. He could only imagine what Agents Walker and Piermont would think about this latest turn of events. Was it possible they still believed he was personally involved in setting these bombs? Last time Griff had supported him, but Declan sensed his boss was quickly losing his patience with the lack of viable leads.

Despite the lateness of the hour, the building was brightly lit up, indicating an unusual amount of activity. He parked and headed inside, finding Griff and the two FBI agents waiting for him.

"About time you showed up," Agent Walker groused.

Declan held on to his temper with an effort. "I was at the hospital with a key witness," he said without apology.

Agent Walker scowled, but Agent Piermont offered a smile. "How about we go someplace private to talk?" she suggested.

Griff grunted and headed over to the same interrogation room they'd used earlier that day. Hard to believe that only sixteen hours had passed since Tess had discovered the bomb beneath her desk.

"I could use a cup of coffee," Declan announced. "Anyone else interested?"

"Sure, I'll come with you," Agent Lynette Piermont said, jumping to her feet.

As he poured two cups of coffee, Declan wondered if she always played the role of good cop. Agent Piermont added a good dose of cream and sugar while he sipped his black.

"Long day, huh?" she asked with obvious sympathy.

He shrugged, unwilling to be drawn into whatever game they were playing. "For you, too, I'm sure."

"Tough case," she agreed.

He turned and headed back to the interrogation room, suddenly annoyed with the small talk. He wanted to get this over and done with so he could head back to Tess.

"So you found another bomb, the third in one day," Agent Walker said without preamble.

Declan folded his arms across his chest and nodded.

Agent Walker stared at him, letting the silence drag out for several interminable seconds. Declan held his ground; he knew how to use these same interview techniques, too.

"How was it that you went to Greenland Park in the first place?" Agent Walker finally asked.

Declan took another bracing sip of his coffee before trodding through the same story he'd given Griff earlier. His boss remained silent as he explained how Tess had heard from her brother and gone out to meet him.

"We've run a check on Bobby Collins," Agent Piermont interjected. "Seems he has a couple of disorderly conduct tickets on file."

Declan shrugged, thinking about the disorderly conduct citations he had gotten himself as a teenager. He'd actually done worse things, but was lucky enough not to get caught. Joining the marines would have been impossible if he'd had a significant criminal record. And despite everything, he was glad he'd been given a chance to turn his life around.

"Sounds like this Bobby Collins is now your number-one suspect," Agent Walker said. "You need to bring him in for questioning."

Declan mentally counted to ten before he spoke, keeping his tone even. "And we will, as soon as we find him."

Agent Walker scowled. "If you knew Ms. Collins had

a brother, why didn't you put the APB out on him earlier? Maybe we could have avoided this latest bomb if you'd done your job."

Declan glanced at Griff, but his boss's bland expression didn't give anything away. Was Griff siding with the feds? "If you recall from my earlier report, we had a viable suspect, the guy wearing a green baseball cap who was not only seen at the scene of the elementary school, but was literally in the area minutes before the bomb exploded. Are you suggesting that I should have ignored that suspect to follow up on Bobby Collins?"

Spoken out loud, the idea sounded twice as ridiculous. The glimpse of a smile played across Griff's face as the two agents exchanged a frustrated glance.

"So tell me...when did you first decide that Bobby Collins might be a potential suspect?" Agent Walker demanded.

Declan shrugged. "Not until I found the bomb beneath the picnic table at the designated meeting place. There was no reason to suspect him earlier."

"I need to be notified immediately once you have Bobby Collins in custody," Agent Walker declared. "Understand?"

Declan had the ridiculous urge to laugh but managed to keep a straight face. "Of course. Is there anything else? Has your investigation unearthed any leads?"

The agents exchanged another frustrated glance. "We're finished here. Don't forget to turn in your report."

This time it was all Declan could do not to roll his eyes. As if he really needed to be told to do his job? What was wrong with these feds anyway? Surely they had other things to worry about.

He pushed to his feet and turned to his boss. "I'm

going to shower and change before heading back to the hospital. Call if you need anything."

Griff gave him a curt nod, and Declan released a breath he hadn't realized he'd been holding as he walked out the door. He went to his locker to get a fresh uniform, and then quickly used the facilities to shower, shave and change.

He felt 100 percent better as he drove back to Trinity Medical Center. The woman behind the desk recognized him from earlier, and waved him through.

As he strode down the hall toward Tess's room, he frowned when he realized there was a man wearing a navy blue jacket and gray dress slacks peering in through the half-closed doorway.

The guy looked familiar and it took a moment to recognize Allan Gray, Tess's geeky neighbor.

"Hey, what are you doing?" Declan called out sharply.

Clearly startled, her neighbor jerked around, gaping at Declan in surprise. Without saying a word, Gray turned and ran off in the opposite direction.

What in the world was Gray doing here? Spying on Tess? Declan sprinted after him, following as he disappeared through a doorway. Declan covered the distance as quickly as possible, bursting through the same doorway a few minutes later.

But all he saw was a long, empty hallway. There were several doors but he had no idea which one Tess's neighbor might have taken.

Allan Gray had gotten away.

TEN

Tess faded in and out, unable to keep her eyes open for very long, which made it difficult to keep track of what was happening around her.

But every time she opened her eyes Declan was there, sitting in a chair beside her bed. Reassured by his presence, she let herself drift.

Finally she woke up, feeling as if she could actually stay awake for a while. Bright sunlight was streaming through her window and she stared at the clock on the wall in shock. Two-thirty in the afternoon?

Had she really slept for more than twelve hours?

She struggled upright, wincing a bit as her head protested the sudden movement. Glancing over to where she remembered seeing Declan last, she was disappointed to find the chair was empty.

Of course he'd probably gone to work. After all, twelve hours was a long time to expect him to sit by her bedside. Thankfully, Greenland Elementary was closed so she didn't have to report in. Not that she was in any shape to teach anyway. She lifted her hand to her hair and grimaced at the tangled mess.

A nurse entered her room, looking a bit surprised to

find her awake. "Hi, my name is Sally. How are you feeling? I must say, you're looking much better."

"Thanks, I feel better." Tess realized she wasn't in the emergency room any longer but had no memory of being brought to a regular room. "I'd like to get up to use the bathroom."

"Certainly," Sally agreed, coming over to help. "Sit on the side of the bed first, in case you get dizzy."

Tess did as she was told. Sally was right on—the room tilted wildly, but then stopped moving after a few minutes. She braced herself on the bed and remained still, breathing deep and keeping her gaze focused on the bathroom door.

"Are you ready?" Sally asked.

"Yes." Tess hated feeling like an invalid, but she allowed the nurse to assist her into the bathroom. After using the facilities, she insisted on taking a shower and felt much better afterward.

Getting the snarls out of her hair wasn't as easy, and soon she was tired again. She crawled back into bed with a scowl, wondering when the doctor would show up to release her. She was already feeling guilty for being here this long, when all she had really needed was some sleep. And who could blame her after the day she'd had?

"Hey, you're awake," Declan said as he came into the room. He looked amazing with his clean shaven jaw, jeans and button-down denim shirt.

She smiled, unable to hide the fact that she was happy to see him. "Finally, huh? It's good to see you. Any idea when they'll spring me?"

"You're probably going to have to stay one more day," Declan advised. "They were worried about a small head injury they found on your CT scan."

"Really?" She put her hand to her temple, outlining the swollen area gingerly with her fingertips. "It doesn't seem any worse than the lump on the back of my head."

"Two head injuries in one day are serious enough to warrant close observation for a while."

She had no intention of staying here another night, but there was no point in arguing with Declan about that, so she changed the subject. "What did I miss? Have you found Bobby? Has anything else happened?"

Declan shook his head. "No, we haven't found Bobby and the only thing I've done is to write a bunch of reports and be interviewed by the feds."

Her good mood faded at the realization that her brother was still missing. "Did you check to see if Bobby reported to school this morning?"

"Yes, I called first thing. But he didn't show."

Despair nearly overwhelmed her. Where on earth could he be? The only logical explanation was that something bad had happened to him.

"Tess, tell me about your relationship with your neighbor Allan Gray," Declan said, breaking into her troubled thoughts.

She frowned. "What do you mean? We don't have a relationship. He's just my neighbor."

"Has he ever made any romantic overtures toward you?" Declan pressed.

"No, of course not. He offers to help me at times, and we chat if we see each other outside, but that's about it."

"What does he help you with?"

"Neighborly things, you know, like helping me to carry in my groceries or offering to shovel my driveway."

"He's been inside your house?" Declan asked, obviously appalled.

"Only in the kitchen, and it's not a big deal." She shrugged at his stern expression. "Honestly, I rarely take Allan up on his offers because I'm afraid of leading him on, or giving him the impression that we're more than neighbors. I'm nice to him and he's nice to me, that's all."

"So you do sense that he's a little off," Declan mused. "I don't blame you for being wary, since the guy is clearly following you."

Her jaw dropped. "What makes you say that?"

"He was here in the middle of the night, standing outside your room while you were still in the E.R.," Declan explained with a dark frown. "The minute he saw me, he took off. I went after him, but I lost him."

She relaxed and fought a smile. "Allan's not following me. He works as a third-shift security guard here at the hospital. He probably walked by my room and stopped when he recognized me. You're making a big deal out of nothing."

Declan was not amused. "So why did he run off when I asked him what he was doing? Why not come over and talk to me?"

"Maybe because you're scary?"

His scowl deepened. "I'm not scary and I'm telling you, he definitely looked guilty. Don't forget I saw him in my old neighborhood, too, shortly after you crashed. There's something not quite right with that guy and I wouldn't put it past him to plant bombs in the area. For all we know, he's carrying some sort of grudge since high school."

She sobered, thinking about how close she'd come to being seriously hurt when she crashed into the light post after the rock had shattered the windshield. It was strange that Allan would be nearby after that incident, but it had to be a weird coincidence. Because no matter what Declan thought, she couldn't imagine Allan doing something as crazy as setting bombs around the city.

"I'm sure he's not following me," she repeated. "You can't blame the guy for being around while he's working. Do me a favor and find my doctor. I'd really like to get out of here." Seeing Declan's dark scowl, she quickly added, "You know that I need to keep looking for my brother, and I can't do that from a hospital bed."

Flattening his lips, he stared at her for a long moment. "Look, Tess, every cop in the city is looking for Bobby. And they have a much better chance of finding him than you do."

"What?" She did not like the way Declan made it sound, as if her brother was some sort of criminal. "Why? Did you list him as a missing person?"

He winced and averted his gaze. "Not exactly."

A flash of anger burned through her. "You actually think he's guilty of planting that bomb under the picnic table? Come on, Declan, he's seventeen years old! Bobby has no reason to set bombs or try to blow things up. Especially not me!"

"Tess, you have to admit it's possible—"

"No, I don't," she interrupted. "No matter what kind of trouble Bobby is in, he wouldn't hurt me."

"What about the incident last night?" he demanded. "Someone hit you from behind and then robbed you. And you saw Bobby's truck. Why wouldn't he be involved? Clearly he's in way over his head."

"You're way off base. Bobby didn't hit me. It's clear he's in trouble. Maybe his friends turned on him for some reason and took his car and his phone."

"That's ridiculous," Declan scoffed. "You're wearing

blinders, Tess. Trust me, I've been Bobby's age. I know what it's like to get mixed up in the wrong crowd. He could very easily have gotten sucked into something illegal."

She bit her lip and tried not to cry, deeply disappointed in Declan's attitude toward her brother. He was just like Jeff, believing the worst. She sniffed back her tears, turned away and pushed the call light, asking for her nurse.

Declan could believe whatever he wanted to, but he'd never even met Bobby. She knew her brother, had raised him for the past six years. Granted Bobby had a couple of run-ins with the law, but deep down, he was a good kid. She believed Bobby loved and cared about her, the same way she loved and cared about him.

Too bad Declan couldn't trust her judgment. And for the first time since yesterday, she felt completely alone.

Declan left Tess's room, battling a wave of frustration. He didn't like having Tess be upset with him, but he didn't understand how she could be so convinced her brother was innocent after all the circumstantial proof that was stacked against him.

He leaned against the wall just outside her room, waiting while the doctor went in to talk to Tess. There was nothing he could do to stop Tess from leaving, and he hated feeling helpless. Why couldn't she do as he'd asked and stay one more night?

Nothing was more important than keeping her safe, other than finding the perp who'd set the bombs. Unfortunately, so far his investigation was nothing more than one big dead end.

Granted, he'd been mostly focused on Bobby and

Allan Gray, but maybe it was time to look into that Jeff guy who used to date Tess. He needed to cover his bases, and clearing Jeff Berg would give him more time to focus on the people closer to home.

Declan straightened when the doctor came back out of the room. "Are you keeping her another night?" he asked.

The doctor shook his head. "No, she's stable and can do the rest of her healing at home. Although she should take it easy for a while."

Declan signed, thinking that task was easier said than done. "Okay, I'll wait until she's ready to leave."

The doctor turned away, presumably to write the necessary discharge orders. Declan entered Tess's room to find her rummaging in the small closet. "Sit down, Tess, I'll get your things for you."

"I'm not an invalid," she said, gathering her clothes to her chest and then turning to face him. "Are you going to drive me back to the hotel? Or do I need to call a cab?"

Okay, she was obviously still upset with him. So why was he still incredibly drawn to her? "Of course I'll drive you back to the hotel. Nothing has changed. I still intend to keep you safe."

She stared at him for a long moment, as if she wanted to say something more, but she simply turned and headed into the bathroom, shutting the door with a loud click.

He lowered himself into an empty chair to wait for her. His phone rang, and he quickly answered it when he saw Isaac's phone number. "Hey, buddy, what's up? Have you found Bobby?"

"Not yet, which is a little odd considering we have everyone on alert. But I wanted you to know that I talked to Allan Gray this morning—he apparently works as a security guard at Trinity."

"Yeah, Tess informed me of that, as well. But did he explain why he took off running when I yelled out at him?"

"Claims he was worried he'd get arrested for some kind of privacy breach."

Declan shook his head, thinking Gray's excuse sounded pretty lame. "Did you ask him where he was yesterday afternoon?"

"Yeah, claims he wasn't anywhere near the corner where Tess hit the light pole, but I did get a good look at his car. He's driving a beige Chevy, so he could have been the guy you saw."

"Yeah, but it doesn't do me any good if I can't prove it." Declan sighed and rubbed the back of his neck. "At this rate, we'll never nail this guy."

"Deck, it's not like you to have a defeatist attitude," Isaac pointed out. "We'll keep poking at the clues and eventually something will turn up."

"I think we need to broaden our search," Declan muttered. "I'm going to look into that Jeff Berg who used to date Tess."

"Isn't he some sort of principal now?" Isaac asked. "Not a likely candidate for a bomber."

"I know, but there was something in Tess's expression when she mentioned him that sent up a red flag. I get the feeling there's more to that story." The bathroom door opened and Tess appeared, looking pale and drawn. "I have to go, but keep me posted with any updates."

"Will do."

He disconnected from the call and rose to his feet. "Are you ready to go? Do you need to sign paperwork or something?"

"I'll check with the nurse." She pushed her call light

and within moments the nurse came in with the discharge papers. After a few minutes Tess was ready to leave, although she flatly refused to use the wheelchair.

Declan walked beside her, ready to catch her if she fell, but it seemed she was truly fine as they made their way down to the lobby. "Wait here," he suggested. "I'll bring the car around."

"All right."

It didn't take long to drive the car up to the entrance where Tess was already walking outside to meet him.

"Are we going back to the same hotel as before?" she asked as they drove away from the hospital.

He nodded. "At this point there's no reason to move locations—the perp likely set up the meeting at the park because he didn't know where you were. I think we'll stay at least one more night, before moving on." He didn't add that the main reason he wanted to stay was so that Tess could get some much-needed rest.

"Good," she murmured. "I'd like to go to church tomorrow morning."

"Tomorrow is Saturday," he said, wondering if the bonk on her head caused her to be confused.

"I know, but there's usually an early morning service every day."

Okay, so she wasn't confused. "That's fine if you want to go, but I'll go with you."

She slanted him a curious glance. "I'm glad. You might find out that you really like it."

He didn't want to burst her bubble. The fact that he'd prayed while he worked on the bomb beneath the picnic table didn't mean that he planned to start attending church every week.

He steered the subject away from faith and church. "I need to know about your relationship with Jeff Berg."

Tess crossed her arms across her chest, immediately going on the defensive. "Why? I told you that he's not involved in this."

"How can you be so sure?"

She turned and stared out her window for several long moments. "We dated, and then he took a new job. That's all there is to it."

He was convinced she was holding back. "Tess, please. I'm sorry if you think I'm poking my nose in your personal business, but I really need to understand what went wrong between the two of you. If he's innocent, that's fine, because right now I'd like nothing more than to cross at least one suspect off the list."

Tess sighed and shook her head. "There isn't anything to tell."

He'd interviewed enough suspects to know that wasn't true. "If a guy is happy and thinking of spending the rest of his life with a woman, he's not about to look for a new job in another state. Which means that something wasn't right between the two of you."

"We weren't serious," Tess protested. "And Jeff was very ambitious. I knew he wanted a principal position."

She wasn't making this easy. "How was his relationship with Bobby?"

Her flinch was so subtle that he almost missed it. "They didn't get along," she admitted frankly. "But understand that Bobby's attitude didn't help much."

"I'm sure your brother was very protective of you."

She nodded grimly. "Yes, that much is true. But Jeff repeatedly told me that I was too soft on Bobby and that I needed to be stricter with him."

He sensed he was treading on dangerous ground. "Maybe that's just the way he was raised."

"No, that's the way I was raised," she admitted. "My father was strict to the point I used to feel sick to my stomach every time he got angry with me."

He scowled at that. "Did your father abuse you?"

"Not physically, but he was a total control freak. And he didn't hesitate to yell and scream if I stepped out of line. I spent most of my spare time in the library since it was the only safe haven I had to escape the tense atmosphere at home."

Suddenly Tess's reaction to his commands yesterday made sense. "I'm sorry," he murmured. "That must have been rough."

She lifted her shoulder in a careless shrug. "Maybe I was too lenient with Bobby, but I didn't appreciate the way Jeff used to yell at him, either."

Declan tightened his grip on the steering wheel. "Did Jeff do more than yell?" he asked carefully.

Tess pursed her lips together and reluctantly nodded. "I think so," she said in a low voice. "One day I was late coming home and Jeff was already at the house when I arrived. Bobby was sporting a black eye. Jeff denied hitting him but admitted that they'd argued. Bobby wouldn't say anything one way or the other." She released a shuddering breath. "I refused to go out with him that night and Jeff told me that was fine because he'd only come to tell me that he'd accepted a principal position in St. Louis."

Declan found it hard to believe that a man who'd dedicated his life to leading teachers had actually hit a teenager. "Did you report him? Or call the police?"

Tess shook her head. "No, Bobby convinced me not to. He admitted that he'd instigated the argument. I guess

I was worried that somehow Jeff's story would change and Bobby would be the one thrown in jail."

Declan nodded, understanding her logic. He remembered several times he'd gotten in trouble just for being in the wrong place at the wrong time. Once the cops tagged you as a troublemaker, it was difficult to recover.

But this new information swirled around in his head. Was it possible that Jeff was worried Tess had the power to ruin his career? Would he take drastic steps to keep her from talking about what had happened with Bobby? It seemed like a long shot, but he couldn't afford to totally discount the possibility.

He pulled into the parking lot of the hotel and then turned to face her. "Maybe I should pay Berg a visit?"

"I'd rather you didn't," Tess said with a frown. "I don't trust him not to turn everything back to Bobby. Right now it's the word of a principal against that of a troubled teenager. Besides, as much as Jeff turned out to be a jerk, I still can't imagine him running around the city planting bombs as a way to get back at me."

Declan sighed. "You could be right…it does seem to be a bit of a stretch. But someone is trying to hurt you, Tess, and we need to figure out who that could be before he succeeds."

"How do we know that I'm the target?" she asked. "I've been thinking about this a lot, and you're in as much danger as I am. Maybe more, since you're the one who ends up dealing with the actual bombs."

He scoffed at the idea. "I doubt it. The other members of the SWAT team are just as much at risk as I am."

"I heard Caleb and Isaac talking about the fact that you're the main bomb guy. And didn't you work at the minimart when you were in high school?"

He stared at her in surprise. "Yes, but you worked at the custard stand."

"You used to come to the custard stand all the time, even though you didn't buy anything."

Declan swallowed hard. He didn't want to admit that he'd gone there to get a glimpse of Tess.

"Think about it, Declan. What better way to get back at you than to keep planting bombs? And you said yourself, your sister was at the minimart when the bomb went off. Maybe we should be looking at someone who's holding a grudge against you."

Declan didn't know what to say, because he couldn't deny the possibility she was right. All the bomb sites were places where he'd hung out as a teenager.

His gut clenched with dread. What if the only reason Tess was in danger was him?

ELEVEN

Tess glanced at Declan, who was staring intently through the windshield, clearly deep in thought. She was glad his focus had shifted away from Jeff Berg.

She couldn't believe she'd been stupid enough to go out with Jeff in the first place. Even in the beginning, she hadn't appreciated his stringent attitude toward Bobby. Just thinking of the way Jeff had hit Bobby made her furious all over again. A wave of helpless guilt washed over her. She knew she should have called the police while the bruise darkening her brother's eye was still visible, proof that Jeff had punched him. Even if Bobby had started the fight, she should have defended him.

At the time, she'd been afraid that Jeff would claim Bobby hit him first, somewhere a bruise wouldn't show. And considering the two disorderly conduct citations Bobby had already racked up, she suspected the police would side with Jeff, a respected assistant principal of the local middle school, rather than believe her brother.

Was that the real reason Bobby had skipped school and then disappeared? Because she hadn't done a better job of protecting him last summer? Her cheeks burned with shame at the thought of Bobby blaming her.

It was too late to go back and fix the past; all she could do was to focus on the future. She sent up another silent prayer. *Please, Lord, please keep Bobby safe and show him the way home. Amen.*

"Let's get inside," Declan said, finally breaking the silence.

She nodded and pushed her car door open. She knew she needed to keep looking for her brother, but she was out of ideas as to where to search next.

Had Bobby gone to the church to find her note? She really wanted to go and check, but she worried that going to church tonight as well as going in the morning might cause Declan to be suspicious as to her true motive.

Yet at the same time, she had to know one way or the other. Somehow, she just knew that if Bobby was in trouble, he'd go to the church they'd attended together.

Using her magnetic card key, she opened her door and went inside. Declan surprised her by following her into the room.

"Are you hungry?" he asked. "We can go out for something to eat."

"Not really, I had a late lunch. But you go ahead… I'm sure you're hungry."

"No, I'm not leaving you here alone," he said stubbornly. "We'll order in when you're ready."

Tess sank down on the edge of her bed, trying to ignore the ache in her head. Sitting here doing nothing didn't suit her.

"I changed my mind," she said abruptly. "I'd like to go back to church tonight, instead of waiting until the morning."

His eyebrows rose. "Okay," he said. "But I'd like to eat something first if that's all right with you. And you should probably take more pain meds, but not on an empty stomach."

She felt bad making him skip a meal, so she gave in. "All right, but all I need is some soup."

He looked as if he wanted to argue, but he shrugged. "Okay, rest for a few minutes while I find somewhere that delivers."

She stretched out on the bed, intending to just close her eyes for a few minutes, but the next thing she knew almost an hour had passed. She had no idea that having a head injury would cause her to feel so exhausted.

"Declan?" she called as she swung upright on the edge of the bed. The connecting door was open, but she couldn't hear anything.

"I'm here," he said quickly. He strode through the doorway with a tray of food. "I ordered you some chicken noodle soup and scrambled eggs."

"Thanks." She stood and met him over by the small table in the corner of the room. "Did you already eat? Is that pizza I smell?"

"Yeah, I ate already," he said, ducking his head as if embarrassed. "Sorry about the pizza fumes…I hope they don't make you sick."

"I'll be fine," she assured him. She ate the lukewarm soup and eggs while Declan surfed the internet. Her brief nap had restored her appetite.

"Are you sure you're up to a walk to the church?" he asked when she'd finished. "We can wait until tomorrow. I still have some research to do on my laptop and you look as if you could use more sleep."

Tess had to admit it was tempting, but she forced herself to shake her head. "I'd like to go tonight, but you don't have to come along. I'm sure I'll be fine—the church is only a few blocks away."

"I don't want you to go alone, so I'll come with you," Declan said, although she could see the flash of disappointment in his eyes. "Just give me a few minutes to shut down."

"Sure." Tess used the time to freshen up in the bathroom, splashing water on her cheeks in a vain attempt to bring some color to her pale face. Her headache had eased a bit, which she hoped was a good sign.

Declan had carried his computer into his room, returning less than five minutes later. He took her hand as they left the hotel. She told herself that this gesture didn't mean anything other than the fact that he was likely worried that she'd fall flat on her face. But despite her efforts to convince herself otherwise, the warmth of his hand surrounding hers was very distracting as they walked to the church.

"Why is it so dark?" she asked, glancing up at the clouds hovering in the sky.

"Supposed to rain, but not until later."

Tess couldn't help wondering if she was crazy to think Bobby had come to church to find her note. It could be that this was nothing more than a wild-goose chase. Although enjoying the fresh air was nice and refreshing.

If nothing else, sitting in church would help her feel closer to God, at least for a short time.

"Let's try not to stay too long," Declan cautioned as she walked up the stairs to the main doors. "I'd rather not get caught in the rain."

"Are you going to wait in the back?" she asked.

"No, I'm coming up front with you."

To her chagrin, Declan followed her all the way to the

front of the church, and she wondered if he would have done this if they had been sitting through a regular service. Somehow she doubted it. As she went into the pew, she brushed her fingers in the corner where she'd left the note, but it wasn't there.

Because the cleaning staff had found it? Or because Bobby had? The possibilities swirled around in her mind and she wanted more than anything to believe the latter.

Declan bowed his head in respect as Tess prayed. He wondered if she was still praying for her brother, and decided that adding something of his own wouldn't hurt.

Lord, help us find Bobby before it's too late.

He opened his eyes, feeling a little foolish. What made him think that God would listen to his entreaties? But just like when he'd prayed while defusing the bomb, he felt a sense of peace.

"I'm ready," Tess murmured after what seemed like only a short time had passed.

"Are you sure? There's plenty of time." They'd only been there for about fifteen minutes, and he was worried she'd resent him for making her leave so soon.

"Yes, I'm sure."

He stood and made his way out of the church pew, waiting for Tess to precede him down the aisle. She stood for a moment at the end of the pew, her head bowed, and he wondered if she was feeling dizzy again.

But before he could ask her, she straightened and stepped away.

Outside, darkness had fallen, mostly because of the dark clouds obliterating the sky. When Tess shivered, he put his arm around her shoulders. To his surprise, she leaned against him as if grateful for the support.

No doubt her headache was back. He wanted to point out that they shouldn't have come, but he stopped himself. The last thing he wanted to do was to act like her father. He understood now that the way she'd rebelled against his edicts before was because of her experiences with her father. Barking orders was a way of life in the marines, but of course he understood that civilians like Tess didn't have to listen.

Somehow he needed to make sure she understood that the only reason he told her what to do was to keep her safe and not that he was a control freak like her father.

Although as soon as the thought formed, he knew that wasn't entirely true. Because he was a man who liked to be in control. He needed to control the things he could because when he went into active crime situations, he was forced to react to whatever was going on.

Tess went tense and he dragged his thoughts back to the present. "Did you hear that?" she asked in a whisper.

He mentally smacked himself in the head for losing his concentration and exposing them to possible danger. He stopped and listened, holding Tess close to his side.

The wind was picking up, whistling through the trees. But he didn't hear anything else. He turned and swept his gaze across the area behind them, but couldn't see much in the darkness.

"I'm sure it was just the wind," he murmured reassuringly. He began walking again, wishing he could pick up the pace. Tess must have shared his sense of urgency because she walked faster than she had on the way over to the church.

A soft thud reached his ears and he reacted without thought, pulling his Glock even as he pushed Tess back into the shadow of the trees. Within seconds he had her crouched behind a tree, while he stood in front of her, wishing he had his night-vision goggles to help penetrate the darkness.

But even though he waited patiently, he didn't see anything move or hear any other sounds. There was absolutely no indication that there was actually someone behind them, tracking their every move. Although he couldn't afford to discount the possibility.

He silently promised himself that if Allan Gray showed up, he'd arrest the guy for stalking. Enough was enough.

But the seconds stretched into a minute, and then two. He hesitated, debating between calling for backup and getting Tess back to the hotel as quickly as possible. They were less than thirty yards away from the bright lights of the hotel.

"Declan, do you see anything?" Tess whispered.

"No." He turned toward her and put a hand under her elbow to help her stand up. "We need to get back to the hotel. Are you able to run?"

"Yes," she answered quickly.

"Stay as close to the trees as you can," he murmured. "And have your key ready."

She gave a jerky nod and he hoped he wasn't making a mistake by running for it. But it went against the grain to call his team when he was armed and they had barely thirty yards to go to reach the safety of the building.

He moved to the right, keeping Tess hidden in the trees. Soon they ran out of tree coverage and without his saying a word, Tess put on a burst of speed, running toward the hotel and jamming her card into the slot in the door.

Keeping right behind her, he mentally braced for the

sound of someone coming after them, but he didn't hear anything and within minutes they were safely inside the hotel. He shut the door behind him, as Tess sank against the wall, breathing heavily.

He reached out for her, intending to offer comfort, but the moment his arms wrapped around her, the embrace went from friendly to intense.

There was no way to know who moved first, but somehow he was kissing her and even more astonishing, she was kissing him back.

Tess clung to Declan's shoulders, losing herself in his kiss. She could have stayed in his arms for hours, but within a few minutes, he gently pulled away and she reluctantly let him go.

She missed his warmth as he stepped back, running a hand through his hair. "I'm sorry, I don't know how that happened."

His apology didn't make her happy. "I'm not sorry, so don't worry about it."

His gaze clashed with hers, and a strained tension rippled between them. This time, she broke the connection by turning away.

"Excuse me," she murmured, escaping into the bathroom. She closed the door and dropped down onto the commode, trying to calm her racing pulse. It bothered her that Declan regretted kissing her, especially since she'd secretly dreamed of being with him again since their first kiss ten years ago.

Even then, Declan had been her knight in shining armor. Saving her from Steve Gains and a potential sexual assault.

Declan had been a year older than her, and of course

she remembered seeing him at the minimart and hanging out at the custard stand, his rebellious long hair and black leather jacket screaming defiance. Yet despite his troublemaker reputation, he'd never been anything but nice and polite to her.

Ironic that all those years ago, she'd been safer with the town rebel than she had been with Steve Gains, the town golden boy. Declan's true personality had shown through that night, the way he'd stood up for her and had taken on Steve Gains. She'd realized that much of Declan's tough attitude had been a cover for his true nature.

What she didn't know was why.

She gave herself a mental shake. Enough worrying about Declan, she told herself firmly. Her brother had to remain her top priority. Her note that she'd tucked into the church pew was gone, but that didn't mean Bobby was the one who'd found it.

She buried her face in her hands, battling a wave of helplessness. What if Declan insisted on switching hotels? Bobby would never find her.

When she'd first heard the noise behind them, she wondered if it could be Bobby, but when the sounds stopped and no one appeared, she figured she was imagining things. But then they'd both heard it again, the barest thud of a footstep. What did it mean? Surely if Bobby had found her, he would have come forward right away?

Unless he was in trouble and was worried about being arrested. She didn't want to think the worst but forced herself to acknowledge that the way Bobby had been missing for the past two days wasn't encouraging.

Maybe it was a good thing that all the police in the area were looking for him. Even if he ended up in jail, at least she'd feel better knowing where he was.

She pulled herself together with an effort, rising to her feet and taking a deep breath before opening the bathroom door. When she stepped into the room, she was surprised to see that Declan wasn't there.

Was he already planning their next move? She racked her brain, trying to think of an excuse that would convince Declan to stay here at least for another night or two.

Long enough for Bobby to find her.

The sound of muted voices wafted through the connecting doorway. Tess rose and walked over, straining to listen.

"I need to know where Allan Gray is," Declan was saying in a low tone. "I think he's following Tess again."

She closed her eyes, despair washing over her. If Declan thought Allan Gray had been stalking them, then for sure he'd make them leave. There was a long pause before Declan spoke again. "So you're saying he's been home this whole time? That it's not possible for him to have waited outside the hospital for us and followed me to the hotel?" His voice rose sharply. "Are you confident enough about this to put Tess's life on the line if you're wrong?"

Several more tense moments of silence passed. Tess clenched her fingers together tightly, waiting for Declan to say something to whomever was on the other end of the line.

"I hope you're right, Isaac," Declan finally said in a weary tone. "And let me know as soon as you hear anything about Bobby."

He disconnected from the call and then lifted his head, catching sight of her hovering in the doorway.

"They still haven't found my brother?" she asked.

Declan grimaced and shook his head. "Not yet."

She nodded, understanding that Declan wanted to find Bobby just as much as she did. Although for a very different reason.

"Good night," she said, pushing away from the doorway.

"Tess, wait." She paused and turned around to face him. He stared at her for a long moment before he said the words she'd been dreading to hear. "Pack up your things. We need to move to a different hotel."

"Not tonight," she protested.

"We can't ignore the fact that we may have been followed here," Declan pointed out. "What if our perp is out there right now, planting another bomb?"

The stark reality was too much to ignore. She didn't want to leave because of her brother, but was she willing to risk her life?

Or Declan's?

The answer to both of those questions was a resounding no. Tears pricked her eyes and she blinked them away before Declan could see them.

"Give me a few minutes," she murmured. She turned around and went into her own room, closing the connecting door behind her. She needed some time alone.

She sniffed loudly, wiping away the dampness around her eyes. It was so frustrating that she couldn't do more to find her brother.

All she could do was to continue praying for him.

But somehow even praying for Bobby didn't lift the heavy sense of dread that shrouded her. After several long moments, she stood and forced herself to pack her meager belongings together.

There was a faint noise outside, and she frowned and

crossed over to the window. There it was again, a slight pinging noise.

She instinctively turned off the lights and waited a few minutes for her eyes to adjust to the darkness. When she heard the third taping sound, she moved the heavy curtain over the window just enough to peer outside.

The window looked over the front parking lot and she scanned the area carefully. But nothing seemed out of place that she could tell. There were several cars parked out front, but none directly in front of her window.

A slight movement caught her eye, and she realized there was a figure crouched near the side of a black truck, mostly hidden in the shadows. She blinked and stared, trying to get a good look at the person's facial features. The way the person was crouched down, she couldn't even tell if it was a male or female.

But then the figure lifted his head and his arm, tossing another pebble at her window. Relief overwhelmed her, making her knees go weak.

Bobby! Her brother had found her!

TWELVE

Tess's heart was pounding with anticipation as she opened her hotel room door as quietly as possible and slipped outside. "Bobby?" she called in a whisper. "It's me, Tess. Are you out there?"

"Yes, I'm here." Bobby rose to his feet, and the moment she saw him, she rushed over to throw her arms around him in a huge hug.

"Thank heavens you're safe!" she whispered, clutching him tightly. "You have no idea how happy I am to see you."

"I found your note, Tess," Bobby said.

"I'm glad," Tess murmured. "I've been so worried."

"I'm sorry, sis. I'm so sorry, for everything."

She reluctantly released him and stepped back so she could try to read his eyes. "What happened, Bobby? How much trouble are you in?"

Her brother let out a heavy sigh. "I'm not in as much trouble as Mitch, that's for sure. I thought we were friends, but I guess not." Her brother's tone was bitter.

She couldn't deny feeling glad that Bobby wasn't sticking by his friend Mitch. "Start at the beginning," she suggested. "I went to pick you up from school, but you weren't there…"

"Yeah, we decided to go off campus for lunch and Mitch wanted to skip class the rest of the day. I tried to argue with him, but he wasn't listening."

"What happened next?" she asked.

"He talked me into heading over to the park for a while. Then, out of nowhere, Mitch demanded money to buy drugs. I refused to give him a dime, told him that he needed to go into rehab to get clean. At first, Mitch seemed okay, but as soon as we were about to leave the park, he caught me off guard and slugged me." Bobby raked a hand through his hair, then continued. "Next thing I know, he took off with my phone and my truck. I tried to find him, even went to his house, but he wasn't anywhere…."

"Go on," she prodded gently, trying to keep a tight rein on her emotions. Despite the inner turmoil that she was feeling right now, she needed to remain calm, and composed so he'd tell her the whole story from start to finish.

He cleared his throat. "By this time, it was really too late to go back to class, so I didn't bother. I really thought Mitch would come back and give me the truck keys after he got what he needed, but after an hour or so passed, I knew things were bad. Eventually I walked home, but then I saw your sign on the door, and I've been hiding out ever since."

Tess narrowed her eyes at him. She could see the dark bruises on Bobby's face, but as much as she loved her brother, she couldn't help wondering how much of his account was really true. "Why didn't you call the police?"

Bobby shrugged and stared down at his feet. "At first

I didn't want to get Mitch in trouble, and then I was worried that they wouldn't believe me."

Tess tamped down a flash of annoyance. She knew Bobby had a deeply ingrained mistrust of the police ever since his last arrest for disorderly conduct, but he needed to get over it already. Granted the last time he'd been cited he caught a raw deal, as he was truly trying to help a girl who was being threatened by her ex-boyfriend. But of course, the police didn't believe Bobby and ended up giving him a ticket instead of citing the guy who'd started the mess in the first place.

But now the fact that her brother hadn't gone straight to the authorities would make him look bad. And she couldn't deny a tiny sliver of doubt that Bobby had in fact gone along with Mitch, at least in the beginning. "So you weren't the one who knocked me out and stole my money?"

"What?" Bobby's shock was too real to be faked. He grasped her arms, staring at her intently. "No! Tell me what happened."

Tess knew her attacker must have been Mitch, hopefully acting alone. "I received a call from your phone and I thought it was you on the other line asking me to meet you at Greenland Park because you needed money. Except when we got there, we found a bomb under the picnic table." Seeing Bobby's eyes widen even farther, she drew a breath and continued. "Declan dealt with the explosive while I went back to his car. I was supposed to return to the hotel, but then I found your truck. When I looked inside, the truck was empty, but someone came up behind me and knocked me out. When I came to, all my cash was gone."

"That jerk," Bobby muttered darkly. "Mitch is going

to pay for hurting you. I can't believe he actually mugged you!"

"Don't say things like that," she admonished him. "You're not going to make him pay or do anything else about this. We'll let the police handle it. Which is what you should have done right away. With your statement, I'm sure we can convince the authorities to arrest Mitch."

"I hope so." Bobby shuffled his feet and dragged a hand through his too-long reddish blond hair. "I'm sorry I disappointed you, Tess."

"Oh, Bobby." She sighed and gave him another quick hug. "I know it's been rough the past couple of months, but you have to learn to trust in the system, okay?"

Bobby shrugged, nodded and then changed the subject. "Who's Declan?"

Tess hoped her blush wasn't too noticeable. "He's a friend of mine from high school, who just happens to be part of the Milwaukee County SWAT team. He's been keeping me safe."

"Yeah, I noticed."

"How would you know?" she asked with a frown, trying to understand how her brother had figured that out.

"I saw you two together."

"That was you back there? Following us from church?"

Bobby nodded. "Yeah, but as soon as your bodyguard went into cop mode, I backtracked." Her brother grimaced. "I can't believe you're friends with a cop."

"Trust me, Declan is one of the good guys." She prayed her brother would learn to trust the police. "We'll get through this, Bobby. Always remember that I love you and I believe in you."

Bobby managed a crooked smile. "I love you, too, sis."

She gave her brother another hug, closing her eyes in

relief. *Thank You, Lord! Thank You for keeping Bobby safe and showing him the way home.*

Declan glanced at his watch for the fifth time in ten minutes. What in the world was taking Tess so long? He understood she didn't want to leave, but they didn't have a choice.

His goal was to keep her safe. Maybe his imagination had been working overtime on the walk back from the church. It was possible that the only thing he'd heard was the wind whipping through the trees. But he wasn't going to take a chance with her life.

Tess was clearly getting tired of being on the move, and he didn't blame her. He knew that she was still feeling the effects of her concussion. She needed to rest and relax, two things that were difficult to accomplish when you were constantly running from one place to the other.

He straightened, realizing she might have fallen asleep again. Maybe that was why she wasn't ready to go?

He hated the thought of waking her up if she had indeed fallen asleep. Yet she could sleep as long as she needed once they'd gotten settled in a new hotel.

Five minutes, he promised himself. If she hadn't opened the connecting door by that time, he'd have to use his second key to get into her room.

Tess wouldn't be happy to know he actually had a key to her room, especially considering the way he'd kissed her. But since he'd paid for both rooms, the clerk hadn't batted an eye when he asked for one.

He still couldn't believe he'd lost his head like that. The same way he had ten years ago. Granted, their brief kiss the night he'd driven her home after rescuing her from Gains hadn't been nearly enough. He'd thought about kissing her often during those first few weeks after graduation, but then he'd joined the marines and he had bigger things to worry about, like staying alive.

So why had he kissed her again, tonight? He shouldn't have taken advantage of the situation. For one thing, she'd had a concussion. For another, she was his responsibility to keep safe. Getting emotionally involved with Tess was not part of the plan.

Okay, he'd made a mistake by kissing her tonight. But he couldn't allow himself to make another one. Even if Tess had seemed annoyed when he'd apologized for taking advantage of her. Did that mean she'd enjoyed the embrace as much as he had?

Don't go there, he reminded himself. *Stay focused.*

He went through his notes one more time, still frustrated by the fact that Isaac had confirmed Gray had actually been at home during the time he and Tess were making their way back from church. But interestingly enough, it appeared that Jeff Berg had taken a short personal leave of absence from his brand-new job.

Had Jeff come back here to exact his revenge on Tess? Declan had instructed Isaac to put out a notice that Jeff Berg was a person of interest in the bombings.

More than five minutes had passed, so Declan took out his spare hotel key and stepped outside. But before he could walk over to Tess's door, he stopped abruptly when he saw she was outside, talking to a young man who towered over her by a good twelve inches.

It took a minute to recognize the young man as her brother Bobby.

"Tess!" His tone was sharper than he intended. "What do you think you're doing?"

She jumped around at the sound of his voice and then

stepped protectively in front of her brother, as if Declan were the enemy instead of the guy who'd pledged to watch her back.

His fault, for sounding like a marine drill sergeant. He mentally kicked himself for reverting to his military mode. But he'd been so surprised to find her outside talking to her brother as if nothing had happened.

"Don't yell at me," Tess said defiantly. "My brother needs help. He's as much a victim of a crime as I am."

Yeah, right. Declan reined in his temper. "Let's get inside the hotel, okay? I don't like having you out here unprotected."

"I can protect my sister," Bobby said arrogantly. "We don't need you."

Declan fought for control, when he really wanted to give the kid a piece of his mind for what he'd put Tess through during his disappearing act. He glanced at Tess, hoping she would see reason. "Please, let's go inside and talk, all right?"

"No one followed us here," Tess said wearily. "Bobby was the one behind us, so there's no need to worry."

Somehow the knowledge that her brother was the one who'd followed them wasn't exactly reassuring. "Don't enable him. He needs to be held accountable for his actions," Declan said gruffly. Ignoring her withering glare, he took out his phone, planning to call Isaac. "It's probably better if we go down to the station to talk."

"What? You can't be serious. Didn't you hear me? Bobby is the victim of a crime!"

"I heard you," he said, striving to remain calm.

"Come on, Tess, let's get out of here," Bobby said, tugging on her arm. "We don't have to stay here with *him.*"

"Bobby, wait, just give me a minute, okay?" Tess

gazed at Declan as if imploring him to listen. "Don't you remember what it was like to be Bobby's age? To have everyone automatically assume the worst about you? Can't you give him the benefit of the doubt? At least until you've heard his side of the story? Please?"

Declan blew out a sigh, realizing she was right. He did remember what it was like to be Bobby's age, but he'd earned his title of being the town troublemaker and he was pretty sure Bobby had earned his, too. Maybe he could wait a few minutes to hear the kid's side of the story. "All right, fine. But let's talk inside."

"Please, come with me," Tess said to Bobby. "I don't have my car, so it's not as if we can just drive away."

Her brother scowled but gave a tight nod. "Okay, but if he calls to have me arrested, I'm outta here. I'll be fine on my own."

Since that was exactly what Declan had intended to do, he couldn't blame the kid for his response. But he'd made Tess a promise to listen to Bobby's side of the story, so he would. But if the kid tried to lie to them, he wouldn't hesitate to cuff him.

Because whether Tess realized it or not, he was going to do whatever he had to in order to protect her, even from her brother, if necessary.

Tess kept a hold on Bobby's arm, as if he might run off if she let go, while they followed Declan inside the hotel room.

Bobby remained tense and she suppressed a sigh, knowing she would have to be the buffer between the two hardheaded men. Somehow, someway she had to convince Declan to give Bobby the benefit of the doubt.

When the door closed behind her, it seemed the room

shrank considerably, uncomfortably crowded with the three of them in there. She gave her brother a nudge toward one of the chairs located near the desk. She sat on the edge of the bed, forcing Declan to take the chair next to Bobby.

"Bobby, explain everything you told me earlier to Declan," Tess said, breaking the silence.

He repeated his earlier story, and to his credit Declan didn't interrupt. When Bobby finished, she wasn't surprised when Declan went back to clarify a few key points.

"So Mitch is the one who assaulted Tess," he surmised.

"I didn't know anything about that," Bobby said with a frown. "He had no right to go after my sister. If I had known his plan, I would have called the police."

"But you didn't," Declan reminded him.

Bobby exhaled sharply. "No. I know I should have, but you don't understand what Mitch has been through. His mom has...issues."

Tess exchanged a glance with Declan, and he nodded, obviously remembering the way Mitch's mother had been drunk when they stopped by. "I know, Bobby," she said softly. "I went over to Mitch's house to try and find you."

Bobby's face flushed with anger. "You shouldn't have done that, Tess. You have to stay away from there. It's a really rough neighborhood."

She silently agreed, remembering the rock that had shattered her windshield. Was Mitch the person responsible? Or someone else?

"Where were you Thursday evening?" Declan interjected. "That's when Tess went to Mitch's house looking for you, but someone threw a rock at her car, causing her to crash into a light pole. She's lucky she wasn't seriously hurt."

Bobby scowled and jumped to his feet. "Are you accusing me of hurting my sister?" he asked defensively.

Declan raised a hand. "Calm down, Bobby. I'm not accusing you of anything. I was just wondering if you were still with Mitch close to that time, that's all."

The teenager's anger deflated as quickly as it had flared. "The last time I saw Mitch was roughly two-thirty in the afternoon. By Thursday evening, I was back in Greenland Park, hiding out and trying to figure out what to do next."

It broke Tess's heart to think of her brother being all alone without friends or family to help him out. Why, oh, why hadn't her brother contacted the police?

"I believe you," Declan said.

Bobby's head snapped up, his gaze surprised. "You do?"

"Yes, I do. There's no way you'd purposefully harm Tess. The only thing I don't agree with was your decision to avoid going to the police." He pulled his phone out of his pocket. "I'm going to call one of the guys from my SWAT team to put out an arrest warrant for Mitch. Will you provide an official statement about the way he stole your phone and your car?"

"Yeah, I'll give you a statement. But aren't you going to arrest him for assaulting Tess?" Bobby demanded.

"Yes, but we still need more proof to make those charges stick," Declan explained. He started to make the call, but then stopped. "Bobby, did you ever see Mitch building a bomb?"

"What?" His eyes widened in alarm. "No, why? Do you think he's the one setting the bombs?"

Declan shrugged. "Anything is possible. What's the

rumor mill at the high school? Is anyone taking responsibility for the bombs? Or maybe bragging about them?"

Bobby slowly shook his head. "No, although a few of the kids made smart-aleck comments about how it would be nice if the bomber would hit the high school so we wouldn't have class."

"What about any kids in the chemistry class?" Declan asked. "Any of them say anything about how easy it would be to make a bomb?"

"Nah, I didn't hear anything like that, but I took chemistry last year, so I wouldn't have been in there to hear anyone bragging or talking about it."

Tess spoke up. "Bobby, if you know anything at all, please tell us." She gave him an imploring look. "Who was the kid who mentioned wishing classes would be canceled?"

"Ricky Jones, but he's not smart enough to plant bombs. He just talks big, that's all."

"We might have a little chat with him anyway, just in case," Declan said as he rose to his feet. Tess noticed a wince flash over Bobby's face and knew her brother wouldn't have given a name if he'd known that Declan was going to interrogate the kid. He called Isaac, but the call must have gone to voice mail since Declan only said, "Call me back," before hanging up.

"This is really serious, Bobby," Tess said in a low voice. "People have died. The police have to investigate every lead."

"I guess," her brother muttered. "You can't blame me for not wanting to be a snitch."

"I can blame you if you don't tell us something that could help arrest this person," Tess countered.

Her brother sighed. "Okay, okay. I hear you."

Declan swung back around to face them. "Tess, are you ready to go?"

"Go where?" she asked. "I thought we could stay since Bobby was the one who'd followed us from the church."

"There's not a lot of room here, and rather than get a third room, I think it might be best if we all go back to my place."

Tess hesitated, instinctively wanting to squash Declan's offer. But she had her brother's safety to consider. Just the thought of Bobby being alone in his own hotel room caused her stomach to clench in fear. She wouldn't put it past Bobby to disappear again if he somehow thought Declan was turning against him.

"If Tess wants to stay here, then that's what we should do," Bobby chimed in, automatically siding with Tess. She was touched by his loyalty.

Declan didn't say anything but kept his gaze centered on her. "Tess? I promise we'll get to the bottom of who's planting these bombs. But I need you to hang in there with me, at least for a little while longer."

She trusted Declan, and maybe Bobby needed to realize just how much the police could help them. "You're right, going back to your place would be easier," she acknowledged. "Thanks for the offer."

"You're welcome."

Bobby looked as if he wanted to argue, but she narrowed her gaze and shook her head. "Don't, Bobby. I've had a long day and I just want to get some rest."

"Does your head hurt?" Declan asked softly.

"Not too bad," she hedged even though the dull pounding was back.

"The doctor told you to take it easy," Declan reminded her. "You should have stayed in the hospital another day."

"Hospital?" Bobby's voice rose in alarm. "You didn't say anything about being in the hospital!"

"I'm fine, it's just a concussion." She glared at Declan, annoyed that he'd worried her brother with that detail. "All I need is to rest."

"Listen, Declan, you have to find a way to make Mitch pay for what he did to Tess," Bobby said harshly. "That's ridiculous that he hurt her bad enough to send her to the hospital. I can tell you what drugs he's been taking and where he gets them. Maybe that can help you track him down."

Declan nodded. "That would help. I'd like nothing better than to find a way to prove Mitch assaulted Tess, and we can talk more about that later. First, I want to get you both someplace safe. Tess is still in danger from someone planting bombs around the city, and until we know for sure that Mitch is or isn't involved, we can't afford to get complacent."

"Crazy. This is just so crazy," Bobby muttered. "I can't believe someone actually has it out for my sister. Tess doesn't have any enemies, well, except for that stupid ex-boyfriend of hers. He was a jerk."

"Jeff Berg, right?" Declan asked. When Bobby nodded, he added, "Yeah, I'm checking him out, among others. We've found three bombs near Tess, and the others had been planted in places she used to work or hang out in." Declan frowned. "Way too much of a coincidence to ignore."

"I appreciate you watching out for my sister when I wasn't able to," Bobby said solemnly. "She deserves the best."

"I agree," Declan replied. "And I promise I'll protect her with my life if necessary."

Tess felt a tiny flutter in the region of her heart as she watched Bobby and Declan talk, pulling together as a united front in order to protect her. She was glad Declan had dropped his overbearing I'm-in-charge cop attitude, and that he was actually treating Bobby like an adult who had something to contribute. Far different from the way Jeff had treated her brother, and she was ashamed to think she'd dated Jeff for three months when he clearly didn't deserve one ounce of her attention.

Now watching Declan converse with Bobby gave her hope, especially since Declan connected with her brother in a way Jeff never had.

And for the first time in a long while, she found herself believing her brother would be okay. At least if they could get through this nightmare. Bobby would graduate from high school and hopefully then go to college or at least a technical school program. She needed to believe he would have a good future ahead of him.

And she knew that with Declan as a role model, anything was possible.

THIRTEEN

Declan glanced in the rearview mirror at Bobby and Tess in the backseat of his truck as he headed for the highway. She was leaning against her brother, looking relaxed and happy for the first time since he'd been called to disarm the bomb that had been planted beneath her school desk. Despite his earlier annoyance, he was sincerely glad that Bobby had tracked them down at the hotel, although he hadn't been thrilled to hear how Tess had actually left a note in the church stating her exact location. Still, he couldn't deny that her plan had worked. And the kid's concern for his sister rang true, he found himself honestly believing Bobby's story. He planned to call off the arrest warrant on Bobby and put the APB out on Mitch Turner instead. Granted, he'd have to convince the feds, but there would be time to clue them in later.

Maybe now he could focus the investigation on finding Mitch and the bomber. Not necessarily in that order.

He took a long, winding route to get to his place, making sure no one followed them. The closer he came to his neighborhood, the more vigilant he became. About three blocks from his house, he stopped at a red light near a corner gas station. Glancing over, he noticed a beige sedan, much like the car he'd seen Allan Gray driving, parked in front of a pump. A man was in the process of opening his gas tank and Declan peered through the darkness, trying to get a glimpse of the guy's face. When the man turned and looked up directly at Declan's truck, a chill snaked down his spine.

Allan Gray. The instant their gazes clashed, Allan looked away, hunching his shoulders and keeping his back toward the street as he pumped gas.

The light turned green and Declan pivoted the wheel to the right, going the opposite direction he'd originally intended. He went past the gas station and was tempted to turn around and go back to confront Gray, but held back because he had Tess and Bobby with him.

But what was Gray doing on the opposite side of town from where he lived? Trinity Medical Center was located in the general area between the gas station and Gray's house, and there were service stations every couple of blocks scattered around the city. So there was no need for Gray to drive so far out of his way to fill up his tank.

Unless Gray had somehow managed to figure out where Declan lived and had been watching his house? He clenched his jaw and tightened his grip on the steering wheel to control the flash of anger at the thought.

"Declan? What's wrong?" Tess asked.

He tried to relax his facial expression, secretly amazed at how Tess was so in tune to his feelings. After a moment he admitted, "I saw your neighbor Allan Gray at that gas station."

"Really?" She swiveled in her seat in an attempt to catch a glimpse, but the station was well behind them by now. "Must be a coincidence."

He didn't believe in them but didn't bother pointing

that out since there was no reason to scare Tess any more than absolutely necessary. Yet he needed her to be hyper-aware of her surroundings just in case Allan Gray was the man guilty of setting bombs around the city.

"Allan?" Bobby echoed in surprise. "You mean our weird neighbor? That Allan?"

Declan met Bobby's gaze through the rearview mirror. "Yeah, why? Do you know something about him?"

Bobby squirmed in his seat. "I know he has a crush on Tess," he finally admitted.

"How do you know that?" she asked incredulously.

"Come on, Tess, he asks about you every single time he sees me. 'Where's Tess? How is she doing? Is she still seeing that Jeff guy?'" Bobby shrugged. "I knew he wanted to ask you out, but I think he was afraid of being rejected. He seemed harmless, so I didn't think too much about it."

Declan knew his initial instincts about Gray were right. "I don't think he's harmless. Is he obsessed enough to follow Tess?"

Bobby slowly nodded. "Yeah, I could see it. I caught him watching her from his window once. I confronted him, but of course he denied it. I let it go, figuring it was good enough that Allan knew I was onto him."

"Why didn't you tell me?" Tess asked in exasperation.

"I didn't want you to be creeped out about it," Bobby said defensively. "I didn't think he was dangerous."

"I'm not so sure," Declan said in a low tone. "I don't like the way he keeps turning up when least expected. I need to get Isaac and Caleb to help me follow him a little more closely. There's something off about that guy and his bizarre fascination with Tess."

"I'll help," Bobby volunteered.

Declan hesitated, not wanting to alienate Tess's brother, yet at the same time, he didn't need a teenage amateur to mess things up. "What I really need from you, Bobby, is to help me protect Tess. I can't be with her 24/7, especially when I'm called away for SWAT team business. I feel much better knowing that you'll be there, watching over her."

Bobby looked a little disappointed, but then he nodded. "You can count on me to help keep my sister safe."

"Good." Declan drove around the block twice before turning into his driveway. "Don't get out until the garage door has closed," he cautioned as he pulled inside.

Bobby and Tess waited until it completely closed behind them before they slid out of the truck. Declan led the way inside, turning on the small kitchen light over the sink and gesturing for them to sit at the table, which was out of sight from the main living area.

"I need for the two of you to stay low, especially at night when it's dark outside. I don't want anyone watching from outside to see you."

Bobby surprised him by nodding in agreement. "It's a good idea. We'll stay well hidden."

Tess looked less than thrilled. "It's going to be hard for us to find our way through a strange house in the dark."

"I'll help you and since it's late anyway, you two should probably get some sleep. We can discuss this more in the morning."

Tess reluctantly agreed. Declan led the way upstairs to the second floor, with Tess and Bobby behind him. He turned on the bathroom light so that they could at least see where the bedroom doors were located.

"My twin nieces usually share this bedroom here," he said, indicating the room off to the left. "There are two beds in there and I think it's best for the two of you to stay together at least for tonight."

"Sounds good," Tess agreed in a weary tone. She looked pale and drawn and he knew her head must be hurting her, even though she never once complained.

He resisted the urge to pull her into his arms for a reassuring hug. The kiss they'd shared just a few hours earlier was way too fresh in his mind.

"Come on, Tess. You can have first dibs on the bathroom," Bobby said, urging his sister forward. "Good night, Declan."

"Good night." Declan headed back downstairs. He waited a few minutes while Tess and Bobby got settled before grabbing his truck keys and slipping out to the garage.

He intended to find Allan Gray. It was about time he turned the tables on who was following whom.

Tess woke abruptly from a sound sleep, her heart pounding with fear. She couldn't figure out if she'd dreamed the noise or if she'd actually heard someone moving around in Declan's house.

She glanced over to see Bobby was sprawled on the twin bed against the opposite wall of the room. He was sound asleep and snoring softly. She relaxed a bit, glad that the noise, if she'd really heard it, wasn't from Bobby leaving. But what had made that sound?

Tess silently crept out of bed and made her way to the hallway, feeling along the wall as she went. There weren't any lights on downstairs, and she paused at the top of the stairs, straining to listen.

Was someone in the house? If so, she needed to get Declan, but she didn't want to wake him up in the middle of the night if the noise she'd heard was nothing more than her overactive imagination.

She didn't hear anything beyond the beating of her own heart and she slowly relaxed. But now that she was up, she realized she was incredibly thirsty, so she slowly descended the stairs, wincing as one of them creaked loudly beneath her foot.

Just as Tess reached the bottom step, a dark shadow loomed before her and hard hands grabbed her shoulders, causing her to let out a squeak of alarm.

"Tess? What are you doing?"

It took a minute for Declan's familiar voice to register in her mind. "Me?" she asked in a whisper. "You're the one who woke me up by making noise down here!"

"You shouldn't have come down here alone," he muttered. His hands loosened but didn't release her and she enjoyed the warmth of his touch, wishing she could make out the expression in his eyes.

"I wasn't sure if I had imagined it or not," she admitted.

"I'm sorry, I didn't mean to wake you."

She put her hand on his chest, realizing that his clothes were slightly damp. Was it raining outside? Had the noise she'd heard been the garage door closing? "Where did you go?"

There was a long pause before Declan answered, "I went looking for your neighbor."

She was surprised at that. "Did you find him?"

"Not right away. First I went to his house, but he wasn't there. Then I came back to make sure he wasn't hanging around watching my place. He wasn't in the vicinity, but I eventually found his car in the parking lot of the hospital. I called the hospital—he's working the graveyard shift tonight."

She wished he'd get over Allan Gray already. "I know you suspect Allan, but I really don't think he's the one setting bombs," she said. "He's smart, but not the destructive type."

She heard Declan sigh and when he dropped his hands from her shoulders, she immediately missed his touch. "You could be right," he murmured. "But I still think it's odd that he's always around, even in areas where he shouldn't be."

She rubbed her hands over her bare arms, feeling the chill in the air. "Maybe, but like I said, I can't see Allan as a big threat."

"Don't underestimate him, Tess."

Declan's serious tone made her shiver. "I won't." She moved to step around him, but his hand shot out to clasp her arm, stopping her.

"Where are you going?" he asked.

She rolled her eyes. "To get a drink of water, if that's okay with you."

"Oh, sure. No problem."

Declan followed her into the kitchen and she felt a bit self-conscious as she filled a tall glass of water from the fridge. She downed half the glass and then took it with her to head back upstairs.

Declan hovered nearby as she paused outside the doorway of the spare bedroom. "Good night," she whispered.

"Good night," he echoed.

She put her hand on the doorknob but then turned back toward him. "Declan? Thanks for believing in Bobby and for being so nice to him."

"He's a good kid at heart," he said gruffly. "And I can't deny he reminds me of myself at that age."

She smiled. "You weren't as tough as you wanted everyone to believe."

"I was tough," he protested. "I only showed my softer side with you."

There was a strange intimacy in the air and Tess wanted to reach out to Declan, to tell him how much she was starting to care for him, but he stepped back, abruptly breaking the moment. "See you in the morning," he said, before turning and walking into his room.

She sighed, wondering if the attraction she felt was one-sided. Was he avoiding her on purpose? Maybe, since Declan had been the one to break off their kiss.

She needed to keep her emotions in check. Declan was just being nice to her…nothing more. It would behoove her to remember that, because there was no point in setting herself up for a broken heart.

Sunlight pouring through the window woke Tess the following morning. She blinked, and then sat up when she realized the other bed was empty and she was alone in the room.

For a moment panic seized her by the throat, but then she heard the muted sounds of voices coming from downstairs. Bobby was still here; he hadn't left.

She closed her eyes and sent up a quick prayer of thanks to God for bringing her brother home. She headed into the bathroom, grateful that her headache was almost completely gone. A hot shower and change of clothes made her feel like a new person.

The scent of bacon and eggs made her stomach growl and she went down to the kitchen, pleasantly surprised to find Bobby and Declan huddled around a laptop computer, obviously working, their empty plates evidence of a shared breakfast.

"Hey, sis, how are you feeling?" Bobby asked when he saw her.

"Much better," she admitted.

"Are you hungry?" Declan asked with a smile. "Your brother offered to cook this morning."

"There's plenty of bacon left…how would you like your eggs?" Bobby asked, jumping to his feet. "Scrambled? Over easy?"

She was taken aback by the offer, since her brother had never bothered to cook when it was just the two of them at home. "Over easy would be awesome."

"Coming right up," Bobby said, heading over to the frying pan sitting on the stove.

Bemused, she sank into a chair next to Declan. "What are you guys working on?" she asked.

"Bobby was giving me information on Mitch Turner," he said, pointing to the computer screen. "Here's his social media page, where he has several photos where he seems to be under the influence."

"Doesn't he understand that anyone can see this stuff?" she asked, frowning at a terrible shot of Mitch looking completely stoned.

"These photos can only be seen by his friends, but yeah, it's crazy that he puts it all out there."

"Tell her about my truck," Bobby said from the stove.

"You found it?" she asked hopefully.

"Yeah, it was left abandoned and out of gas at the end of a dead-end street, not far from Greenland Park," Declan said. "We have the crime scene techs going over it now, looking for hair, fingerprints, et cetera."

"That's wonderful news!" Tess exclaimed. "I'm sure Mitch left something incriminating behind."

"Yes, but that's still a long ways from proving that he's the one who assaulted you," Declan cautioned. "Remember that Bobby and Mitch left the high school together in the truck, so the evidence would have to be something more than just fingerprints or hair. But it's a step in the right direction."

Her brief flare of hope died as she realized Declan was right. They needed something more than just proof that Mitch was in the truck. "What if they found hair and fingerprints on the steering wheel? Wouldn't that indicate that he was driving?"

"Yes, but it's still his word against Bobby's. Don't worry, we'll get him."

"Your eggs are almost finished, Tess," Bobby said. "Do you want toast, too?"

"Sure." She couldn't help thinking that Bobby's new helpful attitude had to be the direct result of being around Declan. She'd done her best in raising Bobby after their parents' deaths, but clearly having a man's influence meant more than she'd realized. Especially a guy like Declan.

Bobby handed her a plateful of eggs, toast and bacon. "This looks delicious, thanks so much."

Bobby's ears turned red and he shrugged off her gratitude. "It's no biggie."

She let it go, sensing he was embarrassed and maybe he hadn't wanted Declan to know that cooking breakfast was not the norm.

"Do you know this guy standing next to Mitch?" Declan asked abruptly.

She leaned forward, trying to get a look at the photo.

Bobby sat down on Declan's other side. "Yeah, that's Ken Rogers. He graduated last year," her brother said.

"He's wearing a green baseball hat," Declan said, glancing over at Tess. "Do you think this could be the same guy you saw near the maple tree at the school parking lot?"

The bite of toast lodged in her throat and she swallowed hard before leaning over to look intently at the picture. "I don't know," she admitted. "Ken's hat has a Green Bay Packer emblem on the front, but I think the other guy's hat was plain."

"Here, look at these photos again," Declan suggested. She stood next to him, surprised to see that several of the close-up shots that Nate had taken from the surveillance camera were uploaded on his computer.

It wasn't easy to concentrate on the photos with Declan's musky scent filling her head, but she did her best. "He's not the same guy, I'm almost sure of it," Tess said. "See this picture? There's no emblem on the front of his cap, and you can see that his hair is brown or dark blond, not nearly as dark as the kid standing next to Mitch."

"Okay, you're right," Declan acknowledged. "If only we could get one solid lead on this guy."

Tess reluctantly returned to her seat to continue eating, while Bobby and Declan went through the photos from the crime scene. She was secretly relieved when Bobby didn't recognize the suspect, either.

Declan's phone rang, interrupting them. "Yeah, Isaac, what's up?"

There was a brief pause before Declan shot to his feet so fast he knocked his kitchen chair over. "Really? I'm on my way."

"What's wrong?" Tess asked.

"I have to go. They arrested Mitch Turner," Declan said excitedly. "This could be the break in the case we've been looking for."

"Can I come with you?" Bobby asked.

"I need you to stay here with Tess." Declan picked up the chair he'd knocked over and glanced between the two of them. "I don't like leaving you here alone, but hopefully this won't take long. I'll be back as soon as possible."

"We'll be fine," Tess assured him, standing next to Bobby.

"I hope he confesses to assaulting you," her brother muttered. "He needs to pay for that."

Tess couldn't stop herself from reaching out to gently squeeze Declan's arm in lieu of hugging him. She didn't say anything to stop him from going, but she had a bad feeling that Mitch could easily turn everything around onto Bobby. She could only hope that Declan would find a way to get to the truth.

FOURTEEN

Declan watched as Isaac questioned Mitch Turner about the events that took place over the past few days. Mitch looked pretty bad—he was pale, sweaty and shaky, and Declan figured the kid was on the verge of going through withdrawal from whatever drugs he'd been taking.

"Tell me again how you ended up with Bobby Collins's phone?" Isaac said patiently.

Mitch shifted in his seat and tapped his fingers on the desktop. "Bobby gave it to me. Just like he loaned me his truck. He's lying if he's telling you something different."

"So where's Bobby now?" Isaac asked. "Why did he leave you with his stuff?"

Mitch looked confused for a moment and it was clear to Declan that the kid's brain wasn't firing on all cylinders. "Uh, he had to go home. His sister told him to come home."

"How did his sister do that?" Isaac asked. "You had his phone, so how did he talk to his sister?"

"I gave him his phone when she called."

"And when was that?" Isaac murmured, leaning back in his chair.

"I don't remember." Mitch glanced around as if looking for a way out.

"And how did Bobby get home?"

"I drove him."

"See, that's where I have trouble with your story," Isaac said with a puzzled frown. "Why would Bobby let you drive him home, leaving him without his truck or his phone? Doesn't he normally drop you off at your place?"

"Yeah, but this was different." Mitch shifted again and his finger tapping became more pronounced. "I needed a favor."

"You needed to buy drugs."

Mitch nodded but then caught himself. "No way, man, that's not true."

"I have to tell you, you don't look so good," Isaac continued. "Are you sure you're feeling all right?"

"Yeah, man. I'm fine." Mitch swiped away a trickle of sweat rolling down the side of his face. "Maybe I am sick. I have the flu. Yeah, that's it. I'm sick with the flu. I need to go home."

Declan blew out a frustrated breath. Even if the kid did confess to assaulting Tess, a decent lawyer would get him off if he was indeed going through withdrawal. They'd be better off getting Mitch admitted to the hospital and talking to him again when he was sober.

"Pretty sad, huh?" Caleb asked from beside him.

Declan nodded, humbled by the fact that he'd narrowly escaped ending up just like Mitch Turner. Joining the marines had been the best decision he'd made. Without the discipline of being in the service, he didn't think he'd be where he was today. "Yeah, his mother is an alcoholic, too, so the deck was pretty much stacked against him."

Caleb grimaced and shook his head. "Raising kids

these days is scary. I'm already worried about Kaitlin's future."

Declan glanced at him in surprise. Caleb's six-year-old daughter was adorable, so why on earth would he be worried? "I'm sure Kaitlin will turn out just fine."

"I hope so," Caleb muttered. "It kills me to see how many kids' lives are destroyed by drugs. And they're getting hooked younger and younger. Noelle insisted on putting Kaitlin in a private school, and I'm glad we did. I'll take all the help I can get."

"I hear you." Declan tried to ignore the tiny flash of envy at Caleb's life with his new wife and daughter. His buddy had narrowly escaped being wrongly imprisoned for murder, so Caleb certainly deserved to be happy.

Declan glanced at his watch, unwilling to leave Tess and Bobby alone for too long. "I need to get back. There isn't much more to do here, since Mitch isn't in any condition to be interviewed. He probably needs to get to the hospital sooner than later."

"I agree. We found drugs in Mitch's pocket, so we can arrest him on possession for now. He also had a good two hundred in cash on him. We should be able to add a charge for intent to sell."

It wasn't as good as getting him for assault, but Declan was willing to take it. For now. "We need to get a warrant to search Mitch's house. There's a chance he might have had something to do with the bomb that was found in Greenland Park."

"Isaac already has a team out there checking it out," Caleb assured him. "Do you have any other leads yet?"

"I still think Allan Gray is involved," Declan admitted. "He's obsessed with Tess, and I think he's been following her. And there's always Jeff Berg, too. I'm still trying to figure out why he took a leave of absence from school."

"I'll work on the Jeff Berg angle," Caleb offered. "I know Isaac was trying to keep an eye on Allan Gray, as well. You're not in this alone, Deck. Griff told us about the feds, and I just want you to know we're here for you."

"I know and I appreciate the help." Declan knew he was lucky to have friends like Caleb and Isaac. "I don't suppose the feds have come up with anything useful yet, have they?"

Caleb shook his head. "Not that they're willing to share."

That figured. The FBI tended to keep their information to themselves. "All right, call me if anything changes."

"Will do."

Declan headed back outside to his truck, anxious to get back to his house. The thought of Tess and Bobby waiting for him made him think about what it might be like to have a family of his own.

Ridiculous to go there. He'd made a conscious decision not to have a family because he was too much like his father to take the risk. Yet somehow that reason didn't seem good enough anymore. Granted, he'd lost his head when his buddy Tony was shot and killed right next to him, but that was four years ago now, and he hadn't had a drop of alcohol since.

Would that change if he was in a relationship? He didn't want to think so but was afraid to hope.

Why was he even thinking about this? There was no guarantee that Tess would be interested in him. She deserved someone better, that was for sure. Not Jeff Berg or Allan Gray, but there had to be plenty of single men who'd be interested in her.

Still, the very thought of Tess being with Isaac or Griff or any of the other single guys from the SWAT team didn't sit well with him, so he forced himself to stop thinking about Tess as a woman he was interested in.

Tess was in grave danger. He needed to stay focused on that fact. But right now he was fresh out of new leads. He'd really hoped that Bobby might recognize the guy with the green ball cap, but so far the guy was still a mystery man.

He drove home, intending to do more research. They needed a break in this case soon, before another bomb was set and more innocent lives were put at risk.

Tess finished cleaning up the breakfast dishes and then went back to the kitchen table, to review the photos on Declan's computer again. She went through each of the images, slowly and deliberately. The guy in the green ball cap still seemed familiar. Why couldn't she place him?

She rubbed her hand over her eyes and pushed the laptop away. Maybe she needed to stop trying so hard to remember. Since they hadn't gone to church services this morning, Tess went upstairs to get her Bible.

Bobby glanced at her when she came into the room. "I can't stop thinking about Mitch," he admitted. "I wish I could have gone along with Declan."

Tess picked up her Bible and then turned to face her brother. "You can trust Declan. I'm sure he'll let us know what happened with Mitch."

"I wish I would have turned Mitch in to the police sooner," Bobby confessed. "If I had, he never would have been able to attack you."

"You can't think like that," she chided. "I've made a

lot of mistakes, too, but all we can do is to learn from them and move forward."

"I guess you're right." Bobby waved a hand at her Bible. "I know I wasn't always good about going to church, but I prayed a lot after Mitch took off and left me alone. Going to church helped me cope. I was there twice before I stumbled across your note."

She smiled. "I'm glad to hear that. You need to believe that God is always there for you. I can read a few passages to you if you're interested."

He shrugged and then nodded. "Okay."

Tess sat on the edge of her bed and began to read from the book of Psalms. She expected her brother to lose interest, but he seemed to be paying close attention. In fact, they were so engrossed in the passages that she didn't realize until she'd finished that Declan was standing in the doorway listening in, as well.

"That was great," he said. "I always thought the Bible would be dull and boring."

"Tess knows how to make it interesting," Bobby said proudly, before changing the subject. "So, what happened with Mitch?"

Declan shrugged. "He didn't admit to assaulting Tess, but he's been arrested for possession with intent to sell. They were calling an ambulance to take him to the hospital when I left, because he seemed to be going through withdrawal."

"He's such an idiot," Bobby muttered, obviously disappointed that Mitch hadn't confessed. "You would have thought he'd stay away from drugs after seeing his mother drunk all the time, but maybe this will force him to get the help he needs."

"We'll pray for him," Declan said, surprising Tess. Did

that mean he believed in God and the power of prayer? She was thrilled at how he'd listened to her reading from the Bible and hoped that he'd continue on this path, even after they'd gone their separate ways.

That thought was depressing, so she shook it off. "Praying for Mitch is a great idea." Tess took a deep breath and then bowed her head. "Dear Lord, we ask that You heal Mitch Turner's addiction and show him the way to God. Amen."

"Amen," Bobby and Declan echoed simultaneously.

Tess smiled and felt a deep sense of contentment inside her. Being with Bobby and Declan together was nice, despite the fact that there was still a crazy bomber on the loose.

"Is there something we can do to help you find the guy who's after Tess?" Bobby asked as he crossed over to Declan.

He shrugged. "I wish there was. Maybe walking through the case again with the two of you will help."

"Sounds good to me," Bobby agreed.

"Go ahead, I'll be down in a little bit," Tess said.

Bobby and Declan clattered down to the first floor and she took a few minutes to include Declan and Bobby in her prayers.

Tess spent a few minutes in the bathroom, brushing her hair and putting on a coat of clear lip gloss before heading downstairs. She couldn't deny she wanted to look nice for Declan, and gave herself a mental scolding as she reached the living room.

She paused, listening to his deep voice as he talked to her brother. Her intent wasn't to eavesdrop, but when she heard Declan saying something about joining the marines, her temper flared.

"What were you telling Bobby?" she demanded as she marched into the kitchen. "I hope you weren't encouraging him to join the service."

"Calm down, sis. Declan was just telling me what worked for him, right? I didn't know he'd been in the marines."

Declan didn't say anything, and the warm, tender feelings she'd had toward him earlier quickly vanished.

"Bobby, we talked about this, remember?" Tess said, giving her brother an imploring look. "You said you'd be willing to give college a try. I get that joining the marines made sense for Declan, but you have other options. I have money set aside for your college tuition."

"I know I have options, Tess. There's no need to jump all over me."

She wanted to smack Declan for even putting the idea of joining the armed forces in Bobby's head in the first place. Why couldn't he leave well enough alone? Bobby was the only family she had left in the world, and the last thing she wanted to do was to risk losing him in some Third World country. Surely Declan wanted something better for his own kids?

She knew she was overreacting so she tried to pull back her anger. "Don't do anything rash without talking to me, okay?" she said to Bobby. "Please?"

"I won't," Bobby promised.

She nodded, took a couple of deep, calming breaths and finally looked at Declan. "I thought you guys were going to review the case."

"We are. Have a seat...you can listen in, too."

Tess dropped into the chair closest to her brother. Declan cleared his throat and began reviewing the facts of the case.

"There have been a total of five bombs so far, the first one at the minimart, the second at the custard stand, the third beneath Tess's desk—"

"What?" Bobby interrupted. "I didn't know that the bomb was planted beneath Tess's desk. The only thing I heard was that it was at the elementary school."

Tess felt some of her anger melt away remembering how Declan saved her life just two days ago.

"There was a fourth bomb planted near your sister's car, too," Declan continued. "And the fifth one was found under the picnic table at Greenland Park. Each of these targets has a link to your sister."

"Don't forget, you're linked to some of those targets, as well," Tess said.

Declan nodded. "All of these sites are places that kids tend to hang out, so that was one of the reasons that I thought someone like Mitch, or one of his buddies, may have had something to do with them."

Bobby shook his head. "Like I mentioned before, I never heard anything about this at school. If someone there is involved, they're not talking about it."

"Either way, I believe the bomber is someone local, or the targets would be different. They'd be bigger, like a baseball game, a festival, the theater or a music concert."

Tess's earlier contented mood evaporated. She knew that the rest of Declan's SWAT team were investigating the leads they had so far, but it seemed as if there was nothing more they could do, other than to wait for the bomber to make his next move.

Declan pushed restlessly away from the kitchen table. Talking through the case wasn't helping the way that he'd hoped, and he hated feeling helpless. Maybe he should be the one following Allan Gray. As far as he was concerned, the guy was at the top of his suspect list.

His phone rang and he was relieved to see that the caller was Caleb. "Hey, what's up?"

"I found out why Jeff Berg is on a leave of absence—his mother has been admitted to a local hospice, as she's apparently dying of cancer. I think we can take him off the list of suspects."

Declan let out a heavy sigh. "You're right. I guess that's a good reason to be on a leave of absence. Did Mitch say anything more before you shipped him off to the hospital?"

"Nah, he was babbling a bit and not making much sense. According to his doctor it'll be several days before we can talk to him again. And Isaac's team didn't find anything other than the usual drug paraphernalia at Mitchell's house, either."

Declan tried to look on the bright side, but it wasn't easy. "So the only real suspect we have left is Allan Gray."

"Don't forget the guy in the green ball cap, who may not be Allan Gray at all," Caleb said. "It's not like you to be so fixated on a suspect like Gray. Must be because he's Tess's neighbor."

"Point taken," Declan acknowledged, knowing he was letting his personal dislike of Gray get in the way of cool logic. It wasn't as if he had a reason to be jealous of Allan, not after the way Tess had shot daggers at him after she overheard his conversation with her brother. He knew she was mad, but she didn't realize Bobby had broached the subject first. Apparently her brother had already talked to an army recruiter, a small detail he obviously hadn't shared with Tess.

"I put the guy's basic description, as much as we could identify anyway, through the system to see if there are any other known bombers that might match it, but so far, nothing has popped." Declan knew that it was a long shot, since they didn't have an accurate height, weight or eye color to add.

"I can't think of anything more we can do," Caleb admitted. "I'm going home to spend time with my family. Let me know if you need anything."

"All right, thanks, Caleb." Declan disconnected from the call and glanced at Tess. "Jeff Berg's mother is dying of cancer, so that's why he's back in town."

"Poor Jeff," Tess murmured, her gaze full of sympathy.

Bobby grimaced. "I didn't like him much, but I feel bad for his mother."

"I was thinking," Tess said slowly. "We should go through our high school yearbooks. It's possible that seeing some of the photos of our classmates might jog our memories."

Declan lifted his eyebrows in surprise. "That's a great idea, Tess. I meant to do that earlier, especially because I want to get a look at Allan Gray. Give me a few minutes to go upstairs and dig them out."

He took the stairs two at a time, trying to remember where he'd stored his stuff from high school. Had to be in one of the boxes he'd stashed in the back of his closet.

He should have thought of this sooner, even though it was probably a long shot. What were the chances that the bomber was someone they went to school with? Still, doing something was better than nothing.

He found the yearbooks, blowing the dust off before carrying them downstairs. As he set them on the kitchen table, his phone rang again. This time, the caller was Isaac.

"What's up?" Declan asked. "I thought you and Caleb were heading home to enjoy a day off."

"They called in another bomb, Deck. It's at the Greenland Grand Movie Theater."

A chill snaked down his spine as Isaac's words sank in. His sister, Karen, worked there. Was she working today? He didn't know, but if she was, this would be the second time she was in the path of a bomb. He strove to remain calm, even though his stomach was clenched with fear. "I'm on my way."

"What's wrong?" Tess asked.

"I have to go, another bomb has been found at the movie theater where my sister works." He didn't want to leave Tess and Bobby alone, but he didn't have a choice. His sister and other innocent lives were at stake. He grabbed his truck keys off the table. "You both need to stay here and keep hidden until you hear from me."

Tess's eyes were as large as saucers, but she nodded her agreement. "I'll pray for you."

"Be careful," Bobby added.

He gave a curt nod and rushed out to his truck, jamming the keys into the ignition and peeling out of his driveway, praying he'd get there in time.

Please, Lord, keep my sister and everyone else at the movie theater safe from harm.

FIFTEEN

Tess watched Declan leave, feeling helpless. She couldn't imagine what he must be going through, knowing his sister's life could be in danger once again.

She closed her eyes and prayed for everyone's safety. When she opened her eyes, she was surprised and humbled to see that Bobby had been praying, as well.

Her brother flashed a sheepish grin. "Declan needs all the help he can get."

"I know." She didn't want to make a big deal out of it, so she gestured toward Declan's computer. "We can't sit here doing nothing—we need to figure out who is behind setting these bombs."

"We're not exactly trained investigators," Bobby reminded her. "But I agree that we need to try and do something to help. I still think Allan Gray could be involved." Bobby pulled Declan's computer around to face him. "Maybe Allan's on social media."

Tess reached for the yearbooks. "I'll start going through these. Maybe a picture of a younger version of Allan will spur a memory."

She opened the first book, which was Declan's freshman year. She would still have been in the middle school then, as she was a year younger. Once she found Declan's picture, she could hardly believe how young he looked. He wore his hair shorter then, but there was still a hard edge to his gaze, as if he'd already seen too much. She knew Declan had lived in the trailer park. Was being poor part of the reason he copped an attitude? Or was there more to the story?

She went back to find a picture of Allan Gray and winced at the photograph that was less than flattering. Poor Allan had suffered a bad case of acne and his hair looked unkempt. She stared at the picture for a long moment, vaguely remembering something about Allan having a sister. But was she older or younger?

Tess opened the other yearbooks, going through the *Grays,* searching for Allan's sister. She found a photograph of Alice Gray, who was a freshman during Declan's junior year. But there was no photograph of Alice in Declan's senior yearbook. Tess went back to the junior year and found a section in the back of the book where there was a list honoring the three students who had died that year. Two of them died in a terrible car crash, but the memorial for Alice only mentioned how she would be missed by all who knew her.

Tess sat back, remembering the incident now that she'd seen the memorial. Alice Gray had been found dead of a drug overdose. She'd taken a hodgepodge of pills from the family medicine cabinet. And if Tess remembered correctly, Allan had been the one to find his sister the following morning.

Was it possible that Allan somehow held Declan or the entire town responsible for his sister's suicide? Maybe this wasn't about Tess after all, but was actually all about

Alice. Maybe Allan *was* savvy enough to set the bombs around the city.

As she went back to see Allan's picture she stumbled across a photograph of Steve Gains, the guy who'd attempted to assault her after the prom. Looking at him after all these years made her feel sick to her stomach. How could she have been so blind as to his true nature? Steve had been the star pitcher for the Greenland Gophers baseball team. He'd been offered a full scholarship to Arizona State University based on his talent. But she hadn't heard much about him after that; it was almost as if he'd dropped off the face of the earth.

She paged through the yearbook and found the group photograph of the entire baseball team. Their uniforms were white-and-green pin-striped pants with green jerseys and green baseball caps.

Abruptly she straightened in her seat, the tiny hairs on the back of her neck lifting in alarm. Steve Gains! Was it possible Steve was holding a grudge against Declan after all this time? It seemed ridiculous, yet she knew the person in the ball cap seemed familiar. The hair color and body type were the same. Steve Gains had to be the man in the green baseball cap that was captured on the video outside the school parking lot.

Maybe this wasn't about Alice Gray's suicide after all.

"Bobby, we need to find Declan's boss, Griff Vaughn, right away," she said, leaping to her feet in a rush.

"Why? What happened?"

"I think I found the bomber, and he has a good reason to hold a grudge against Declan. We need to hurry. It's possible they can find and arrest him outside the movie theater."

"Who?" Bobby asked skeptically.

"This guy here, Steve Gains." She tapped the photograph in the yearbook. "It's a long story that we don't have time to get into now. There isn't a moment to lose."

"Okay, but how are we going to get to the sheriff's department without a vehicle?" Bobby asked.

"Maybe we can take a taxi or something." Tess paced the small area of Declan's kitchen. "I don't think calling the guys from Declan's SWAT team will help, because they'll all be out at the movie theater."

"Just a minute." Bobby tapped on the keyboard of the laptop. "There's a bus stop a few blocks down the road. That will take us within a couple of blocks of the sheriff's department."

"Do you have a couple of bucks for the tickets?" she asked. "My cash is gone."

"Yeah, I have some money that Declan loaned to me."

Tess wondered why Declan had done that, but there wasn't time to get into it now. "Let's go." She didn't want to wait a second longer.

Tess led the way out through the side kitchen door, but she'd barely stepped outside when a large man holding a gun grabbed her roughly by the arm.

"Hi, Tess. Did you miss me over the past ten years?"

Her heart leaped into her throat as Steve Gains leered down at her, his eyes ice-cold with hatred. She wanted to shout at Bobby to run, but before she could move, Steve brought his hand down hard on her temple.

And for the third time in as many days, pain exploded in her head seconds before darkness claimed her.

Declan approached the ticket sales counter dressed in his full SWAT gear, beads of sweat trickling down his spine. Karen's eyes were wide with fear, but she sat completely still in her seat despite the bomb that was planted beneath the counter.

The setup was very similar to the one he'd rescued Tess from. Was it really just a few days ago? He couldn't afford to think about Tess and Bobby now. The first thing he'd done when he arrived was to send Isaac back over to his place to watch over them.

Just as Tess had done, Karen managed to activate the device when she sat down behind the ticket counter. He couldn't ignore the fact that there were four different ticket counters at the theater, which meant his sister had been targeted on purpose.

Tess was right: The bomber must be someone who hated Declan enough to target the people closest to him.

He smiled at his sister reassuringly. "Hang in there, okay? I'm going to find a way to get you out of here."

Karen's smile was tremulous. "Declan, if anything happens to me I want you to take custody of Jenny and Josie."

"Nothing's going to happen," Declan promised. He didn't want to point out that if something happened to Karen, he'd likely die right alongside her. Because no matter what happened, he wasn't going to leave her here alone.

"I don't want Craig to get custody," Karen insisted. "He drinks and spanks them."

"Karen, I need you to calm down. We're going to beat this thing, okay? Now give me a few minutes to see what we're dealing with."

Karen didn't look pacified, but she didn't say anything more. Declan blew out a heavy sigh and knelt down on the floor, focusing his attention on the explosive device. It was almost an exact replica of the one that had been planted under Tess's desk, although he couldn't afford to assume the wiring inside was the same, as well.

In fact, he suspected the outside was made the same on purpose just so that he'd go down the same path in disarming the device.

He nudged Karen's seat out of the way as much as he dared, to make room to work. "It's the same perp," Declan said through his mic to Caleb.

"Roger, Deck. Can you disarm it?"

"Affirmative." He injected confidence in his tone to reassure his sister more than anything.

He found himself praying as he quickly identified and removed the dummy wires. *Please, Lord, guide me on the right path to saving my sister and other innocent lives today. I need Your strength and courage to assist me. Please show me the way!*

Soon Declan was down to the three wires that consisted of the timer, the trigger and the ground.

For a moment panic seized him. What if he made a mistake? Jenny and Josie would be motherless and whoever had set this bomb would eventually find Tess and Bobby. And the deaths wouldn't stop there. For all he knew the perp would move on to even bigger targets. He couldn't bear the thought of having so many lives resting on his shoulders.

"Deck, is everything okay?" Caleb asked through his headset.

"Yeah, two minutes and counting." Declan swiped his hands down the sides of his pants, trying to rein in his turbulent emotions. Failure was not an option. And he wasn't alone; God was with him.

A sense of peace washed over him, despite the timer that continued to count down ominously. He really did believe that God was guiding him and knew he had to trust his instincts. By now, he knew exactly what the bomber was thinking when he created these devices. He could almost sense what had gone through the perp's mind.

Declan lifted the wire cutters and clipped the wire located between the timer and the end of the device. Instantly the clock went dark.

"I think I have it," he muttered. Two wires were left and he held his breath as he clipped the second wire that was closest to the timer.

Nothing happened. No explosion. No boom. He'd managed to successfully disarm the device.

"Move your knee away from the side of the device," Declan instructed.

"Are you sure?" Karen asked anxiously.

"I'm sure."

Karen slowly eased her knee away from the trigger.

"Now slide your chair away from the counter," Declan told his sister. "Easy, now."

Karen whimpered a bit but did as he instructed, pushing her wheeled chair away from the counter. When she was far enough away, she rose shakily to her feet. "Thank you, Declan. I was so afraid I'd end up in the hospital again, or worse."

He got to his feet and wrapped his arms around her in a big hug. "You're welcome. Now go home and hug your girls for me."

"I won't forget this," she whispered.

"I know," he murmured. He cleared his throat and stepped back, clicking on his mic. "Caleb, I'm sending my sister out now. The device has been disarmed, but we need to get this thing into a reinforced box as soon as possible."

"Roger, Deck. Good job," Caleb responded. "As soon as your sister is clear, I'll bring in the box."

"Have you heard from Isaac?"

"Negative, but I'll check in with him soon. Right now we have to focus on the device."

Declan suppressed a flash of irritation. He knew the bomb was important, but he thought it was odd that he hadn't heard from Isaac. Surely his buddy would have at least checked in to say everything was okay?

He knelt back down to figure out the best way to get the bomb detached from the underside of the ticket counter. This wouldn't be as easy as cutting through a metal school desk. The counter was roughly two inches thick. How did the perp get the bomb attached anyway?

"Deck, are you there?" Caleb asked.

"Affirmative, what's up?"

"Isaac is at your place, but Tess and Bobby aren't there."

"What?" he asked sharply. "What do you mean? They have to be there. Make sure he checks the entire house, including the basement."

"Isaac has confirmed the house is empty, including the basement," Caleb said in a calm tone. "Do you have any idea where they might be?"

"No, I told them to stay there until they heard from me. Are there signs of a struggle?"

"Negative. Deck, why don't you come out here? I'll take over inside."

Declan didn't have to be told twice. The bomb might have been neutralized for the moment, but it was still dangerous. He could hear his boss arguing through his headset, demanding Declan stay to finish the job.

But Declan pulled off his headset, refusing to listen.

Griff could fire him if he wanted, but no way was he going to sit here while Tess and Bobby were missing.

He could only pray that nothing bad had happened to them.

Declan pulled into his driveway behind Isaac's truck. Isaac came out to meet him. "They might have left on their own, Deck."

He didn't want to believe it, although he'd already tried calling and texting without a response. "Are you absolutely sure that there's no sign of foul play?"

Isaac spread his hands wide. "Not that I could tell. Take a look for yourself."

Declan brushed past his teammate to go inside. The first thing he noticed was the yearbooks spread out across the table. The books were closed, but he wondered if maybe Tess had been looking through them for clues. Had she found something incriminating against Allan Gray?

He swept a glance over the room. Nothing else seemed to be out of place. However, the kitchen chairs had been pushed in, which struck him as odd. If Tess and Bobby had left in a hurry, would they have bothered to make sure the chairs were neatly tucked against the table?

The laptop computer was closed, and he lifted the screen and pushed the start button to bring it to life. There were two different search tabs open, one for local bus routes and another for a popular social media website, but he couldn't tell if Bobby had found anything of importance.

"I don't like it," he muttered darkly. "Why on earth would they leave? And on a bus? To where?"

"Maybe they were trying to get out to the movie theater," Isaac suggested. "Could be they stumbled upon some sort of clue."

"Call Caleb, see if they showed up there after I left." Declan pulled one of the yearbooks closer, half listening as Isaac made the call. He opened it up, searching for a picture of Allan Gray.

The image didn't spark any memories and he battled a wave of helplessness. He didn't have time to sit here trying to retrace the steps Tess and Bobby had taken. He needed to know they were safe.

"No sign of them at the movie theater," Isaac confirmed. "Griff's not too happy with you, either."

Declan shrugged. "I did my part, Caleb, and the rest of the team can get the device out of there."

Isaac blew out a heavy sigh. "Look, Deck, there's nothing more we can do here. I'm sure Tess will get in touch with you soon."

Declan shook his head. "I can't let it go. Something's just not right. The kitchen chairs are neat, but the yearbooks are spread all over. Was the door locked when you arrived?"

"No," Isaac admitted. "But if they left in a hurry, they may have forgotten to lock the door behind them."

Declan walked back over toward the door and peered along the door frame. It took a few minutes for him to find the crimson stain. "Does this look like blood?" he asked hoarsely.

Isaac came over and rubbed his finger across the stain. "Maybe."

"They didn't leave of their own accord, I'm sure of it." Declan spun around and went back to the yearbooks. If they had in fact been taken by force, surely they would have tried to leave some sort of clue behind.

"What are you looking for?" Isaac asked.

"I don't know, but hopefully I'll figure it out when I see it."

Isaac joined him in searching through the yearbooks. "Hey, Deck, check this out."

"What?" Declan glanced over at the yearbook Isaac had open.

"This page was bent over. Do you think either Tess or Bobby left it like this on purpose?"

Declan peered at the page, realizing that the point of the page was right next to a photograph of Steve Gains.

Gains? The guy who'd tried to assault Tess on prom night? Suddenly everything made sense and he mentally kicked himself for not considering the possibility sooner.

This creep would be crazy enough to carry a grudge against him, and using Tess to get to him would be the icing on the cake. Poetic justice, at least in Steve's mind.

"Steve Gains has Tess and Bobby," he said in a choked voice. "And I think he's the bomber, too. We have to find him, before it's too late!"

SIXTEEN

"Tess? Wake up, sis. I need you to wake up!"

The urgency in Bobby's voice cut through the fog that seemed to have shrouded her mind. Tess blinked and lifted her head, wincing at the pain in her neck and temple as she tried to peer through the dim light. "Bobby?"

"Thank God you're all right." The anguish in his tone made her think she must have been unconscious for a long time.

It took a few minutes for her to realize that she was sitting in a chair with her arms bound behind her back with something that felt sticky, like duct tape. Bobby was sitting across from her, no doubt tied up in a similar manner. Her shoulders ached from the stress of her arms being wrenched behind her, but the pain was not nearly as bad as the throbbing in her head.

She probably had another concussion, on top of the one she already had. She was really annoyed at the way these losers kept hitting her in the head.

"Where are we?" she asked in a whisper.

"Some cabin in the woods," Bobby murmured. "I'm sorry, Tess. He held a gun on you, so I didn't dare try to get away. I didn't want to risk your life."

"It's okay, Bobby," she assured him, even though she secretly wished her brother had saved himself. Unfortunately, there wasn't anything she could do about it now. Maybe together they could find a way out of here.

She struggled against the duct tape tying her wrists together, biting back a cry as pain reverberated up her arms. Was duct tape really that strong? Or had Steve used something else first and then added the duct tape as a precautionary measure?

"Is Tess finally awake?" Steve Gains's harsh voice echoed through the sparsely furnished cabin.

Tess turned her head toward Steve's voice, swallowing hard when she noticed he had a boxlike device along with several other items spread out on the rough-hewn table across the room. Her heart sank as the implication hit home.

Steve was planning to build another bomb. And she had no doubt this time he intended to kill her and Bobby. She hated to admit that Steve's timing was perfect. He must have purposefully set the bomb at the movie theater to keep Declan busy saving his sister, clearing the way for him to come after her and Bobby. And even once Declan managed to defuse the bomb at the movie theater, there was no way he could know where she and Bobby were being held. Steve wasn't even one of Declan's top suspects.

Her stomach clenched with nausea. They were on their own.

"I don't understand what's going on, Steve," Tess said, trying to placate the man who clearly held a grudge for all these years. "Why are you doing this?"

"You just don't get it, do you?" he asked sharply. "My life is over and it's your fault! And Shaw's, too!"

Tess fought to control her instinctive reaction to his absurd allegation. Why on earth would anything that happened to Steve Gains be her fault? He was the one who tried to assault her, not the other way around.

"Obviously you've been setting these bombs around the city, but I still don't understand why," she said. "It's not as if the innocent people you've involved are responsible for what happened to you."

"This town turned its back on me a long time ago," Steve said, sneering. "I was kicked out of college, did you know that? And then a couple of those snotty sorority chicks accused me of raping them, so I was arrested and thrown in jail. Do you have any idea what it's like inside the joint? Do you have any clue what I've been through?" His voice and facial expression reflected the depth of his desperation, and for a moment she felt bad for him. "And then just a few months before my release, I see a picture of Declan and some other cop being called heroes because they saved some kid. Well, I've shown him."

"I'm sorry, Steve. But now that you're home, I'm sure things will get better."

"Liar!" he shouted, a wild look in his eyes. Tess swallowed hard, wondering if he was going to lose it and simply kill them outright. "Being here is even worse! I've been turned down for every job I applied for! The minute they found out about my prison record, I wasn't worthy enough to wipe the mud off their shoes. Well, now they'll be sorry for the way they treated me. I'll show them who's in charge around here. And it's not Shaw!"

Tess glanced helplessly at Bobby, wishing there was some way to get through to Steve. But how? Apparently he was too far gone to listen to reason. Somehow he'd rationalized that all the failures in his life were because of her and Declan. She swallowed hard, knowing her initial instincts were right. Declan was the real target. No doubt, Steve planned to use her and Bobby as bait.

And she didn't want to think that this time Steve might succeed in building a bomb Declan couldn't defuse.

"Declan will find us," Bobby spoke up confidently. "He's smart and you won't be showing the people around here anything except how pathetic you are once you're back in jail. If you were smart, you'd leave now while you have a head start, because if you wait much longer it'll be too late."

"I'm not going back to jail!" Steve shouted. And for a moment his eyes narrowed thoughtfully as if he was seriously considering his options. Had her brother's harsh words penetrated Steve's irrational obsession? Was he thinking of taking Bobby's advice and leaving them alone?

But no, Steve abruptly turned back to the items he had strewn across the table, clearly intending to create the bomb as soon as possible.

Tess closed her eyes against a wave of despair.

Please, Lord, help Declan get here in time. Please keep me and Bobby safe in Your care. We ask for Your grace and mercy, in this desperate time. Amen.

Declan scrubbed his hands over his face, battling duel waves of fear and worry. He had to find out where Steve had taken Tess and Bobby. But so far his internet searches hadn't come up with any clues.

"We need to call the feds," he said, looking over at Isaac. "They have better resources than we do."

"All right, keep searching while I make the call."

Since no addresses had popped up under Steve's name,

Declan tried to find his parents. But he didn't have a clue as to what their first names were, and there were more than one Gains in the online white pages listing.

"We may have to go to each place ourselves," Declan muttered as he listened to Isaac's one-sided conversation with the FBI. He jotted down the addresses that were closest to Greenland High School, although truthfully, Steve's parents could have moved at any point in the past ten years.

"Agent Piermont is going to get back to us," Isaac said after he'd disconnected from the call.

"So she believes me about Steve Gains being the bomber?" Declan asked.

Isaac grimaced. "I wouldn't go that far. She thinks your theory is far-fetched but agreed it was a lead worth following up."

Declan sighed and continued working on his list. "We have three addresses here for the last name Gains. We don't have time to sit around waiting for the feds to get back to us. We need to start checking these places out now."

Isaac hesitated and then slowly nodded. "Okay, should we split up? Caleb and the rest of the team are still working with getting the device out of the theater, but we can ask Griff to free up a couple of the guys."

Declan shook his head. "I don't think so. The boss isn't too happy with me at the moment. Let's wait to see what the feds come up with first. For now we'll split up. You take this address here and I'll take this one." Declan tore the sheet of paper he had into two parts before handing the lower half to Isaac.

"Keep in touch," Isaac said as they strode outside.

"I will. And let me know as soon as you hear from the feds," Declan said.

"Will do."

Declan punched the first address on his list into the map application on his phone. Driving to the small house that was located in a nice but older neighborhood didn't take too long, and he was encouraged when he saw there was a car sitting in the driveway. At least someone was home.

Still dressed in his SWAT gear, Declan approached the front door of the Gains household. He hoped his official attire would help elicit the cooperation of the occupants inside. He knocked and waited impatiently for someone to answer the door.

The seconds stretched into a full minute before the door opened a crack. "Yes?" a frail voice asked. "What do you want?"

Declan smiled at the elderly woman who answered the door. "I'm sorry to bother you, ma'am, but I'm looking for Steve Gains. Are you his grandmother?"

"Eh?" The elderly woman leaned closer to the door while still hanging on to the frame for support.

"I'm looking for Steve Gains," Declan repeated in a louder tone. "Does he live here with you?"

"Stevie? No, he doesn't live here." The woman wrinkled her brow. "I think he's still in Arizona."

There was no point in arguing with the poor woman; it was clear she hadn't seen Steve anytime recently. "Where do Steve's parents live? Do you know their address?"

"His father still lives on Elmwood Parkway, but I don't think he's home. George? *George!* Has Ronnie come back from California?"

Declan winced as she shouted to her husband. He

glanced down at the slip of paper in his hand. The third address on his list was on Elmwood Boulevard, not parkway but close enough.

"That's okay, thanks for your help," Declan said as he turned away. He jogged back to his car, grabbing his ringing phone as he slid into the seat. "Steve's father lives at 1107 Elmwood Boulevard," he said to Isaac.

"You work fast. Agent Piermont just called to confirm that, as well. But she also told me that Steve spent the past seven years in jail, so now they believe he could be the bomber."

Declan felt a surge of satisfaction, but knowing that Steve was the guy behind it all was one thing. Getting to him before he hurt Bobby and Tess was something else.

"Steve's father has a fishing cabin located about forty minutes away near Percy Lake," Isaac continued. "The address is 659 Range Road."

Forty minutes? He didn't like the sound of that. "Steve could be at his father's house, too, since it sounds like he's not home. Why don't you go over to the parents' place in case Steve is there and I'll head up to the cabin on Percy Lake?"

"You should have backup with you. Do you want me to call the feds?" Isaac asked.

"Yeah, we need all the help we can get. I'll let you know as soon as I reach the cabin. If you find Steve before me, let me know."

"Roger that. Be careful, Deck."

"You, too." Declan disconnected from the call and quickly programmed the new address into the GPS application on his phone. Twisting the key in the ignition, he flipped on the red lights on the top of his vehicle and then gunned the engine, backing quickly out of the driveway.

He needed to get to the cabin in less time than forty minutes. And he hoped and prayed that Tess and Bobby could hang on long enough.

Tess glanced nervously at Steve as Bobby inched his chair closer to hers. How much time did they have before Steve finished his bomb? She had no way of knowing for sure.

Bobby groaned under his breath as he struggled against the bonds that held his wrists together. If he was tied as tightly as she was, he would only end up hurting himself.

"Be careful," she murmured in a low tone. "He'll hear you."

Bobby shook his head and continued to fight the duct-taped rope that Steve had used to tie them up. She tried to do the same, but the pain radiating through her head and shoulders made it impossible.

She dropped her chin to her chest, fighting a strong sense of hopelessness. The odds were overwhelmingly stacked against them. She'd prayed over and over again, but still Steve continued working on the bomb he was creating and she knew it was a matter of minutes, not hours, before he'd put his destructive plan into place.

"Come on, Tess. Don't give up," Bobby coaxed. "We're not beat yet."

She looked up at her brother, struck by the way Bobby had matured over the past few days. In the face of adversity, he'd grown into a confident young man, a far cry from the troubled teen she'd worried and prayed about.

Tears pricked her eyes at the thought that he might not live to graduate from high school, attend college, fall in love or get married.

She pulled herself up short. *Enough wallowing in self-pity, already!* Bobby was right—they weren't beaten yet. In fact, the way he was moving his left arm indicated he might be close to getting loose.

"I left Declan a clue about Steve," her brother confessed in a low tone. "We have to believe he'll get here in time."

"Really?" Tess didn't try to hide the admiration in her tone. "Very smart, Bobby. I'm proud of you."

Her brother flushed and ducked his head as if embarrassed. "I'm sorry for everything I've done over the past few years, Tess. I know I wasn't the easiest person to live with. But I promise that once we're out of here, I'll make it up to you."

Tears threatened again. "I love you, Bobby. No matter what happens, you need to remember that."

"Right back at you, sis."

Praying in earnest, she watched as Bobby continued to work against the restraints holding his wrists together. She wasn't sure what they could possibly do against Steve Gains, who was armed not only with a gun but with the bomb he was making.

But there was a chance that with the right set of circumstances, Bobby could catch Steve off guard. All they needed was a little luck and a lot of faith.

Declan slowed his speed and shut off the red and blue lights as he approached Ranger Road. He made the trip in less than twenty minutes, and Isaac had already called him to let him know that there was no one at Steve's parents' house.

He knew he'd find Gains at the cabin, hopefully along

with Bobby and Tess. What better place to build bombs than out in the middle of an isolated cabin on a lake?

When the GPS on his phone indicated he was two-tenths of a mile away from the cabin, he pulled off onto the shoulder and shut down the engine. He set his phone to vibrate and tucked it in his pocket before climbing out of the car. Reaching into the backseat, he grabbed his M4 .223 sniper rifle and his Glock. He took the time to load them before closing the door softly and heading off on foot.

Declan wanted to get to the cabin as quickly as possible, but he couldn't afford to let Steve see him, either. Thankfully the area around the cabin was full of trees and brush, so he set off on an angled path from the road in the same general direction that the cabin was located.

He walked slowly, peering through the brush for the cabin. Had he gone past it by accident? No, there it was, a log cabin nicely camouflaged behind the trees with its brown logs and green trim.

The cabin was about a hundred yards away, but he was hesitant to go any closer. Slinging his M4 over his shoulder, he climbed a nearby tree for a better position.

Declan was sweating by the time he settled in the branches of the large tree. It was early enough in September that there were plenty of leaves clinging to the branches, which provided decent cover, but they also blocked his view. Moving carefully, he pulled his M4 off his shoulder and brought the business end up so that he could peer through the scope. It took him a few seconds to pinpoint the cabin, and his breath lodged in his throat when he saw a man with his head bent down, working on something that was on the table.

The guy had to be Steve Gains. And a sick sense of

urgency hit as Declan realized Gains was building another bomb.

Where were Bobby and Tess? The window along the front of the cabin was wide, and he carefully tracked along the bottom edge until he caught a glimpse of two figures seated in chairs on the other side of the room.

Bobby and Tess! They were still alive, although clearly bound to their respective seats.

His phone vibrated with an incoming call, and he braced himself in position prior to answering it. "Yeah?"

"Is Steve there?" Isaac asked.

"Affirmative. He's building a bomb and he has Bobby and Tess, too."

"The feds are on their way and so am I," Isaac informed him. "ETA is less than fifteen minutes."

Fifteen minutes was an eternity if Steve was anywhere close to finishing the bomb. "Okay, but I can't guarantee I'll wait if Gains makes a move. Get here as soon as you can."

"Understood."

Declan disconnected from the call and put his phone back in his pocket. He lifted the M4 again and found a niche in the tree branches to help steady it. He didn't want to think about the fact that he wasn't the best sharpshooter on the SWAT team. Granted, he'd been working hard to improve, but everyone knew that his area of expertise was defusing bombs, not hitting the center of a target at a hundred and fifty yards.

Sweat trickled down the sides of his face as he watched Steve Gains through the scope. The man abruptly stood, a sinister smirk spread across his face. He turned and said something to Bobby and Tess. Was he telling them the bomb was finished? Was he taunting them with his plan of killing them?

Declan tightened his grip on the M4, knowing that if the bomb was in fact finished, there wasn't a moment to lose. Right now he had the element of surprise on his side. If he waited too long, Gains could move away from the window and his opportunity to take him out would be gone.

Declan drew in a deep breath, knowing he had to shoot twice, once to break the window and then a second time to hit his target. He adjusted his aim for the trajectory of the bullet and slowly pulled the trigger.

The M4's retort pierced the air as the window of the cabin shattered. He took his second shot a millisecond later and then stared through the scope, desperately looking for Steve. Had he missed? Dear Lord above, he couldn't have missed!

There was no sign of Gains. Declan didn't dare believe he'd actually hit his target.

"Help us!" a female voice shouted. Tess? He moved the scope and saw that Bobby had thrown himself across Tess in an attempt to protect his sister.

"I'm coming!" Declan shouted. He swung the M4 back over his shoulder and quickly descended from the tree. "Where's Gains?"

"He's hit! Hurry!"

Declan swung down to the ground and took off running toward the cabin. He pulled his Glock and flattened himself against the side wall next to the door. He twisted the knob and shoved the door open while keeping out of sight.

"Look out, he has a gun!"

Everything happened so fast it was nothing more than

a blur. He tucked and rolled through the doorway, in the direction where he estimated Tess and Bobby were located. A gunshot echoed through the cabin and he quickly brought up his Glock and aimed again at Steve Gains who was lying on the floor drenched in blood.

He shot Gains a second time and the man finally fell back, his gun dropping uselessly to the floor. Declan quickly ran over to retrieve Gains's gun, checked for a pulse, not surprised that it wasn't there before looking over at Tess and Bobby, relieved when he didn't see any blood.

"Are you both okay?" he asked as he came over to help straighten Bobby's chair so that he was off Tess.

"We are now," Tess said in a wobbly voice. "Thank heavens you made it in time."

"The power of prayer," Declan murmured as he dug in his pocket for a knife to cut them both loose.

The danger was over. Tess and Bobby were safe. The sounds of sirens indicated his backup would be here shortly.

Thank You, Lord!

SEVENTEEN

Tess bit back a cry of pain when Declan cut through the binds holding her hands behind her back. Red spots danced in front of her eyes as her arms fell uselessly to her sides. For several long moments she waited for the pain to recede and the blood to circulate normally before she could move. She watched as he freed Bobby, as well.

"Tess? Are you sure you're okay?" Declan asked, coming back over to help her stand.

She swayed and Declan hauled her close. Gratefully, she leaned against him, absorbing his strength. "I'm just so glad you made it here in time," she murmured.

"Me, too," Declan admitted, resting his cheek on her hair. "I was worried sick that I'd be too late."

"Steve was going to kill all of us," she confided. "He blamed you and me for everything that went wrong in his life."

"He won't hurt anyone ever again," Declan promised.

There was a commotion from outside and Tess glanced up to see Bobby heading over to the doorway. "Hey, it looks like the rest of your team is here," Bobby said.

Tess caught Declan's gaze. "I guess you should go out

and fill them in," she said, stepping back to move out of his embrace.

"Tess…" Declan's voice trailed off as he cupped her cheek in his palm. "There's so much I want to tell you."

She smiled gently. "I have some things I'd like to tell you, too, but let's finish this up first, okay? We can talk more later."

He surprised her by giving her a quick, tender kiss, before releasing her. Her heart raced and she had to take a deep breath to calm herself before she crossed over to stand next to Bobby. She glanced at Steve Gains's body lying in front of the table covered in blood, and then quickly averted her gaze.

"Good job, Deck," Isaac said as he crossed over to kneel beside Steve.

"Not really, I didn't want to kill him. Now we'll never know exactly what was going on in his head."

"You may still get that chance to talk to him, because I'm pretty sure he still has a pulse." Isaac glanced up. "Get the ambulance crew in here, now!"

"What? I checked for a pulse," Declan protested.

"Maybe it stopped momentarily from shock," Isaac said.

Tess and Bobby stepped back out of the way so the ambulance crew could get to Steve. The two paramedics quickly went to work, one starting an IV and hanging fluids while the other one applied pressure to the gunshot wound.

"I hope he makes it," Declan muttered. "I'd really like to know his true motive."

"I can tell you what he told us about why he was doing this," she offered. "He ranted a lot before he finished working on the bomb."

"We'll take over the interviews from here," a woman said, stepping forward. She was dressed in a navy blue suit, her long dark hair pulled back severely from her face, and it took Tess a moment to realize she was one of the FBI agents Declan had mentioned.

Declan and Isaac glanced at each other, and Tess could tell they weren't happy about the feds interfering with the case.

"Please come with me," the FBI agent said.

She shot Declan a helpless glance, before reluctantly following the female agent outside to the clearing around the cabin.

"I'm coming, too," Bobby said loyally.

The agent stopped several feet away from the front door of the cabin and began to rattle off a series of questions. Together Tess and Bobby relayed their account about how Steve had accosted them at Declan's house and brought them here. Agent Piermont kept interrupting them, so it took far longer than it should have to get through all the details.

"Apparently Steve's father had a criminal record for sexual assault, too," Agent Piermont informed them.

"Did I hear you right?" Declan asked as he came over. "Steve's father also served time for sexual assault?"

"Yes, although it was a long time ago," Agent Piermont admitted. "His mother left when Steve was five years old, leaving his father to raise the boy alone. I have to wonder if the son learned a little too much from his father."

Declan paled and nodded, turning abruptly away. Tess frowned and started to follow him, but just then the ambulance crew came outside rolling Gains on the gurney. Within moments, the ambulance whisked the perp away to meet up with the Flight For Life helicopter that was landing somewhere close by. The roar of the chopper blades made it difficult to hear anything that was going on. When Tess turned back to find Declan, she noticed he was talking to his boss, the two men wearing matching solemn expressions on their faces.

Tess sucked in a quick breath as Declan handed over his handgun and a rifle to his boss, before turning away and crossing over to meet them.

"What happened?" she asked. "Are you in trouble?"

"Normal operating procedure in a police shooting," he said, waving off her concern. "I've been cleared to head home since I'm officially on administrative duty."

Tess didn't like the sound of that. "What is wrong with your boss? Doesn't he realize you saved our lives? If you hadn't shot Steve, who knows what would have happened? This lunatic was getting ready to plant the bomb between me and Bobby."

"Hey, it's okay, Tess. They have to investigate no matter what," he said softly. "You already gave your statement to the feds so Griff and the rest of the brass will eventually find out that the shooting was justified. It'll just take some time to get through all the forensics that will support my case."

"I still don't like it," she muttered. "They should know you well enough to realize you wouldn't shoot unless you had no choice."

"Come on, let's go home." Declan held out his hand and she gladly took it, ignoring Bobby's smirk.

The ride back to Declan's house was relatively quiet, and Tess gratefully leaned back and closed her eyes, willing her splitting headache to go away. She hadn't mentioned it to Declan, because she knew he'd make her go back to the hospital to be checked out, and she already knew from her first visit that there wasn't much they could do about her concussion anyway.

"Are you sure you're okay?" Declan asked.

"Just tired and sore, that's all."

"She needs to rest," Bobby spoke up from the backseat. "She's been through a lot."

Tess must have dozed, because it seemed like barely five minutes later that Declan was pulling into his driveway. She knew she should insist on going home, but she didn't have the energy to argue with him. Before she could move, Declan had come around to open the passenger door.

"Come on, let's get you upstairs to get some sleep," he said.

"I can walk," she muttered.

Declan ignored her protest and wrapped his arm around her waist to assist her as Bobby went ahead and opened the doors. Declan helped her upstairs to the second-floor bedroom that she'd been sharing with Bobby.

Once she reached the bedroom she gratefully sank into the bed, barely noticing that Declan left her alone, softly closing the door behind him.

When Tess woke up again, the room was dim and through the window she could see the sun was low on the horizon. Gingerly sitting up at the side of the bed, she was grateful to note that the throbbing in her head had faded to nothing more than a very minor ache. After freshening up in the bathroom, she made her way downstairs. She could hear voices outside and had to smile when she realized Declan and Bobby were outside grilling dinner.

She opened the door and then froze, when she heard their conversation.

"Tess doesn't know about my meeting with the army recruiter," her brother was saying.

"You need to talk to her, Bobby. You know she cares about you."

"But she doesn't want to hear my side of it," her brother argued.

"You still need to discuss this with her."

"Yes, you do need to talk to me," Tess said as she opened the door and stepped outside. She shot Declan a narrow glare. "I thought I asked you to stop encouraging him to join the service."

Declan lifted his eyebrows. "I didn't encourage him, Tess. Go ahead and ask your brother when he went to visit the recruiter. He'll tell you that it was well before any of this happened."

Tess didn't want to believe it, but she knew Declan was probably right. Bobby and Declan had only been together for the past two days, and there had been no time to visit a recruiter considering all the events that had taken place in the past forty-eight hours. Still, this was the second time she'd overheard Declan and Bobby talking about the armed forces, and as far as she was concerned, that was two times too many.

"Well?" she asked, looking at her brother.

Bobby ducked his head and shuffled his feet. "Mitch and I visited with the recruiter the first time in April. But then Mitch started using drugs, so I went to see the recruiter again by myself right before school started."

Tess's heart sank at her brother's words. "I thought we had this conversation, Bobby. I thought you agreed that you'd give college a try."

Bobby shrugged. "I know that's what you want me to do, Tess, but I'm not sure college is the right choice for me. And look at Declan. He went from the marines to being a cop! Joining the service worked out fine for him."

Tess was so angry she could barely think straight. "Declan's situation is different."

"No, it's not…you just don't understand."

Tess didn't want to have this conversation here. Clearly she and her brother needed to have a heart-to-heart conversation, alone. "I'd like to go home, Declan. Now."

"Come on, sis, you're overreacting."

Tess folded her hands over her chest. "Either you agree to take us home, or I'll call Caleb or Isaac for a ride. Your choice."

"I'll take you," Declan agreed in a subdued tone. "Just let me take the burgers and brats off the fire so they don't burn."

"I was looking forward to eating them, too," her brother muttered loud enough so she could hear. "It's been hours since breakfast."

Tess turned away, feeling helpless. She couldn't bring herself to ignore her brother's need to eat dinner. He'd been through a lot today, too. "Fine, we can eat first and then go home." Without waiting for a response, she went back inside and shut the door behind her. Fighting tears, she sat down at the kitchen table and held her head in her hands.

She didn't want to lose her brother to the army. And if Declan cared about her at all, he wouldn't encourage her brother to join the service.

Which only made her realize that Declan might not feel the same way she did.

The moment he'd burst through Steve's cabin door to

save them, she realized how much she loved him. She always had a soft spot for him back when she was in high school, but they'd gone their separate ways. Being with him these past few days made her realize she loved the man he'd become. And up until now, she'd also loved the way he'd been such an awesome role model for her brother.

But that was before all this. If her brother joined the army, she'd never forgive him.

Apparently she'd have to find a way to move on with her life, without Declan.

Declan flipped the brats and burgers, wondering if he'd blown his chance with Tess after the way she demanded to be taken home.

"Don't worry about my sister," Bobby told him. "She'll get over being mad at you. One thing about Tess, she can't hold a grudge for very long."

Declan wasn't too sure about that. He stared blindly down at the grill. Had Bobby taken his willingness to talk about the service as encouragement? That hadn't been his intention. Joining the marines had worked for him, but then again, his home life had been very different.

"I'll go talk to her," Bobby offered, obviously anxious to make amends. "I'll make sure she knows this is my decision and not yours."

Declan watched as Bobby disappeared back inside the house. When the brats and burgers were cooked to his satisfaction, he removed them from the grill and piled them on a platter. He carried it inside. Tess and Bobby were seated next to each other and he winced when he saw that Tess had been crying.

He set the platter down on the counter and turned to

face them. "Look, Bobby, there's something you need to know before you make this decision. I did join the marines, but at the time I was mainly trying to escape my father." A muscle twitched in his cheek. "You see, my old man was a mean drunk. My mother left him and took my sister with her, and my dad used to smack me around until I was old enough to defend myself."

"Wow…that must have been rough," Bobby said sympathetically.

"It was. Maybe if my mom had stuck around, things would have been different. So I'm going to be honest with you here—if I'd had the same support system you have with Tess, I'm not so sure I would have enlisted."

"But you said that it was an honor to serve our country," Bobby protested.

He couldn't bear Tess's accusing gaze. "Yes, it is an honor to serve our country. But you also need to understand just how many men and women have died for their country. My best friend, Tony, was standing right next to me when he was shot and killed."

He heard Tess gasp in horror, and as much as he wanted to stop, he knew it would be best if they knew the truth about everything.

"When my tour was up, I lost control of my life," Declan continued. "Tony's death had been difficult to deal with. He had a wife and a son. Why was he the one to die that day? I kept thinking it should have been me."

"Oh, Declan," Tess cried. "That must have been awful, but you know that it's not up to us to question God's plan."

He shrugged. "I didn't have faith back then. I spent months trying to drown my grief in the bottom of a whiskey bottle. And when my sister came to find me, I lashed out at her in anger. Thankfully I didn't hurt her, but it was then that I realized that I'd become my father." Baring his soul like this wasn't easy, but he owed it to Tess to convince her brother that he had other options. "Bobby, you have your sister's faith, love and support. Just make sure you're joining the army for the right reasons, and not as a way to escape."

"Man, I'm sorry to hear about your friend," Bobby murmured in shock.

"Tony was a good man, and there are still days I think that it should have been me who died instead of him."

Tess surprised him by jumping out of her seat and coming over to wrap her arms around his waist. "Declan, I'm sorry for everything you've had to go through. I'm sure your sister understood that you were in pain, hurting over the death of your friend."

He couldn't stop himself from hugging her back. "Thanks, but that's no excuse. I sobered up and decided then and there that I wouldn't drink again. I attended the police academy and graduated at the top of my class. But it wasn't easy to move on." He swallowed hard. "When I heard that Steve's father had a history of sexual assaults, it reminded me that my father's blood runs in my veins, too. Don't you see how similar we are? Steve's mother abandoned him, too."

"Declan, don't you dare compare yourself to Steve. And you're not your father, either. I could see the goodness in you the night you rescued me from Steve's assault. I'm sorry that your father hurt you, but can't you see how different you are from him?" Drawing a breath, she continued softly. "You've made the decision to make something of yourself, to serve our country and to give back to your community. You've learned about faith and have accepted God's calling. I'm proud of the man you've become."

His throat closed with emotion and he pulled her close, hoping and praying that Tess would be willing to take a chance on him. "Thanks," he managed. "Does this mean you'll give me the opportunity to prove how much I care about you?"

Tess tipped her head back to smile up at him. "Of course, Declan. Because I care about you, too."

The timing wasn't perfect, but Declan decided that if he was going to bare his soul, he might as well go all the way. "Good to know, because I love you, Tess. For years I told myself that I didn't want a family, but that was just an excuse to avoid relationships. When I realized Steve had you, I knew how much I loved you. And I hope and pray that someday you'll learn to love me, too."

Tess smiled, her eyes filling with tears. "You don't have to wait, Declan. I love you. I love you very much."

"I'm glad," he whispered before capturing her mouth in a deep, heart-stirring kiss.

Bobby cleared his throat loudly, forcing Declan to lift his head, ending the kiss. Tess blushed and pulled out of his embrace as if she'd completely forgotten her brother was still in the room.

"I'm glad you guys have made up," Bobby said drily. "And you've convinced me not to jump into anything, especially since my priority should be to make sure I graduate before I weigh my options."

"That's a good approach," Tess agreed.

"Absolutely. And I want you to know that Tess and I will be there to help you in any way we can," Declan added.

"Okay, great. Now can we please eat dinner?" Bobby asked with a pleading gaze. "I'm starving!"

Declan grinned and Tess broke into giggles. Even though he wanted nothing more than to discuss his future with Tess, including putting her through medical school if that was what she really wanted, he knew there was no rush.

For now, he was grateful for the precious gift he'd been given. Tess showed him the way to his faith and had offered her love.

And that was good enough for him.

EPILOGUE

"I now pronounce you man and wife!" Pastor Tom said jovially. "Declan, you may kiss your bride."

Tess blushed as Declan bent down to kiss her, keenly aware of the fact that the entire congregation was watching them. She was thrilled that this was the first day of their new life together.

"I love you," Declan murmured as he lifted his head.

"I love you, too," she whispered back.

"We already know that," Bobby pointed out in a loud whisper. He'd stood up as Declan's best man, and she was thrilled at how her brother had turned his life around. He'd been accepted at a junior college for the next fall but had also joined the National Guard, as a reservist. It was a good compromise and she knew that Declan's influence had helped her brother make the right decisions.

"You both look so happy," Karen gushed, swiping at her eyes. Tess had asked Declan's sister to be her maid of honor, and of course Declan's twin nieces had insisted on being flower girls.

She was thrilled to have their entire family together.

"Are you ready?" Declan asked.

"Yes." She took his arm and together they walked

down the aisle. He took her off to the side and gave her a big hug before the rest of the wedding party joined them in the receiving line.

"Are you sure you don't want to try to get back into medical school?" Declan asked for at least the fifth time since they'd agreed to get married. "Because I don't mind supporting you and I think you'd make a great doctor."

"I'm sure," she said. Maybe that had been her dream once, but not anymore. Maybe she'd been looking for an excuse to escape her father, too. "Declan, please believe me when I say that having a loving husband and a family is all I need to be happy."

"I promise I'll do whatever I can to make you happy." He pulled her close for another kiss, and this time, she didn't care if everyone stared at them.

This was their first day as husband and wife. And Tess was looking forward to spending the rest of her life with Declan and any children God blessed them with.

* * * * *

WE HOPE YOU
ENJOYED THIS

LOVE INSPIRED® SUSPENSE
BOOK.

Discover more **heart-pounding** romances of **danger** and **faith** from the Love Inspired Suspense series.

Be sure to look for all six Love Inspired Suspense books every month.

Love Inspired® SUSPENSE

SPECIAL EXCERPT FROM

Love Inspired
SUSPENSE

*A K-9 cop must keep his childhood friend alive
when she finds herself in the crosshairs of a
drug-smuggling operation.*

Read on for a sneak preview of
Act of Valor *by Dana Mentink,*
the next exciting installment in the
True Blue K-9 Unit *miniseries, available in May 2019
from Love Inspired Suspense.*

Officer Zach Jameson surveyed the throng of people congregated around the ticket counter at LaGuardia Airport. Most ignored Zach and K-9 partner, Eddie, and that suited him just fine. Two months earlier he would have greeted people with a smile, or at least a polite nod while he and Eddie did their work of scanning for potential drug smugglers. These days he struggled to keep his mind on his duty while the ever-present darkness nibbled at the edges of his soul.

Eddie plopped himself on Zach's boot. He stroked the dog's ears, trying to clear away the fog that had descended the moment he heard of his brother's death.

Zach hadn't had so much as a whiff of suspicion that his brother was in danger. His brain knew he should talk to somebody, somebody like Violet Griffin, his friend from childhood who'd reached out so many times, but his heart would not let him pass through the dark curtain.